The passions, scandals and hopes
of two fabulously rich families...

Welcome back to the glamorous and cutthroat world
of Australian opal dealing, in this first of
two collections featuring Miranda Lee's bestselling
six-book series, HEARTS OF FIRE.

It all began in SECRETS AND SINS...

Seduction & Sacrifice
Desire & Deception
Passion & the Past

Now the Whitmore Saga continues with...

Fantasies & the Future
Scandals & Secrets
Marriage & Miracles

Relive the romance

by Request®

Three complete novels
by one of your favorite authors

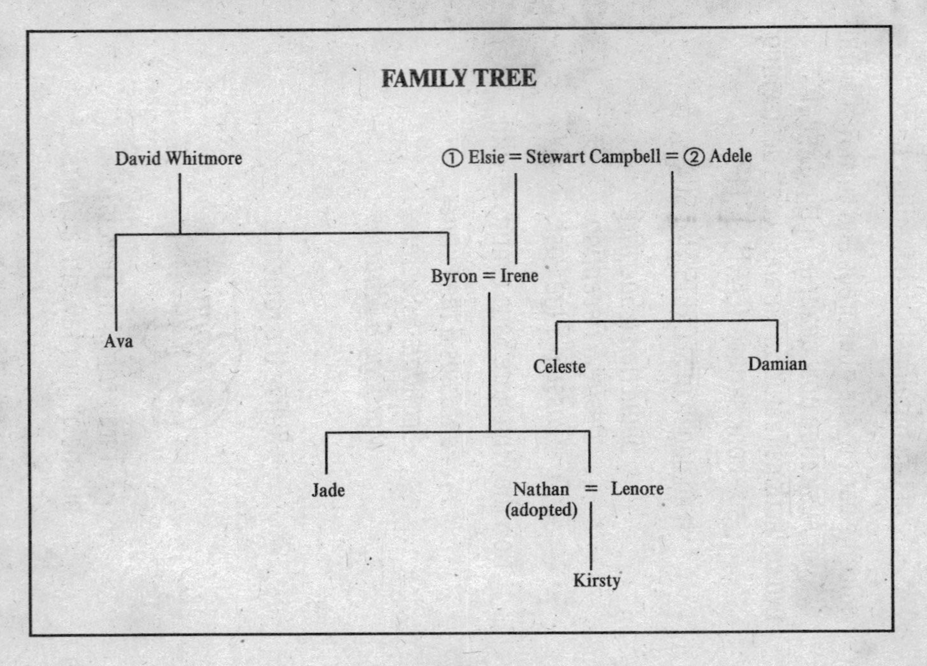
FAMILY TREE
David Whitmore
① Elsie = Stewart Campbell = ② Adele
Byron = Irene
Ava
Celeste
Damian
Jade
Nathan (adopted) = Lenore
Kirsty

Miranda LEE

FORTUNE & FATE

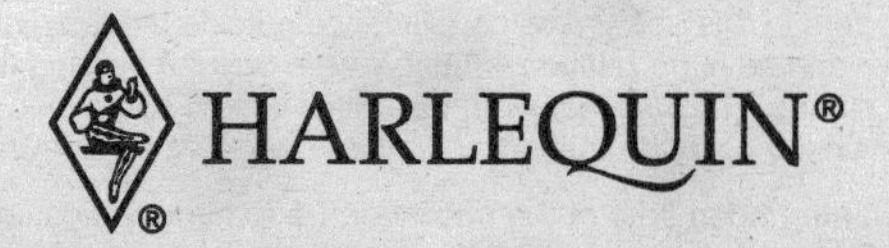

TORONTO • NEW YORK • LONDON
AMSTERDAM • PARIS • SYDNEY • HAMBURG
STOCKHOLM • ATHENS • TOKYO • MILAN • MADRID
PRAGUE • WARSAW • BUDAPEST • AUCKLAND

HARLEQUIN BOOKS

by Request—FORTUNE & FATE

ISBN 0-373-18513-8

Visit us at www.eHarlequin.com

Printed in U.S.A.

CONTENTS

FANTASIES & THE FUTURE

CHAPTER ONE

AVA WAS SITTING at her easel, paintbrush in hand but her mind a million miles away, when her brother stormed into her studio-cum-sitting-room.

'Ava! I can't find my favourite tux. It's certainly not hanging with my other suits. I've looked damned well everywhere. Would you have any idea where it could be?'

Ava's startled face was quickly filled with a flustered guilt. 'I—er—I took it to the dry cleaners a couple of weeks back. Remember, you got a wine stain on it from Jade's wedding?'

'And?' Byron growled ominously.

'I…um…forgot to pick it up.'

Byron didn't say a word. He simply glared at her for a second, shook his head in total exasperation, then spun on his heels and stormed out again.

Ava jumped up, her palette sliding from her lap and crashing to the parquet floor. With a groan of dismay, she dithered, then decided to ignore the palette and raced after her brother. 'I…I'm sorry, Byron,' she called after him as he marched along the upstairs hallway, 'It won't happen again. I promise.'

'That's what you said the last time,' he threw back over his shoulder before abruptly grinding to a halt and whirling around to face her. 'This past six weeks has been nothing but one disaster after another. God knows why I let you talk me into giving you a chance at running this household. I suppose I was swayed by your argument that since there was only the two of us pathetic old Whitmores left living in this great empty barn of a house you could possibly manage. But that was just wishful thinking!'

'*You* might be pathetic and old,' Ava countered, finding her temper at long last. 'But I'm not! I'm only thirty and I think I've done rather well considering I've had no experience with housework. I certainly don't consider a small memory-slip such as forgetting to pick up some dry cleaning a *disaster!* Frankly, Byron, I was hoping you'd be encouraging, rather than bullying. Melanie assured me you'd changed since the accident, but I can see you're still the same unsympathetic, insensitive chauvinistic tyrant you've always been!'

Her outburst concluded, Ava was on the verge of subsiding into her usual wimpish mush when Byron laughed. His reaction took her by surprise and she simply stared at him.

Laughing, her brother looked a long way from being old and pathetic as well. Though rising fifty, he was a fine figure of a man, his extremely tall, broad-shouldered frame kept in shape with hard sessions in his own private gym downstairs. Admittedly, his wavy black hair was sprinkled liberally with grey, but it was still thick and lustrous. His strongly chiselled face was as handsome as ever, despite a few lines, and his blue eyes, now glittering with a dry amusement, were still holding women in thrall.

Recently, Byron had started dating a divorcee named Catherine who was in her mid-thirties and quite stunning-looking. Ava, however, could not stand the woman, who was a first-class snob and very patronising in her manner. She obviously fancied herself the next Mrs Byron Whitmore—no doubt she was already auditioning for the part since Byron had stayed overnight at her unit a couple of times already—but Ava knew that if such a marriage ever took place she would move out of Belleview.

Where she would go, she had no idea. She had no real money of her own until she married, Byron having control of her sizeable inheritance till that unlikely event occurred. Meanwhile, all she had was a very modest allowance, though Byron's daughter, Jade, *had* given her all her mother's jewellery to do with as she liked. But it still sat, untouched, in the safe in the library. Ava didn't want anything to do with anything that had belonged to Irene.

'I knew you had some spirit somewhere, Ava,' Byron surprised her by complimenting. 'You are my sister, after all. So Melanie thinks I've changed, does she? That's the pot calling the kettle black, don't you think? I'm still getting over our prim and proper ex-housekeeper being a closet vamp and ensnaring one of the most famous sportsmen in the world! Next thing I'll find out *you've* been having an affair with the chauffeur on the sly!'

'We don't *have* a chauffeur!' Ava retorted. 'Though maybe it would be a good idea if we did. Then you wouldn't have to stay over at ladies' places simply because you've had a few drinks, and I'd have someone to run me around doing all the chores I have to do these days!'

Ava's heart beat faster at such a thought. It had been one of her recurring romantic fantasies over the years, being a beautiful heiress who hired a gorgeous young Italian to be her chauffeur, then fell in love with him. Italians figured largely in all of Ava's fantasies. She found their darkly brooding looks and macho attitude to women very exciting.

Of course nothing too sexy or sordid ever happened in her fantasies. Being a virgin and terribly shy with the opposite sex, Ava had never got beyond picturing herself hugging or kissing a man. Was this perhaps because she could never imagine herself taking her clothes off in front of one? Or his finding pleasure in her short, top-heavy, roly-poly figure?

'Over my dead body!' Byron pronounced quite testily, his amusement fading as quickly as it had come. 'A lot of chauffeurs are sleazy gigolo types on the make. I wouldn't let you within a hundred miles of the sort of good-looking but unscrupulous young creep who usually applies for such a position!'

'As if *any* good-looking young man would look at me twice,' Ava muttered, 'I'm no Celeste Campbell.'

Ava could have bitten her tongue out for having mentioned that dreaded name. Byron's eyes darkened, a muscle twitching along his jawline as he battled to control his temper. There'd been a short time, after the attempted robbery at the ball a couple of months ago, when he had spoken of his scandalous sister-in-law with a certain reluctant admiration. Her defence of herself that night, using her undoubted skills as a martial arts expert, had clearly impressed him. Or maybe, since she'd just bought back the Heart of Fire—the opal that was rumoured to have somehow caused the original feud between the Whitmores and the Campbells—he'd decided to try to let bygones be bygones.

But such was not to be. Celeste had come to the hospital to visit Melanie, who'd accidently been shot during the drama, with her new chauffeur in tow. It had quickly become clear to all Melanie's other visitors—which included both Byron and Ava—that the handsome young man was the latest toy-boy lover of the glamorous head of Campbell Jewels. Any hope of reconciliation had been dashed with Byron raving all the way home that the woman was a disgrace to her sex.

'A woman like Celeste can look after herself,' he bit out now. 'Whereas an innocent like you, my dear, would be easy meat to the type of conscienceless young stud *she* eats for breakfast. There will be no chauffeur here at Belleview. Please do not bring the subject up again!'

'I wouldn't dream of it.'

Byron's expression softened at her suddenly depressed tone. 'Poor Ava…I'm a beast to you sometimes. I don't mean to be, love. I really don't. You do know I always have your best interests at heart, don't you?' He slipped an arm around her shoulders and pulled her to his side. 'Am I forgiven for snapping at you?'

Ava felt tears pricking at her eyes. 'Yes,' she mumbled.

'Then I must go. I'm supposed to be at Catherine's by eight. By the way, don't worry about breakfast for me tomorrow. I'll—er—drive straight to work from there in the morning. You'll be all right on your own, won't you?'

'Of course,' she said stiffly. 'I'm a grown woman, Byron. Why wouldn't I be all right?'

His small smile suggested that, while she was a grown woman in years, she wasn't at all in experience.

'In that case I'll be off now. Everything's locked up downstairs. I double checked. See you tomorrow evening.'

Ava just managed to smother another exasperated retort. Double checked the doors. Truly! 'Goodnight, Byron,' she said with crisp politeness. 'I hope you have a good time.'

'I will.'

Ava's mouth set into a mutinous pout as she watched Byron stride off down the hall. I'll just bet you will, she thought crossly. Everyone in this family's having a good time lately but me. You're having an affair with the coolly beautiful Catherine. Melanie's settled in an English mansion with her dashing racing driver husband. Jade's married her billionaire boyfriend and Nathan—God bless his black heart!—seems to have managed so far to hide his true self from his gloriously innocent child-bride.

Ava's irritation sustained her till Byron disappeared down the stairs and she was faced with the unpalatable thought of actually staying home alone all night in this big barn of a house. The prospect did make her a little nervous, but to have admitted as much would have only confirmed her brother's opinion that she was still a child in a woman's body.

The front door banging confirmed that she was indeed alone, a shiver of nerves running through her. This only irritated her further. Good lord, what did she think could possibly happen? If some mad rapist broke in, he would take one look at her and run for his life!

With a scoffing laugh, Ava whirled and strode back into her empty studio, where she swooped up the palette from the floor and banged it down on the side table beside the easel. Crossing her arms, she studied the watercolour she'd been working on, finding no satisfaction in the half-finished landscape. Something wasn't right. The balance of shape, or the colours she'd chosen. Or perhaps it was the subject-matter. She'd tried to paint that particular scene many times.

Her dissatisfaction with it grew and soon she was reefing it off the easel and almost throwing it against the far wall with all the other unfinished paintings. Naturally they were turned away so that she didn't have to look at them.

Ava flopped down on her old sofa, punching the cushions with frustration. Dammit! Why can't I ever be a success at anything? I really thought I could handle the running of the house. I really thought I could…

Ava's mental haranguing was terminated abruptly by the sound of a door banging somewhere. Her blue eyes flung wide, her heart jumping into her mouth. Had Byron come back for something? Was there a window open, perhaps? Or was she about to be murdered in her bedroom?

'Auntie Ava!' a female voice sang out. 'Where are you? It's only me, Jade!'

The blood hardly had time to flow back into Ava's face before her exuberant niece popped her highly arresting head into the studio. 'Ah, there you are!' she grinned, dark blue eyes sparkling beneath a shock of spiked white-blonde hair, huge golden hoops hanging from her ears.

Jade's grin faded to a puzzled expression as she pushed the door right open and stood there, frowning over at her aunt. 'You do realise your television set isn't on. Auntie, don't you?'

Ava got to her feet with a weary sigh. Jade had that effect on her sometimes, the girl's vibrant energy making her feel old, though she was grateful for the company. 'I was just resting,' she said.

'Aren't you feeling well?' Jade asked worriedly.

'I'm quite well. I'd be even better, however, if your father was a bit easier to please.'

'I know just what you mean, Auntie. I do feel sorry for you. What you need is to find yourself a husband like I did and get out of here.'

Ava had to laugh. *Her,* find a *husband?* 'I'm sure Kyle wouldn't like to think you married him just to move out of home.'

A naughty smile pulled at Jade's generous mouth. 'Oh, I don't think he thinks that.' She patted her gently rounding stomach. 'I married him for other reasons.'

Ava did her best to ignore the unexpected stab of pain and envy in her heart.

'Come and talk to me, Auntie,' Jade went on blithely, 'while I have a look to see if any of the clothes I left behind will fit a mum-to-be.'

They trundled along the hall into Jade's room, where Ava sat on the side of the bed while Jade began rummaging in wardrobes and drawers.

'So how's the housekeeping going?' she asked, folding a huge T-shirt and placing it on a chair. 'You managing OK?'

'Fair enough, but I doubt your father would agree. Of course I can't cook anything too complicated yet so we have a cook come in every night. I make breakfast, though, and I do most of the general housework, though a lady comes in on Mondays and Fridays to do the ironing and the heavy cleaning.'

'I'm impressed, Auntie. After all, you've never been all that domesticated, have you? Not that I'm much better. I have trouble boiling water.'

'Don't exaggerate, Jade. You're a very smart girl. Your father is very proud of you and the way you've turned around Whitmore's. He says you're a born marketing person.'

'Pops said that? Goodness, then I must be good, mustn't I?'

'There are many meanings of the word "good".'

Jade looked over at her po-faced aunt and laughed. 'You're a card, Auntie.' She pulled a very sexy black bra out of a drawer and held it up. 'Hmm, perhaps I should take this home. I might need to start wearing a bra soon.' She tossed it on to the growing pile on the chair. 'So tell me, what's my dear father been up to that's bugging you besides picking on everything you do or don't do?'

'He's having an affair, for one thing. With that Catherine person he's been seeing.'

Jade shrugged. 'You can't blame him for that. He's still a relatively young man. What is it about her that you disapprove of so much?'

'She's a snob.'

Jade laughed. 'So's he.'

'Yes, but not the same sort of snob. Byron has class, and...and...standards.'

'Goodness, I must meet this Catherine. And soon! I think I have the right venue too. Kyle and I want to give Pops a party for his fiftieth birthday. It's next week, you know?'

Ava was stricken with guilt. 'Lord, I forgot!' Her groan was full of self-disgust. 'I forget *everything*. First, I forgot to buy the toilet paper last week, then I didn't give Byron an important telephone message, and then I forgot to collect his favourite suit from the dry cleaners. That's not all, either. Yesterday I went out shopping, forgetting that the lawn-mowing man was due. Naturally, he wasn't able to get in the locked gates and wasted a lot of time waiting around for nothing. He rang up later and was so rude I told him not to come again. Of course I haven't told Byron this last bit yet. I haven't dared. God, no wonder he thinks I'm hopeless,' she finished wretchedly.

'Poppycock!' Jade refuted. 'You're not at all hopeless. Everyone forgets things sometimes, especially when one is new at a job. What you need, Auntie Ava, is to have a little more faith in yourself!'

A little more faith in myself? Ava sighed. When had she ever had that? Had there ever been a time when she'd viewed the future with confidence, when she'd been brimming over with exuberance and optimism, when she *hadn't* taken the line of least resistance?

Not that she could recall.

Why was that? she wondered. She'd been a pretty child, with big baby-blue eyes and bouncing soft brown curls, and not unintelligent. She'd been able to read by the age of three. People had commented on how bright she was. Good at games, too. Goodness, she'd been able to swim like a fish as soon as she could walk. Now, hardly a day went by without her tripping over something. As for swimming…her body hadn't seen a swimming costume in years!

She should have turned out so very different from the unprepossessing, overweight, accident-prone, timid creature that she was these days. Where had it all gone wrong?

'The reason you think you're hopeless,' Jade resumed, almost as though she had read her aunt's mind, 'is because my darling mother told you so every single day of her life, as she did me. She didn't get the desired result with me because I'm a chip off the old block, so to speak, but you're a real softie, and she hurt you much more than me with her horrid putdowns. But she's gone now, Auntie. She can't hurt you any more. As for Pops…he's all bark and no bite. Just ignore him. Look, I have to get a plastic bag to put these these in. I won't be long.'

Jade strode confidently from the room, Ava happy to have a few moments to herself. What a whirlwind that girl was. But so smart, and so sure of herself. Ava did so admire the way she'd always stood up for herself, even if some of her antics as a teenager had been hair-raising. Ava never had the nerve or the courage to be that kind of rebel. Either that or she'd had it knocked out of her very young.

She sighed over the circumstances that had placed her at the age of seven in hands other than her own loving parents. Her father had died of cancer when she'd been five, her mother shortly afterwards of a heart attack, leaving her to be raised by her older brother, Byron, unfortunately at a time when the family company had been facing financial ruin and he'd been working twenty-hour days. Two years later, he had married Irene Campbell.

It had been rumoured right from the start that Byron had hoped the marriage would merge Campbell Jewels and Whitmore Opals—thereby rescuing Whitmore Opals—but somehow he'd got his wires crossed. Stewart Campbell had left everything, including total control of Campbell's, to his second wife, Adele, who had apparently detested Irene, and was quick to cut her out of the estate in favour of her own children, Celeste and Damian.

Fortunately for the family's fortunes, Whitmore's had rallied—this was during the years before Celeste took control of Campbell's and resurrected the old feud—and in the end it hadn't mattered that Irene Campbell had brought nothing to the marriage but her own sweet self.

Ava's top lip curled up at this description of Irene. Only with Byron had Irene ever been sweet, and even then the word was inadequate. Irene had loved Byron with a love that was sickeningly obsessive. He was her prince, her god, her reason for living. In his presence, she'd been a totally different creature from the one who inhabited Belleview when he wasn't there. In his absence, she'd given new meaning to the word 'sour'.

Yes, Jade was right, Ava conceded. The deterioration of her self-esteem could be laid directly at Irene Campbell's feet. How insidious that woman had been, with her subtle but relentless sarcasm. Criticisms were delivered with a dry laugh, or a saccharine smile, but the effect had been the same. One was left feeling a failure. While Jade had fought back, *she'd* shrivelled up like a hothouse flower, turning to food for comfort, then retreating into her fantasy world. Worst of all, she had allowed Irene to convince Byron that his sister was a homely little nincompoop who couldn't possibly attract a member of the opposite sex, so of course any chap who showed an interest in her had to be a gold-digger!

The memory of what had happened with James when she'd been twenty was just too painful to recall, perhaps because on that occasion Irene had been crushingly right. After that incident, she'd eaten more cream cakes. And more chocolate bars. And more packets of crisps.

Her life had deteriorated to a perpetual round of useless diets that never lasted and binges that did. Her once very real intention to get a job of some sort had vanished along with what was left of her self-esteem. It was much easier to stay in her room and pretend she was going to become a famous artist one day. Byron had even had the bedroom next to hers converted to a studio so she could pretend with some flair.

And while deep in her subconscious she believed she did have some talent, nothing she ever painted really pleased her. Whenever she got dangerously close to finishing one of her watercolours, something about it would dissatisfy her and she would put it aside. She had never, ever really finished a painting. Not once!

'Here I am again.' Jade hurried back into the room and stuffed the pile of clothes into a large plastic bag. 'I must go, Auntie. I'll talk to Pops tomorrow at work about his party and I'll give you a ring sometime. Whatever, keep Friday week free. If we don't have a party we'll all go out to dinner.'

Ava walked Jade down to the front door, making sure all the doors and the front gates were locked after she left, a look at the lengthening lawns reminding her she would have to do something about them. No matter what Jade said, Ava accepted that she was a bit hopeless sometimes. She shouldn't have forgotten the lawn-mowing man was due yesterday. Her memory was atrocious!

It was to be thanked she couldn't create a similar problem with the gardener. Mr Potts had been with them for years and had his own key, since he lived down the road and came and went at all sorts of odd hours. At a pinch he might mow the lawns once or twice if she asked nicely, but he was getting old and the lawns were extensive. No, she couldn't ask him to do that.

But who?

She'd already searched Melanie's little black book where their former housekeeper had written down all manner of casual helpers she had hired at some time or other. But there wasn't one lawn-mower man among them.

Byron would simply have rung around the neighbours and asked them whom they used. But Ava cringed at doing so herself. They would probably laugh at her behind her back—which they were probably already doing anyway. Poor stupid Ava, trying to run a house. What must Byron be thinking of?

A shudder ran through her.

No, she would just have to look in the *Yellow Pages* and simply take a stab in the dark. What was the worst that could happen? The man might be inefficient or unreliable. If so, she would simply fire him and try again. If at first you don't succeed…

Steeling her churning stomach, Ava stood up, squared her shoulders and marched through the family room into the kitchen where the telephone books were kept. Five minutes later Ava was still scanning the pages of the business directory, a frown on her face. She'd never dreamt there were so many lawn-mowing services. She was dithering over which one to choose from, when a boxed ad down in a corner caught her eye. It said:

Morelli's House and Grounds Maintenance Service. No job too small or too large. Reasonable rates and reliable workmen.

'Morelli's,' she whispered aloud, liking the way the name slid off her tongue.

Now Ava knew an Italian name when she saw one.

She stared down at it for a long time, aware that her heart was beating faster all the while. She knew it was ridiculous to be drawn to an advertisement simply because it carried an Italian name. There again, she had to hire someone…

Her hand shook slightly as she dialled, her throat drying as she waited and waited for someone to answer.

'Morelli's House and Grounds Maintenance Service. How may we help you?' said a female voice with a heavy Italian accent.

Thrown slightly by a woman answering, Ava dithered. 'Oh…I— er—I…'

The woman at the other end sighed heavily. 'If you are one of Vincente's *lady-friends,*' she said caustically, 'then let me tell you something. My son is soon to be engaged to a nice Italian girl and will not be sleeping in any of your beds any longer!'

Ava's head snapped back as her lips parted in a gasp. She stared down at the receiver while the sounds of a heated argument—fortunately or unfortunately in Italian—blared forth for all who could decipher it.

Finally, a male voice, very attractive but not carrying a trace of an accent, came on the line.

'Hello. Vince here. Sorry about that. Let me assure you,' he said in a dry tone, 'that I have no fiancée-to-be, Italian or otherwise. Who is this, by the way?'

'Oh! My…my name is Ava Whitmore,' she stammered. 'We—er—we need someone to mow our lawns, and I was wondering if…if…'

'Where do you live?' he interrupted efficiently.

'St Ives.'

'How much lawn is there?'

'Well, they're quite large really.'

'How long does it usually take to do them?'

'Three or four hours at least.'

'That big, eh? We charge twenty dollars an hour.'

'That...that's fine.'

'When would you like us to come?'

'M...Mondays would be best, I think. The previous man used to come on a Monday.'

'Lawns shouldn't need mowing every week at this time of the year. Let's see now... Yes, I can slot you in next Monday at nine.'

'*Next* Monday?'

'Something wrong with next Monday?'

'Well, no, not really, except that the man didn't come *last* Monday, and they really do need doing. If...if they're not done soon, Byron will begin to notice and there'll be hell to pay!'

There was a short sharp silence during which Ava regretted running off at the mouth like that. Whatever must Mr Morelli be thinking of her?

'Sounds like an emergency,' he said at long last, and Ava sighed with relief.

'Yes, it is,' she agreed hastily. 'Byron's very particular about things.'

'I presume this Byron is your husband?'

'Oh, no, he's my big brother. You—er—know what big brothers can be like,' she added with a nervous little laugh.

'Actually, no,' he drawled. '*I'm* the big brother around here, and it's not an easy job, I can tell you. Now about your lawns, Miss Whitmore, I'm afraid I haven't got anyone available tomorrow. Not unless...'

Another short silence seemed to hang in the air. Ava couldn't for the life of her understand why she was holding her breath. All she knew was that she was.

'It's all right, Miss Whitmore,' he resumed crisply. 'I'll come over and do them myself. No trouble. Just give me your address and everything's sweet.'

Ava let out her long-held breath, and told him Belleview's address. Then she added their telephone number in case there were any unforeseen complications. When she hung up a minute later, she stayed staring down at the telephone for ages. Finally, she turned and walked slowly back upstairs to her bedroom, her madly beating heart sinking back to harsh reality when she caught a glimpse of her reflection in the mirror.

What a fool she was. A silly fantasy-filled fool!

Ava sagged down on the side of her bed, but she refused to cry. She simply refused to.

At least the lawns will be mown by the time Byron gets home tomorrow night, she told herself. Things could be worse. And she supposed it would be quite interesting to see an Italian Casanova in the flesh.

Ava went to bed wondering just how many ladies' beds Mr Vincente Morelli had slept in.

CHAPTER TWO

GEMMA LET HERSELF into their bayside unit, instantly aware that Nathan was home—then quickly aware he was not alone. The perfume that teased her nostrils was not one she ever used. Since Kirsty didn't go in for exotic scents, Gemma had to discard any hope that the female her husband had brought home with him was his teenage daughter.

Every feminine instinct she owned screamed out that their visitor was none other than Lenore, Nathan's ex-wife. Gemma knew it was impossible to avoid the woman altogether. Even if she weren't Kirsty's mother, Nathan was directing her in the lead role in a play of his at the moment. But did he have to bring her into their apartment when she wasn't there with them?

Marshalling every ounce of composure she owned, Gemma walked across the foyer and opened the double doors that led into the large living area. The scenario that met her eyes might have been perfectly innocent, but Gemma surveyed it with dark jealousy in her heart.

Nathan was sitting next to his ex-wife on one of the blue and white striped sofas that flanked the cedar fireplace, half-drunk glasses of Scotch on the low table in front of them. Though they weren't touching, their body language bespoke an intimacy that made a lie of Nathan's repeated assertions that he felt nothing for Lenore any more. Their knees were pointed towards each other, their heads bent low.

Lenore's wide green eyes jerked up and around at Gemma's sudden entrance, their shimmering suggesting recent tears. Gemma gave Nathan a speculative look as he stood up, but his handsome face was as coolly unreadable as it always was.

'You're home late, darling,' he said, sweeping a blond lock back from his forehead as he came forward to give her a peck on the cheek.

'Not really,' she returned. 'Hello, Lenore.'

Up close, Lenore's eyes were red-rimmed and bloodshot, indicating a lot of tears. Suspicion turned to guilt as it struck Gemma that something awful might have happened.

'Is...is Kirsty all right?' she asked anxiously.

When Gemma had first come to Sydney from Lightning Ridge, Nathan had hired her as his teenage daughter's minder. Kirsty had been going through a difficult time after her parents' divorce, and, while Gemma had been six years older than Kirsty's fourteen, they had become close. Their friendship had been strained, however, when Gemma had married Nathan, and it was only recently that they had been reconciled.

'She's being a typical teenager,' Nathan said drily. 'Can I get you a drink, darling? Some white wine perhaps?'

'What? Oh, yes...please. That would be nice. But what has Kirsty done to make Lenore so upset?'

Nathan shot a look at Lenore, who sighed rather theatrically. It reminded Gemma that Nathan's ex-wife was a talented actress, not to mention a very beautiful one, her striking face, glorious red hair and model-slim figure mocking her thirty-four years.

Gemma always felt gauche compared to Lenore's ultra-sophisticated appearance, which was probably understandable since she was only twenty and had been brought up by a rough and tough old miner in a dirt dugout at Lightning Ridge. Hardly finishing-school material.

But she'd rather hoped time might have cured her of feeling inferior. After all, no one could fault her own appearance these days. Her shoulder-length dark brown hair was cut expertly to frame her face. And her once too curvaceous figure had slimmed down to a perfectly acceptable hour-glass. As for her clothes...they came from the best Double Bay boutiques.

'Kirsty's found out about my affair with Zachary Marsden,' Lenore confessed. 'She's very angry with me. She...she's demanding to be sent to boarding-school.'

Gemma gaped. Nathan had told her ages ago that Lenore was having an affair with a married man, but *Zachary Marsden?* Zachary was Byron's best friend *and* solicitor. He had a pretty little wife, Felicity, and two sons.

The news rocked Gemma's faith in humanity—and men in particular. Could they ever be trusted where sex was concerned? Or women like Lenore, for that matter?

Lenore sighed again. 'I can see Nathan wasn't lying when he assured me he hadn't told you. Look, I know it sounds bad, Gemma, but Zachary and Felicity haven't been happy for years. Felicity was the first to ask for a divorce, too. She's fallen in love with some man she met in a music shop. Not that I deny having loved Zachary for a long time...' This, with a pained glance Nathan's way.

'We...we've all been keeping our relationships secret till Zachary's younger son, Clark, finishes his HSC this year. Then Felicity and Zachary are going to separate officially. Meanwhile, I've been meeting Zachary on the quiet. He...he dropped in to rehearsals to see me late this afternoon. Unfortunately, Kirsty had the same idea after school. She—er—walked in on us in one of the dressing-rooms.'

'I see,' Gemma said, and sank down on the other sofa, a shocked expression on her face.

Lenore took one look at her and laughed. 'No, I don't think you do, love. Maybe one day, but not yet.' She stood up, smoothing down the wrinkles in the tight black skirt she was wearing. Her blouse was cream satin, tucked in at the waist, her whole outfit showing the slender elegance of her tall, willowy figure. Gemma suddenly felt fat, which was ridiculous. She'd lost even more weight recently and was slimmer than she had ever been.

Lenore picked up the black jacket that was draped over the back of the sofa and threw her ex-husband a rather wry smile. 'Thank you for all your help, Nathan. You've been surprisingly sweet about this. Marriage seems to agree with you. I'll let you know what happens with Kirsty,' she said as she dragged on the jacket.

Nathan came forward, handing Gemma her glass of wine then straightening to address the woman he'd once been married to for twelve years. 'I think you'll find that after Kirsty calms down enough for you to really talk to her and explain the situation she'll change her mind about boarding-school. But if she doesn't, you could always send her to St Brigit's for years eleven and twelve. Jade loved it there for some weird and wonderful reason.'

'Now you've really surprised me,' Lenore said, smiling that sensuous smile of hers. 'I thought you despised boarding-school.'

'I do...for eight-year-olds. But two years at this stage in Kirsty's life isn't an eternity.'

'*One* year seems an eternity sometimes,' Lenore said wearily. 'Well, goodbye, you two. Look after Gemma, Nathan. She looks a little tired. Bye, Gemma love.'

'B-bye, Lenore,' Gemma stammered, her insides churning over Nathan's solicitous treatment of this woman whom he'd once claimed could feel love and lust at the same time for different men. Female intuition kept warning Gemma that Lenore was a danger to her marriage. She might love Zachary Marsden, but she had once lusted very much after Nathan. Maybe she still did.

Nathan returned from showing Lenore out with a preoccupied expression on his face. He swept up one of the half-empty glasses of Scotch up and drained it.

Gemma's fingers tightened around her wine. She sipped

it with small, untasting swallows. 'How long were you and Lenore here before I got home?' she asked tautly.

For a moment there was a frozen silence, then Nathan said in the coldest voice, 'Are you implying what I think you're implying?'

'I'm not implying anything. I'm simply upset to find that you talk to your ex-wife more than you do to me.'

His sigh was full of exasperation. 'Only about our daughter. Look, I'm sorry if you resent it, but I did give you the chance a few weeks ago to start a baby of our own, and what did you do? Put on a tantrum about my having dared to throw away your pills without asking you, after which you went out and bought some more.'

For a second Gemma felt guilty, but Nathan's choice of the intimidating word *tantrum* brought a flash of rebellious resentment that quickly overpowered any such remorse. 'You just don't see that what you did was wrong, do you, Nathan?' she burst out, slamming the wine glass down on the coffee-table and getting to her feet. 'You *never* see that anything you do is wrong.'

'I wouldn't say that,' he said darkly. 'But my motives are always for the best.'

'Are they, Nathan? I wonder...'

When she went to brush past him, his free hand shot out to grab her upper arm. 'What do you mean by that?' he demanded to know, his fingers biting cruelly into her flesh underneath her sleeve.

Gemma winced with pain and tried to pull her arm free but his hold only tightened. For a man who looked the epitome of urbane elegance, he was remarkably strong. 'You're *hurting* me!' she protested.

'Then tell me what you meant by that remark!'

'Nothing. I...I meant nothing. I was angry. I say lots of silly things when I'm angry.'

'Don't lie to me, Gemma. Don't ever lie to me!'

'I'm *not* lying. Nathan, stop this! You're...you're frightening me.'

'Not as much as you're frightening me, my darling wife.'

'What do you mean?' she rasped.

'I mean precisely this. I wouldn't want ever to find out that you're cheating on me, sweetheart. Because if I ever do, I'd hate to imagine the consequences. If you want out of this marriage, then just say so. Up front! No sneaking behind my back. No playing me for a fool. Do I make myself clear?' His grip on her arm tightened even further, and she had to bite her lip to stop the cry of pain.

Suddenly, he released her, his angry face slowly smoothing to a semblance of his usual composure. Gemma's eyes were round upon him, the throbbing in her arm still there to remind her of what had just happened. But it was his *words* that had frightened her the most. He did not expect their marriage to last. He expected her to leave him. He'd expected it right from the start!

Why?

Because he didn't love her? Or because he didn't think she loved him?

Both, she guessed with a madly beating heart. Melanie had spelt it out for her one day when she'd asked the other woman for advice about her marriage. Right from the start Gemma had been worried about their lack of true intimacy or communication. Nathan never talked to her, never told her anything about himself or his writing or what he did when they weren't together. All he ever seemed to want her for was bed.

Melanie had expressed the opinion that a lot of people married for the wrong reasons. For lust, not love. If it was just lust between them, she'd said, then one day, they would wake up and there'd be nothing there.

Was that what Nathan was expecting? For them to wake up one day and find nothing there any more? The thought appalled her!

'There's a letter for you,' he said, his casual tone belying his violence of a moment before. 'I put it on your dressing-table. I think it's from that old lady out at Lightning Ridge.'

Despite her inner distress and confusion, Gemma felt an instant brightening. 'Ma?'

'Must you call her that?' he ground out. 'She's not your mother.'

'She was more of a mother to me than my real one!'

'True. *She'd* have to get the wooden spoon for motherhood, that's for sure!'

Gemma stared at him. He sounded as if he *knew* her mother. Yet that was impossible! At her behest, Nathan had hired an investigator to try to uncover the identity of the woman who'd given birth to her, and who had subsequently disappeared from the face of the earth. But the mysterious Mary Bell on her birth certificate existed nowhere else but on that document of lies. Neither was her dead father—alias Jon Smith—registered anywhere, except on his illegally obtained driver's licence.

But of course his real name had been Stefan. She'd found that out when she'd discovered that old photograph shortly after his death. Which reminded her...

'Nathan, you never did give me back my photograph. You know...the one of my mother.'

'The one you *think* is your mother, don't you mean? You don't really know one way or the other.'

Gemma frowned at her husband. 'Is there something you haven't told me, Nathan? Did that investigator find out something you don't want me to know?'

'What makes you think that?'

Nathan's evasion of her question with another question rang warning bells in her brain. That was what he always did when he didn't want to answer her.

'I'm not sure,' she said hesitantly, though her heart was racing. 'A hunch, I guess. You do like making decisions for me, don't you? I could well imagine you keeping something from me because you think it's for the best.' My God, could he know who her mother was and hadn't told her?

She stared at him and her voice, when she resumed, was shaking. 'Nathan, you haven't done that, have you? You know how important it is to me to find out my mother's identity, no matter what...*don't* you?'

'Yes, of course, darling,' he soothed, putting down his glass and coming forward to draw her into his arms. More warning bells rang. This was plan B when plan A didn't work. Make love to the silly little idiot to shut her up.

'I would never do anything to hurt you, Gemma,' he crooned. 'You know that.'

Those treacherously seductive lips covered hers, and, to her shame, her pulse leapt. But her distress was far greater than her desire to lose herself in that dark erotic world her husband could create so easily, so she pulled her mouth away, sending a deeply resentful glare up into his wickedly handsome face. 'That won't work this time, Nathan. I do not want to make love. I want to know what you've been keeping from me, what you know that I *don't* know.'

His head lifted, his steady gaze showing not even a hint of agitation. 'I know a lot of things that you don't know, Gemma,' he drawled. 'But nothing *you'd* want to know, I assure you.'

'You will swear on your own mother's grave that you don't know the identity of *my* mother?'

There was a tiny twitching at the corner of his beautiful mouth, but nothing else. 'I do so swear,' he said, and Gemma let out a shuddering sigh of relief.

'Happy now?'

She stared up into his suddenly cold eyes and felt a chill run right through her. He might have told her the truth just now but he didn't always. Of that she was certain.

'I'm going to go and read my letter,' she said stiffly, and, whirling, fled to their bedroom, relieved when Nathan didn't follow her. If he'd come after her and started one of his ruthlessly successful seductions, she wasn't sure what she would have done. They hadn't made love for over a week, due to her time of the month last week, and she probably would not be able to resist him indefinitely.

Nathan had once vowed to attune her body to his demands, and she couldn't deny he'd done that. And more! She'd found herself lately getting addicted to his making love to her in a less than gentle fashion. In fact, when she was in the right mood, she found his more aggressive attentions so exciting that she lost all control. Oddly enough, this often coincided with their having an argument. Since their life together lately had become punctuated with verbal spats, this type of lovemaking was happening more and more. She sometimes wondered if Nathan goaded her on purpose to make her more amenable to his savage kisses and caresses, not to mention the more adventurous type of position. She still lacked the courage to take the initiative in the bedroom, but she certainly didn't object to whatever he wanted to do to her.

It was only afterwards that she sometimes worried over what had transpired between them. Was it her own lack of control that bothered her? Or Nathan's? Admittedly, there were times when he seemed beyond reason, beyond ever being told to stop. Still, she never did want him to stop, did she?

Now she glanced nervously at the bedroom, suddenly fearful of Nathan bursting in. But the door remained closed and, finally, Gemma gave a strangled sob which perversely sounded disappointed. God, what was to become of her? She couldn't live with Nathan, and she couldn't live without him!

Remembering Ma's letter, she hurried over to pick up the rather grubby envelope and tear it open. Ma seemed to be her only link with down-to-earth reality these days and the only other female whose advice she could possibly ask. Melanie was no longer around, Ava had no real-life experience, Lenore was definitely not on her list of potential confidants, which only left Jade, who wasn't much older than herself and was so wrapped up in her new husband that Gemma didn't like to bother her with her own mixed-up troubles.

Besides, she wasn't at all sure Jade would be sympathetic. When Gemma and Nathan had recently attended Jade's small garden wedding at Belleview, Jade had come up to her afterwards, given her a big hug and told her that if Kyle loved her as much as she knew Nathan loved *his* new wife, then she'd be delirious with joy! Jade might have always had a tendency to exaggerate with her larger-than-life personality but there was no doubt she believed her adoptive brother was truly in love at long last.

Which made her the only one, Gemma realised with bleak bitterness.

Except perhaps Byron...

Byron seemed to have faith in their marriage. There again, Byron wasn't the most intuitive of men, from what she had seen. Or the most sensitive. Look at the way he treated poor Ava!

Gemma sighed as she thought of Byron's sister. It wasn't *her* fault that the caterer at Jade's wedding had got the number of guests wrong and delivered food for two hundred guests, instead of twenty. But anyone would think it was, the way he'd carried on. The man needed some woman to come along and sort him out, someone like...like...Celeste Campbell! Now there was a woman who wouldn't be bossed or bullied, who would give as good as she got—and a bit more besides!

But any hope of that happening was pie in the sky, Gemma realised drily. Though a person would have had to be blind not to sense there was something between those two. The night of the Whitmore Opals ball, when Celeste had stunned everyone by showing up, the air had crackled with electricity every time she came within three feet of

Byron. As for Byron...he hadn't been able to take his eyes off his outrageous but undeniably gorgeous sister-in-law, even if she was his main business rival and supposed deadly enemy.

Gemma would have liked to have been a fly on the wall when whatever had happened between those two had happened. It must have been pretty dramatic, and pretty dreadful; whatever it was!

She'd also have liked to have been a fly on the wall during Nathan's growing-up years. She'd always believed the answer to his secretive and highly complex personality lay in the past, but he had no more intention of telling her about that than he had of discussing her *own* past with her.

Sighing, Gemma pulled out Ma's letter and started to read. A minute later, she was jumping off the bed and racing out to find Nathan, who was standing at one of the windows, staring out over the darkening waters of Elizabeth Bay, another drink in his hands.

'Nathan, guess what?' she burst out.

Nathan turned slowly, one of his eyebrows lifting in a droll fashion. 'What?'

'You know that man out at Lightning Ridge who assaulted me years ago? The one who scared me to death the day we first met?'

'Yes...'

'He's dead! Got in a fight with another miner, and had a stroke or something. Ma says it's good riddance to bad rubbish!'

Nathan took an idle sip of his drink, his eyes never leaving her face. 'I couldn't agree more. But you seem inordinately pleased. I never took you for a creature who would relish revenge.'

'It's not revenge, Nathan, but relief. Now I can go back without being afraid.'

Nathan's glass stilled mid-way to his lips. 'Go back?'

'To Lightning Ridge. I promised Ma I'd come back and

visit her. Not only that, I always wanted to ask a few questions around town by myself. Not that I wasn't grateful about you hiring that private investigator. But you don't know what Ridge people are like. They wouldn't take kindly to some slick city fellow asking them personal questions. I'd have a much better chance of finding out the truth about my parents if I were alone.'

'You really think so, Gemma?'

'I *know* so. Please…don't try to stop me from doing this, Nathan. I've quite made up my mind.'

A few moments passed while Gemma stood, breathlessly waiting, and Nathan lifted the glass to drink once more. Now his eyes were glazed, as though he were thinking about something a long way away. Suddenly, he snapped back to the present.

'When were you thinking of going?' he asked.

Gemma expelled her long-held breath. 'Friday week. I thought I could take the morning flight and come back on the Monday afternoon. That way I'll only have to take two days off work. I haven't been at the shop long enough to ask for real holidays, but if I work some extra Saturdays, then…'

'Good grief, Gemma!' Nathan suddenly snapped. 'You're one of the family. Do you honestly think Byron wouldn't give you some time off? All you have to do is ask. There's no need to grovel around like some silly little salesgirl.'

'I wasn't going to grovel, Nathan,' she countered, hurt by his attitude. 'It's called acting with integrity and consideration, not grovelling. I don't like to take advantage of my position as your wife. Neither do I like to let people down. We're short-staffed right at this moment. Gloria's come down with the chicken pox. Hopefully, by Friday week, she'll be back on deck.'

'You're *too* considerate. Believe me, those girls at the shop would stick the knife in your back as quick as look at you.'

'Yes, so you keep telling me, Nathan,' Gemma said wearily. 'But it's me I have to live with, not them. If they do nasty things, that's their problem. I have to be true to myself.'

Nathan exploded with a type of black exasperation. 'God! How on earth did someone like you come out of...out of...someone like your father? It doesn't make sense!'

'Maybe I'm more like my mother than my father,' Gemma suggested, which brought a harsh laugh from her cynical husband.

'You don't believe that any more than I do, Gemma. She deserted you as a baby, left you with that bastard to bring you up. Would a sweet, kind and caring creature do that? I don't think so.'

'You don't know what circumstances led my mother to do what she did,' Gemma defended, but lamely. Down deep, she thought pretty well the same as Nathan. If she ever came face to face with her mother, she might just slap that face. 'She...she probably died soon after I was born.'

'You don't believe that.'

'No...no, I don't.'

'Why?'

Gemma shrugged. 'I think it's the way Dad spoke of her, on the rare occasions he did speak of her. He used to say, "She's a slut, your mother". Not...she *was* a slut.'

'That's splitting hairs, isn't it?'

'I suppose so, but it's what I feel. Sometimes all one has to go on is what one feels.'

'Yes,' Nathan said, nodding slowly. 'You're right. But sometimes, one feels what one *wants* to feel, not what is real.'

Gemma was still thinking about her mother being alive or dead, when Nathan suddenly materialised in front of her, taking her shoulders in his hands and pulling her hard against him.

'And what is it you can feel right now?' he rasped.

His hungry kiss cut off any answer she might have given, his expertise taking advantage of her slightly disorientated state of mind. With all her recent doubts tumbling through her mind, she began to battle against what her body instinctively yearned, which was simply to sink against him and let mindless desire take over. Valiantly, she held herself stiffly in his arms, resenting the way her lips automatically fell apart for his silkily seductive tongue, the way her heartbeat revved up in tune with his.

But he was too strong for her, too merciless, too knowledgeable of her body's weakness. She shivered when he trailed an almost tender hand up and down her spine while his other hand caressed her buttocks. Slowly, he pleated her skirt upwards till cool air met the gap between the top of her stockings and her skimpy satin underwear. When his fingers found bare flesh at the top of her thighs, then slipped under the elastic of her panties and began an intimate and highly expert exploration, her defeat was inevitable.

Arousal surged its insidiously heated path along her veins, her memory tempting her with how it felt when it was the full length of his desire invading her, not those tantalising teasing fingers. At long last, she moaned a moan of a total and tortured surrender, and Nathan gave an answering growl of triumph.

'Tell me you love me,' he whispered into her trembling mouth.

'I love you,' she said. Obediently. *Blindly.*

'Here, then,' he demanded hoarsely. 'On the floor... Now!'

'Yes,' she agreed wildly, even as he was already pulling her down on to the carpet and dragging at her underwear.

But later, as she lay beneath his sprawled body and listened to the desire draining from him in harsh dry gasps, Gemma hated the power Nathan had to make her do and say things like some puppet on a string. Was this love? Or some other dark force? A darkly destructive force that was like a summer storm, full of heat and wild electricity, building and building till it exploded into a sudden and dramatic downpour.

But unlike a summer storm, after which the sun came out and everything was warm and clean and peaceful, Gemma didn't feel warm, or clean, or peaceful at that moment.

Nathan's weight rolled from her and she buried her face into the soft pile of the carpet, cringing when he pulled her clothes back into place.

'I'll run you a bath,' he said from what seemed a long way away. He must have stood up. It sounded as if he was fixing his clothes. A zip was closed abruptly.

'Please don't,' came her muffled protest. 'I...I'd rather have a shower.'

'Suit yourself. Call me when dinner's ready. I'll be in my study.'

Gemma flinched at the sound of the door closing firmly behind him. Five minutes later, she was standing under a hot shower, trying to wash every bit of him from her body.

CHAPTER THREE

IN THE END, AVA WAS GLAD Byron had stayed the night at Catherine's. It meant he wasn't around to comment on her nervous state that following morning.

Ava didn't try to reason why Vince Morelli's coming to mow their lawns at nine o'clock should be putting her in such a tizz. Her subconscious understood the reason only too well. In fact, her *conscious* brain wasn't confused, either. This was as close as she was ever going to come to one of her fantasies coming true.

She dithered over what she should wear. A glance through her bedroom window showed the beginnings of a pleasant, delightfully mild spring day. Sydney was sometimes at its best in September and the forecast had predicted a top temperature of twenty degrees, with light sea breezes.

Ava pulled out a pair of lightweight black trousers that she had bought recently from her favourite boutique, favourite because it specialised in fashion for big women, clever fashion that flattered and hid faults to perfection.

Ava believed she had a lot of faults to hide, despite her now busier lifestyle's having stripped quite a few pounds from her previously very tubby body without her even trying. She'd had no time for dieting. Not so much time, either, for stuffing herself with all the junk foods she usually craved.

So when she pulled on the black trousers the elastic waist didn't have to nearly expire from stretching to get around her middle. Eyes widening with surprise, she raced to inspect her semi-naked self in the full-length mirror on the back of the wardrobe door, something she hadn't done in donkey's ages.

What she saw startled, then thrilled her. Goodness, she really didn't look too bad. Not exactly svelte, she thought ruefully as she pinched the spare tyre just above her waist. But her hips, bottom and thighs had trimmed down more than she'd realised. Must be all the running up and down stairs she'd been doing!

As for her bust…it was actually beginning to look like a *bust,* instead of a mammoth continuation of flesh from her neck to her waist. She cupped her breasts with her hands, lifting them and pressing them together. Now that was a *cleavage,* she thought naughtily. Then dropped them when the oddest physical sensation shot through her. It was almost as though she'd had an electric shock.

Ava's blue eyes widened when she noticed her nipples standing erect, goose-bumps having formed all over the pink circles around them.

She stared at them for ages before the compulsion to touch one finally overpowered her natural shyness. Her finger shook as it approached the taut peak but it would not be denied. Contact brought a sucked-in gasp. Ava wasn't sure if she liked the feeling or not. Her fingertip gently rolled the pebble-like point and Ava felt her whole insides contract.

My God! How could touching something up there make things happen down there? But it did. It definitely did! Her eyes shut and her lips fell softly apart as she touched her nipple a second time. The same thing happened.

What would it feel like if a man did this? she wondered as her heart began to beat faster. Maybe a gorgeous young Italian named Vincente…

A shudder of involuntary pleasure ripped through her and Ava's eyes shot open, shame heating her cheeks. She had gone too far. Far too far. She was becoming wicked in her old age. This type of behaviour was something she had never indulged in before. Never! And she wasn't going to start now.

Flushed and flustered, she spun away from the mirror, hurrying to drag on her bra. The confining cotton and lace, however, kept her hotly aware of her still erect nipples, and, much as she tried telling herself she *was* wicked, some secret part of herself revelled in this newfound sensuality. Finding something to team with the black trousers became a battle between her outraged conscience and her baser instincts.

In the end, she realised none of her clothes were sexy anyway, so she settled for a multicoloured jacket-style blouse which had slimming black panels inserted in each side, black lapels and cuffs. The bright design of the rest was mostly in blues and yellows, with a dash of lime-green. The buttons were black.

Ava had found, since frequenting her favourite boutique and listening to the advice of the salesgirls there, that separates with long-line tips did wonders for her short body, padded shoulders minimising her usual tendency to look top-heavy. She'd also been advised to wear really high heels to give her more height, but Ava thought that was tempting fate. She had enough trouble staying upright in flatties. But she compromised occasionally with mid-height heels. Actually, her habitual clumsiness had improved lately with all the running around and physical tasks she'd been doing. Maybe practice did make perfect.

Finally, Ava's attention turned to her face and hair. She'd had her short brown curly hair streaked a golden blonde for Jade's wedding, and it had seemed to be a hit with everyone, if you could believe their compliments. Razor-cut short at the sides and back, the hairdresser had left it longer on top, a body perm giving her natural curls more controllability. It looked equally well brushed back off her face, or with a softly wavy fringe flopping towards one eye.

Ava chose the former style that morning, then proceeded to make up her face with more attention than she had in years at that hour of the day. Some navy blue eyeshadow around her eyes deepened their bright blue colour to rich sapphire, especially once she stroked layers of black mascara along her long curly lashes.

That was one area of her looks where she had fared as well as Byron, Ava thought. Her eyes. Her mouth was passable as well, though it wouldn't have looked *any* good on a man. It was small, with a bow-shaped top lip and a softly full bottom lip. It was the mouth of a child. Or a southern belle. Slightly pouty. Ava decided for the first time that day that she rather liked it. She glossed it in generously with a deep coral lipstick that had a high lustre.

Her double chin, though, did not find favour, even if it wasn't as jowly as it had been a few weeks ago. Ava turned side on, patting it upwards, but it still drooped down when she stopped. Sighing, she searched through her box of earrings for something that would distract from her jawline without looking too ridiculous in the daytime. She settled on drops in the same lime-green that was in the jacket.

Her level of nervous excitement precluded breakfast, though she did have a couple of cups of coffee before settling down in front of the television to wait for nine o'clock to come round. The gates were already open and she was beyond housework. There wasn't much to be done anyway, what with Byron having spent the night elsewhere.

Which reminded her…

Ava jumped up and hurried out into the kitchen and over to the noticeboard on the wall where Melanie had always jotted down reminder notices and messages. Picking up the attached pen, Ava wrote PICK UP BYRON'S SUIT FROM THE DRY CLEANERS in big bold letters.

There, she thought smugly as she slotted the pen back into place. That should do it!

Ava was on her way back to the family-room when she

heard the sound of a vehicle crunching to a halt on the gravel driveway at the side of the house. A quick glance at the kitchen showed less than a minute to nine. It seemed Mr Morelli was either habitually punctual, or he wanted to make a good impression on the first day.

Ava didn't care either way. She was simply glad he'd shown up at all! Tradesmen didn't have the best reputation in the world for doing that these days.

Her relief was short-lived, however, quickly replaced by a fluttering stomach and a whirling head. Maybe fantasies were best kept in the imagination. What if Mr Morelli proved to be a dreadful disappointment in the looks department—five feet two inches tall, with a portly belly and a droopy mustache?

Most unlikely, she decided with a ruthless logic that surprised her. Would his mother have reacted as she had on the telephone last night if her son didn't have women throwing themselves at him in droves? No, Vincente Morelli was going to be good-looking all right. Ava could see him now. Tall, with black wavy hair, flashing black eyes and a cruelly sensual mouth that lifted at the corner when he smiled his coolly seductive smile.

She knew the type. Their glamorous images had filled the screen in all those Italian films she'd gobbled up over the years, the ones with subtitles and darkly handsome heroes—often in period costume—who smoldered at fanholding heroines across the palatial rooms of white-walled villas overlooking a crystalline blue sea.

Ava sighed. How she adored those movies!

The side doorbell rang, and Ava froze. Oh, God…

The doorbell rang a second time eventually and she forced her jelly-like legs to move in the direction of the sound, to make her way past the laundry and around the corner to the left where the corridor ended abruptly in a white wooden door. Steeling herself, Ava clasped the brass knob, turned it then wrenched open the door.

Ava tried hard not to stare.

The man standing a few feet from the side door wasn't darkly handsome at all.

Because he simply wasn't dark. Other than that, he *was* handsome. Incredibly so.

'M…Mr Morelli?' she queried, her still stunned eyes rolling over his light brown wavy hair, golden bronzed skin and velvet-brown eyes.

'That's me,' he replied quite curtly, those same velvet eyes hardening for some reason as they flicked over her. 'I take it you're the lady I spoke to last night? Miss Whitmore?'

'Yes…yes, I'm Ava Whitmore.'

'God, I should have known better,' he muttered under his breath before sighing a disgruntled sigh then arching his left eyebrow at her.

Ava blinked back at him.

'I suppose you'll want me to call you Ava,' he went on with the most peculiar note in his voice. If she didn't know better she'd think he was being sarcastic. As for the way he was looking at her…there was something oddly contemptuous in it.

She frowned her confusion. 'Will I?' she said blankly.

He stared at her for a long moment before frowning himself. Ava found herself noting the details of his face, now that the initial shock of being confronted by such a gorgeous creature was receding.

He had a big face, feature for feature. A man's face, dominated by a stubbornly square chin complete with cleft in the middle. It would have been a hard face if it hadn't been for those incredible eyes and that full, slightly feminine bottom lip which was protruding at the moment in a pensive pout. His blackly brooding expression brought her back to his odd comment.

'You…you can call me Miss Whitmore,' she offered tentatively, 'if you'd prefer.'

His smile, when it came, wasn't anything like those mockingly cynical ones her fantasy men always delivered. It was wide and flashing, reaching right up to his eyes which twinkled down at her in some secret amusement. Smiling, he looked about twenty-five, but her guess was that he was a good few years older.

'No. Ava it is. I'm glad we got that sorted out.'

What sorted out? she wondered.

'You were certainly right when you said you had a lot of lawn,' he went on after a brief glance around. 'I'll be lucky to be finished by lunchtime. Well, I'd better get started. Nothing will get done if we stand around chatting all day. I'll knock when I've finished.' Throwing her a final fleeting smile, he turned and began striding towards the combi-van parked under the elm that shaded that side of the house.

'Mr Morelli,' Ava called out.

He spun round, and she could have sworn a dark wariness clouded his eyes for a second. 'Yes?'

'I…I have to go out later for a while. But I should be back before noon. Would you rather I pay you now just in case you finish earlier than you expect?'

'I can't see my doing that. Besides, I won't know what to charge till I'm finished. And could we make it Vince? My father was Mr Morelli.'

'Vince,' she repeated, much preferring the romantic-sounding Vincente his mother had called him the previous evening. Yet the name did suit him. It was a strong name. And very male. Just like him.

'Your father's passed on?' she asked gently, not wanting to finish their conversation just yet. Or was it that she didn't want to stop looking at him just yet?

There was certainly plenty to look at in his lawn-mowing garb of chest-hugging white T-shirt and washed-out blue jeans, both of which lovingly followed every contour of his macho and very muscular body. Not that he was muscle-bound. Just superbly toned and honed. And very watchable.

'Eight years now,' he admitted, if a little reluctantly. 'He was a good man. I miss him.'

When he didn't follow this up with any questions about her own father or family, Ava got the hint. He wanted to get on with his work, not make idle chitchat. She began to feel self-conscious, not to mention a little guilty.

'I'm sure you do,' she murmured. 'Look, I won't hold you up any further. Ring the bell here when you're finished.'

'Right.'

Despite her resolve to dash inside and stop making a potential fool of herself, Ava stayed standing on the doorstep, watching in dry-mouthed fascination while Vince slid open the side-door of the van and lifted out a lawn-mower, then an edger, both heavy items, but both placed on to the grass without undue effort. When he noticed her still there, he threw her a puzzled look. 'Is there something I can do for you?' he asked, that peculiar wariness back in his eyes.

She blushed at the thought that automatically slid into her mind. God, but she was shameless today. Simply shameless!

'I...I was just wondering what the ladder was for,' she improvised wildly, indicating the extension ladder roped to the roof. 'I mean...how often would you need a ladder to mow lawns?'

'Not ever as I recall. But we Morellis don't just mow lawns.' And he pointed to the sign on the side of the van. *'Morelli's House and Grounds Maintenance Service'*. 'We wash windows and clean out gutters and paint roofs and keep swimming pools crystal-clear, as well as all manner of handyman jobs.'

'You do? Oh...oh, that's good then, because I'm sure we need most of those things done around here.'

Vince's laugh was dry. 'Well, I can't do them all today. Fact is I can only give you this morning. I've already had to shuffle my normal schedule around like crazy to fit you in because you sounded pretty desperate on the telephone last night. But I'll put you down as a spring-cleaning client and line up one of my brothers to come over and tackle the rest on a regular basis. Will that be all right?'

'I suppose so…' Why did she have to sound like a little girl whose daddy had just said he couldn't make it home for her birthday?'

'We'll talk about it after I've finished the mowing, OK?' Vince said brusquely. 'I really must get started.'

'Yes…yes, of course.'

Ava forced herself to go back inside but almost immediately she dashed upstairs and went round all the windows, seeing which one gave her the best unimpeded view of Vince Morelli mowing. Her own studio won hands down for the back lawn, but she would have to venture into Irene's old bedroom once Vince moved round to the front. An intimidating thought, and one she pushed aside since he was thankfully starting on the back lawn.

How utterly gorgeous he was, she sighed as she spied on him through the lace curtains. She could keep looking at him for hours on end. Gradually, her earlier thought about going to pick up Byron's dry cleaning this morning was pushed aside.

The sound of the telephone ringing first startled, then annoyed Ava. It seemed fate didn't even want to allow her the harmless pleasure of just *looking* at a real live fantasy man.

Muttering, she hurried out into the hallway, where they kept an upstairs extension on a marble-topped cedar console that matched the one in the foyer downstairs. She couldn't imagine who it could be ringing her at this early hour.

'Yes?'

'Ava? Is that you?'

'Of course it's me, Byron,' she snapped irritably. 'Who else would it be?'

'Lord only knows. It just didn't sound like you for a moment. You sounded all breathless, as if you'd been running.'

'Maybe I've taken up jogging.'

'Are you being sarcastic? Ava, what's got into you lately?'

'Maybe I'm growing up at long last, Byron,' she returned, pleased with herself for standing up to her domineering brother. 'What is it that you wanted, anyway?'

'What? Oh—er—I wanted to remind you to pick up my suit from the dry cleaners. Catherine and I are going to the opera on Friday night.'

'It's only Wednesday.'

'Yes, well, better safe than sorry, wouldn't you say?' came his dry remark. 'You've got a memory like a sieve.'

Ava bristled. 'I can't go today. I'll go tomorrow.'

'Why can't you go today?' he demanded to know.

Ava was going to invent some white lie but at the last second another spurt of defiance had her deciding to tell the truth—in part. 'I have a man here mowing the lawns,' she stated firmly. 'And when he's finished I want to be here to talk to him about getting some other jobs done that need doing around Belleview.'

'The man's here mowing the lawns? On a *Wednesday?* Doesn't he always come on a Monday?'

'The last chap did. I got rid of him and hired someone new, someone who's a bit more...versatile.' Ava was glad Byron couldn't see the fierce blush that zoomed into her cheeks at that moment, or the amazing thoughts that entered her head. She wondered if 'versatile' had ever had that sort of connotation before.

'You hired someone *new?*' Byron huffed and puffed. 'And you didn't discuss it with me *first?*'

Ava counted to ten before replying. 'Melanie wouldn't have had to discuss such a thing with you. Why should I?'

'Melanie was competent at that type of thing,' he growled. 'Whereas you're...you're...'

'Just as competent,' Ava argued, though her voice had begun to shake. 'Or I will be soon, if you keep your bib out of things and give me a fair go!'

'Ava!'

'Oh, do stop "Ava"-ing me, Byron! It's beginning to give me the pip.'

'The *pip?*'

'And stop repeating everything I say. Look, I know you think I'm a nincompoop. You've told me often enough. But you're wrong. I'm quite intelligent, really.'

'Well, of course you are. You're a Whitmore!'

'Not to mention your sister,' she reminded him pointedly. If there was one thing Byron could be relied upon, it was standing up for the family name. Nevertheless, Ava decided to change the subject. She was still rather sensitive when it came to his and other people's opinion of her intelligence, not to mention competence.

'Did you have a pleasant evening?' she asked, half fearful of hearing news she didn't want to hear. She knew Byron had been lonely since everyone had married and moved out of Belleview, but the thought of Catherine as her sister-in-law made Ava want to puke.

'Quite pleasant, thank you.'

Ava wasn't sure if her brother's stiff reply was a reluctance to admit, even to his sister, that he was sleeping with that woman, or evidence that the evening had not gone all that well. She prayed the latter was the case. Doubtful, though, since they were off to the opera together in two days.

'Now look, Ava,' Byron resumed abruptly. 'About this new fellow you hired to work around the place. What do you know about him? I mean, how did you find him?'

'He came highly recommended,' Ava lied outrageously. 'Please give me credit for some common sense.'

Silence from the other end.

'I must go, Byron. I think Mr Morelli's finished out the back and I want to make sure he trims the weeds around the terrace before he starts on the front.'

'You...you certainly seem to have everything in hand.'

'I do. Goodbye, Byron.'

'B-bye…'

Ava smiled as she hung up, never having heard Byron sound so hesitant when speaking to her.

She was still smiling when she walked downstairs and made her way out through the sliding glass doors of the family-room to the back terrace, intent on doing exactly what she'd told Byron she was going to do.

Perhaps she wasn't watching where she was going. Her eyes *were* searching for her fantasy man. Perhaps it was the unaccustomed heels that were her undoing. Whatever, she caught her heel in something, lurched forward, then totally lost her balance.

Her fall might have been relatively harmless if it hadn't been for the heavy wooden outdoor furniture just in front of her. As she went down her head connected with a sharp corner of the table. She sprawled down on to the cobblestones, totally winded yet seemingly otherwise OK. But as she lifted her head, blood began to pour forth from her forehead in large drops.

Drip. Drip. Drip.

Ava stared down at the growing red puddle. It was only when she straightened and it began to run down into her eyes that she screamed.

CHAPTER FOUR

'GOOD GOD, WHAT HAPPENED? *Hell!*'

Ava couldn't really see. But she could hear the shock in Vince Morelli's voice. Suddenly, something soft was being pressed hard against her forehead and her knees were crumpling. Yet she didn't strike ground this time. Strong arms scooped her up and gently laid her down on some nearby mown grass.

'You're lucky I heard you scream,' he muttered. 'I wouldn't have if the mower had been going, but I'd stopped it to do some of the edges. Put your hand here while I mop some of this blood out of your eyes.'

He placed her hand over the mound of soft material that he'd pressed against her forehead. 'Keep it firm,' he advised. 'It'll stop the bleeding.'

He began dabbing gently around her eyes. She blinked madly to find Vince leaning over her, a blood-stained handkerchief in his hand, a concerned look on his face, and not a stitch on above the waist. His white T-shirt was, at that moment, pressed against her forehead, but it took a few dry-mouthed moments for Ava's befuddled brain to reach this conclusion, but once she did, she gasped, her fingers lifting.

'Your shirt! It'll be ruined.'

'Stuff the shirt. Keep pressing hard for a little longer,' he insisted, covering her hand with his and exerting gentle but firm pressure. Ava could feel the calluses on his palm against the back of her hand and oddly it was this awareness more than his beautiful bare chest that sent a shudder reverberating right through her.

'What happened?' he asked. 'Did you trip over something?'

Ava's whole chest contracted as a huge wave of dismay flooded in. Of course she had tripped. *And* fallen. *And* hit her head. Clumsy-clot Ava strikes again!

Tears filled her eyes.

'Hey! Don't cry. You'll be all right. Head wounds always bleed like mad. You should have seen me one day when a bloke dropped a brick on my head. I thought I was a goner by the amount of blood, but when it was all cleaned away the actual damage was quite small. I'll bet you've only got a little nick. Still, I think I'd better carry you inside. You're awfully pale. Shock, probably. Is there anyone else at home?'

'No. No one.'

He picked her up as if she were a feather, Ava blinking up at him in awe as he carried her through the sliding glass doors that led from the back terrace into the family-room. He lowered her carefully on to the largest of the leather loungers. 'There we are. Now, no fainting on me.'

'No,' she croaked.

'Good girl.' His gentle hand on her shoulder plus his soothing smile did amazing things to her already squelchy stomach. Sighing, she closed her eyes.

'Do you want me to call your doctor?' he asked.

The thought of old Dr Handcock tut-tutting over yet another of her accidents filled Ava with dismay. Her shudder must have betrayed her reluctance for Vince said, 'You probably don't need one. As I said before, you'll be surprised how small that cut will turn out to be. Still, I think you could do with a nip of brandy,' he said firmly. 'Where should I look, Ava? You must have some brandy around here somewhere.'

Her eyes fluttered open. 'There…there's some in the drawing-room.'

He glanced around the huge family-room with its several exits. 'Which way's the drawing-room?'

'Out there.' She pointed to the door leading out into the main downstairs hall. 'Turn right and it's the second door along on the right. There's a large rosewood drinks cabinet over against the far wall. You…you can't miss it.'

'Right. You stay right there, madam. No doing the fandango while I'm gone either.'

This brought some low laughter from her lips. But no sooner had Vince disappeared than the tears started anew, rolling softly down her cheeks. He was probably right about her being in shock. Suddenly, she just couldn't stop crying, no matter how hard she tried.

'Now what's all this about?' Vince cajoled gently when he returned to sit beside her, a half-filled glass in his left hand. 'I left you laughing and I come back to find you crying again. Just as well I brought you a hefty slug of brandy. You obviously need it.' Sliding a large palm underneath her neck, he tenderly tilted her head upwards till her quivering bottom lip found the edge of the glass. 'Open up, Ava, and take a good gulp.'

She did exactly as she was told, though it made her splutter a bit.

'Another,' he ordered.

This time, the brandy slid down smoothly.

'Again…'

Her wet lashes fluttered surprise up at him and his returning look was reproachful.

'Ava, you bad girl,' he rebuked, though with humour in his voice. 'If I wanted to have my wicked way with you, I certainly wouldn't pick now, would I?'

Or any other time for that matter, Ava thought bleakly. He was just being funny, trying to cheer her up. But instead of being cheered, a depression settled deep in her heart. A man as stunningly good-looking as Vince would never want to have his wicked way, or any *other* way, with someone like her. Not in a million years.

Suddenly, she became very conscious of his large strong hand cradling the back of her head, of his half-naked body leaning over her. He was so close and so overwhelmingly male that Ava's heart automatically began to beat madly in her chest.

She found her schoolgirl reaction humiliating in the extreme. What a fool she was, a silly stupid fat fool!

But she couldn't seem to help her rising pulse-rate any more than she could help all the futile fantasies this man had evoked since the moment she'd called him the previous evening. In desperation, she gulped down some more brandy, hoping that would bring if not total composure, then some Dutch courage with which to handle this highly embarrassing situation.

'I think you've had enough,' he warned when she went to drink some more. 'No point in getting tipsy now that you've got your colour back in your face.'

Ava didn't doubt it. Her cheeks felt as if they were burning up. *She* felt like she was burning up.

Vince placed the near-empty glass down on the coffee-table then turned back with a serious look gathering on his handsome face. 'I think it's time I had a look at what you've done to this head of yours… Yes, just lie back, close your eyes and try to relax… I'm sure it's nothing too bad…'

Ava's eye-closing had nothing to do with Vince's advice and everything to do with not wanting to look upon his naked chest any longer. Never had she seen a man's shape so perfect, both in structure and proportion. His handsome face was distracting enough. His body was sheer male beauty, compelling her to wonder what it might be like to possess such a man, to be able to touch him at will. And have him touch her…

Ava had no personal experience to fall back on—only a mind full of images from movies she had seen and books she had read—but she was positive that making love with Vince would be a magical experience. Not that that magical experience would ever be hers.

A strangled sob punched from her throat just as he gingerly lifted the rolled-up T-shirt from her head.

'What is it? Did I hurt you?'

Her eyes flung wide open and when she saw his concern it struck Ava what a self-pitying self-absorbed selfish creature she was turning into. Here was this man, being so sweet and kind and generous, and what was she doing? Mooning over some pathetic fantasy which was so far out of whack from reality that it wasn't worth even *thinking* about, let alone getting upset over. If every plump, homely woman succumbed to tears and a crippling depression every time a gorgeous man wasn't attracted to her, then the world would have ground to a halt yeas ago.

Get real, Ava, she berated herself sternly. And pull yourself together!

Self-disgust had her finding some inner steel at long last.

'Not really,' she said with an apologetic smile. 'I'm just a big baby.'

'Aren't we all at times like this?' he teased gently. 'My mother says I'm a dreadful patient. I never catch a simple cold. I'm always dying with the flu!'

Ava's heart flipped over at his engaging grin. She soothed herself with the knowledge that no woman could be completely immune to charm like this, let alone a love-starved spinster like herself.

'Let's see now,' Vince was saying. 'Yes, just as I suspected. Not too bad at all. I don't think it'll need stitches. Fortunately, it's behind your hairline so there won't be any visible scar. Still, some disinfecting wouldn't go astray. You'd better direct me to your medicine cabinet. As opposed to the drinks one this time,' he added with another of his heart-stopping smiles.

Ava swallowed before finding a relatively calm voice.

'Melanie kept a first-aid kit in the kitchen somewhere, but I'm not sure exactly where…'

'Who's Melanie? Your sister?'

'No, I don't have any sisters. There's just my brother and me. Melanie was our previous housekeeper.'

'Previous, as in passed away?' he asked tentatively.

'Goodness, no. She left to get married a few weeks ago. I've been trying to do her job ever since. Not altogether successfully in my big brother's opinion,' she finished with a weary sigh.

'Much as I have sympathy for big brothers, Ava—being one of the poor misunderstood brigade myself—yours does sound a right pain in the neck. I have a feeling he and I wouldn't get along too well. Still, I doubt we'll have to worry about that, will we? Now, where else but ''somewhere in the kitchen'' do you keep disinfectant in this place?'

'There's some in my bathroom upstairs, but it…it's…'

'Upstairs,' he finished drily before grinning again. 'No trouble. Upstairs we go!' Vince jumped to his feet, scooped her up into his arms and began carrying her in the right direction. 'I know where the stairs are,' he explained blithely. 'Saw them on my journey to the drawing-room.'

'You can't carry me all that way!' Ava protested breathlessly. 'The stairs go on forever, and my rooms are right at the back of the house, and I…I'm too heavy!'

Vince's expression was startled. 'You? *Heavy?* Good grief, Ava, you're a tiny little thing.'

'In height maybe,' she muttered miserably. 'But not in weight.'

'So you're not anorexic. Believe me, that's a pleasant change these days. Besides, Italian men like their women nicely rounded, didn't you know that?' He looked down at her, brown eyes twinkling.

Ava stiffened in his arms, knowing he was just being polite and hating the way her silly heart had leapt with his cavalier though patently false flattery. If she wasn't careful here, she might stupidly start thinking there was more behind Vince's words than mere kindness, which was surely the way to a broken heart.

Vince made his way carefully up the sweeping marble staircase without appearing to notice her emotional discomfort, his apparent ease of carrying her making her concede that she certainly couldn't be as fat as she once was. But she was still carrying far too many pounds. She knew it and nothing he could say would change the truth.

'You said your room was down the back here?' he asked when they were halfway down the upstairs hall. 'Which door?'

'The last on the right.'

Amazingly, he supported her with one arm while he turned the knob and pushed open the door to her studio.

'Just put me on that divan over there,' she suggested, shuddering with relief as his arms finally slid out from under her. When he rolled his shoulders on straightening, flexing one of his hands, she knew the effort of carrying her upstairs and opening that door without dropping her had been far greater than he'd made it look, the mortifying realisation making her shrink inside.

Yet at the same time something hardened within her, a new iron-clad determination finally to do something about her weight and body. She would not only lose a good few *more* pounds, she would exercise and tone up all the flabby flesh she'd abused and neglected over the years. Byron's gym downstairs had everything she needed. It was just a matter of application and discipline. Come tomorrow she would start!

But she would not do it for any man, came her second astonishing resolution, not even Vince. She would do it for herself! Never again was she going to feel as rotten as she did at this moment. For now, however, all she wanted was for him to go, so that she wouldn't have to endure any more of his bittersweet pity.

'I'm sure I'll be all right now,' she began shakily. 'I can get the disinfectant myself. Thank you for all your help, Vince. You've been most kind but you...you'd better get back to your mowing.'

'Don't be ridiculous, Ava. I couldn't possibly do that. I'd worry all the time that you were passed out on the floor up here. No, the mowing can wait a while longer. The lawns aren't going anywhere. I'll do them later.'

'But...but you said you could only give me this morning?'

'That was before your accident. Accidents force people to rearrange their priorities, and you, Ava, have become priority number one for me today. I'll ring up and cancel what I had on this afternoon so that I can stay here and look after you till you're fit to look after yourself.'

'But...but...'

'Don't argue with an Italian man, Ava. It leads to nothing but a sore throat and total frustration. We're well known for being as stubborn as mules, especially when we know we're right. Come now,' he continued with a drily amused note in his voice. 'You wouldn't really expect me to leave you to fend for yourself in this death-trap, would you?'

'D-death trap?'

'God, yes. Never been in a house with so many things to knock into or so many slippery floors, not to mention all those atrocious marble stairs. They're downright dangerous.'

'It's *Italian* marble,' she pointed out, not sure if she was thrilled that someone else found the house an accident waiting to happen, or piqued that he was criticising Belleview, which was considered one of the finest homes in Sydney. 'Italian marble is the best in the world!'

'Quite a lot of things Italian are the best in the world,' he said with a wicked glitter in his eyes, 'but that doesn't mean they can't be dangerous if used incorrectly.'

'Most people don't have trouble with the stairs,' she mumbled. 'Only me...'

'What do you mean, only you? I had the devil of trouble keeping my footing.'

'Only because you were carrying me.'

Her disgruntled tone brought a dark glance and she would have given anything to know what he was thinking. 'Now look here, Ava,' he said after a few seconds' black silence. 'If I say the stairs are damned dangerous then they are! Look, why don't you have a carpet strip run up the middle and along that hallway outside? A deep blue would go nicely with all the grey and white. Match those pretty blue eyes of yours too,' he added, looking straight in those eyes with something close to admiration.

Ava gulped in an attempt to control her over-the-top pleasure at this new compliment which she couldn't entirely dismiss. She *did* have pretty blue eyes. Her view of her appearance was not so jaundiced that she refused to acknowledge her one good asset. But surely pretty blue eyes weren't enough to attract a man like Vince.

Confusion reigned supreme in her heart till she reasoned that even if Vince didn't *look* like a typical Italian lover-boy, he was quite capable of acting like one. No doubt flattery for females flowed from his lips quite easily, and without great thought to their effect. Still, she couldn't help pinking with pleasure at his comment, which brought another sharp glance. Clearly, Vince Morelli wasn't used to women blushing at his tossed-off lines.

'I...I don't think Byron would approve of my changing the décor around here,' she said lamely.

'That brother of yours is beginning to sound like an ogre! But enough of him for now. If we don't clean and disinfect that cut soon, it will form a scab. Where's the bathroom you told me about?'

'Through that door.'

Ten minutes later, Ava's wound had been gently but expertly administered to, she had taken two aspirin Vince had also found in the bathroom cabinet and was lying back on the roomy old divan resting, while Vince was out in the hallway, making a couple of phone calls. Any further protests over the time he was wasting on her had been ruthlessly dismissed and Ava finally decided to wallow in this one-time experience of being cosseted by the sort of man who had previously only existed for her in a movie or in her mind.

She was not foolish enough to think there was anything behind it but a quirk of fate. And she knew that when today was over their time spent together was going to be nothing but a pleasant memory. Vince had already told her that this was the one and only time he'd be mowing her lawns. In future, one of his younger brothers would be mowing them, as well as any of the other chores she needed doing around Belleview. But he *was* going to finish mowing her lawns later today. He'd promised. Meanwhile for the rest of the morning he seemed prepared to pander to her every whim.

'Everything's fine,' he announced on returning to the studio. 'I'm free for the entire day.'

'You shouldn't be putting yourself out so much,' she said, though not meaning a word of it. 'I could have called Byron. He'd have come home to look after me. Or sent someone round...'

'Don't be silly. I'm rather enjoying playing Good Samaritan. It's not my usual role, I can assure you.'

'Oh? What's your usual role?'

He laughed. God, he had a beautiful laugh. And a beautiful smile. And a beautiful everything. Sometimes life could be so unfair, Ava thought with a sudden stab of pain.

'Probably something akin to your Byron,' he said ruefully. 'My family says I've become a tyrant in the years since Dad died. They think the power has gone to my head.'

Ava frowned. 'The power? What power? What do they mean?'

He shrugged. 'Being head of the family, I suppose. Having to be responsible. To make decisions. Whatever. By the way, since I'm going to be here for a few hours, you wouldn't have a T-shirt I could borrow, would you?'

Ava couldn't very well tell him that she would much rather he stay exactly as he was. With his request, her eyes automatically went to his bare chest, one last hungry glance encompassing everything from the glorious bronzed colour to the rippling muscles to the arrow of golden curls that directed her gaze down to the flat planes of his stomach, not to mention the cheeky navel peeping above the waistband of his almost indecently tight jeans.

Ava stopped her wandering eyes right there, but she could not stop her imagination, or the heat creeping up her neck and into her face. 'Of course,' she said hurriedly, hoping Vince was interpreting her high colour as embarrassment and not what it really was.

'I'm sorry,' she went on hastily. 'I didn't think. I should have offered you something to put on before. I'm really sorry...'

'No, *I'm* the one who's sorry. I've embarrassed you by bringing your attention to my half-dressed state.' His sigh showed regret, his expression similarly apologetic. 'You're a genuine lady, Ava Whitmore, and you make me feel a heel.'

'A...a heel?'

'For the way I spoke to you when I first arrived, not to mention the things I thought.'

'What did you think?' Ava asked, both puzzled and intrigued.

'Damn, but it's hard to explain without sounding incredibly arrogant...' he groaned at the bewildered look on her face. 'One look at those innocent eyes should have told me the truth but I guess I've become cynical over the years. And you *did* waylay me with one of the usually reliable warning signs.'

Warning signs? Warning signs for what?

Her eyes widened further.

'I jumped to conclusions and I damned well shouldn't have. I'm really sorry.'

Ava's confusion and curiosity made her speak out with a most uncharacteristic impatience. 'Vince! For pity's sake, stop apologising and just tell me the truth, whatever it is.'

'All right, all right, I'm simply trying not to shock or offend you, that's all. I can see how far off the mark I was now. I guess I'm a little rusty at recognising the truth now that I'm not mowing lawns any more.'

He wasn't? Ava wondered what he was doing here, then, but she didn't like to distract him at this moment by asking. There were far more important things to find out.

'You've got no idea, Ava,' he continued with a grimace of distaste, 'just how many bored and neglected rich women there are around Sydney, and a lot of them look upon men like me as easy meat.'

'Easy meat?' she repeated with a suddenly dry mouth.

'There must be a type of grapevine among some of them,' he swept on, ignoring her raspy murmur. 'These women find out which of the tradesmen working in their area are young and reasonably attractive, then they deliberately go out of their way to hire you. The first sign you have that your primary function in being there is *not* to fix the taps or mow the lawns or clean the pool is when they answer the door first thing in the morning all glammed up. Full make-up, jewellery, perfume, sexy clothes, the works!'

Ava's mouth went dry when she thought of her attention to her appearance that morning, and the way Vince had looked her over when she'd answered the door. She recalled the coldness that had come into his eyes, then his later flashes of wariness. My God, he actually had thought for a while that she…that she…

'*Then,*' he stated with a contemptuous curl of his top lip, 'they purr at you to call them by their first names, they hang around so that you're within view all the time and finally, when you're finished, they try to get you to come inside or stay longer on some thinly veiled pretext. They offer you a cool drink, or the use of the shower. I've even had them suggest a refreshing dip in their pool. But believe me, you're not expected to do any of those things alone, and if you're stupid enough to fall for one of those lines then you've *crossed* an invisible line, and you're not expected to leave till the lady of the house is well satisfied with your services. If you do leave, you lose that client pretty damned quickly!'

'R-really?' Ava croaked out, not sure if she was shocked or fascinated that there were women in this world who actually made their fantasies come true. Of course, she didn't condone such tacky and immoral behaviour, but it did have a certain appalling appeal.

'Really,' he confirmed. 'Which is why when you answered the door looking so smart at nine o'clock this morning, I thought…' He broke off with a shrug. 'Yes, well, I've already apologised for what I thought and now that you understand why I thought what I thought, I think we'll finish with that unfortunate topic, don't you?'

All she could do was nod.

His smile seemed relieved, as though he was glad to get that off his chest, his still deliciously bare chest. Ava started wondering if he'd ever accepted any of those women's offers, if he'd ever crossed that line, but she didn't dare ask him. His derision over their behaviour suggested that he hadn't, but when that scathing remark of his mother's popped back into her head Ava had second thoughts. What ladies' beds had Mrs Morelli been referring to? Regular girlfriends, or some of his rich-bitch women employers?

Ava's gaze focused once more on Vince's semi-nude male body and she swallowed convulsively. Clearly, it was in the interests of her sanity if he put something on. *Pronto!*

She sat up, swinging her feet over the side of the divan.

'What in hell do you think you're doing?' Vince growled, rushing over to pick up her sandalled feet and place them back where they came from. 'You're not ready to get up yet. Lie back down. And you shouldn't have these still on…'

Ava froze when he started removing her sandals, gritting her teeth each time his fingers brushed against her flesh.

'There's blood on this one,' he said brusquely. 'I'll wash it for you.' He glanced up at her, eyes narrowing. 'There are some spots of blood on your top too. We'd better get it off as well and I'll soak it in cold water. Blood can be the devil to get out if you let it set in for too long. I'll just go and find you something to change into.'

'Oh, but you can't! I mean…I…I…'

He sighed at her obvious fluster, her reaction seeming to exasperate him mildly. 'Really, Ava, I realise you might not be keen on my rifling through your drawers but this is no time for excessive modesty. Agreed? Not only that, I have to find something for myself. I presume you have some of those one-size-fits-all T-shirts among your clothes?'

She was back to nodding. Her T-shirts would easily go around his broad shoulders and chest.

'Good. That is your bedroom on the other side of the bathroom, isn't it?'

Another nod.

'I thought as much. You just lie here and rest. I'll be back shortly. You won't jump up the moment I turn my back, will you?'

She shook her head.

'Lost your voice, have you?' he teased softly.

Her smile was pained. She had an awful feeling she'd lost more than her voice. She just might have lost her heart as well.

'When I get back we'll see if we can find it again. I want to know all about you, Ava Whitmore,' he said warningly, beautiful brown eyes glancing around the studio. 'You're a very intriguing lady. But most of all I want to know what's behind those mysterious damned canvasses stacked up against that wall over there!'

CHAPTER FIVE

A COMBINATION of cold common sense and healthy cynicism came to the rescue of Ava's heart while Vince was absent from the room. This wasn't love, she told herself sternly. It was fascination. Infatuation. Desperation and frustration. Not only was Vince Morelli a walking dreamboat, a fantasy in the flesh, a real live Latin lover, he was also the first man in years to be this nice to her. So of course she was smitten by him. Any idiot woman would have been, but especially *her* brand of idiot who was already besotted with Italians anyway.

So Ava lay there on the divan, bravely determined not to harbour any false hopes where Vince's excessive attentions were concerned. She was well aware that her unfortunate—or was it fortunate?—accident had sparked an uncharacteristic Sir Galahad instinct in him which he was unexpectedly enjoying. Hadn't he virtually said as much? But it wouldn't last. Dreams never did. Neither did fantasies. There always came that awful moment when one woke up and reality returned.

Her stomach curled over when Vince reappeared. Her black T-shirts had never looked anything like that on *her*.

'This do for you?' he asked, holding out a thankfully slimming black and white striped shirt that had been one of the mainstays in her casual wardrobe for years.

'Fine,' she said, taking it from his outstretched hand. 'Could you—er—turn away while I change?' The thought of him seeing what she was hiding under her clever clothes made her shudder inside.

'Of course,' he agreed, though Ava thought she detected a hint of dry amusement in his eyes as he turned away. No doubt not too many of the women he knew wanted his eyes averted from their bodies. And neither would she…if she felt for a moment he could look upon her semi-bared flesh with admiration and not revulsion.

Her fingers fumbled with the buttons of her jacket and she almost swore at her clumsiness in doing such a simple task as removing one top and putting on another. Her eyes kept darting to Vince's broad back. So nervous was she that he might turn around before she was finished that when he did make a sudden move, she gasped. But he kept his back to her as he walked across the studio floor towards the stack of unfinished, turned-around paintings leaning against the far wall. 'Do you mind if I have a look at these?' he threw back over his shoulder.

She did. But if she said so, he might stop and turn around and she was only just now struggling into the black and white blouse. In her defence, it wasn't easy undressing and dressing half lying down and she hadn't done the buttons up yet. 'Not at all,' she said breathlessly. 'But none of them is properly finished and they're not very good.'

He didn't say a word to that, simply picked up the first and turned it around to stare down at it. Gradually, he turned them all around, spreading them along the wall till Ava's watercolours formed a highly original if embarrassing border.

'I told you they weren't very good,' she murmured uncomfortably when his silence continued. His head twisted round to throw her a frowning look. 'And who the hell told you that?' he said sharply, before sighing his irritation. 'No don't tell me. I can guess. Dear old Byron—'

'No!' she protested, quite fiercely, feeling guilty that somehow she had given Vince the wrong idea about Byron.

Her brother might occasionally be a pain, as Vince had suggested, but he was never deliberately cruel. He'd actively encouraged her in her painting, told her she was very talented. Her not really believing him was not *his* fault! 'Byron has always praised my paintings,' she defended staunchly.

'Then who?' Vince demanded to know. 'Who was ignorant enough, or mean enough, to criticise your work to such an extent that you've never finished even one of these truly glorious pictures?'

'G-glorious?'

'Yes, *glorious!*' He snatched one up and strode back over towards the divan. 'Take this one for instance. Look at the light you've captured...the sense of peace and utter stillness. *Look* at it, woman! This is sheer exquisite beauty!'

Ava stared, wide-eyed, at the gentle landscape of the valley in the national park behind Belleview, painted in the soft greys and blues of a pre-dawn light. It was the closest she had ever come to really finishing one of her paintings, only a small patch in one corner needing some work to be complete. Ava recalled she had been especially happy with this one. Happy enough to maybe show it to someone. Till Irene had come in one day, taken a quick look and made a scoffing sound.

'Good God, Ava,' she'd said, that horridly scornful note in her voice, 'when are you going to try painting something other than these pathetic little bush scenes? It's not as though you ever finish any of them. Still, I suppose you've got nothing else to do and it's not as though anyone other than the family ever sees them. Just as well, eh?' she'd laughed, then swanned out of the room and off to one of her charity luncheons.

All the optimistic joy had drained out of Ava and she had put down her paintbrush, stood up and carried the painting over to where she'd put all her other unfinished canvasses. Vince was the first person to have looked at it since.

Now she stared at it again herself and, while her eyes told

her it *was* rather good, something deep inside her refused to believe it. Surely Vince was exaggerating. He'd been flattering her all day. A bitter resentment flared, making her snap at him.

'Please don't patronise me. It's not necessary. That picture is sheer unadulterated rubbish. Why don't you just say so? I can take the truth.'

His straight brown brows lifted in surprise then drew together. '*Can* you?'

'Yes,' she retorted, her small rounded chin lifting indignantly.

'Not that I can see,' he countered. 'I've just *told* you the truth.'

'Oh, for pity's sake!'

His searching gaze grew more thoughtful on her face. 'You really think this painting is rubbish, do you?'

'Yes, of course it is. I just said so, didn't I?'

'And all these others?' His free arm swept round in a circle to encompass the rest of her work.

'Those, even more so!' she spat contemptuously.

'Then why haven't you got rid of them?' he persisted with merciless logic. 'Why would you want to keep a motley collection of unfinished rubbish? Any reasonable person would have thrown them away. Or is it that you need a constant reminder that you're an artistic failure?' he threw at her with sudden harshness. 'That you have no talent at all!'

His sneering words launched Ava on to her feet, her blue eyes blazing. 'I *do* have talent!' she burst out, hating him for making her admit it, hating him for making her face the unfaceable, that she had allowed Irene to destroy her confidence and faith in that talent, had allowed that horrid woman to spoil the artistic future she might otherwise have had.

'Yes, you damned well do!' Vince reiterated strongly. 'So why *haven't* you finished any of these? What in hell's the matter with you, Ava Whitmore? Are you a coward or simply a fool, to believe whoever it was who told you differently?'

Ava plopped back down in the divan, stunned by her own outburst as well as Vince's relentless inquisition. The unexpected surge of angry defiance that had propelled her to her feet flowed out of her as quickly as it had come, replaced by a bleak misery. 'Both,' she sobbed. 'Both…' And her head dropped down into her hands.

Yet no tears came. Perhaps she was beyond tears, beyond anything. God, what a hopeless mess she'd made of her life.

'Go away,' she croaked out. 'Oh, please just go away…'

Vaguely, she heard Vince mutter something that sounded suspiciously like a four-letter word. Then he was squatting before her, taking her hands away and forcing her dry-eyed but haunted face out of hiding.

'I'm sorry,' he said gently. 'I'm an insensitive blithering idiot, going at you hammer and tongs like that. But I'm not sorry for what I said. I meant every word. And at least you admitted you *do* have talent. Believe me, Ava, when I tell you that I do not patronise people. Or flatter them. I'm far too egocentric for such niceties. If you doubt me, ask my mother. Or my sister. Or even my brothers! They'll vouch for my nasty side.'

'You could never be nasty,' she husked, shaking her head from side to side.

His laughter was low. 'You'd better believe it. I can be a real mean son of a bitch when I want to be. But you seem to bring out the best in me. I hope I can also bring out the best in you.'

Her eyes lifted, long lashes blinking. 'What…what do you mean?'

'I mean I hope I can restore the confidence in your talent that that bastard—whoever he is—destroyed so thoughtlessly.'

'Bitch,' she muttered bitterly. 'She was a bitch, not a bastard.'

Vince's sigh was expressive. 'Of course. I should have guessed. A woman. A jealous bitch of a woman.' He sounded even more vehement in his condemnation than Ava. 'And does this bitch have a name?'

'Irene,' she whispered, as though just saying her name might conjure her up like a bad spirit.

'Irene...' Vince came up off his haunches and sat down on the sofa beside her, still holding her hands. 'Tell me about this Irene. Who she is and what she did to you.'

Later, Ava was to wonder how she could have told a virtual stranger so many personal details, but at the time she would have told him anything. Maybe the brandy on an empty stomach had loosened her tongue, or maybe it was having a sympathetic listener at long last. Whatever, she must have spoken for over twenty minutes, telling Vince quite a lot about her growing-up years, but especially the part Irene played in forming the person she was today.

'But surely Byron must have known that his own wife was a wicked witch?' he asked, frowning. 'You make it sound as if he was ignorant of her true nature.'

'He was, in a way. She was so clever, Vince, so very clever. Byron never witnessed her real wickednesses, only her occasional black mood. But then, Byron made allowances for her moods, because of her being diagnosed a manic depressive.'

'Manic depressive, my foot! The woman was just a jealous vindictive bitch.'

'Jealous? But what did she have to be jealous of with me? Irene was a highly intelligent and beautiful woman whereas I'm...' She broke off, shaking her head. 'That doesn't make sense, Vince. She couldn't have been jealous of me. And surely not of her own daughter! Remember, she was just as mean to little Jade as me.'

'Maybe jealous is the wrong word. Maybe warped and

twisted better describes her. Who knows what makes some women sour on life, Ava? But I've known quite a few who are. They seem scared that other people might find the happiness they think they've been cheated out of, so they make sure everyone around them is as miserable as they are. Reading between the lines, I would say your brother did not love his wife, Ava. Not as she wanted to be loved. But I would say *she* loved *him* obsessively. Tell me, was Byron a faithful husband?'

'Oh, yes! Byron would never commit adultery. Never! He's very strict on that kind of thing.'

'Even in those last years, when his wife was away a lot in those rest-homes you told me about? You did say she was in there for weeks sometimes.'

'Yes, she was...' Ava's confidence in Byron's celibacy wavered in the knowledge of his present affair with Catherine. She'd been rather shocked that her almost prudish brother had launched into such an open sexual liaison. There again, he had changed since Irene's death. Loosened up quite a bit. Look how he'd accepted Jade becoming pregnant to Kyle before they were married.

'What about this Melanie you mentioned?' Vince asked. 'Your previous housekeeper. Could he have been having an affair with her?'

'Lord, no!' She laughed her incredulity at such a thought. 'No, no, you're quite wrong there. Besides, Melanie was only with us for a couple of years. We had another woman before that. A Mrs...um...Parkes...' Ava's voice trailed away as she recalled the abruptness with which Byron had despatched Mrs Parkes. Had he been caught out in an indiscretion with her? Beverley Parkes had not been an unattractive woman...

'I can see you're having second thoughts about your brother's moral rectitude,' Vince said somewhat drily. 'Believe me, Ava, when it comes to sex there aren't many men who can resist temptation, especially if they're frustrated at the time and an attractive woman offers herself to them on a silver platter.'

Ava stared at Vince, her mind jumping to all those rich woman who had propositioned him. Had he slept with any of them? Surely not. He'd been contemptuous of such women earlier. Why be contemptuous if he'd accommodated their wishes?

'Let's not talk about Byron any more,' she said, keen to change the subject. 'Or Irene for that matter. She's dead. If I'm still a failure then I have no one to blame but myself.'

'Dead right,' Vince agreed, making Ava's head jerk back in shock at his bluntness. His smile, however, was soothing. 'You've just had your first and last therapy session. Now it's time to change, madam. No more excuses. So what's the first thing you're going to do?'

'Er—finish that painting?'

'That and all the others! And then?'

'Then?' she repeated blankly.

'Then you're going to *do* something with them, aren't you?'

'Am I?'

'For pity's sake, must I hold your hand the whole way?'

Ava flushed furiously, and Vince groaned. 'God, I've done it again. Badgered you shamelessly when really it's none of my business. But dammit, Ava. I hate to see a nice sweet lady like you suffering from having been put down so cruelly all her life. I think if that Irene wasn't already dead and gone, I'd strangle her myself!'

Ava didn't doubt it. When annoyed at something, Vince was all volatile temperament, like most Italians. Maybe that was why she'd always found them so enormously attractive, because they embodied everything she wasn't. Outgoing. Passionate. Highly emotional. Being the wife of a man like Vince would be very exciting, she imagined. Both in bed and out…

'I'm going to give you the name of someone, Ava, whom

I want you to promise me you'll make an appointment to see.'

'Who?'

'A Mr Giuseppe Belcomo. He's a very successful artist in his own right and an exceptional teacher. Owns a small gallery in Gordon where he holds exhibitions of his students' work from time to time. I'm sure he'll take you on when he sees what you've already accomplished on your own.'

'You really think so?' she asked, sounding and feeling unsure.

'I know so. But you'll have to watch him. He'll try to seduce you. He always tries to seduce his attractive female students. Not that you should worry about it unduly. He's seventy-three next birthday.'

Her laughter was rather dry. She didn't think she would have to worry, even if he'd been thirty-three.

'And what does that mean?' Vince immediately pounced, his handsome features distorted by a disgruntled frown. He slanted her a suspicious look. 'I'm not sure I can trust you to call Giuseppe, do you know that? I think I'll contact him myself and have him drop by. Yes, that's a much better idea. He can see all your work without your having to cart it over to his place. What night would be the best night for him to call round?'

'Can't...can't he come during the day?' Ava asked, knowing she had no hope of deflecting Vince from this but worrying about Byron's reaction. Much as she claimed her brother was enthusiastic about her artistic talent, she wasn't at all sure about putting his support to the test.

'Nope. I'm coming too to make sure you don't fob Giuseppe off. And to make sure he behaves himself! But I can't come during the day for the rest of this week. My days are full. They'll be even fuller after today,' he finished ruefully.

Ava felt dreadful at this reminder of Vince's wasted time. 'I told you not to stay,' she pointed out in a pained voice.

'Look, Vince, I'm not sure any of this is such a good idea. I mean...I...I...'

One look at his face had her voice drifting to nothingness. 'All right,' she amended with a resigned sigh. 'Call your friend. But Friday night is the only night that suits.'

'I didn't realise you were such a social butterfly,' he said on a puzzled note. 'From what you'd told me, I got the impression you lived a rather quiet life.'

Ava now regretted the extent of her confession to Vince.

'I do,' she admitted stiffly. 'It's just that I'd rather Byron not be here when you come.'

'And you say he's not an ogre,' Vince muttered.

'He's not! He's just...*difficult*...sometimes.'

'That's a euphemism for ogre if ever I've heard one. But it's your life, Ava, and I wouldn't dream of causing you any unnecessary hassle. I'll bring Giuseppe over Friday night, if he's free. If he's not, I'll call you and we'll find some other time your saintly sibling is absent. I'll be calling you tomorrow anyway to see how your head is faring. Have you got a headache now? You're frowning at me.'

'No. No, I haven't,' she realised with some surprise. To be honest, she'd almost forgotten about the accident. It was hard to concentrate on anything with Vince making such astonishing statements. Why on earth was he bothering to be so sweet to her?

'Good!' he pronounced. 'Look, I think I'll pop down the road and buy us both some lunch. I'm hungry and so must you be. Is there anything special you like to eat for lunch?'

'Not really,' Ava said, amazed at this next realisation that she hadn't given food a thought all day. If this kept up, she would indeed lose some weight. 'A salad sandwich?' she suggested.

'Done! And I'll get us some juice to drink. Is there anything else you'd like me to do for you while I'm down at the shops?'

'Er—which shops are you planning on visiting?'

'The shopping centre just a few blocks down the road. You must know the one I mean.'

'Yes, I do.' Byron's suit was there. 'Do you think you could pick up some dry cleaning for me?'

'Sure.'

'It's not too much trouble?'

He gave her an exasperated look. 'For pity's sake, woman, the way you carry on, I'm beginning to think no one's ever done anything for you in your life!' He flashed her a frowning look before muttering something and shaking his head. 'What's the big deal, anyway? I'll already be down there, won't I?'

'Yes, I suppose so....'

'Then just give me the ticket and stop arguing. *God!*'

'I'll have to get off this divan to get it.'

'Can't I get it for you?'

'No,' she said weakly, cringing inside.

'Why ever not?'

'Because I...I can't remember where I put it. It's downstairs s...s...somewhere,' she stammered as she always did when she felt stupid.

Vince raised his eyebrows to the ceiling. 'You artistic types are all alike. Absent-minded and airy-fairy.' His sudden grin disarmed the rapidly gathering feelings of inadequacy and stupidity. 'But where would the world be without its artists? It'd be pretty dull filled up with just us physical types, wouldn't it?'

'Oh, I don't know,' Ava murmured when, as she attempted to stand, Vince slid a helping arm around her. She wasn't sure if her light-headedness was due to the bump on her head or Vince's touch. A couple of fingertips were brushing the underside of her left breast. Whatever, a dizzy spell struck and her knees went from under her. Once again, she found herself swept up into those big strong arms, her own arms automatically snaking around his solid neck for extra support. Her fingers contacted some soft wavy ends, Vince's hair being rather long at the back.

'This…this is getting to be a habit,' she croaked on their way downstairs.

His eyes dropped to hers. 'Well don't get used to it. I only do this on Wednesdays, and only during the first week of spring.'

'Oh…'

'Of course…all rules are meant to be broken,' he said as he stepped carefully on to the foyer floor.

Ava stared back up at him, her lips parting slightly as her heart jolted into a gallop. For a second his stride faltered completely, an odd cloud darkening his warm brown eyes. Ava's senses swam under their narrowed gaze and she could have sworn his arms tightened around her, lifting her slightly closer to his mouth. The thought that he was going to kiss her brought a widening of her eyes and a mad acceleration to her already pounding heartbeat.

But she was deluding herself, as usual, his next words indicating he'd only been rearranging his cumbersome load after the hazardous walk down the elongated marble staircase.

'I thought this house was dangerous before,' he muttered quite testily. 'I didn't know just how dangerous.'

Ava's disappointment was acute, as was her embarrassment. Why on earth would a man like Vince want to kiss her? She had to be losing her mind! 'I…I'll buy some carpet for those stairs as soon as I can,' she promised for something to say to cover her shame.

'What? Oh, yes…the carpet. You do that, Ava. And if you need someone to install it for you, Morelli's Maintenance employ an excellent man who's a dab hand at that kind of job. His name's Roger White.'

'I…I'd rather have you, Vince,' she said, not wanting another stranger around the house. He was already going to send over one of his brothers next Monday for the lawns. 'Don't you do that sort of thing?'

He hesitated, then smiled. It was a most peculiar smile. 'No...no, I don't do that sort of thing.'

When his face assumed a closed look Ava didn't like to persist, but she was left with the odd impression that he wasn't talking about installing carpet.

'I'll send Roger out to do the lawns next Monday as well,' Vince said abruptly, his legs resuming their long stride as he crossed the foyer.

'But I thought you were going to send one of your brothers?'

'I was...but I think Roger will suit you better all round. He's a good man. Yes, a very good man.' Vince carried Ava through the family-room and out into the kitchen where he frowned at the wall clock. 'Good God, is that the time? One o'clock? We'll have to get a move on here. Now where do you think you might have put that infernal ticket?'

CHAPTER SIX

GEMMA GLANCED AT HER WATCH. One o'clock. At long last, she thought with a weary sigh. Lunch.

Normally, time at work flew for Gemma. She loved showing customers the beautiful designer opals that Whitmore's had for sale in this particular shop. Being in the foyer of the exclusive Regency Hotel, the range of jewellery they kept here was very upmarket, much more so than their other Sydney store down at the Rocks whose clientele was mostly made up of the less affluent tourists wanting to buy a simple opal ring or pendant to take home.

The sort of person who came into the Regency store was more interested in purchasing an opal that would serve as both an item of jewellery and an investment. Over fifty per cent of their customers were wealthy Japanese, which was why Gemma had had to learn Japanese before Byron had allowed her to work there. She'd had to study very hard to become even passably fluent in the language at her time of starting as a sales assistant a few months back, but since then constant use had improved her fluency in leaps and bounds. Gemma felt great satisfaction in this and was usually keen to serve as many Japanese customers as possible.

Any other day she would have been pleased when a large group of Japanese walked in, as had happened a couple of hours back. Today, however, Gemma hadn't felt like smiling politely all the time and having to concentrate on what was being asked of her. She'd been at screaming point by the time they'd all finally trundled out, not even the extent of her sales making up for the stress of the long and demanding encounter. At least now she'd be able to escape and go for a quiet walk, away from people and noise, to somewhere she could just sit and think.

Turning from the counter, she signalled the manager that she was off to lunch, then walked quickly through the curtain into the back room where she lifted her cream woollen blazer off the coat rack and drew it on over her classically simple forest-green dress. Her shoulder-length hair, she noticed in the mirror on the wall, was still tidy, its clever cut making it curve naturally around her face in soft bangs. Her make-up needed a touch-up and after doing that she automatically sprayed on some of the Arpège perfume she kept in her bag at all times.

Her grooming complete, she looped the long strap of her tan handbag over her shoulder and left the shop, mouthing a smiling farewell to Peta and Graham, who were both busy with customers. Her long legs moved her tense body swiftly across the hotel foyer, out through the revolving doors and down the ramp to spring sunshine and fresh air.

Gemma stood for a second and breathed deeply, till she caught a strong whiff of the carbon monoxide from the steady stream of taxi exhausts as they pulled up and left the hotel. Wrinkling her already pert nose, she shuddered, then determined not to breathe too deeply again till she reached the really fresh air of the Botanic Gardens. In five minutes, she'd be there, provided the lights were kind.

She walked quickly, head down, unaware of the man who'd followed her out of the hotel, and was still following her, an intense look on his strikingly handsome face. When Gemma had to stop at a set of lights, he momentarily fell back into a nearby doorway, his narrowed gaze never leaving her.

Her inner agitation had been clear to him from the moment she came out of the shop door. Hopefully, this meant that her marriage to Nathan Whitmore was as rocky as his information suggested it was. He hadn't wanted a woman this much in years, hadn't *waited* for one for this long. Ever. But waiting, he was finding, could be an extremely strong aphrodisiac. And he could do with one these days.

Simple sex with a woman was beginning to pall. It was all too damned easy for a man like himself. Amazing what a combination of good looks, wealth and reputation could achieve without any real effort on his part. Women seemed very keen to accommodate him in just about whatever way he fancied. Well…a certain type of woman did.

Only he didn't fancy that type any longer. Where was the challenge in that? There was no sense of triumph in a gold-digging slut coming across on the first date. Or in laying a whip across the bare buttocks of an amateur whore. Even his affairs with the wives of the businessmen he met in his position as sales and marketing manager for Campbell Jewels were beginning to bore him.

But what if he could possess Nathan Whitmore's lovely young bride…?

It had always piqued him that he'd never been able to seduce that bastard's previous wife. Lenore was a beauty too, but unfortunately too streetwise to fall for his lines of approach. Damian's hatred of Nathan Whitmore had grown with his lack of success with Lenore, but he had no intention of failing this time. Gemma Whitmore was no Lenore. How could she be at only twenty?

He could still recall the first moment he'd seen her at the ball in that exquisite dress, looking incredibly sensual yet sweetly innocent at the same time. There was no doubting that that lush body of hers had never experienced anything like what he wanted to make it experience. The thought of Nathan Whitmore capturing such a delicious virgin for himself rankled. Where had he found such a prize? From talking to her later at the ball, Damian had seen first-hand just how innocent she was, how sweetly trusting and naïve.

His loins contracted fiercely as he imagined what it would

be like to have her at his mercy, in hearing her whimpering cries, be they either of pleasure or pain. God, yes, he'd give anything for that...

The lights turned green and Gemma stepped off the kerb, only to have someone tread heavily on her heel from behind so that she stumbled and sprawled on to her knees on the pedestrian crossing. A couple of people asked if she was all right, one man stopping to put a supporting arm around her waist as he helped her back on to shaky legs. When he picked up her bag which had slipped from her shoulder, then went to hand it back to her, she found herself looking up into a pair of incredibly beautiful and familiar black eyes. They rounded immediately with the same startled recognition as her own.

'Mrs Whitmore!'

'Damian.' His name escaped her lips on a shocked whisper, her eyes wide upon the man her husband had warned her never to speak to again, under any circumstances.

Damian was Damian Campbell, younger brother of Celeste Campbell, the scandalous woman head of Campbell Jewels. In his late twenties, he was as handsome as the devil and supposedly as wicked, if Nathan and her in-laws were to be believed. But when Gemma had met him for the first time at the Whitmore Opals ball two months ago she'd seen no evidence of that wickedness.

OK, so he probably shouldn't have approached her on the sly the way he had, or told her Nathan didn't really love her, that he'd married her for one thing and one thing only. But she couldn't deny the sincerity of his concern for her, or his offer of friendship, if and when she might need it. While she had hotly denied his assertions about Nathan at the time—had literally run away from the disturbing claims—she now worried that he might be right.

Gemma had been married to Nathan for nearly six months and their relationship hadn't grown in any way except sexually. Maybe *he* was satisfied with the way he'd turned her into his sexual puppet, pulling her strings this way and that, but she wasn't. Lately, he'd focused their relationship on the physical more than ever, their lovemaking having taken on a dangerous edge by his choice of time and place, not to mention position.

But where in the early months of their marriage Gemma had always felt wonderful after they'd made love, sometimes now she was left feeling awful. Nathan could be quite cold to her afterwards, as though he almost despised her for having responded as wildly as she had. Was that the way a man really in love acted?

The sounds of horns honking had Damian urging her back on to the pavement, a speeding taxi just missing her. He shook an angry fist after the driver. 'Have a bit of common decency, you impatient bastard!' he shouted before turning worried eyes upon a trembling Gemma. 'Are you all right, Mrs Whitmore? God, you're shaking and you look awfully pale. Let me take you somewhere where you can sit down.'

She was incapable of stopping him from taking her arm and guiding her into a nearby coffee lounge, solicitously seeing her seated at a small table for two against the far wall before sitting down opposite. A waitress materialised by his side almost immediately and Damian ordered two coffees plus a plate of mixed sandwiches.

Seeing the way the attractive young waitress was visually gobbling up her extraordinarily handsome male customer, plus a fleeting glimpse at the way Damian momentarily eyed *her* up and down, sent some of Nathan's warnings tumbling back into Gemma's mind.

The man is a rake…no conscience…decadent…shocking reputation…a home-wrecker…have nothing to do with him. Ever!

Nathan would undeniably contend that this was a contrived meeting. But if Damian Campbell had evil intentions towards her, then why had he waited nearly two months to put those evil intentions into action?

Still...she supposed it *was* possible. He might have followed her, deliberately trodden on her heel, pretended to be surprised on seeing her...

With the waitress's departure, Damian swung still concerned eyes upon her, his anxious gaze raking her face before bestowing a relieved smile upon her. 'You're looking better already. I hope you like coffee. I can easily change it to tea if you prefer. And I ordered us some sandwiches. I was just about to buy myself some lunch when I ran into you, but I'm afraid I have to be back at the office in...' he glanced at his wristwatch '...half an hour.'

Damian's open relaxed chatter flooded her with relief. At the same time, irritation that she'd begun to think like Nathan welled up inside her. Did she honestly want to be like her husband, looking upon everything with a world-weary cynicism? He denigrated every single man who even so much as looked sideways at her. In his opinion, the whole male sex was wickedly waiting in the wings for her to give them the slightest cue or come-on before launching into a ruthless seduction.

Seeing Damian in the flesh again was a reassurance in itself. His extraordinary handsomeness was not to Gemma's personal taste, but still, here was a man who could have just about any single woman who took his fancy. Why would he be bothered chasing after a married woman who, even if she was being besieged with doubts about her husband's love, was still very much in love with that same husband?

'You haven't bolted yet,' he suddenly teased, black eyes twinkling with a wry amusement.

'No,' she admitted.

'Don't tell me. The boss is out of town this week and you can't get caught.'

A guilty colour slashed across her high cheekbones. 'Not at all,' she denied. But it was true, in a way. It was Wednesday, and because of a matinée performance at the theatre where *A Woman in Black* was to be staged, rehearsal today was being held at a small theatre out in the suburbs. There was no chance of Nathan dropping in at the shop unexpectedly this afternoon, or of her being caught drinking coffee with Damian Campbell. 'I don't like you talking about Nathan like that,' she reproached. 'It's not nice.'

'Sorry.'

Gemma looked over at him. He didn't sound or look at all sorry, and his boyish grin was very disarming. She found herself smiling back at him.

'I think you might be as naughty as everyone says you are,' she said, her voice shaking a little. *She* was shaking a little, as though it were *her* behaviour that was naughty. But why shouldn't she have coffee with a man? she thought mutinously. Nathan had more than damned coffee with Lenore!

Damian laughed at her remark. 'I've been called a lot of things, but never naughty. At least, not since kindergarten.' Sparkling black eyes caressed hers across the table, Gemma feeling slightly discomfited by the feeling of intimacy he'd managed to convey so quickly. There was something about Damian's eyes that was very magnetic. Once they locked on to you, you couldn't seem to look away.

Gemma had to make a real effort to drop hers down to the white tablecloth.

'Nathan found out about us, didn't he?' Damian said.

Her chin snapped up. 'There is no *us,* Damian,' she protested huskily.

He said nothing for a few seconds, that hypnotic black gaze boring into her till she felt almost light-headed. When his eyes finally slid away, an odd shudder rippled through her, almost as if she'd been physically released from some hidden force-field.

'No, of course not,' he said coolly. 'I only meant that he'd found out I'd spoken to you privately at the ball.' Now his gaze returned, penetrating and unsmiling. 'I'll bet he gave you an earful about me...

'Yet you're still sitting here,' he added slowly and with a sardonic arch to one of his straight black brows. 'Why is that, I wonder? Could it be that little Gemma doesn't quite believe everything her husband dishes out to her these days? Has she decided to buck the hand that feeds her? And dresses her? And *undresses* her...?'

Gemma shot to her feet just as the waitress arrived with their order on a tray. Under the other girl's startled look, she sank back down into her chair, deciding to depart in a more decorous fashion once the girl had gone. But during the time it took for the waitress to place the sandwiches and coffee on the table, then ask coyly if the gentleman wanted anything else, her anger dissipated somewhat.

Besides, she was rather curious about Damian's antagonism towards Nathan, and vice versa. Was it simply an extension of that old feud between the Campbells and the Whitmores? Or something more personal? It reminded her of the bitter enmity between Celeste Campbell and Byron. No one seeing them together could believe their mutual hatred was solely based on an argument their fathers had had over forty years before. It was too spiteful, too intense.

'I'm sorry,' Damian apologised again once they were alone. And he seemed to mean it this time. 'I shouldn't have said that.'

'No,' she agreed. 'You shouldn't have.'

'I just get mad when I think of a lovely young lady like you married to a man like Nathan Whitmore. Do you take sugar in your coffee?' he asked, holding the small silver tongs out to her after gently dropping a couple of cubes into his cup.

She took them and dropped one cube in, all the while wanting to ask further questions about Nathan but worrying over the wisdom of listening to things about her husband from an obvious enemy. Damian might lie. She wanted facts, not malevolent or exaggerated gossip.

'You have a habit of making nasty cracks about the sort

of man my husband is,' she said while stirring her drink. 'But you don't really know him, do you?'

His laughter was harsh and dry. 'I know him a damned sight better than you do.'

She stiffened. 'I find that hard to believe. I'm his wife!' How odd, she thought, that as soon as someone else deigned to criticise Nathan she immediately leapt to his defence.

'You think because you've been married to the man a few measly months that you know him? Lenore was married to Nathan for over a decade and she never got to know him.'

'How do you know that?'

'With a few drinks under her belt, Lenore has a habit of using the nearest listener as a substitute therapist. I happened to have been by her side at a few parties over the years and I heard quite a lot about Nathan's failings as a husband. Not in the bedroom, mind. I concede he's well versed in boudoir skills. Which is only reasonable, given his—er—colourful…upbringing.'

'Meaning?"

Damian's black eyes glittered as they travelled over her frowning face. 'Surely you know about his mother, don't you?'

'I know she was a drug-addict, and that she died when Nathan was sixteen.'

'Is that all he's told you?'

'I…I know she never married Nathan's father…'

Damian chuckled darkly. 'My dear, she didn't even know who Nathan's father *was,* from what I've heard.'

'Who have you *heard* these things from?' she gasped.

'From a reliable source, I can assure you.'

'Are…are you talking about Lenore?'

'No.'

'Who, then?'

'Does it matter?'

'I think it does, if you expect me to believe you.'

'I see… Well, I certainly do expect you to believe me,

Gemma my sweet. In fact, I'm counting on it.' He picked up his coffee and took a sip, holding her gaze over the rim of the cup. 'Irene told me.'

'I...Irene?' Shock made Gemma sound vague.

'You don't know who I'm talking about?' Damian seemed surprised. 'Goodness, the Whitmore clan has certainly kept you in the dark, haven't they?'

'Of course I know who Irene was,' Gemma bit out. 'She was Byron's wife.'

'And my half-sister.'

'Oh. Oh, yes, I forgot.'

'So have most people, but Irene and I always did have a certain...rapport. Mother never could stand her, and neither could Celeste. Frankly, she was an incredible bitch with them, but she was always a sweetie to me. I could understand her, you see. Maybe we shared some similar genes from dear old Papa.'

When Damian stopped for a moment, his face deep in thought, Gemma also fell silent, her thoughts revolving. She was quite intrigued by these revelations about the woman who would have been her mother-in-law, had she not been accidentally killed in a boating accident last year. But no one around Belleview ever spoke of Irene Whitmore, except very briefly in passing and not at all kindly.

'Irene always told me everything,' Damian continued after sipping some more coffee. 'Believe me when I say I know a hell of a lot about your beloved Nathan.'

'From Irene's point of view, you mean,' Gemma inserted with another sharp frown. 'Let's face it, Damian, from what I've heard, Irene was not the nicest person in the world. Ava told me she could be very jealous and vindictive.'

'Ava *would*,' he laughed drily. 'Poor old Ava! Still...she's quite right, to a degree. Irene *was* given to moments of vengeance: some called for, some not. But she loved that bastard Byron Whitmore, and didn't deserve to be kicked in the guts the way he kicked her. I don't blame her one bit for going to bed with his golden-haired boy.'

Gemma stared at him, her face paling.

'Have I shocked you again?' he said in a darkly dry voice. 'Poor Gemma...you really don't know anything, do you? Hasn't anyone told you of your Nathan's ingrained penchant for older women? When Byron found him after his mother's death, he was the live-in lover of some ancient old actress who boasted openly of her young lover's sexual prowess and stamina.'

Gemma's hand lifted to her clammy forehead as Damian droned on and on. She could hear what he was saying, but the room seemed to be receding, her stomach rolling over and over.

'Given Byron's adultery with a certain relative of Irene's who shall remain nameless, who could blame her for having a little fling with the gorgeous young Nathan? He was, as I've already explained, well trained in meeting the needs of more mature ladies. Irene certainly gave him a ten when she was telling me all about their sneaky nocturnal romps.'

Damian watched a green-gilled Gemma race for the ladies' room, knowing that he'd just delayed his chances of any imminent seduction in favour of a more immediate pleasure. But how he'd adored seeing those innocent eyes widen with revulsion and horror. And who knew? Perhaps his revelations might achieve the other end as well? Maybe they would give her the impetus to leave that bastard. If she crossed that high moral line he pretended to live by.

I'll offer her a position in one of our stores, Damian planned. And accommodation in one of the many blocks of units Campbell's own. At a reduced rent, of course. Something she can afford but which won't make her suspicious of my intentions. A girl not long left Lightning Ridge wouldn't have any idea of the rents in Sydney.

All might not be lost after all, he mused as he watched her come back to the table, white-faced and shaken.

'I...I can't stay,' she blurted out. 'I just can't...'

He picked up one of her limp hands, holding it fast against her rather weak struggle to free herself. 'Yes, you can,' he said firmly. 'You can do anything you want to do. You are a beautiful person, Gemma. And a good one. You deserve better than the life you're living. Get out before it destroys you, before *Whitmore* destroys you!'

She wrenched her hand away, snatched up her bag and bolted for the door, not looking back.

Damian's sigh was frustrated. Perhaps he'd over-played his hand. Laid it on too thick. It was always difficult to know how far to carry a lie.

Not that everything he'd said was a lie. Not by a long shot. Nathan Whitmore was a corrupt bastard all right. And a cruel one. What he'd done to Irene had been unforgivable. Blackmail was the lowest of the low. Even he had never stooped to such tactics.

Though it could have a certain appeal in certain circumstances. Yes, he would give the matter some further thought...

'Has the lady left already, sir?' the pretty waitress asked huskily. 'She didn't drink her coffee.'

Damian looked up and into her eager blue eyes.

Not much of a challenge. But the encounter with the delectable Gemma had aroused him. Besides, the thought of going back to that bloody office this afternoon was untenable. Celeste was in a foul mood, and he wasn't exactly in her good books since she'd found out about his bribing those Japanese tour guides. But dammit, he had to get some extra money somehow. He'd had a dreadful run at poker lately.

Yes, there were plenty of better ways to spend the afternoon than putting up with his bitch of a sister hauling him over the coals again, or asking him about that stupid opal she'd bought. How would *he* know how, when, where and why the damned thing had turned up again?

Focusing his magnetic black eyes upon the waitress, he flashed her a winning smile. 'What time do you finish here, darlin'?'

CHAPTER SEVEN

AVA WAS STILL IN A DAZE of delight when the telephone rang. Vince had not long left, after spending the entire day looking after her every whim and want, yet still completing the lawns and edges. His promise to call her the following day and let her know about Giuseppe's proposed visit on the Friday evening had still been ringing in her ears when the cook arrived to prepare the evening meal. The woman had given Ava a frowning look when she'd asked her what she wanted cooked that evening and Ava had said, 'Any old thing. I'm really not hungry.'

Ava had ignored the woman's mutterings and was swanning up the stairs when the jangling sound of the telephone had cut into her rampant fantasies about her blossoming romance with the most gorgeous, sexiest, sweetest, kindest man who ever drew breath.

'Damn and blast,' she muttered irritably, hating having to abandon the mental image of Vince partnering her to next year's opal ball. She'd be divinely slim and svelte by then—in her mind—wearing a figure-hugging black gown and quite taking everyone's breath away with her slender elegance and astonishingly handsome companion.

The imaginary scenario dismissed, Ava had a moment of dithering as she tried to make up her mind whether to go back downstairs to the extension in the foyer or to keep on going to the one in the upstairs hall. Further irritation descended with the unpalatable realisation that such a simple decision was rattling her. Even her making up her mind to keep going upstairs didn't make her feel any better.

Did someone as weak-willed as herself possess the fortitude and stick-at-it-ness to put into action all these new resolutions Vince had sparked in her today—exercises to be done, paintings to be finished, classes to be taken?

'And carpet to be put on these infernal stairs!' she grumbled aloud when her foot almost shot out from under her on the top step. Frustration launched her into potentially reckless strides which brought her with surprisingly safe swiftness down the corridor to the hall telephone. Glaring at the nuisance of a thing, she snatched the receiver up to her ear. 'Yes?'

'Ava?' The female voice on the other end sounded very unsure.

'Yes,' Ava snapped. 'Who is this?'

'It's—er—Gemma. Have I caught you at a bad time?'

Guilt consumed Ava. What was wrong with her, snapping like that? Gemma must think she was dreadfully rude. But with her forcible return to reality, Ava had had to face that her silly dreams about Vince were just that: dreams. They would never come true. And this time, reality had made her angry as well as depressed.

'I'm sorry, Gemma,' she apologised. 'I didn't mean to bite your head off. I...I'm a bit off today. I—er—fell over this morning on the back terrace and cut my head open. Isn't that just like me?'

'Oh, dear, that sounds nasty. Are you all right? Did you get the doctor? Would you like me to come over? I've just got home from work and Nathan's not home yet but I could quite easily leave him a note and drive over.'

Ava's guilt increased, if anything. She hadn't been trying to gain sympathy by telling Gemma about her mishap, just trying to find an excuse for her bad manners. But what a sweety that girl was. She'd endeared herself to everyone at Belleview from the first moment she'd set foot in the place.

Never had Ava known such a kind, generous, soft-hearted girl. She was far too good for the likes of Nathan!

'No, no,' she blurted out. 'I wouldn't dream of making you come all this way when you've just got home from work. I'm fine. Really. It didn't even need stitches. I'm just mad at myself for being so clumsy all the time. But what about you, Gemma? You don't usually telephone for nothing. Is there something wrong?'

'Oh—er—not really. I…um…I wanted to ask you a few things, but if you're not feeling well then I think perhaps I…I—'

'I'm feeling perfectly well,' Ava cut in firmly. 'You'll make me feel terrible if you hang up without asking me what you wanted to ask me. I'll worry and you wouldn't want that, would you?'

'No…'

'Ask away, then.'

'It's rather awkward, really…'

Ava knew she was not the most intuitive person when it came to tuning into other people's emotions. She'd lived her life far too much as a dreamy outsider. But suddenly, Gemma's smothered distress communicated itself to her and her chest tightened with instant concern. Yet oddly enough, she felt flattered too. Someone was turning to her for advice, and help. She determined to do her very best to soothe this sweet girl's fears, if she could.

'It's about Nathan,' Gemma went on hesitantly.

Well, of course it was, Ava thought ruefully. She should have realised that immediately.

'And…and Irene…'

Ava blinked her shock. Nathan and *Irene?* Good God, did the girl mean what she thought she meant?

'I…I'm not sure I understand what you mean,' she said, hoping against hope she was getting the wrong vibes here.

'Please, Ava, I don't want you to protect me from the awful truth. Someone told me today that Nathan and Irene were once lovers. I was hoping you might be able to tell me if it's true or not. Please tell me if you do. It…it's important.'

'Good lord, Gemma, I…I'm speechless! Nathan and Irene…*lovers?* Whoever said such a scandalous thing to you?'

'Never mind who said it. Is it *true?* You once told me that Nathan had bewitched every woman at Belleview at one time or another. Just who were you referring to?'

'Heavens, I was exaggerating! I didn't mean literally everyone. A few of our cleaners over the years have gone ga-ga over him. I myself developed a schoolgirl crush at one time. And so did Jade.'

'I know about Jade.'

Do you? Ava wondered, her very good memory providing a picture of a half-naked Jade in Nathan's arms by the pool less than a year ago. Still, that was before Nathan had met Gemma. To give the man credit, he did seem to be crazy about his young wife, as she was crazy about him.

'It's Nathan's relationship with Irene that concerns me,' Gemma added tautly.

'Then let me assure you it was a very cool one. Irene and Nathan barely tolerated each other at best. Irene barely tolerated *most* people.'

'I see… Then you have no evidence or suspicions that anything of a sexual nature happened between Nathan and Irene? I'm talking about not long after Nathan came to live with you all at Belleview, when he was quite young.'

'I've never heard of anything so disgusting!' Not that Nathan wasn't capable of having an affair with an older woman, Ava conceded with a silent ruefulness. She'd long known about his being the live-in lover of some actress in her forties when he'd been barely seventeen.

But he hadn't had an affair with Irene. She was sure of it. Irene had, if anything, always been a little afraid of Nathan, who had a way of looking at you back then that was quite frightening. Byron used to excuse his protégé's remote coldness as perfectly normal for a lad of his background. And maybe he had been right. But Ava herself had often felt uneasy in his presence. There were dark layers to Nathan's character that she believed no one had ever seen, which was perhaps just as well.

But nothing would be served by telling Gemma that. Gemma had asked if she had any hard evidence of Irene and Nathan being lovers and that was the question she was answering.

'It's a lie,' she said convincingly. 'Truly, Gemma, I'm shocked that anyone would even suggest such a thing. Who is making such a scurrilous claim?'

'I...I can't tell you that.'

'Why not?'

'I just can't,' the girl said in such a wretched voice that Ava became very worried. Who could it be?

An inspiration struck. Could Irene have told this vicious lie to someone at some stage in order to make trouble? Irene had hated seeing anyone happy. Had she perhaps told Lenore while she was still married to Nathan, thereby putting the nail into the coffin of that already rocky relationship? But if that was so, what on earth was Lenore doing telling Gemma? Surely she wasn't trying to get Nathan back, was she? She didn't love him. No, that couldn't be it. Who, then?

Anger at this malicious snake in the grass fuelled Ava to speak sternly.

'Don't believe anything Irene might have told anyone, Gemma. That woman couldn't lie straight in bed at night. She was evil. *Evil,* I tell you!'

'I see,' Gemma said, still sounding upset. 'But just say it *did* happen. I mean...if Nathan did go to bed with her, it probably wasn't his fault. He...he was very young at the time, with Irene the older party. If the situation was reversed, and it was a man with a much younger adopted daughter, then people would blame him, wouldn't they? They wouldn't blame the girl...'

Ava's heart went out to Gemma. Oh, how that girl loved that man. Why, she was prepared to forgive him *anything!* But she shouldn't have to forgive something that hadn't happened.

'Gemma,' Ava advised firmly, 'you have to forget what this person has told you. I can assure you that it is not true! I can only think that he or she is trying to make trouble between you and Nathan, for whatever reason. And I certainly wouldn't be bringing this matter up with Nathan. He'll only deny it, and rightly so. But where would that leave you? He'd be furious to think you'd been discussing him behind his back. You know what he's like.'

'Yes,' Gemma sighed. 'I do...'

Ava frowned. 'Aren't you happy with him, dear?'

She found Gemma's reluctance to answer very telling. So that was how the land was lying, was it? Well she couldn't say she was surprised. Good husband material Nathan wasn't. It just showed you that all the good looks and sex appeal in the world couldn't make up for other things.

Ava stiffened slightly when her mind unexpectedly filled with an image of Vince. Now why, she asked herself, would thinking about Nathan make her think of Vince? They were not at all alike. Vince wasn't just a good-looking hunk. He was a genuinely warmhearted and decent man. He and Nathan were as different as chalk and cheese.

'Marriage is never easy, Gemma,' she said, not from experience but from observation.

Gemma laughed. 'Oh, I know that, Ava. *Now.* Yet I thought when I married Nathan that all my dreams had come true.'

'And it's more like a nightmare?'

'I wouldn't go that far...'

'Much as I'm not your husband's biggest fan, Gemma, I

think there's much in his past to explain the man he is today. That mother of his was a shocker, from what I've heard.'

'Yes, I realise that,' the girl sighed. 'I just wish he'd tell me about his past himself…'

Ava didn't think Nathan was ever going to do that.

'I…I love my husband very much,' Gemma went on, a catch in her voice, 'but I think he has a lot of problems he has never faced.'

Ava had to agree. 'Men have great difficulty facing their shortcomings, my dear. Be patient. Nathan is not all bad. If anyone can teach Nathan to love, it's you.'

'I hope so, Ava. Anyway, thank you for giving me what I think is some very good advice. I'll try to be more patient and understanding.'

'Thank you for asking me. Not too many people ask silly old Ava for anything.'

'You're not silly or old at all!'

Ava smiled at how surprised Gemma sounded at her own words.

'Er—how are things going with the housekeeping?'

'I have my ups and downs. Literally,' she added drily.

Gemma laughed. 'Oh, you *are* funny.'

'Funny? *Me?*'

'Yes. You have a delightfully dry sense of humour. I must go. Nathan's just come in. Look after yourself, and thank you again.'

Gemma replaced the receiver and looked up, staring straight into a pair of beautiful but cool grey eyes.

'Who were you talking to?'

Gemma tried not to bristle, but did Nathan have to sound so suspicious?

'Ava,' came her succinct reply.

'*Ava?* And you think she has a delightfully dry sense of humour? Come on, now. Who were you *really* talking to?'

Gemma clenched her teeth hard in her jaw. It was one thing to promise patience, another to practise it.

'I was talking to Ava. If you don't believe me, call Belleview and ask her yourself.'

He kept surveying her in that same cool fashion, his face not betraying any of the frustration she knew must be bubbling over in hers. But she did so wish he wouldn't do things like this. All her earlier sympathy and understanding was vanishing in the face of his unjust suspicion.

'I believe you, darling. Is there any reason I shouldn't?' He turned away and strode across the foyer into the living-room. 'It's just that it's not like Ava to ring,' he threw back over his shoulder as he continued on over to the bar. 'Is there anything wrong at Belleview?'

'She had a fall today.'

'God, not another one. Is she hurt?'

Gemma hovered in the open doorway, anxious now to escape Nathan and any further inquisition. 'She pretended she wasn't. Look I must—'

'Did she want you to go over?' Nathan cut in.

'No.'

'Then why did she ring?'

Gemma sighed. 'Just to talk.'

Nathan's glance was sardonic. 'Ava never does. She spends her whole life in that fantasy world of hers.'

The family's attitude to Ava had long irked Gemma.

'Well, if she does, then who could blame her?' she snapped. 'Byron puts her down all the time and you're not much better. You ought to be ashamed of yourselves. Ava's a nice lady, and not at all as stupid as you make her out to be. Byron is particularly patronising. Look at the way he made her feel small about that mistake over the catering at Jade's wedding. It wasn't all Ava's fault yet she got the total blame. One day, she'll rebel and shock the life out of all you Whitmores, you wait and see!'

'You're a Whitmore too,' Nathan said wryly. 'Or had you forgotten?'

She glared at him across the room. 'Am I supposed to read some hidden meaning in that remark?'

'Not at all.' His face was bland as he picked up his drink. 'Can I get you something to drink? You look like you could do with one.'

'No, thanks. I was just about to run myself a bath.'

'What a good idea. You certainly need something to relax you. You're very uptight. Ava's little chat doesn't seem to have put you in a very good mood.'

Gemma swung away before she made another revealing retort. She hurried into her bedroom where she stripped off her jacket and dress, muttering while she hung them up in her wardrobe. Why did he have to make that sort of double-meaning remark all the time? Why did he have to make it *obvious* he didn't trust her any more? What had she ever done to inspire a lack of trust in her love?

The memory of her meeting with Damian Campbell at lunch today slid into her mind and she bit her bottom lip. Nathan would not believe that she'd run into him by accident. Even if he did, he would still be furious with her for having stayed and listened to what Damian had to say.

God, she wished she hadn't. She'd been terribly upset for the rest of the day, finding it hard to concentrate at work. Her phone call to Ava had been made out of desperation to find someone who could deny Damian's appalling claim about Nathan and Irene. To be honest, Ava had surprised her with her firmness and sound advice. The woman was not at all the absent-minded eccentric she'd imagined her to be.

But despite Ava's reassurances, there still lurked within Gemma's mind the slim possibility that Nathan might have been seduced by Irene. As for his having openly lived with some woman old enough to be his mother...Gemma found that thought both repulsive and disturbing.

'Mmm. Nice slip, that.'

Gemma whirled to find Nathan leaning against the door-jamb, lazily surveying her body in its ivory satin petticoat. He lifted his drink to his lips, his narrowed gaze continuing to take in the curves of her womanly body as he emptied the glass.

Gemma swallowed, not wanting Nathan to start anything with her right now. She was still having trouble dealing with what she'd found out about him today.

'You've lost weight lately,' he remarked as he continued his slow appraisal of her body. 'Aren't you eating properly during the day?'

She flushed guiltily at the reminder that she'd had no lunch at all that day. 'I...I thought I could do with losing a few pounds.'

'Don't.'

'Don't what?' she countered sharply. 'Don't think?'

'No, don't lose any more weight. In fact, I want you to put some back on. I liked you the way you were.'

'Yes, sir. I'll get to it right away.'

She could feel his eyes upon her as she kicked off her shoes and started to roll down her tights.

'Are you spoiling for a fight, Gemma?'

'No, of course not,' she muttered, recalling how their arguing always ended the same way lately, with Nathan intent on proving that there was one area where she never argued with him. That was the last thing she wanted. 'It's...it's been a long day,' she went on, not looking up. 'We're short-staffed at the shop and every man and his dog seemed to want to not only buy opals today but to see everything we had in the place.'

'Poor darling... Maybe you'll need someone to wash your back for you, if you're that tired...and a glass of your favourite wine. I'll go and get you some.'

Gemma's head jerked up, her mouth opening to protest, but Nathan was gone. Groaning, she went into the bathroom, put in the plug, turned on the water and poured in a whole stack of bubble-bath. If she had to endure Nathan coming in while she was naked in the bath, she was going to make sure he couldn't see a thing. Stripping off, she lowered herself carefully into the rising water and was well covered by rapidly multiplying bubbles when Nathan showed up with a tall glass of chilled Riesling.

'Thank you,' she said as he handed it over. 'Don't worry about my back. I'm going to soak.'

'So I see.' He leant back on the corner vanity, arms crossed. 'Are you all set for your trip back to Lightning Ridge?'

Gemma found herself growing tenser by the second. 'I've booked the flights. And I've written to Ma.'

'You haven't got your hopes up, have you? You do realise you probably won't find out anything.'

'Yes, but I have to try. And I'm going to keep trying,' she insisted.

'You're wasting your time,' he muttered. 'Just as I'm also wasting mine in here. I think I'll go order us some food from our favourite Thai restaurant. Clearly you're too tired for anything tonight, even cooking.' And he stalked from the room.

Gemma didn't know whether to feel relieved, or perturbed. Nathan was like a pendulum. Push him and he invariably came back to knock one off one's feet. Gemma had a feeling that she might have just pushed a little too hard.

CHAPTER EIGHT

AVA SAID NOT A SINGLE WORD to Byron that Wednesday night about either her fall or Vince, knowing both subjects would inspire critical and condescending comments that she just didn't want to hear. When she combed her hair with a fringe, it completely covered the cut, so there was nothing to notice. Not that her brother ever really looked at her. He did say grudgingly in passing that the new man seemed to have done a good job with the lawns, then was unflatteringly surprised to find that his suit had been collected from the dry cleaners.

Ava was content to spend the evening quietly with her memories of the most remarkable day she had ever spent. Not to mention the most remarkable man.

If it hadn't been for Vince's promise to bring his art-teacher friend by in a couple of days, Ava would have swiftly slotted Vince into the section of her mind reserved for fantasy men. But his impending visit on the following Friday night kept him right in the realms of real live men.

And real live men had real live eyes, she was forced to accept by the time she went to bed. Her meagre weight loss of late had not transformed her from an ugly duckling into a graceful swan. She had a long way to go before she would be really pleased with what she saw in her mirror. But dam-mit, she aimed to give it her best shot this time. Not with a silly crash diet either. That never worked. She had to tackle her weight problem another way.

Ava fell off to sleep that night full of determination, waking the next morning with her new optimism still intact. As soon as Byron went to work, she was down in his gym, working out on just about everything she could manage. A few minutes on the exercise bike, then on the step walking machine, then on the trampoline. She even did some chest and leg presses. If it had been warmer, she might have jumped into the pool for a few laps. But it wasn't. Not that the pool was in a fit state to be swum in. That was another of the jobs that had to be seen to before too long.

Ava felt so exhilarated after her hour of exercises that she went through the housework like a whiz, *and* without knocking into a thing. Breakfast was a sensible plate of muesli with fresh fruit, followed by black coffee and no sugar. She winced at the bitter taste but drank it anyway, telling herself she would get used to it in time. Ten-thirty saw her about to dash out to visit her favourite boutique for fatties when the telephone rang. Normally, she regarded the intrusive sound with irritation, but this time, she raced to answer it with a suddenly fluttering heart.

It might be Vince. He'd promised to ring some time today.

But it wasn't Vince. It was Nathan.

'Hi, there, Ava,' he said in that smoothly elegant voice of his. 'I wanted to find out if you were all right.'

'All right?' she repeated blankly, thrown by Nathan telephoning her. He'd never done so before.

'Didn't you have an accident yesterday? Wasn't it you on the telephone to Gemma when I came home last night?'

'Yes…yes, that was me. And yes, I did have a small fall.'

'Gemma and I were concerned about you, love. We would have come over if you'd needed us, you know.'

Ava was at a loss for words. This wasn't Nathan at all. She wondered if she'd missed something along the line.

'Ava? Are you still there?'

'Yes, Nathan. I guess I'm a bit speechless. I'm not used

to the male members of my family making solicitous phone calls, or enquiring about my well-being.'

Nathan laughed. 'Gemma said you had a dry sense of humour. I'm beginning to see what she means.'

'Gemma is sweet.'

'Not like her husband, eh?' he drawled.

'You *can* be nice, Nathan. When it suits your purposes.'

'How calculating you make me sound.'

'If the cap fits…'

There was a short sharp silence, during which Ava had a few moments to ponder this surprising new side of herself. Normally, she would never dare to speak to anyone like this, let alone Nathan. What was happening to her?

'You've never liked me much, have you?' he finally said in his usual cool fashion.

Not true, Ava thought. There was a time when I was madly infatuated with you. But that was a long, long time ago.

'It's hard to like someone you don't really know.'

'You know me pretty well.'

'No one knows you, Nathan.'

His low chuckle sounded bitter. 'My, my, now you've really surprised me, Ava. You have hidden depths.'

'Not as hidden as yours.'

She heard him suck in a sharp breath, but when he spoke again, his voice was chilling. 'I think we might leave this conversation right there, Ava. Clearly your bang on the head hasn't in any way impaired your brainpower. Though perhaps a word of warning might be in order.

'Don't ever presume to meddle in my affairs, especially my relationship with Gemma. I wouldn't like you to think you would tell her anything that might be misconstrued. Do I make myself clear?'

'Are you threatening me, Nathan?' Ava was astonished to find that her voice was quite calm, even though her heart was beating madly.

'Advising you, that's all.'

'Then let me give you a piece of return advice. I've had it up to my ears with other people telling me what to think and say and do. I will do as I please from now on. Do *I* make myself clear?'

She hung up before he could say another word. And even though she was trembling from head to toe Ava felt highly satisfied with herself. Finally, she hadn't quivered in her boots when someone had shot at her. She'd shot right back, and done it with style!

Yet once her sense of personal triumph faded, Ava was left worrying about Gemma. That marriage was doomed, as any marriage to Nathan was doomed.

Ava might have brooded over Nathan and his marriage to Gemma for ages if the telephone hadn't rung again. Nevertheless, her hand reached to lift down the receiver in a somewhat distracted fashion and her 'hello' was a mite vague.

'Is that the answer of a confident, up-and-coming artist?' demanded a gruff male voice.

'Vince!'

'Right in one. How's the head this morning?'

'Oh—er...' For a second she was tempted to claim a splitting headache. It would be nice to hear soothing sympathetic words, to have Vince fussing over her again, even if it was only over the telephone. But a deeply ingrained honesty waylaid her before her tongue could put the temptation into action.

'It's fine,' she said with a sigh.

'Are you sure? You're not just saying that?'

She laughed. 'No, Vince, I'm definitely not just saying that.'

'In that case why aren't you up there in that studio of yours, finishing some of those paintings?'

'Goodness, what a slave-driver you are!'

'Well, you don't become successful in life sitting on your

bum. Up and at it, Ava. When I get there tomorrow night, I want to see at least my painting finished and ready for framing. You know the one I mean. I want to buy that one.'

'You want to *buy* it?'

'How else am I going to get it? I wouldn't expect you to give it to me for nothing. Or isn't it for sale?'

'I…I hadn't thought about it. I guess it is.'

'Good. How much?'

'How much? I…I have no idea. How much do you think it's worth?'

'Good God, woman, is that any way to get a fair price for your pain, sweat and tears? Look, how about you ask Giuseppe to put a price on it and I'll pay whatever he says it's worth. Fair enough?'

'He'll probably say it's worth nothing,' she muttered. 'But I don't understand, Vince. Won't you be here when Giuseppe's here?'

'Afraid not. He refuses to look at an artist's work at night. So he's dropping by Friday afternoon instead, if that's all right with you.'

'Yes, of course it is,' she said with much more confidence than she was feeling at showing her work to an expert. He'd probably take one look at her paintings and want to throw up.

'Good. Can't stay and chat. I'm ringing you from my car phone and I'm just turning into the building site now.'

'What building site?'

'The one I'm working on at the moment. I'll see you tomorrow night around seven. That's not too early, is it?'

'Seven will be fine,' she said, her heart fluttering when she suddenly realised she would be alone with him again.

'You're very accommodating, do you know that? But I like it. See you then, Ava, and promise me you won't go running down those damned stairs.'

'I promise.'

'Have you ordered the carpet yet?'

'No.'

'Do it today.'

'Yes, Vince.'

'Bye. See you tomorrow night.'

'Bye, Vince, and…thanks…'

He didn't hear her thanks because he'd already hung up. Ava took some time to hang up herself. It was as though by keeping the telephone to her ear she might pick up some lingering vibrations of Vince's amazing energy and drive. His enthusiasm and confidence were catching when she was actually talking to him, but as soon as she hung up the old insecure Ava raised her ugly head again. Her head began spinning with all she had to do that day. There were clothes to buy, paintings to finish, carpet to order, more exercises to be done, fat-free dinner menus to plan…

She took a revitalising breath then picked up her car keys and headed for the garages. One step at a time, Ava, she kept telling herself. One step at a time.

The following morning—Friday—Ava could hardly take even one step. She woke to find that every muscle in her body had seized up, like an old car engine without any oil. Getting out of bed was agony. In the end she rolled out, groaning aloud as she put her full weight on to knees that refused to straighten.

A long Radox bath achieved a measure of mobility, as did some gentle stretching. By mid-morning, Ava felt almost human. A representative from the carpet manufacturer she'd contacted the previous day came in person to show her a wide selection of samples. She picked one, a subtle grey, not the royal blue Vince had suggested, telling the man that she would place the order on the following Monday after her handyman told her how much she would need.

Of course, she would eventually have to mention what she was doing to Byron—even Melanie would not have installed new carpet without consulting him—but she would put off the inevitable for a few days yet. If the worst came to the worst, and he vetoed carpet on the stairs, she would use it to carpet her studio. She was rather fed up with the polished floor in there too.

Friday noon saw her sitting at her easel, staring at the painting Vince had so admired. A few dabs of sky in one corner and it would be finished. The paint was mixed, her brush was ready, but every time the brush approached the picture her hand began to shake. It was incredible!

Finally, she had no choice but to put the brush down and abandon the idea. Vince would be so mad with her, but better not to finish it than ruin it completely. Maybe she was suffering from a crisis in confidence. Maybe she was nervous about what this Giuseppe person was going to say about her work. A real artist would surely see faults Vince would not even begin to see. There again, perhaps her nerves had nothing to do with her painting. Perhaps they were due to the prospect of seeing Vince again that night, but for undeniably the last time.

For what was to keep him coming back after tonight? Absolutely nothing. Men like him didn't date women like herself, no matter how accommodating they were, she thought bitterly. Or how hard they worked to make themselves look as good as they could.

Her mind turned to the new outfit she'd purchased yesterday, a silk trouser suit in a bronze colour. The loose-legged culottes and cleverly cut jacket top flattered her figure, the colour complementing her golden-blonde hair colour. She'd also purchased drop earrings in the same gold that rimmed the self-covered buttons of the jacket, as well as low-heeled bronze shoes. Most of this month's allowance had been reduced to zero in one fell swoop.

Still, it had been worth it if she could face Vince tonight looking as good as she possibly could. She'd need all the confidence she could muster, Ava reckoned, after Giuseppe's visit this afternoon. Lord, whatever had possessed her to put her so-called talent on the line like this? Seven-twenty that night saw a primped, preened and perfumed Ava sitting stiffly in an armchair in the family-room, her eyes on the flickering television screen but her ears straining to hear the sounds of a car arriving on the gravel driveway. She'd deliberately turned the volume down so that she could hear more easily. Minutes ticked away, her tension increasing with each silent second, dismay only a heartbeat away. Was he simply late, or had he decided not to come? Surely he would have rung if he couldn't make it? Surely he…?

What was that?

A shudder of relief reverberated through Ava as she recognised the crunching of a vehicle coming to a halt outside the front steps. She jumped up and began to run, stopping only when she encountered the slippery marble on the foyer floor. The prospect of sliding on her bottom over to the front door filled her with horror. But it was her sudden vision of her flushed, excited face in the mirror on the wall that really brought her up with a jolt.

Get a hold of yourself, you stupid fool. Where is your pride? Since Vince has been kind enough to come back a second time, the least you can do is present yourself with some dignity, not like some flustered over-exuberant schoolgirl.

Tempering her face into what she hoped was an elegantly cool expression, Ava had just enough time for her galloping pulse-rate to calm to a respectable trot when the front doorbell rang. Swallowing down the last persistent symptom of her nerves, she walked regally over to the front door, opening it with what she hoped was a smooth flourish.

'Sorry I'm late, Ava,' Vince said as he strode in, a frustrated scowl on his handsome face. 'I had a small problem with my car, which meant I had to drive one of the trucks.' He waved an impatient hand at the battered utility parked in front of the house. 'Damned thing ran out of petrol in the middle of the Pacific Highway. I'm going to kill whatever brother of mine is responsible when I get home.'

'But isn't it your fault if your car ran out of petrol?' Ava asked, rather confused by his outburst.

'It wasn't *my* car that ran out of petrol!' he explained frustratedly. 'One of my brothers borrowed that for the night. Probably Marc, now that I come to think of it. Presumably to impress the latest fluffy-headed female he's taking out. That boy has no taste! Naturally, with a hot date on his mind, he wouldn't have had his brain in gear when he finished for the day and forgot to fill up the petrol tanks as he's supposed to at the end of the week in readiness for the following Monday.'

Vince pushed up the sleeves of the black sweatshirt he was wearing and propped his hands on his hips, drawing Ava's gaze to his jeans-clad legs. Not the same tight blue ones he was wearing the other day. These were a faded grey, but just as tight.

'Once I realised my car was missing,' he grumbled, 'and I was running late, I just jumped into the first vehicle I could find and took off, not looking at the gauge. I nearly blew a gasket when it put-putted to a stop in the middle of an intersection.'

'So I can see. But all's well that ends well, Vince. You're here safe and sound and you're not too late, so calm down,' she soothed. 'It's not worth getting so het up about, is it?'

Vince glared at her for a moment, before a wry smile tugged at his lovely mouth. 'You're so right, Ava. I guess I'm a bit stressed out tonight. Today's been hell at work and I was worried that you might think I wasn't coming. So tell me…what did Giuseppe say?'

Ava's lips began to twitch with a sudden unexpected sense of mischief. 'Well, first of all he wanted to know why you haven't told him what a fine-looking woman I was…'

'That randy old devil! I knew I shouldn't have let him come here without me!'

'And then he asked me if I'd be interested in modelling for his anatomy classes…'

'Good God, is there no stopping that man? You do realise his models pose in the nude, don't you? What did you tell him?'

Ava's laughter was incredulous. 'No, of course.'

'Thank God for that. Can't have you posing nude.'

Ava bristled. 'And why not, pray tell?'

'Why not? What do you mean, why not! Who knows what one of those male students might do after ogling you all night? You might get crudely propositioned, or raped, or worse!'

'Oh, truly, Vince,' she dismissed scornfully. 'Do you really think some man is going to go into a lust-induced rampage after seeing me in the nude?'

Those beautiful brown eyes of his blazed with angry lights as they raked over her. 'Why not? As Giuseppe said, you're a damned fine-looking woman. Don't underestimate your attractions, Ava. There's a lot of men out there who like a well-rounded female. Italians are especially partial to voluptuous curves.'

Maybe so, but not the one standing in front of me.

His sudden grin distracted her from imminent depression. 'Look, why are we arguing about a hypothetical situation? You've already said no to the modelling offer. What I want to know now is what Giuseppe said about your *paintings!*'

Ava's soul flooded with the same emotion she'd felt when Giuseppe had pronounced his considered opinion.

'Oh, that...'

She turned away to close the front door, only turning back to face Vince when the hot wave of remembered pleasure was firmly under control. The temptation to grin fatuously was incredibly strong. Instead, she looked Vince straight in the eye and smiled an understated smile.

'He loved them. He wants to give me an exhibition.'

CHAPTER NINE

AVA HAD ANTICIPATED that Vince would be pleased. Giuseppe's opinion had, after all, validated his own. Men always liked to be proven right. What she hadn't anticipated was that his pleasure would take such a physical expression. Clearly, she had underestimated his Italian heritage and the highly emotional and demonstrative nature it had planted firmly within his macho body.

'I knew it!' he exclaimed, and, with an excited whoop, picked her up bodily and whirled her around the foyer, which was thankfully spacious or they might have come to a sticky end. By the time he finished the whirling around by planting her down and giving her a bear-hug, Ava was left extremely breathless and just a little on the warm side.

'What fantastic news!' He pulled back from the hug to grin down at her, his large hands still curled around her upper arms. 'And what am I up for to buy my painting? What has that old rogue demanded that I pay?'

'Nothing,' she said, her voice a little shaky.

Vince's hands dropped away and Ava breathed a sigh of relief.

'*Nothing?* That doesn't make any sense! Giuseppe's no fool. If he wants to give you an exhibition it's because he thinks you're going to be very successful, especially in a commercial sense. People will want to buy your paintings in droves, Ava. You can count on it.'

Ava found herself flushing with pleasure. How wonderful it was to have people believe in you, she realised. And what a difference it made to one's confidence. After Giuseppe had left she'd sat right down and finished the painting Vince especially liked, then gained nothing but total satisfaction from looking at it. All those imagined faults had been just that. Imagined.

'If I am ever successful, Vince...' she began.

'*When* you're successful, Ava,' he corrected. 'There is no if about it.'

She smiled her surrender to his single-minded confidence. 'OK. *When* I'm successful, I'll always remember who started me on my way. None of this would ever have happened without you.'

'Rubbish!' he denied, though she thought he looked pleased by her words.

'You don't know what your faith and support has meant to me. I would never have had the courage to show anyone my work on my own. Which is why I didn't ask Giuseppe to put a price on your painting. I want to give it to you, as a token of my gratitude. Please...don't say no...'

Ava choked up at this point. Perhaps because of all that had happened to her today, or because her offer had the sounds of goodbye attached. She wasn't sure which. But the renewed realisation that their friendship was swiftly drawing to an end might have had something to do with the lump filling her throat.

'I wouldn't dream of saying no,' Vince said with gentle softness, bending to press a tender but totally unloverlike kiss on her forehead. 'Thank you, Ava. It will have pride of place in my collection.'

Ava was forced to clear her throat and to blink rapidly. 'Your...collection?' she asked, dragging up a blandly curious expression from somewhere.

'Yes. I've purchased something from every one of Giuseppe's student exhibitions over the past few years. I'm no expert but I know what I like. And I value Giuseppe's opinion. I have no doubt that in years to come my collection will be extremely valuable. Meanwhile, it gives me enormous pleasure.'

'I'm sure it does. Goodness, what are we doing still standing here in the foyer?' she exclaimed before she burst into tears. 'You must think me a simply dreadful hostess. Come along into the drawing-room and I'll get you a drink. Or some coffee, if you'd prefer.'

'I would prefer coffee, but not the drawing-room. That room's only fit for musical soirées. I much prefer the kitchen.'

'Whatever you say,' Ava shrugged.

'Are you going to take lessons from Giuseppe?' Vince asked on their way through the family-room.

'Definitely. He's going to teach me oils too. I've always wanted to learn oils.'

'When do you start?'

'In a couple of weeks.'

'And when will the exhibition be?'

'Not for quite a while. I have to finish all those paintings and do a few more, he says. Perhaps early in the New Year.'

Once they arrived in the kitchen, Ava astounded herself by being able to make coffee and talk at the same time. Normally, she needed total concentration for such tasks to be completed without mishap, though at least this time she did not have to arrange things on a tray or carry that tray anywhere. All she had to do was set up cups and saucers on the breakfast counter where Vince was already perched.

It was the rotten telephone ringing that was her undoing. Ava jumped at the sound, coffee beans spilling from the spoon she was holding. She stared down at the brown stain spreading on the white counter. Groaning, she lifted mortified eyes to Vince without thinking, her personal agony at her clumsiness there for him to see. He was off his stool in a jiffy, quickly coming round to take the still trembling spoon out of her hand.

'Isn't it just like an artist not to be house-trained!' he

teased gently, already cleaning up the spill with a sponge from the sink. 'Heads in the clouds, all of them. You need someone to look after you.'

When he smiled over at her, Ava found herself staring deeply into those velvet-brown eyes, her heart squeezing tight. What a wonderfully warm person he was. Despite his claim that he'd been acting out of character last Wednesday, Ava suspected that he was always a kind-hearted man, generous with his time and his friendship, quick to help someone out when they were in trouble or in need.

'Aren't you going to answer the phone?'

Ava flushed her embarrassment. 'Yes, of course,' she mumbled, and turned away to lift the receiver down from the wall.

'Hello,' she said tautly.

'Hi, there, Auntie.'

'Jade!'

'Don't sound so surprised! I did say I'd ring you. About Papa's fiftieth, remember?'

'Yes...yes, of course. What did you decide?'

'Well, believe it or not, I've talked him into the idea of a party, after promising faithfully that it won't be too large or too formal. Kyle and I are going to have it here on our houseboat. I'll organise some buffet-style food and Kyle will have plenty of champers on hand.'

'And Byron's really agreed to this?'

'Reluctantly. I think he hates being reminded that he's fifty but we couldn't very well let his half-century go by without celebrating it, could we? Anyway, he's agreed to come and he's going to bring darling Catherine. Frankly, I'm dying to meet her.'

'You might die *after* meeting her.'

'Brr. Do I detect a little chilliness there? What's wrong with her besides her being a snob? Is she a right bitch, is that it?'

'I think I'll let you judge for yourself on that score.'

Jade laughed. 'That's sitting on the fence, but I won't press. Now I want you—plus a partner, please, Auntie—to be here next Friday night and no arguing. If you don't know anyone you can ask, then hire yourself an escort.'

'Hire myself an *escort?*' Ava repeated in a shocked voice before remembering there were other ears in the room. 'Jade, don't be ridiculous,' she hissed. 'I…I'll just come alone.'

'Oh, Auntie…'

'What time do you want me there?' Ava asked crisply.

Jade sighed. 'Any time after eight will do, but really, Auntie, you're going to spoil my numbers. Everyone will be here with someone.'

'Well, that's just too bad. Since it's not a sit-down dinner, who's going to notice? Now I must go. I have a…' She just bit back the word visitor and finished with '…I have coffee getting cold. See you next Friday night, Jade.'

'Oh, all right,' her niece said in a dispirited voice. 'But if you can think of someone, Auntie, do please bring him.'

Ava hung up and turned a falsely bright smile Vince's way. 'Sorry about that. Family problems.'

'Yes, so I gathered. How do you take your coffee?' he asked, having busied himself while she was talking.

'Black, with no sugar.'

His glance over his shoulder was sharp. 'Didn't you take it white on Wednesday?'

'Oh—er—sometimes I take it white and sometimes I take it black.'

His narrow-eyed glance carried suspicion. 'Mmm. I hope that's right and you're not on some stupid diet.'

'I don't diet any more,' she defended staunchly. 'I've given it up.'

'Why would you ever want to diet anyway?' Vince muttered. 'As I said before you have a very attractive, womanly body. There's far too many skinny women around these days.'

Ava laughed. 'I'll bet the women you date are all slim.'

'The women I choose to date are all people. They have minds and personalities as well as bodies.'

He glared over at her and she glared right back.

'Sure, Vince. But I'll bet they just happen to have beautiful slim bodies as well.'

'You're a fool, Ava Whitmore,' he bit out. 'A damned fool.'

'So I've been told often enough.'

Vince winced at this, closing his eyes with a low groan. When he opened them again, their expression was disgruntled. 'Here,' he said, pushing her cup of coffee towards her.

'Thanks.'

The cup was up to her mouth when his next words were delivered, making her hand tremble uncontrollably.

'I'll take you to wherever you have to go.'

Ava lowered her coffee carefully to the counter before she spilt it all down her front.

'What's the occasion?' he went on coolly.

Ava had to admit her own voice sounded just as cool, but inside she was shaking. 'Byron's fiftieth birthday party. His daughter and her husband are holding it. She wants everyone to bring someone, but I...um...'

'You're between boyfriends at the moment,' Vince finished for her.

Ava stared at him. Vince knew damned well that she didn't have a boyfriend from all she'd told him on the Wednesday. OK, so she hadn't told him about her humiliation with Byron despatching all her potential admirers by calling them gold-diggers, the last one justifiably so. But she'd said enough for him to read between the lines and conclude she didn't have men friends queueing at the door to ask her out!

'Actually, I'm between girlfriends myself at the moment,' Vince elaborated casually, 'so taking you is no trouble. I know what it's like, arriving alone when you're supposed to have a partner. Damned embarrassing.'

Ava could not for the life of her imagine Vince ever being at a loss for a partner. There would have to be any number of women in his life who would jump at the chance to go out with him.

No...he was just playing Good Samaritan again. And this time, she couldn't bear it.

'What's wrong?' he asked sharply when she didn't answer. 'Won't I do?'

She almost laughed. But no...actually, he *wouldn't* do. Aside from the fact she hated being the object of pity, everyone's eyes would fall out of their heads if she walked in with someone as gorgeous as he was. Jade would presume she *had* hired him and Byron would look upon him with outright suspicion, assuming Vince had his eye on Ava's inheritance. As for the rest...Ava could imagine their reactions would all be somewhere between Jade's mercenary assumption and Byron's cynicism.

'I would be proud to take you *anywhere,* Vince,' she said in an emotion-charged voice. 'But that is not the issue here. The issue is that I'd rather go alone than feel you were taking me out of charity. Or pity.'

'Pity!' Vince exploded. 'Of all the stupid...pathetic... stubborn' His hands shot out to grab Ava by the shoulders, shaking her good and proper. 'I do not take women out out of *pity!* I take them out because I like them, damn it, and don't you forget it. *Pity...*' His lovely mouth twisted with scorn as he dragged her against him and kissed her quite savagely, his lips ravaging hers before he released her rather roughly, leaving Ava wide-eyed and breathless.

'God, I'm sorry,' he muttered, raking agitated hands back through his hair. 'I didn't hurt you, did I? I didn't mean to do that, believe me. I don't know what came over me.'

It took Ava a few seconds to collect herself enough to provide an answer to his confusion.

Anger.

He'd lost his temper at being accused of something he wasn't guilty of. That kiss had been an act of outrage, not passion. His kindness had been called pity and he'd reacted with typically Italian over-the-top emotion.

'No,' she said tautly. 'You didn't hurt me.' Not physically…

'What time shall I pick you up?'

Ava's breath caught. He really meant to go through with it, then?

'Don't give me any more lip, Ava,' Vince warned. 'I'm taking you and that's that.'

Ava's new sense of self warred with her pride. She didn't like the thought of Vince taking her simply because he'd backed himself into a corner. Neither did she like the image of herself turning up at that party alone.

'What time, Ava?' Vince prompted curtly.

'Yes, yes. Would—er—eight be too early for you?' Byron would be long gone by then, if he had to go over and pick up Catherine at her beachside apartment at Palm Beach. He might not even come home at all after work, just go straight from the city to Palm Beach. God, was this really happening? Was she actually going to walk into Byron's party with Vince on her arm?

'Eight will be fine,' he gruffed. 'Is this do formal or casual?'

'Dressy, but not formal. Wear a suit or a jacket.'

'Right.' He scooped up his coffee-cup and drained it. 'Now I think I'd better get out of here before I do or say something further I might regret.'

Ava was offended but tried not to show it. 'I…I have to get your painting for you. It's upstairs.'

'In that case I'll wait at the front door while you get it.'

'Oh… Very well… If you like…'

'I don't like but it's what I'm going to do.'

'Must you talk in riddles?'

'It's the fact that you think I'm talking in riddles that makes it a necessity.'

Ava threw her hands up in the air. 'You might as well be talking Greek.'

'Don't you mean Italian?'

For a second they glared at each other, till simultaneous laughter erupted from both of them.

'I don't know what I'm laughing at,' she managed at last, hugging herself.

'Neither do I,' he responded, a wry grin on his face. 'But does it matter? Life can't have too much laughter in it.'

Ava stared at him. God, no wonder she loved Italians. She'd never felt so alive as she did at this moment. Suddenly, she didn't care what her family thought next Friday night. To hell with them all!

Not only that, it was slowly coming to Ava that next Friday would not be the end of things where Vince was concerned. Since she was going to become one of Giuseppe's students, and Vince was obviously a close friend of his, then she might see some more of him. Who knew? Maybe he'd also come back to mow her lawns if and when this Roger person was indisposed. Romance didn't figure in her thoughts—when it came to reality, Ava was a realist—but she would settle for anything where this man was concerned. Absolutely anything!

'I'll go get that painting,' she tripped happily, and turned to hurry off, returning with it to find Vince already out on the porch, the front door open. 'Here it is,' she said, and handed it to him all rolled up. 'I finished it for you.'

He unrolled the canvas and stared at it silently for a few moments, before rerolling it and looking back up again. 'This is a most generous gift. I'll treasure it always. Now I must go, Ava. See you at eight next Friday night,' he said, then whirled to hurry down the steps, giving an oddly frowning look as he climbed in behind the wheel. The engine of the ancient utility shuddered into life and he was off, his sudden acceleration sending a spray of gravel out behind him.

Ava stared at the empty driveway long after the car had gone. Very slowly she turned and went inside, pressing the button on the wall to close the gates. What had Vince been thinking when he'd frowned at her just now? Had he been comparing her to the other women he'd dated over the years? Was he going to be slightly ashamed to be seen with her? Did he regret offering to take her to Byron's party?

Maybe all three, she accepted bravely. But she refused to let it get her down. There were seven days before next Friday night. Seven days and seven nights. Surely some considerable improvement in her appearance could be accomplished in that time if she were determined and dedicated enough.

If Vince was generous enough to take her to Byron's party then she was going to make sure he was proud to be with her. With a bit of luck, at the same time, she might just be proud of herself!

CHAPTER TEN

GEMMA AND NATHAN STOOD silently together, waiting for the boarding announcement for the flight to Lightning Ridge. Outside the terminal a cool breeze was blowing, the sun not yet up. Inside, it was comfortably air-conditioned, but Gemma was experiencing her own inner chill. She'd never flown before and she was very nervous.

'There's nothing to be nervous about,' Nathan surprised her by saying. She hadn't mentioned her nerves for fear of giving Nathan an excuse for her not to go at all. 'Driving's more dangerous than flying. Take a few deep breaths and try to relax your muscles and limbs.'

She did so and did, indeed, feel better. But her thoughts were still tense, returning to the semi-argument they'd had the night before and which remained unresolved in her mind. She must have made some sort of worried sound, for Nathan threw her an exasperated look and said, 'What's wrong now?'

'I just wish you'd told me about Byron's party tonight,' she said unhappily. 'If Jade hadn't dropped into the shop yesterday I'd never have known. I think she was put out that you hadn't told her I wouldn't be there.'

'Don't worry about Jade, Gemma,' came her husband's firm reply. 'She'll survive. I wasn't going to let you put off your trip for the sake of a last-minute idea of Jade's. Byron doesn't even *want* a party and he fully understands why you won't be there. I explained the situation.'

Gemma suppressed a sigh. When was Nathan going to

realise that she had the right to make her own decisions about things like this? But no…he kept keeping things from her because he still thought he knew best. Perhaps that was one of the main reasons she was going to Lightning Ridge to make her own enquiries about her background, because underneath she was afraid Nathan knew something, and was keeping it from her.

Yet now that the moment was at hand she wondered what on earth she thought she was going to achieve. Her assertion that Lighting Ridge people would talk to her more openly than a city detective might be true, if there was anyone who knew something in the first place. Ma didn't, and she'd been her neighbour for years. The only possible person Gemma could think of was old Mr Gunther, and he was as close-mouthed as a clam.

'I'm probably wasting my time, anyway,' she muttered dispiritedly.

'I think so,' Nathan agreed. 'But hopefully it will get this obsession about your mother out of your system once and for all.'

Gemma automatically bristled, but said nothing this time for fear of another argument. Really, Nathan had been surprisingly good about this trip. She'd expected him to object, to find a million reasons why she couldn't fly off on her own. Even this morning, she'd been half expecting him to announce at the last minute that he would come with her, party or no party. But he hadn't and for that she was grateful. She could do with a few days on her own, away from him.

She'd been under a lot of stress since the day she'd run into Damian Campbell. Much as she'd tried to be patient with Nathan—as Ava had suggested—the various claims Damian had made about him kept gnawing away inside her. She longed to ask Nathan straight out about them, longed for him to confide in her, longed for him to prove his love for her by trusting her with his past.

But she knew he was never going to do that. Not voluntarily. He was going to keep doing what he'd always done, pretending he was a perfectly well-adjusted man with no dark secrets, using that cool façade of his to hide all the hell that had to be buried deep inside. She'd glimpsed that hell occasionally, especially in moments when his emotional guard was down, as it was when he was furious with her, or sexually frustrated. Then, the devils would be momentarily unleashed from his soul, making him a volatile yet at the same time touchingly vulnerable human being.

Gemma frowned at this last thought. Maybe that was what she'd been doing subconsciously of late, trying to make Nathan angry so that he would explode into that more vulnerable being. Instead, he'd been remarkably tolerant of her behaviour, either ignoring her inflammatory remarks or just not reacting to situations that would normally have annoyed him. In a way, this uncharacteristic tolerance was beginning to bother Gemma, especially when it came to Nathan's response to her avoiding sex lately. The Nathan of a couple of weeks ago certainly wouldn't have mildly accepted her excuses and walked away. He would have forced the issue. Didn't he want her any more? Was that it? Or was he using some sort of reverse psychology?

'Are you sure that old lady friend will be there at the airport to meet you?' Nathan asked, breaking into her muddled thoughts. His worried tone was so much like the old overprotective Nathan she knew and loved that Gemma smiled a type of relief at him.

'Yes, of course she will. Ma's very reliable. Gosh it'll be so good to see her again. Good to see the old home town again too.'

Nathan gave her an incredulous look. 'Surely you haven't been homesick for Lightning Ridge, and that awful dugout you used to live in!'

'Hardly, but it'll be nice to go back, visit old places.'

'You do realise it will be very hot compared to Sydney? You haven't taken all winter clothes, have you?'

Gemma laughed. 'Nathan, what an old fusspot you can be sometimes. Do you think I didn't think of that? I've been looking after myself for years, you know.'

'In a fashion,' he conceded, though grudgingly, which brought an exasperated sigh from Gemma.

'Now don't take offence, darling,' he drawled, sliding his arms around her waist and drawing her close. 'I enjoy fussing over you, just as I enjoy buying you things. Both are my way of showing you how much I love you. All I want is for you to be happy, Gemma. Always remember that...' His head dipped to sip softly at her lips.

It had been so long since Nathan had kissed her like this, so softly and tenderly, that Gemma was startled by her immediate and very fierce response. An electrical current raced through her veins, accompanied by a charge of emotion that brought home to Gemma that her own feelings for Nathan would never change. She loved him. She would *always* love him, no matter what.

Her arms sneaked around his neck, her fingers splaying up into his hair, her tonguetip darting past her softly parting lips to contact *his* lips in an inviting and seductive gesture. Nathan groaned and swept her hard against him, deepening the kiss so that soon they were swirling away in a whirlpool of passion that made them both oblivious of where they were.

Till the words 'Lightning Ridge' spoken over the intercom filtered through to Gemma's brain.

She reefed out of Nathan's torrid embrace, her face hot, her head still spinning. 'I...I have to go,' she choked out breathlessly.

'No, you don't,' he ground back. 'You can stay with me. Forget Lightning Ridge! We'll drive up to Avoca, spend the next four days alone together at the beachhouse, have a second honeymoon.'

'I can't, Nathan,' she said, shaken by how much she was tempted. 'Ma's waiting for me. And what about your rehearsals for the play, not to mention Byron's birthday party tonight?'

'To hell with the play, and to hell with Byron's birthday party!'

She laid a quivering hand against his frustrated face. 'You don't meant that...'

He dragged in then expelled a shuddering sigh. 'No, I suppose not. Go, then. Leave me to my misery and loneliness.'

Her laughter was low but full of satisfaction. Nathan did love her. They were going to be all right.

'When I get back we'll plan a weekend away together,' she promised. 'Meanwhile, why don't you throw yourself back into some writing over the weekend? Drag out that play you put aside.'

'Yes...yes, I might do that.'

'I must go, Nathan...I love you...'

'And I love you too, darling. See you Monday.' He waved as she moved off through the gate with the small line of people.

She waved back once, then walked on, her spirits low. Monday was four days away. Four lonely days.

God, I don't want to go!

The sudden impulse to run back was so strong she halted and glanced back over her shoulder.

But Nathan wasn't there. He'd already left. With a resigned sigh, she kept on going.

AVA WAS A NERVOUS WRECK by the time Friday evening came. She had never felt so excited about something in all her life, yet at the same time agitated.

A brutal inspection in the dressing-room mirror that morning had confirmed she hadn't worked wonders over the previous week. She'd worked a darned *miracle!*

Ava had resisted looking at herself too closely all week, though she'd noticed her face getting thinner, and had sensed a great change beneath her increasingly baggy clothes. But the full-length mirror revealing that literally *pounds* had dropped away in some places and she actually had a *shape!* Of course she'd almost killed herself with working out, and she'd been ruthless in her eating habits, sticking to fresh fruits, grilled meat, steamed vegetables and high-fibre breads with no added margarine.

Nothing sweet had passed her lips. Every time she had a craving—which was often—she would mentally picture Vince arriving to pick her up for the party, and the craving would be resisted. A man was great motivation, she'd found. At least…a man like Vince was.

Ava had left the buying of an outfit till the Friday morning, not going to her boutique for biggies this time, but an ordinary boutique which also had a wide range of lingerie. She still wasn't model material—not by a long shot—but with the aid of a figure-shaping corset in stretch cream satin, she looked very well in a deep coral suit whose semi-fitted jacket and slimline skirt made the most of her still buxom figure. The jacket had a low, heart-shaped neckline which showed quite a bit of cleavage, and when Ava had said she would fill it up with a necklace the sales assistant had shaken her head in disapproval.

'Why distract from your best asset?' the girl floored Ava by complimenting. 'If you've got it, flaunt it!'

Ava had left the shop in a state of elation, her next port of call being her hairdresser, who had oohed and aahed, not just over the clothes, but over her client's much slimmer figure. She'd assumed Ava had been to an expensive health farm, expressing wide-eyed admiration when Ava said she'd done it all by herself at home.

Ava had returned from her shopping and hairdressing expedition with her confidence high but her bank balance in the red. If she kept this up she would definitely have to sell some of Irene's jewellery to make ends meet. After all, none of her clothes fitted her very well any more. In another week or two, she would have to buy a whole new wardrobe. What an exciting thought!

Her happiness, however, was replaced by apprehension as the time to get ready approached. In deference to her nerves, she started early. Unfortunately, her agitated state tended to make her quicker—or maybe she moved faster these days. Whatever, by seven-thirty she was putting in her gold drop earrings and slipping her feet into a pair of strappy gold sandals which hadn't seen the light of day for years but which had never gone out of fashion.

Nevertheless, they were quite high, and Ava figured she could use her spare half-hour getting used to them. What else was there to do? Byron's birthday gift was wrapped, his card written on. There was no one in the house to talk to or show off to—Cook had been given the night off and Byron, as expected, hadn't come home after work, choosing to go straight to Catherine's.

Ava made sure the gates were open then spent the time walking carefully around the house, practising being elegant and smiling fatuously at herself wherever she could see her reflection. God, but she did look good! She still couldn't believe it.

What would Vince say? she wondered breathlessly. Would he be surprised? Pleased? Or wouldn't he even notice the change?

Byron hadn't all week. There again, she did go round the house in sloppy clothes, so she couldn't really blame him. He should see some difference tonight, though. So should every other member of her family. What would *they* say? Maybe they'd be too busy gawking at Vince to really notice the difference in her.

She wondered what Vince would wear. Having never seen him in anything other than jeans, she was rather looking forward to seeing what he looked like dressed more formally. Still, he would look fantastic in anything.

Her feelings of excited anticipation grew with each passing second, her eyes constantly returning to one of the many clocks around the house. But clocks were like watched pots, Ava found out that evening. They never seemed to get a move on. Every time she checked the grandfather clock in the hall, the hands had hardly moved. She paced up and down, up and down, till she was so darned competent in those high heels she could have done the tango across the marble foyer and not missed her footing once.

The doorbell ringing out of the blue almost gave Ava a heart attack. The moment was at hand at last. Dear God, please let him like how I look. Please don't let him say anything critical. And please, stop me from *shaking!*

Ava soon realised that all her shaking was inside, for she managed to make it to the door and open it with surprising panache. Vince's back was to her at first. He must have turned to admire the front gardens, which looked spectacular at night when the lights marking out the circular driveway were on, as they were at that moment. The pond in the centre looked especially enchanting, with its water lilies beginning to bud.

'You're right on time,' she said, her polite smile freezing on her lips when Vince turned, something happening inside her chest when he looked straight at her. It felt like a vice had suddenly been clamped around her heart. She gulped and dropped her eyes from that too handsome face and those too beautiful brown eyes.

His clothes, she noted after a couple of blank seconds, could have been put together from the pages of a style magazine for men. Tailored beige trousers covered his long muscular legs, a tan leather belt marking out his trim hips. A smart cream linen sports jacket made his broad shoulders look broader, underneath which lay a dark brown shirt in a very sexy silky material. The two top buttons were undone and Ava's eyes were irrevocably drawn to the smattering of golden curls at the centre of that well-remembered bronzed chest.

In jeans, Vince had been a handsome hunk. In these clothes he was something different entirely, suave and sophisticated, with a more subtle sexy appeal which still evoked in Ava yearnings impossible to control. She tried to stop her eyes from filling with raw hunger as she looked him over but she was doomed to failure. Her only consolation was that he seemed too busy staring at *her* to notice her appallingly revealing inspection. Was that admiration in his eyes, or exasperation?

'My God, Ava, what have you been doing to yourself?' he exclaimed at last.

'Doing?' she repeated. My God, her heart was pounding so hard she was sure she was going to faint. Thank the lord she was holding on to the side of the doorway. 'What...what do you mean?'

'You know damned well what I mean, woman. You've either been on one of those fool crash diets or you've been deceiving me all along by wearing clothes a couple of sizes too big.'

'Oh...oh, you mean my weight loss,' she returned, her inner agitation increasing. Why was he angry with her? 'Well, actually, I—er—haven't been on a diet at all. I've been working out.'

'Working out?' he repeated, still scowling.

'Yes. You know. Sit-ups and things.'

'Sit-ups and things?'

Vince's attitude finally got to Ava, her inner agitation suddenly bursting forth into open frustration. 'Truly, Vince, must you repeat everything I say?' she exclaimed irritably. 'And why sound so puzzled? I'm sure you know what sit-ups are. What's the matter? Don't you like the way I look?'

His narrowed gaze raked over her from head to toe again

before he gave a dismissive shrug. 'What's not to like? You look gorgeous and you know it.'

Ava was taken aback. What an odd way to give a compliment! It was not at all what she had hoped for. *Nothing* he had said since she had opened the door was what she had hoped for.

'Gee whiz, thanks,' she said, her voice sharp with hurt and disappointment. 'You scrub up pretty well yourself. Amazing what the right clothes can do, isn't it?'

Vince cocked his head on one side, his thoughtful expression slowly being replaced by a rueful smile. 'Amazing what the loss of a few pounds can do to a woman's personality. I hope you're not going to turn into one of those rich bitches, Ava. If you are, then I suggest you turn back the clock. I much prefer the woman I first met.'

Ava was so startled by this remark that she just stood there, her thoughts whirling. How could he possibly have preferred that blimp?

'Tell me, Ava,' he went on with a quiet ruthlessness, 'is there anything you should tell me about this party tonight? I have an awful feeling there's some hidden agenda I don't know about.'

Ava frowned her confusion. 'Why on earth would you say that?'

'I'm not sure. But you must have had a mighty powerful reason for the agony you've obviously put yourself through this past week.'

Ava stared straight into Vince's eyes and battled hard to keep her composure. Oh, Vince.... Don't you know? Can't you see? I love you. I wanted you to be proud to be with me...

Shock at having finally admitted she loved Vince—even to herself—had Ava sucking sharply inwards. Immediately, Vince's gaze narrowed on her face and she had to struggle even harder to keep her equilibrium. Letting out her breath slowly, she was quite proud of the cool dignity of her answer.

'Perhaps I was simply tired of the way my family perceived me, Vince. But, more importantly, I was tired of the way I perceived myself. There comes a time when one has to stop blaming others for what you have become, especially when that person is dead. Irene has no power over my life now. You and Giuseppe have given me back my confidence over my painting, but *I* have set out this past week to get back my confidence as a woman. What you're seeing is a brand-new Ava who wants to be everything she can be, who wants to live life to the full. Hopefully, she'll never become a bitch, but she won't be walked over any more either. I'm only sorry you don't seem to find her to your liking.'

Vince gave a dry chuckle, a sardonic smile lifting one corner of his mouth. 'Not to my liking... Oh, Ava...what rubbish you talk sometimes. You've always been to my liking. And you always will. Don't you know that?'

Ava was still blinking her utter astonishment when Vince took her quite firmly by the upper arms and lifted her right off her feet, carrying her back inside the foyer where he kicked the door shut and lowered her back to the floor.

'Not to my liking...' He laughed again before releasing her only long enough to sweep his arms around her waist, drawing her hard against his body while his mouth bent to cover hers in a very thorough and blisteringly hungry kiss.

A low moan punched from Ava's lungs as the reality of what was happening to her took hold. This was no fantasy. This was for real. Vince's arms around her were real; his kissing her was real; his tongue, which at that moment was doing incredible things, was very real.

It only took Ava a few mind-blowing seconds to recognise that reality was far better than any fantasy, especially when that reality was Vince.

Another highly sensual moan fluttered from deep within her throat which had the wonderful effect of making Vince gather her to him even closer, if that were possible. They already seemed glued together. Ava decided dimly that she must have died and gone to heaven.

When Vince's mouth finally broke from hers, she gazed dazedly up into his flushed face, at eyes glittering with naked desire, lips still apart and panting heavily. Having never encountered rampant male passion at close range before, she wasn't sure what to think, or do. All she knew was she wanted him to kiss her again, wanted him to keep holding her, touching her…

'You should never look at a man like that, Ava,' he growled.

'Like what?' she asked breathlessly.

'Like you want him to ravage you.'

'Maybe I *do* want you to ravage me,' she whispered shakily.

My God, had she just said that? Had she really?

Her lips fell apart in shock at her own boldness. Falling in love had made her go mad! Or was it Vince's kiss that had done that; had driven her to a place where common sense and decorum no longer mattered, only what one wanted deep within one's soul, *and* one's body?

He glared down at her, eyes narrowing. 'Have you been drinking?'

'No.'

'Little girls shouldn't play with fire,' he warned darkly.

His condescension sparked some healthy fire and spirit. 'You kissed me first,' she reminded him accusingly. 'And I'm *not* a little girl! I'm a grown woman.'

His eyes dropped to her cleavage. 'Mmm. You're certainly right there.'

Ava gasped when his fingers followed his gaze and he started undoing the top button on her suit jacket.

'What…what are you doing?'

'Undressing you,' he muttered thickly. 'It's very hard to ravage a woman with her clothes on.'

'But...but you can't! I mean...not here. Not like this!'

He stopped, a frown momentarily clouding the intensity of his concentration. 'Why not? Aren't we alone? God, don't tell me the ogre's somewhere around!'

'No, Byron's not here.'

'That's a relief. But you're right,' he pronounced, glancing around. 'We can't make love down here. Nothing but marble for miles. Such an event calls for comfort.'

Ava gasped again when he bent to slide an arm around her knees and another round her waist, scooping her firmly up into his arms. 'We shall retire to your bedroom.'

'But we can't!' she squawked, even while her pulse-rate went haywire at the thought. 'We have to go to Byron's party!'

'We will go to Byron's party,' he reassured her. 'Eventually.' And began carrying her upstairs two steps at a time without the slightest hesitation on the supposedly slippery stairs.

Panic made Ava say the one thing she thought might stop him in his tracks. 'You do realise I'm a virgin, don't you? At *thirty!*' she added with a lashing of self-contempt in her voice.

Vince didn't flinch an inch, or miss a single beat as he strode masterfully down the hallway. 'Is that so? Then we haven't a moment to lose, have we? Can't have this smashing new Ava ending up a dried-up old maid, can we?'

With that, he swept through her open bedroom door and over to the bed.

CHAPTER ELEVEN

AVA'S HEART BEGAN THUDDING madly when he laid her down on the bed. She wanted him to make love to her. But she was so afraid…of everything…

His leaning over to snap on one of her bedside lamps had her lurching up into a sitting position, a horrified look on her face. My God, she didn't want him to be able to *see* her. Not without her clothes on!

'Vince, I…'

'Hush,' he whispered, sitting down on the side of the bed and cradling her face with his large strong hands. 'I'm not going to hurt you.'

'But the light,' she groaned.

'You want it off?'

'Please…'

'Your wish is my command.' He leant over and switched it off again. A gentle light was still filtering in through the open doorway but the room was large and her bed was against the far wall.

His hands refound her face in the semi-darkness, his palms gentle around her throat while his thumbs caressed the corners of her mouth. 'I've been thinking about doing this all week,' he murmured, his thumbs moving to stroke her cheeks while he kissed her.

Ava's thoughts tumbled into turmoil. He'd been thinking about doing this all *week?* That would mean he'd been wanting to make love to the Ava she had been, not just the Ava she was tonight.

'No!' she cried, and wrenched away from his mouth.

'No?' he echoed, disbelief in his voice.

'You...you couldn't have wanted to make love to *her,*' she insisted shakily. 'You *couldn't!*'

'Who?' He sounded totally perplexed.

'Me. A week ago. No man could have.'

His fingers had frozen on her face and she could feel his eyes boring into her. His sigh, when it came, was full of exasperation. 'Oh, Ava...Ava...what nonsense you talk sometimes. How many times do I have to tell you that a few pounds here and there doesn't make a woman unattractive? I was attracted to you the first moment I laid eyes on you. I had the devil of a job keeping my hands off you that day.'

'You did? Honestly?' Ava could hardly believe what she was hearing. Yet why would he lie?

'Hell, yes. There I was with you in my arms all the time and wanting to kiss you like crazy. I only held back because I'd vowed not to get involved with a woman again till I didn't have so much work on my plate. My last relationship broke up because of my lack of leisure time. On top of that, you seemed to be the sort of woman a man has to marry, not have a convenient affair with.'

This last remark had Ava coming down to earth with a thud. 'And now you think I'm the sort of woman a man *can* have a convenient affair with?'

'I think you answered that question downstairs. You're a grown woman who wants to be all she can be, who wants to live life to the full. I, for one, have never subscribed to the theory that a woman should remain a virgin till she marries, however unItalian that might sound. It's unnatural. You want me to make love to you, Ava. No, you *need* me to make love to you. Don't deny it.'

Her blush betrayed her shyness, as well as her arousal. Vince bent to kiss her till she was clutching at him and moaning softly in her throat.

'God knows how you reached the ripe old age of thirty without being whisked off to bed,' he rasped, drawing back to run a tantalising finger over her softly swollen lips. 'Surely there must have been some man along the line…'

'There…there was a young man named James,' she confessed breathlessly, 'when I was twenty. He said he wanted me, but we…we split up before anything could come of it.'

'What happened?'

Ava shrank back at the memory. 'He only wanted me because of my money. He was poor, you see, and I inherit quite a fortune if and when I ever marry. Irene always said that—'

'Enough said!' Vince cut in savagely. 'I don't want to hear another word if you're going to tell me you let that bitch Irene convince you no man would ever want you for anything other than your money. Do you think I'm here because I want your money? Good God, woman, I'm not at all interested in your damned money. I have an adequate amount of my own, thank you very much. All I'm interested in is your body!'

While Ava gaped, Vince groaned, smacking himself on the forehead. 'God, that sounded dreadful, and it's not strictly true either. I like you very much, Ava. You must know that. I think you're a lovely person and I adore just being with you. But I have no time for anything other than a part-time relationship with any woman. Neither am I emotionally equipped at the moment for anything more. What with my family responsibilities and my workload, sometimes I haven't time to scratch myself. There, that's cold hard honesty for you. I'm offering you nothing but a night here and a night there. If that's not acceptable, you'd better say so now before we go any further!'

'You mean you'd stop if I asked you to?'

'Are you asking me to?'

'God, no.'

He laughed and bent to kiss her startled mouth. 'You're

delightful, do you know that?' He kissed her again. 'And delicious…' Another kiss. 'And desirable…' He pushed her back on to the pillows. 'And dangerous…'

A muffled but very passionate groan rumbled in his throat, his hands no longer holding her face but busy on her clothes. Not that he stopped kissing her. Only once did his mouth leave hers and that was when he sat her up to take her jacket right off. Lord knew where he put it. Ava didn't know and she didn't care. By then she was drunk on his kisses, the blood in her veins as intoxicated as though she'd consumed a whole bottle of wine on her own. She'd even stopped worrying what he thought of her body.

A second abandonment of her mouth was accompanied by the ridding her of her skirt and shoes, which left her lying on top of her bed in nothing but her cream satin corset and stockings. When he returned to her side, he didn't kiss her on the mouth. Instead, he pressed heated lips to the base of her throat while he pushed the shoestring straps off her shoulders. When he began to peel the satin garment downwards, his mouth followed, trailing a damp path of kisses over her skin.

Goose-bumps erupted on her arms, Ava shivering with nervous anticipation as his mouth got closer and closer to her nipples. At last the pained peaks were released from their satin imprisonment, bursting upwards in ripe supplication for his waiting lips.

'Oh,' Ava moaned softly when Vince licked over each one in turn, running his tongue around and over them till they were like river pebbles, all hard and slippery.

'Oh, God,' she whimpered when he started a twin torment, sucking one nipple deep into his mouth while rolling the other between thumb and forefinger. His tugging mouth set up another tugging deep inside her, bringing with it a tension that was both exciting and excruciating.

When he stopped briefly to peel the undergarment right down to her waist, then to undo the snap fasteners between her legs, Ava's eyes flung open. She gasped when his mouth returned to capture a still wet nipple, but her gasp was not in response to this, but to the hand that had stayed between her thighs and was busy showing her that nipples ran a poor second when it came to instruments of erotic torture.

She squirmed beneath his ministrations, panting her excitement as he took her closer and closer to she knew not what. Everything was chaos in her mind. All she knew was that she wanted his fingers to stay inside her, to keep doing what they were doing. When her flesh started pulsating against him, he abruptly withdrew, making her cry out in dismay.

'It'll be all right,' he soothed, pressing a brief kiss to her anguished mouth. 'I'll just be a few moments.' The mattress squeaked a little as he swung his legs over the side and stood up.

He didn't take all that long. But it felt like an eternity. She trembled when he pressed his stunningly naked body against the full length of her, then eased her legs wide to accommodate his own. When his hips dug sharply into her thighs she found her knees automatically lifting, her legs finding a natural comfort wrapped high around his waist. His groan of pleasure was music to her ears. She had done something right: without being told, without being shown.

'Are you sure you haven't done this before?' he rasped, propping himself up on his elbows.

'Not even in my dreams,' she whispered.

She could feel his eyes upon her even though she couldn't see them properly. 'I shouldn't be this glad about that, Ava. It goes against everything I told you earlier. But I am. Hopelessly. God, I hope I'm doing the right thing here.'

'Yes, you are,' she insisted wildly, and pressed impassioned lips to his shoulder. 'God, I love you. I…oh, please, Vince…don't stop!'

'I don't think I could at this point, but for pity's sake, don't start confusing this with love, Ava. This isn't love.

It's sex, and it's been bringing men and women together like this for centuries.'

Ava's heart contracted in rejection of this till he started rubbing his body against hers and everything inside her went haywire. Maybe he was right. She'd had little enough experience with love, after all. Maybe it *was* just sex that was making her head spin and her body explode with pleasure.

'I don't care if it is only sex,' she rasped. 'It feels fantastic and I want it. I want *you.*'

'And I want you, sweet Ava.'

'Then just do it. Don't be gentle. Just do it!' And she arched her back, pressing the moistened valley of her flesh against his throbbing desire.

'God, yes,' he groaned and drove that same desire home, Ava's eyes flinging wide as any momentary pain was far surpassed by the most incredibly strong wave of emotional and personal satisfaction. At last, she was a real woman with a real lover, not a fantasy one. At last…

Ava murmured Vince's name, her hands sliding down his back to splay across his taut buttocks. When she pulled him ever deeper inside her, a tortured gasp punched from his lungs.

'Did…did I hurt you?' she whispered.

'Did *you* hurt *me?*' he rasped disbelievingly. 'Haven't you got that the wrong way round?'

'No.' She made a sensuous little circle with her hips. 'I feel fine.'

'You certainly do,' he growled. 'God knows what's in store for me once you get the hang of this, Ava.'

'Do you like your women to move, Vince?'

'I like it when *you* move, Ava. Let's forget my other women for tonight, shall we?'

'Whatever you say.' She smiled in the darkness, happy that she compared well with his previous lovers. Certainly, all her usual clumsiness seemed to have disappeared now she was lying down. She aimed to adopt this position as often as possible, smiling her satisfaction as she arched voluptuously into him.

'I think you should leave most of the moving up to me this first time,' he muttered. 'You're too damned good at it and I'm only human.'

Ava was starkly reminded just how much man Vince was when he did move, each powerful thrust making the breath leave her lungs in gasp after gasp of startled pleasure.

'I'm not hurting you, am I?' he asked thickly.

'No...'

'Good,' he said, and actually picked up what was already a powerful rhythm. 'God, I could get addicted to this,' he muttered thickly. 'I can almost understand why virgins are so prized. At least...ones like you are... Oh, God...'

Ava was incapable of speech. All she could do was cling to him, digging her nails into his buttocks as an intolerable pressure built up within her body. His urging her not to move was ignored as she searched for release, all her insides squeezing tight as her back arched, her hips revolving against his.

When Ava suddenly tumbled over the edge, her mouth gasped wide, her head twisting from side to side on the pillow as a succession of violently pleasurable contractions seized her, their force compelling Vince into an explosive climax that had him shuddering into her for what seemed like an eternity. Finally with a raw groan of utter satiation, he slumped between her breasts.

Ava lay beneath his sagging weight, stunned by the experience, her limbs going limp as a curious wave of exhaustion washed through her. They stayed that way for ages, till Vince startled her by lifting his head to send a wet tongue down the valley between her breasts, then trailing it over to slowly encircle a nipple. It immediately strained upwards, her breath catching.

'You are the most deliciously responsive woman,' he murmured. 'And you have the most luscious breasts. I adore them. Don't you let Giuseppe ever talk you into modelling for him. I won't have my girlfriend parading around naked for other men's eyes. You're for my eyes only, do you hear me?'

Vince's proprietorial possessiveness, plus his calling her his girlfriend, thrilled Ava. Any concern that their affair might be a very short one was pushed firmly aside. 'Yes, Vince,' she agreed meekly.

'Good,' he said, and settled back down on to her body, his face resting between her breasts, his warm breath fanning her right nipple. Ava was shocked by her immediate and very intense desire to have him make love to her again, only a glance at her bedside clock radio distracting her from her desire.

'Vince...' She gently shook him on the shoulder.

'Mmm?'

'We have to go to Byron's party...'

'Soon,' he said, stunning her when he started licking the nearby nipple, making it glisteningly hard in seconds. 'Parties don't start till ten at least.'

'But it's nearly nine. Vince, please...'

Her stomach curled over when he did the same to her other nipple before glancing up at her. She stared up at his moistened mouth and ached to have it all over her.

'Your wish is my command,' he sighed. 'Mind if I use the bathroom first?'

He was gone in a flash, scooping up his clothes on the way. Ava was left lying there feeling oddly empty. Vince's withdrawal from her body had reminded her that he'd used protection, with nothing of him remaining inside her. Stupid as it seemed, she didn't like the feeling. Was it that it echoed how she would feel after their affair ended, as it inevitably would...?

When depression hovered, she brushed it ruthlessly aside. Ava had no patience with such feelings tonight. Tonight she had become a real woman. Tonight she had started really living. Tonight she refused to be anything but happy.

Swinging her feet over the side of the bed, she encountered a reflection of herself in the dressing-table mirror that she would never in her wildest dreams have imagined encountering. Semi-naked body, tousled hair, puffy mouth, wet swollen nipples, and an ache between her thighs that was a mixture of having been ravaged and wanting to be ravaged some more.

But it was her perception of that semi-naked body that surprised her the most. Suddenly she saw her full breasts as lush, not heavy, her rounded stomach as feminine, not flabby, her whole shape as quite desirable, not repulsive.

Who had changed her perception? Vince...

She had so much to be grateful to him for. So much.

Her chest contracted with the realisation that she did love him, no matter what he said about her feelings being only sexual. But she would not say she loved him again. She suspected their affair would be very short if she persisted with that tack.

Her one consolation to the inevitability of a broken heart was that there would be no going back to the timid unfulfilled female she had once been. No one would look at her with pity in future, as though she were a naïve little fool who knew nothing of life and love, who'd been nowhere and done nothing. She was going to make Vince show her everything he knew about life and about sex, she decided. Every single thing!

The sound of the shower gushing forth sent a sudden thought to her mind. Automatically, she shrank from being so bold, till another glance in that mirror reminded her of all she had just resolved. Gathering every ounce of courage she owned, she stripped off all her clothes, then went bravely but somewhat breathlessly into the bathroom.

CHAPTER TWELVE

'I'VE ORDERED THAT CARPET for the stairs,' Ava said as they walked hand in hand down the marble steps just as the grandfather clock donged nine-thirty.

'That's good,' Vince said. 'When it comes, we'll have to christen it.'

Ava stopped and stared at him. 'Do you mean what I think you mean?'

'You don't fancy making love on a staircase?'

Heat zoomed into her cheeks at the image he was evoking. 'Wouldn't it be rather uncomfortable?'

'I'd work something out.'

No doubt he would, she gulped. Hadn't he just shown her that making love did not have to happen in a bed, or necessarily with intercourse as a finale? When she'd dared to join him in the shower, she hadn't known exactly what to expect. A burst of renewed nerves had almost made her turn and run at one stage, but she had steeled herself and taken the plunge.

Vince had been delighted, quickly dashing any worry that he might not find her lush curves so desirable when she was standing up. He seemed to revel in the fullness of her breasts and hips, delighting in soaping up her whole body before inviting her to do the same to him. She'd been a little shy at first till having free rein to touch him at will brought an excited arousal that had her doing things that hadn't featured in any of her fantasies.

Vince had happily abandoned himself to her attentions,

leaning back against the tiles while she unwittingly but quite shamelessly brought him to climax, after which he'd willingly returned the favour. A shiver ran down her spine at the memory of her gasping shuddering release, her legs apart, Vince between them. She would never be able to go into that shower again without recalling her utter abandonment, or Vince's expertise.

She licked suddenly dry lips and felt a surge of renewed desire. His assertion that her feelings for him were strictly sexual began to take on a disturbing element of truth. It was all she could think of when she looked at him, all that she seemed to want now.

'We…we must go, Vince,' she said, a hunted look coming into her eyes.

'I suppose so,' he agreed reluctantly. 'But only if you kiss me first.'

She groaned but did as he asked,, opening her lips to his demands, moaning softly when he crushed her to him. Suddenly, he put her aside, his expression almost angry. 'I always said this house was dangerous. I'm beginning to think it's more dangerous than even I realised.'

'What…what do you mean?'

'Nothing,' he muttered. 'Let's go.'

Ava was glad of the cool night air in her heated face, though she ground to a startled halt when she saw the sleek red sports car in the driveway. It looked very expensive.

'Is this *your* car?'

'Something wrong with it?'

'No, it's just that I thought…I mean…'

'You thought I was a poor lawn-mowing man with dirt under my nails, nothing between my ears and no prospects.'

'I did not!' she protested. 'You're very intelligent and I'm sure you have great prospects!'

'Such blind faith. But you happen to be right. I do have excellent prospects. The car's leased, by the way. I write the rental off as a tax deduction against the family company.

I often use it for business calls. You've no idea how it impresses a certain type of woman client.'

Ava shook her head at him. 'You're a wicked man.'

He hauled her to him and kissed her again. Quite savagely. 'You'd better believe it, honey,' he ground out. 'I *can* be wicked where women are concerned. Don't you ever make the mistake of falling in love with me, do you hear? All I'm good for where you're concerned is what I've just given you, so take it while it's going and when I'm gone say thank heavens for small mercies! Then find yourself a nice man who'll marry you and give you kids and never a moment's worry. There's no future with me.'

Ava swallowed and looked him straight in the eye. 'That sounds awfully boring, Vince. I think I'll take what's going with you if you don't mind, and to hell with the future for now.'

He glared at her for a few seconds then grinned that sexy grin of his. 'A woman after my own heart. Let's go, lover. The ogre awaits!'

They both piled into the Mazda RX7, Ava giving Vince directions to Jade's and Kyle's houseboat—about a twenty-minute trip at this time of night. It would be ten by the time they got there, which would no doubt bring mutters of criticism all round. But Ava rather suspected her being late would be the least of her family's worries once they saw Vince.

Before he'd arrived tonight, she'd been terribly nervous over what they would think. But Vince's lovemaking and the discovery of her own uninhibited sexuality had sparked a recklessly rebellious spirit in her that was as exhilarating as it was a little crazy. When Vince turned from Belleview's driveway and accelerated away with a rush of speed, she threw back her head and laughed.

'What are you laughing at?'

'I'm thinking of the look on Byron's face when I walk in with you.'

'Oh? And what will that look be like, pray tell?'

She did her best to imitate a shocked, disapproving and suspicious scowl.

'That bad, eh? I presume he'll think I'm after you for your money?'

'Indubitably.'

'More fool him. I've a good mind to let him think it, just to teach him a lesson.'

'You won't have to *let* him think it, Vince,' Ava said drily. 'He'll do it of his own accord.'

'But *why?*'

'I didn't always look as presentable as I look tonight, Vince. A little while ago I was much fatter. I was a frump.'

'God, not that again, Ava. You really do have a complex about your weight, you know that?'

'I could show you photographs, if you don't believe me.'

He sighed. 'You would *still* have been a very pretty woman. Besides, a lot of men like women with a bit of flesh on them.'

'Maybe…'

'No maybe about it. Your brother must be as blind as a bat if he thinks no man would want his little sister for reasons other than money. Now look, you're the one who said you're a new woman. In that case, then throw away all those old ideas about your inability to attract a man. Hell, you're one of the sexiest women I've ever met. Lord knows how you remained a virgin till thirty. Not that I'm complaining mind. I aim to take full advantage of your steam-cooker sexuality.'

'My *what?*'

'You heard me. You need sex, Ava, and plenty of it. No don't go giving me one of those reproachful looks. You know I'm right.'

Was he? Ava didn't feel happy about reducing her feelings for Vince to sex. She was sure there was more to it than that. Never in a million years could she imagine doing what she had done tonight with any other man. Love had to play a very large part.

But to say as much to Vince would court disaster. He would run a mile. And she couldn't face losing him just yet.

A rueful smile played on her lips. 'You're a scoundrel, Vince Morelli. But a rather nice scoundrel. And very talented in certain areas.'

'I have an equally talented partner,' he drawled. 'Speaking of talent, I had your painting framed and it's now hanging in a setting befitting its beauty.'

'You did? Where?'

'Not telling. I'd rather show you.'

'When?' she asked excitedly.

'Soon.'

'Oh, you're a tease!'

He smiled. 'Not usually. But I think I could get to like teasing you.'

'If you don't tell me I'll accept Giuseppe's modelling offer,' she tried bluffing.

'No, you won't. I can see that now. You'd be too shy.'

'True,' she sighed.

'By the way, Giuseppe said to tell he wants you to drop by the gallery next Monday. I think he wants to show it off to you.'

'He's sweet.'

'He's an old rogue.'

'You like him.'

'Yes,' Vince sighed. 'I do.'

'How did you two become friends?'

'I used to mow his lawns. One day he asked me to change some light bulbs in the gallery. The ceilings are very high and you need a good ladder to reach the light fittings. Anyway, he was having an exhibition at the time and I was really struck by the paintings. I'd never been interested in art much before but I couldn't stop looking at this chap's work. It was so real! I can't stand paintings where you don't know which way is up. Not that I think they should look like photographs either. But I do like to know what I'm looking at. Anyway, I raked up the money to buy one. That started me on my collection and my friendship with Giuseppe.'

'I'd love to see your collection, Vince.'

'You will. Don't worry.'

'When?'

'Soon.'

She sighed her exasperation at him. 'I can see a change of subject is called for. How old are you?'

'Old enough.'

'Vince!'

'Thirty-two.'

'You look younger. How many brothers and sisters do you have?'

'Four brothers and one sister.'

'And how old are they?'

'Let's see… Marco's twenty-five, Pietro's twenty-three, Paolo's twenty-one, and Giovanni and Claudia are nineteen. They're twins.'

'So they're all grown up, really.'

'Says who?' he growled. 'They're all complete idiots! If I wasn't around to look after them, they'd be in all sorts of trouble.'

'You sound just like Byron when he talks to me. I think big brothers develop a superiority complex that prevents them from seeing their siblings as adults.'

'Could be, Ava. Could be.' He looked over at her and gave a dry laugh. 'But at least such inadequacies of judgement are not transferable. I can assure you, I think of you very much as an adult.'

His eyes went to her breasts and Ava felt her nipples harden immediately. 'Don't…don't look at me like that,' she said shakily.

'Why not?'

'You know why not,' she whispered, and turned her face away.

Vince said nothing, and an odd tension developed in the car which was both sexual and something else. Vince remained silent, and Ava was left to wonder what he was thinking about.

'What other relatives of yours will be at this party tonight?' he said at long last.

Relieved to be talking again, Ava launched into telling Vince all about Jade and Kyle, about their romance and their recent marriage, complete with a baby on the way, after which she moved on to Nathan and Gemma, telling him all about them in as unbiased a fashion as she could. Naturally this meant disclosing quite a bit more about the family in general as well as the family opal business, though Ava stuck to bland facts. Vince wouldn't want to know family gossip.

'I doubt Nathan's daughter Kirsty will be there,' she finished up. 'She's only fifteen. The rest will be made up of Byron's friends and business associates. No more than twenty to twenty-five people in all, Jade said. The houseboat wouldn't cope comfortably with any more guests.'

'It still must be a damned big houseboat.'

'Oh, it's not one that moves. It's quite stationary, parked at the end of a pier. More like a real house sitting on a barge. Hey, slow down! You have to take the next street on the left.'

The Mazda cornered beautifully and soon brought them safely down the winding road to the small bay and the marina where they discovered all of the parking spots along the foreshore seemed to be filled. They crawled along, looking for a space.

'That's Nathan's car,' she said, indicating the navy Mercedes.

Vince braked to a halt. 'Do you think he'll be leaving the party early?'

'Not as early as we're going to.'

This brought a sharp look from Vince. 'Is that a threat or a promise?'

'A fact.'

He glanced over at her. 'You're nervous,' he accused.

'It seems so.'

He reached over and covered her hand with his, squeezing it while he gave her a reassuring smile. 'Don't worry. I'll be by your side.'

That's what's worrying me, she groaned silently.

'I'll park behind the Merc.'

'You can't do that!'

'Why not? I'm not blocking anyone else and you just said the owner won't be leaving early. Lighten up, Ava.'

Ava grimaced, then laughed. If this kept up she'd lighten up a hell of a lot. She felt so queasy in her stomach that eating was out of the question. A drink was in order, though. Maybe several after Byron met Vince. Dear God, whose dumb idea was this?

Vince took her arm for the rather long walk along the pier towards the houseboat which was well lit around the verandas with coloured lights. No one had wandered outside, however. A fresh breeze was blowing off the water and muffled music drifted towards them.

'Pretty spot,' Vince remarked as they walked up the ramp on to the front veranda. 'But expensive. Do we go straight in?'

The houseboat had large windows on three sides but not the side facing the pier. A solid wooden door presented itself to Vince and Ava, who took a deep steadying breath and said, 'I think we'll just go straight in.'

'Right,' Vince turned the knob and opened the door on to louder music, lively chatter and a haze of smoke. He waved Ava ahead of him, stopping briefly to close the door behind her. Before Ava could look properly around the crowded room, Jade came rushing forward, looking her usual outrageous self in a black flared mini dress which hid her pregnancy well but not her neverending legs.

'Auntie Ava, you made it! We were all beginning to worry you might have had car trouble. But don't you look smashing. And you're so slim! Oh, I'm jealous.' Jade's sapphire-blue eyes twinkled as she looked over her aunt's shoulder straight at Vince. 'I see you took my advice, Auntie,' she whispered so that only Ava could hear. 'God, he's gorgeous.'

'And free,' Ava countered just as softly, but quite firmly.

Jade frowned at her aunt.

Ava turned to slide a tense hand through Vince's arm, bringing him forward. 'Vince, meet my niece, Jade.'

'Hi, Jade,' he said, flashing her one of his winning smiles. 'Sorry we're a little late. We lost track of time, something that always seems to happen when we're together.'

Ava had to control the urge to laugh at the look on Jade's face. Kyle's arrival at his wife's elbow helped pull herself together.

'Ava,' Kyle greeted, nodding to her in his usual cool fashion. His impeccable manners meant that he would not dream of commenting on her weight loss. 'That colour looks superb on you. And you *did* bring a friend. Jade was worried you might come alone. I'm Kyle Gainsford, Jade's husband,' he said, extending a hand towards Vince.

'Vince Morelli.'

'Glad you could come.' He turned back towards Ava, a wry smile lurking in those intelligent dark eyes of his. 'Byron was just wondering where you'd got to, Ava. I'm sure he'll be relieved to know you've come to no harm.'

This brought a rolling-eyed glance from Jade, a wide smile from Vince and a spluttering from Ava. Suddenly, all four of them were grinning at each other.

'Oh, my God, here comes Byron,' Ava muttered.

'Don't forget to wish him a happy birthday,' Jade reminded her.

'Byron's present!' she gasped, looking up at Vince. 'I...I left it in the car...'

'I'll get it,' he said, and was gone before she could say Jack Robinson.

'Ava!' Byron boomed. 'Where on earth have you been? I rang the house a while back and—' He broke off suddenly and simply stared at her. 'Good lord, Ava, is that really you?'

'I think so, Byron.'

'But where's the rest of you?'

'Pops, for pity's sake!' Jade groaned.

'Never mind, Jade,' Ava sighed. 'I don't think he even knows he's being rude. I left the rest of me on the floor of your gym, Byron,' she said drily. 'I was wondering when you were going to notice the difference.'

'This is incredible. And I certainly *don't* mean to be rude. But you look so stunningly lovely and so...so...' He seemed at a loss to find an appropriate word.

'Sexy?' Jade suggested, which brought an instant glare from her father.

'Truly, Jade, must you?'

'Must I what? Tell the truth? Auntie looks very sexy tonight. I'm sure Vince thinks so too.'

Byron frowned. 'Who the hell is Vince?'

'My date,' Ava supplied. 'He's gone back to the car to get your present. I left it on the back seat. Which reminds me. Happy birthday, Byron.' She kissed her brother on the cheek, aware that her heart was beating madly with nerves. She wished Byron's opinion weren't important to her but it seemed it was, after all. She was pleased by his reaction to her improved appearance but it was his attitude to Vince that was crucial.

'Might I ask where you met this Vince person?' Byron demanded immediately. 'You've never mentioned him before.'

'He's a friend of Giuseppe's,' Ava said, deliberately sidetracking the truth about her meeting Vince. 'Giuseppe's my new art-teacher,' she explained to her bewildered-looking brother. 'And my patron. He's going to give me an exhibition.'

'An exhibition!' Jade squealed. 'Oh, how exciting! Congratulations, Auntie!' And she gave her a hug.

'Yes, congratulations, Ava,' Kyle added warmly.

'Thank you.'

Byron was still shaking his head. 'I don't understand any of this but I think I need a drink.'

'Good idea,' Kyle said. 'Take Ava and Byron back to the bar, Jade, and I'll wait here for Vince.'

'Whatever you say, o lord and master,' Jade quipped with a wicked grin at her husband, curling her right arm through Byron's elbow and her left through Ava's. 'Time we rescued Nathan and Lenore from Catherine, anyway.'

'Now who's being rude?' Byron grumbled. 'I don't understand why you don't like Catherine. She's a very nice lady.'

'Did you say Nathan and Lenore?' Ava asked Jade. 'Where's Gemma?'

'Seems she went back to Lightning Ridge for a few days. To visit that old lady friend of hers. Nathan says she was a bit homesick.'

'Really?' Ava didn't believe that. Gemma had hated her life at Lightning Ridge. 'But that doesn't explain why Lenore's here. Did you invite her, Jade?'

'No. Nathan brought her. It appears they were working late on the play and Lenore didn't want to go home to an empty house. Kirsty's gone on a camping excursion with classmates for the school holidays. Won't be back for two weeks.'

'I see,' Ava murmured, hoping that she didn't see what she thought she was seeing.

Still frowning her concern, she looked up and met Nathan's cool grey eyes across the room. It took a few seconds for her to realise that the surprised look that came into his face was to do with her revamped appearance. Lenore was standing next to him, looking absolutely stunning in figure-hugging emerald-green. Her hand was on Nathan's arm and they looked very cosy indeed. Poor Gemma…

Ava's gaze slid over to Catherine, who was standing on the other side of Nathan with a glass of champagne in her hand and a haughty look on her face. Always smart and elegant, tonight she was dressed in a cool ice-blue sheath that matched her eyes and was a perfect foil for her glossy dark hair.

'Everyone,' Jade announced brightly as she dragged Ava and Byron over to the threesome at the bar, 'look what Auntie Ava's been up to. She's become all slim and gorgeous.' Catherine and Lenore, who had not been watching Ava across the room as Nathan had, both looked round at once. Lenore, to give her credit, seemed delighted by Ava's new appearance. Catherine was stony-faced, lifting one of her plucked eyebrows in a gesture of droll boredom. Not a word of comment or praise passed her lips.

At least Lenore was not that rude. 'I'm impressed, Ava,' she said. 'I know how hard it is to lose weight. And I just adore that suit. Where did you buy it?'

Trite conversation flowed till Catherine's sharply indrawn breath had everyone's eyes snapping her way.

'What is it, Catherine?' Byron asked. 'Something wrong with your drink?'

'That man,' she rasped. 'The one talking to Kyle. What's he doing here?'

Heads swivelled and Ava saw at once she meant Vince, whom Kyle was gradually guiding their way.

'Why?' she demanded to know, her heart racing. 'What's wrong with his being here?'

Catherine looked most disconcerted. 'He…used to mow my lawns,' she said shakily. 'He…he made a pass at me one day and I had to fire him. It…it all became rather ugly.'

'How awful!' Lenore exclaimed.

Ava saw her brother scowl his disgust over at Vince and her heart dropped to the ground. For a split-second, she had believed Catherine—perhaps because she wasn't a liar herself—but then her faith in Vince's personal integrity came to the fore and she saw Catherine's lie for what it was: the desperate attempt of a woman scorned to save face and have her revenge.

For Vince would never make an unwanted pass at a woman. He would never have to. The odds were it was the other way around. Catherine made a pass at him and when Vince rejected her she fired him out of spite. He'd more or less told her such things had happened to him.

'What the devil *is* he doing here, then?' Byron ground out. 'Who brought him?'

Ava swallowed then lifted her chin, catching a glimpse of Jade's sympathetic face as she did so. 'I did,' she said bravely. 'He's my date.'

'Your *date?*' Byron looked ready to explode. His eyes widened then narrowed with a slowly dawning realisation. 'My God, you hired a new lawn-mowing man the other week, didn't you? Is that him?'

'Not exactly.'

'What do you mean, not exactly?'

'It's hard to explain.'

'Try,' he bit out.

'Not *now,*' she retorted so sharply that Byron's head snapped back. 'He'll be over here in a minute and if any of my family are rude to him I will never speak to them again as long as I live.' Ava faced Catherine with fury in her heart and determination in her mind. She wasn't going to let the bitch get away with spoiling things for her. No way. 'I don't believe what you just said about Vince, Catherine. I know him very well and he would not do what you've just accused him of. I would suggest you refrain from making such slanderous remarks and treat Vince with the respect and courtesy he deserves as my boyfriend. Do I make myself clear?'

A stunned silence descended upon the group with Catherine paling noticeably. 'I will not be forced to be polite to that man.'

'In that case, Byron, you have a choice,' Ava stated firmly, though her voice was shaking. *She* was shaking. 'Either she leaves this party or I do. Which is it to be?'

'Ava, don't be ridiculous. Let's discuss this like adults.'

'Choose!'

'This is crazy! I shouldn't have to make such a choice.'

'What choice?' Kyle asked, smiling at everyone as he joined them with Vince by his side.

'It...it's all right,' Catherine said tautly, but with a vicious look Ava's way. 'I'll do it.'

Ava felt a real surge of triumph. The bitch had backed down. It rather confirmed Vince's innocence, she thought.

Or Catherine's ambition to become the second Mrs Whitmore, added another darker voice. Ava's stomach began to churn again.

'Do introduce Ava's friend, Kyle,' Nathan drawled. 'We're all dying to meet him.'

To Ava the next few minutes were the longest and most difficult in her life. An excruciating tension invaded her during the whole procedure, especially when Catherine and Vince exchanged the coolest of greetings. It was obvious something had happened between the two of them, with Ava's confidence in Vince's innocence wavering in the face of his manner.

'And what do you do for a living, Mr Morelli?' Byron asked pointedly at one stage.

Ava glared at her brother. She'd had enough of this. 'He builds things,' she stated firmly, evoking a startled look from Vince. 'Other than that, his job is to make me happy, isn't it, Vince?'

Vince gave the expectant faces staring at him a slow survey, a sardonic smile coming to his beautiful mouth. *'Sì, mia amore.'* And blew her a kiss in a very Giuseppe-like gesture. 'Your wish is my command, as they say.'

'Then I wish to dance,' she said, not sure if she was angry or amused at his antics. It was obvious everyone thought he was little more than an Italian gigolo.

'Your sister's present, Mr Whitmore,' Vince pronounced, plonking the prettily packaged box of golf-balls in Byron's startled hands before whirling Ava towards the small dance-floor that had been cleared in the middle of the huge room.

'Vince, how could you?' Ava berated breathlessly when he drew her close and set up a slow rhythm that was disturbingly sensuous.

'How could I what?' he said with mock innocence.

'Let them think you are a man of easy virtue.'

He laughed softly. 'You started it.'

'Is...is it true you once mowed Catherine's lawns?' she asked tentatively.

'Yes.'

'She says you made a pass at her...and that she had to fire you...'

'And did you believe her?'

'No...'

'You don't sound so sure.'

'Well, she is very beautiful...'

Vince snorted. 'Beauty is in the eye of the beholder. She's ugly to my eye. And she's the one who made the pass, if you call standing naked before me a simple pass.'

'She *didn't!*'

'She damned well did.'

'And you rejected her, the way you did all the others who tried to seduce you? You know...the ones you told me about?'

'No.'

Ava froze in his arms, her eyes flinging wide. *'No?'*

He shook his head. 'You misunderstand me. I didn't

touch that bitch. But there *was* one woman I didn't knock back. She was much cleverer with her seduction than all the others, much more devious.'

'Oh?' Ava was so glad he hadn't slept with Catherine that she could almost bear some unknown stranger from the past. Though she couldn't help feeling jealous of this creature who had captured Vince's interest with the sort of womanly wiles she herself had only ever dreamt about. 'Who was she, do you mind my asking?'

His eyes locked on to hers. 'Not at all. She's standing right in front of me.'

CHAPTER THIRTEEN

'OH!' AVA CRIED, her cheeks flushing with shocked pleasure first, then a fierce embarrassment. 'But I didn't!' she protested. 'I mean...I did find you very attractive...but I didn't do anything...I mean...other than trying to look nice. I...I wouldn't have even known how...'

His eyes were gentle and teasing as they caressed her flustered face. 'You knew how, sweet Ava, without having to know how. I think you're an instinctive vamp.'

'Me? A *vamp?* Vince, please don't tease me. I hate being teased.'

'I rather like it myself. Put your arms around my neck. I want you closer...' His arms snaked further around her waist and he moulded her against him, one large hand resting firmly in the small of her back, the other stroking possessively over her bottom. By exerting a firm but gentle pressure, her breasts were slowly pressed flat against the hard expanse of his chest, the soft swell of her stomach a convenient cushion for that part of his body which definitely wasn't soft. As he rocked her gently to the music, all sorts of tingling sensations began shooting through Ava. She shivered at the feel of that roving hand on her buttocks, stunned by the thought that she didn't care what he did with it or how he touched her, even in full view of everyone.

'Let's get out of here,' Vince whispered after a couple of minutes' erotic torture.

Ava couldn't believe how fast her heart was beating. 'Where...where would we go?'

'Somewhere private.'

The temptation was acute. Not only was she incredibly excited at the thought of being 'somewhere private' with Vince, but the prospect of staying here at this party and having to parry caustic comments from Catherine or put up with shocked looks from hypocrites like Nathan had little appeal.

Her mind was made up with a swiftness that almost surprised her. Till she finally accepted that the old wishy-washy Ava was no more.

'Yes, I'd like that,' she said firmly. 'Let's go.'

Vince seemed slightly taken aback by her decisiveness. 'Shouldn't you say goodbye to the host and hostess? Or at least the guest of honour?'

'Probably. But I'm not going to. Do them good to see a different side to silly old Aunt Ava,' she said a touch bitterly.

Vince's eyes carried a shocked look. 'Is that how they really perceived you?'

'You'd better believe it.'

He continued to stare down at her, a steely expression slowly replacing his astonishment. 'In that case you're dead right. They deserve no special consideration. Let's go.' Taking her hand, he pulled her past Nathan and Lenore, who had just walked on to the improvised dance-floor together. Ava got a fleeting impression of Nathan sending a worried look after her.

He has every reason to worry, she thought savagely. If she wanted to, she could cause his marriage a lot of trouble. Gemma would not put up with her husband being unfaithful.

'Ava!' came the sharp call when they were halfway along the pier.

Ava ground to a halt and whirled, though still holding Vince's hand. Nathan stood at the other end of the pier, looking as cool and arrogant as he always did. Lenore was nowhere in sight. Clearly he had left her inside while he followed them out here.

'Where the hell do you think you're going?' he shouted. 'We're about to toast Byron's birthday.'

'I'm not stopping you,' she retorted.

'You're not going off with that bloke, are you? After what Catherine said about him? Surely you're not *that* desperate.'

Vince's hold on her hand tightened. 'Shall I dump him in the water for you, Ava?' he muttered.

While Ava had a healthy respect for Vince's physical strength she also suspected that Nathan was a lot tougher than he looked. He was no stranger to solid workouts in Byron's gym, his tall elegant body having not an ounce of extra flesh on it. If it came to a fight, Vince might just have his hands full.

'No,' she whispered. 'Let me handle this. I'm going to enjoy it.'

Ava let Vince's hand go and walked back towards Nathan. She stopped halfway between the two men, schooling her face into a coolly assertive expression that had Nathan frowning.

'Yes, I am going off with Vince, Nathan. But no, I'm not that desperate. We already made love a couple of times before coming here tonight so I'm actually feeling quite relaxed in that regard. It's having to be around my *loving* family that makes me tense and unhappy. You're all so damned insensitive. Not to mention snobbish. Tell me, Nathan, why is it that Catherine's word is automatically believed whereas Vince's isn't? He tells me she lied about him making a pass at her. He says it was the other way around.'

'And you blindly believe him?' Nathan scoffed.

'Take a good look at Vince, Nathan. Do you honestly think he would need to force himself on a woman? I would have thought that you, of all men, would know there are some males in this world who have no trouble attracting the opposite sex. Females flock to them like moths to a flame. Some women are even stupid enough to come back for seconds, even after they've been burnt.'

She gave him a few seconds for that to sink in.

'I won't tell Gemma what I've seen here tonight, Nathan,' she lashed out. 'But someone else might and I hope she dumps you, you unfaithful bastard!'

'I am not unfaithful to Gemma,' he snapped back. 'Goddamn you, Ava, I warned you about trying to make trouble in my marriage.'

She laughed. 'Do you honestly think your marriage isn't in trouble already? I'm just sorry a sweet girl like Gemma ever had to fall for that superficial charm of yours. You're a fake, Nathan Whitmore! But one day that coolly glamorous façade you hide behind is going to break down and the real Nathan Whitmore is going to emerge. God help the woman you're with when that happens. I just hope it's not Gemma!'

Emotion running high, Ava whirled and stalked back to Vince, who had the common sense not to say a word but simply joined her in her angry march back along the pier. He didn't speak till they were back in the car and had travelled a reasonable distance.

'You sure socked him between the eyes, Ava,' he commented quietly. 'Is he really as bad as all that?'

Ava dragged in a deep breath then let it out in a long slow shuddering sigh. 'I'm not sure. Maybe. Probably. God, Vince, I don't really know. No one knows the real Nathan. No one.'

'That's rather frightening.'

'Nathan *is* frightening.'

'He seemed very cool back at the houseboat. Not so cool a moment ago, however.'

'He's like a rumbling volcano lately. One day he's going to erupt.'

'Mmm. He won't erupt all over you, will he?'

'No. I won't be the cause of his eruption.'

'You *do* sound sure of that. Yet he got pretty mad at you back there.'

'It'll take more than a few barbs from me to crack that man open. No, he'll cool down and come out smiling tomorrow. And he'll find a whole lot of smooth lies to tell that pretty little wife of his when she gets back from Lightning Ridge. And she'll believe him, silly fool that she is.'

'Yet you spoke of her in glowing terms when you told me about her earlier. You made her sound a very strong and courageous individual.'

'She is, but she's young and trusting too. And she loves Nathan to death.'

'She sounds like she's headed for trouble.'

'Yes…'

'Hey, don't start getting depressed. You can't live everyone else's life for them, Ava. All you can do is lend a helping hand whenever you can.'

'Is that so? Somehow I don't think you practise what you preach, Vince. You're still trying to live your brothers' and sister's lives for them, from what I've heard. Time to let each one of them stand on their own two feet, don't you think? Believe me, you're not doing them any favours by watching over their every move and giving them unwanted advice all the time. They have to learn by their mistakes.'

His sideways glance was sharp. 'Is that the voice of experience talking?'

'I think I qualify to speak on the subject of being over-protected, don't you?'

'Perhaps. And am I one of the mistakes *you're* learning by?'

Ava blinked wide eyes his way, shock quickly giving way to a justifiable anger. 'Why on earth would you say such a horrible thing? You know how I feel about you. I *told* you! Oh, I know you think I'm a silly naïve fool who's mixing up love and sex but you're wrong. I might have lived the last thirty years hiding away in that mausoleum I call home, but I've seen plenty of life within those walls. I've seen love and hate and sex and lust, and, believe me, I know the differences. I also know the difference between what is fantasy and what is real. I love you, Vince, with a love that is *not* blind. I love you and I'm going to be your lover for as long as you want me.'

Ava was unaware of the tears filling her eyes till a couple started trickling down her cheeks. She dashed them away impatiently. She hated women who cried at the drop of a hat, or to get sympathy, or their own way. Irene had used tears on Byron all the time.

'Are you crying?' Vince asked anxiously.

'No, of course not,' she denied hurriedly. 'What is there to cry over? You never lied to me or conned me, you told me the truth from the start. You have affairs with women. You don't have time for love or commitment. You don't even have time for romance or a long-term relationship.'

'My, don't I sound like a right prize! Don't say any more, Ava, for pity's sake, or I might turn this car around right now and take you home where you belong.'

'Where I belong, Vince, is where I want to be. And right now I want to be with you.'

Narrowed brown eyes slanted her way. 'That sounds like the words of a very grown-up and independent woman.'

Ava's chin lifted as she eyed him back without blinking. 'I think so.'

'Then you don't want to call a halt to our…affair?'

'Not for all the tea in China.'

'That's a lot of tea.'

'You're a lot of man.'

Vince sucked in a startled breath, the red Mazda losing its line for a second. 'Good God, Ava, you shouldn't say things like that.'

'Why not?'

'Damn, but you're beginning to confuse me as well.'

'As well as what?'

'I think you know, you teasing witch.'

'Oh…that…'

'Yes, *that*. Now shut up while I get us to where we're going.'

WHERE THEY WERE GOING was Kirribilli, pulling up in front of a very tall darkened block of flats which was not quite finished, if all the building materials left on site were anything to go by.

'Where on earth are you taking me?' she asked when he took her hand and helped her out of the car.

'To my hideaway.'

'Your hideaway…'

Vince guided her over to a gate in the high wire-meshed fence that ran around the perimeter of the property, where he produced a set of keys and let them in, locking the gate behind them. Ava assumed this must be the building site he'd been working on lately, but she felt uneasy about what they were doing.

'Won't you get into trouble if we're caught, Vince?' she whispered.

'Who's to catch us?'

'Surely these places are patrolled by security guards at night, aren't they?'

'I certainly hope so,' came his reply. 'I pay them enough. Don't worry, I'll give them a call when I get inside and tell them I'm spending the night in the penthouse. Ava, do stop frowning at me. Look, didn't you see the sign on the fence? It says ''Morelli Constructions''. I own this building. I can do with it what I damned well I like.'

'You own this building,' she repeated in a curiously flat tone, the result of her brain going on strike. She hadn't seen the sign. Neither would she have known what to make of it if she had.

Vince was eyeing her confusion with a confusion of his own. 'Ava, you're the one who told your brother back at the party that I built things. I thought that meant you'd found out I was Morelli Constructions. I assumed Giuseppe must have told you.'

Ava shook her head which was already spinning. 'I've never heard of Morelli Constructions.'

'Then why did you say I built things?'

'Because when you rang me the other day, you said you were just turning into a building site. I thought you must have been doing some handyman work there, or some labouring.'

'You thought I was a builder's labourer…'

'Well, yes…I suppose I did. I mean, you did say you weren't mowing lawns any more.'

He laughed and drew her into his arms. 'Oh, Ava… Ava…you are one special person.'

'What *are* you, then?'

'I'm an engineer.'

'You mean with a degree and everything?'

His smile was wry. 'I don't know about the everything but I do have a degree. Took me a few years longer to get it than I originally planned, however. Dad's sudden death put a spanner in the works for a while. He was a good builder, you see, but not a good businessman. Left the family in all sorts of financial trouble. I had to leave university and earn money any way I could, so I started a lawn-mowing and handyman business with my brothers. Had to finish my degree part-time at night. Once I was qualified, Giuseppe had enough faith in me to lend me some money and I started buying land, building blocks of units and selling them. Giuseppe quickly got his money back and I've subsequently done very well for myself.'

'But…but why didn't you tell me any of this before?'

He shrugged. 'I guess it just didn't seem to fit naturally into the conversation without sounding as if I was bragging.'

Ava's heart was filled to overflowing with admiration and love for this man. Not only was he strong and warm and kind, he was charmingly modest. If only he could see that there *was* room in his big heart—and his busy life—for a real relationship with a woman. If only he could see that she would do anything, make any sacrifice to become a permanent part of his life, however small that part might be.

'Look, I didn't bring you here to stand outside in the cold and play true confessions,' he grumbled. 'Let's go inside and be comfortable, at least. Besides, I have something I want to show you.'

Inside, the building was virtually finished, except perhaps for a lot of dust. Vince rang the security firm from one of the red phones on the wall in the foyer and informed them that they should ignore lights in the penthouse, after which they rode the lift up to the top floor. Once there, Vince inserted a special key, the doors whooshing back to reveal a most eerie sight.

A watery moonlight was streaming through the large uncurtained windows of the huge, open-plan, split-level apartment, casting shadows across the floors and walls of the starkly empty rooms.

'I think some lights are called for,' Vince said, and reached for a switch. Immediately, a myriad wall-lights snapped on, *en masse* giving the bare rooms a softly warm glow, but each one directing rays of light on to a painting hanging on the wall underneath it.

Ava quickly realised she was looking at Vince's art collection.

'Come and tell me what you think,' he said with quiet satisfaction in his voice and a hand on her elbow.

Ava allowed herself to be guided across the concrete floors, through the rooms, down various steps and along wide corridors, taking her time to inspect each painting as they ambled through the unfurnished penthouse. Most of the paintings were landscapes, with the occasional still-life thrown in. What they all had in common was an atmosphere of beauty and peace, as well as a delicacy in the colours and brushwork that had a soothing, calming effect. It was a collection designed to relax.

Ava loved it.

After she'd viewed more than a dozen works she broke her silence, turning her admiration to the man whose eyes had chosen them even though there wasn't one by an artist of any note. They were all unknowns, all worth comparatively little at this present time.

'You have marvellous taste, Vince,' she said with warm sincerity. 'You must get an enormous amount of pleasure out of looking at these.'

'I do, now that I've found the right place to put them. I'm going to come and stay here when things get hectic at home. That's why I call it my hideaway.'

'What about furniture? You're going to need something to sit in occasionally, aren't you?'

'I have all the furniture I need for now.'

'You have?' Her head swivelled as she glanced around. 'From what I can see, you haven't any?'

'Oh, yes, I have. There's one room you haven't seen yet. Come...'

He led her down a hallway and into the master bedroom where she could do nothing but stare at the huge bed with a deep wine velvet throwover bedspread and a semicircular black lacquered bed-head complete with built-in accoutrements. She'd never seen so lavish-looking a bed, despite its resting on a bare floor.

'What more could I possibly want?' Vince said. 'I can even lie in bed and look at the stars through here.' He waved at the glass wall which opened out on to a balcony overlooking Sydney harbour.

'Come and try it,' he said, walking over to sit on the bed and pat the quilt. 'It's very soft.'

Ava hesitated, then decided not to be so silly. She went

over and sat down on the opposite side, still feeling rather awkward.

'No, no,' Vince said. 'Take your shoes off and lie down properly.'

Ava shrugged and did as she was told, glancing rather nervously up at Vince. If he wanted to take her to bed this was a rather obscure way of going about it.

'Now look across the foot of the bed at that wall,' he smiled.

She did, immediately gasping upright into a sitting position. For it was *her* painting on the wall. Framed exquisitely in gold, it was lit with not one but two wall brackets which threw a delicate glow upon its surface, bringing out the gentle colours and making it look as she had never dreamt it could ever look. Silent tears of joy and gratitude pricked at her eyes, a lump filling her throat.

'Oh, Vince,' she choked out. 'It's so beautiful…'

He came up behind her, holding her shoulders and kissing her seductively on the neck. 'Not as beautiful as the lady who painted it…'

Ava shivered underneath his kisses, her eyes still on the painting but her mind and body already responding to Vince's touch. 'Stay the night with me,' he said thickly, his lips moving up her throat and along her jawline. 'Don't ask me to take you home…'

He removed her right earring and covered the ear with his mouth, blowing warm air inside, then sliding his tongue into the well. Ava shivered convulsively, and tried to turn her head away, but he cupped her chin and kept it still, driving her mad till, with a tortured cry, she twisted round and gave her mouth to his in total surrender.

'God, you don't know what you do to me,' he groaned as he pushed her back into the pillows and started undoing her jacket. 'I can see I'm going to be rearranging a lot of schedules for you.'

CHAPTER FOURTEEN

GEMMA COULDN'T SLEEP. She lay back in the motel bed, staring up at the ceiling and wondering if Nathan was enjoying Byron's party. God, but she was missing him. Terribly. She'd felt bereft from the moment she'd climbed on to the plane this morning. Not even seeing Ma at the other end had lightened her spirits. Then had come the shock when Ma had taken her back to visit the place where she'd spent most of her growing up years.

Had it always been so appallingly primitive, so *dirty?*

Admittedly, Ma did not keep the dugout in the same condition she had done, but still...

Gemma shuddered just thinking about it. What kind of father had hers been who would bring up a child in such conditions? Gemma had become so distressed this morning even *sitting* in the place that she had found the first excuse she could think of to get out of there. She told Ma she wanted to see Mr Gunther while he was sober—he usually started drinking around noon.

Ma had driven her back to Lightning Ridge and Mr Gunther's ramshackle house, at the side of which was a garage which served as Mr Gunther's workshop. He made a meagre living by buying small uncut opals, then cutting and polishing them and reselling them to the shops around town. Her father had always sold his opals to Mr Gunther rather than deal with Byron Whitmore, claiming city dealers were crooks and would cheat you blind. This was ironic, since Mr Gunther was widely thought of as a mean old skinflint who wouldn't pay a fair price for an opal to his own grandmother.

The meeting with Mr Gunther had been as unrewarding as she'd thought it might be. The old grouch had been uncooperative and unforthcoming. He claimed he knew nothing about her father before he came to live at Lightning Ridge. When confronted with the old photograph of her parents, he'd growled at her that he didn't recognise the woman and he'd always known her father as Jon Smith, not Stefan, and that Jon had never spoken to him about his past or her mother.

'And that's all I told that other chap as well!' he'd finally flung at her. 'Now get out of here and leave me in peace. I don't want any trouble.'

Gemma had mulled over this last statement while she had lunch with Ma in the same café in town she'd once worked in, wondering if the old man was keeping some secret which might get him in trouble with the law if he revealed it. She told Ma of her suspicion but Ma seemed to think he was so paranoid by nature that any questioning would make him react guiltily. He'd been extra secretive lately, Ma had added. Rumour had it he'd bought some new equipment and was probably afraid the tax people might get wind of it and want to know where the money had come from. Like Gemma's father, Mr Gunther never paid taxes, claiming he never made enough money out of opals to be taxed.

Gemma had spent the afternoon in the bar of the Diggers' Rest Hotel speaking to any of the miners who had known her father, but no one could tell her anything about her missing mother or where her father had lived before Lightning Ridge. One miner had assured her that she definitely hadn't come to Lightning Ridge from White Cliffs, since he'd mined in that area regularly for the last thirty years and he knew everyone around that town. He suggested, however, that she might try asking around the opal fields in Queensland and South Australia, or maybe the gold fields in Western Australia, his idea being that maybe her father had been mining somewhere else before coming to Lightning Ridge. Once a miner, always a miner, he'd reckoned.

Gemma thought it was worth a try and resolved to ask Nathan if his investigator had done that. Who knew? Maybe he hadn't. Anyway, she would discuss it with Nathan as soon as she got back home. Which couldn't come soon enough. God, what was she doing way out here anyway, when her life was back in Sydney?

Gemma sighed. She'd grown away from Lighting Ridge. Ma had seen it and said so in her usual blunt fashion at dinner tonight.

'You're a city girl now, love,' she'd said. 'Through and through. But then…maybe you always were…'

When asked what she meant by that Ma had shrugged and said she supposed she meant Gemma's mother must have been a city girl and she'd passed that on to her daughter.

'You're nothin' like Jon,' she'd finished up saying. 'Not even in nature.'

Gemma lay in her motel room now and felt a degree of satisfaction that she wasn't like her father. Who would want to be cruel and mean? Whatever good genes she had, had to have been inherited from her mother…whoever she was…

When depression threatened again—thinking about her mother always depressed Gemma—she swung her thoughts to Nathan and how sweet he'd been to her that morning. Which didn't really make her feel any better.

Perversely, she'd chosen to stay in the same room in the same motel where she had first met Nathan. A silly thing to do when she was missing him so much. Yet in a way it was good to have her memory prompted, to look back and remember why she had fallen in love with him in the first place.

How kind he had been to her that day. And how gallant.

Her father had not long died and she had come here to sell some small opals for pocket money, thinking she'd be doing business with Byron Whitmore. But it had been his adopted son who had opened the door to her, looking so handsome and so very, very different from any of the men she'd known around Lightning Ridge. He'd been deputising for Byron as buyer for the family business while Byron recovered from the boating accident that had killed his wife, Irene.

Gemma recognised now that her fate had been sealed from the moment Nathan had ushered her into this room. She'd been his from that moment, even if it had been several weeks before Nathan had consummated their love for each other.

She groaned when she realised they could have been up at the beach-house at Avoca at this very moment, making love. Instead, she was lying here alone hundreds of miles away, feeling frustrated and lonely.

Gemma rolled over and stared at the bedside clock. Eleven-thirty. Nathan would still be at Byron's birthday party. She wished she were with him.

The idea to telephone him there came out of the blue. What more natural thing than to call, wish Byron a happy birthday then have a chat with her husband? Nathan had told her not to bother to call—he hated telephone conversations at any time—but she didn't think he'd mind this one.

Besides, Monday was such a long way away…

Feelings excited at the thought of even hearing his voice, Gemma snapped on the light, sat up and dialled direct to Jade's number.

The telephone rang several times at the other end before it was answered, a slightly husky female voice saying, 'Hello.'

Gemma stiffened with instant recognition. Lenore. It was *Lenore!*

'Hello?' Lenore repeated.

'I'd like to speak to Nathan, please,' Gemma said, without acknowledging her husband's ex-wife. 'Is he there?'

'I'll get him for you...'

Gemma's head whirled. *Lenore* was at Byron's party? Why? There was no love lost between those two. Gemma was pretty sure Jade would not have invited her. Then how come she was there?

Surely Lenore wouldn't have dared come openly with Zachary Marsden, would she? She wasn't supposed to be seen with him till after his divorce came through. If she had been so bold, then why didn't she acknowledge Gemma on the other end of the line? Why just slink off to get Nathan without saying hello. Unless she hadn't recognised Gemma's voice. The party sounded quite noisy with music and chatter in the background.

'Gemma?' Nathan said brusquely.

Gemma's heart sank. Lenore *had* recognised her voice. How else would he have known who was on the line? The possibility that Nathan had brought Lenore to the party made Gemma feel sick to her stomach.

'Is there something wrong?' he went on. 'You're all right, aren't you? Lenore said you sounded upset.'

Gemma's imminent distress was sidetracked by Nathan making no attempt to hide Lenore's presence at the party. Would a guilty man do that?

'No,' she said, feeling confused now. 'I...I just thought I'd ring and wish Byron a happy birthday.'

'Oh, is that all? I thought you must have found out something about your mother.'

Gemma sighed. 'I'm afraid not. Er—what's Lenore doing at the party, anyway?'

'I brought her. She was awfully depressed about Kirsty going away on some school excursion for a couple of weeks. I thought it would do her good to get out the house and have some company.'

'I thought that was Zachary Marsden's job,' Gemma said tartly.

'Now, Gemma, don't be catty. The poor woman was lonely.'

So am I, she longed to say. Instead, she bit her tongue and tried to be charitable. 'Yes, I suppose so,' she sighed. 'I do wish you were here with me, Nathan. Do you realise I'm staying in the same motel room we met in? It has this big bed in it. Much too big for one...'

'God, Gemma, don't do this to me. Come home, darling. Tomorrow.'

Her heart started to beat faster, which was crazy since he was hundreds of miles away. 'I wish I could,' she groaned. 'But I can't. There's no flight over the weekend.'

'Damn.'

She laughed in an effort to break the tension he was engendering within her. 'You'll just have to write over the weekend, won't you.'

'Bitch,' he said, but softly...seductively.

Gemma swallowed. 'I think I'd better talk to Byron. You're getting me all hot and bothered.'

'He's busy.'

'Doing what?'

'Dancing with Catherine.'

'Oh?' She'd heard he had a new girlfriend, but not much about her. 'What's she like?'

'Good-looking. Rich. Sexy.'

'I hate her.'

'You're not the only one.'

'What does that mean?'

'I'll tell you when you get home.'

'Na-than!'

'Curiosity kills the cat. Promised information brings her back.'

'You're a conniving manipulative devil.'

'Of course. Is there any other way with you?'

She lay down with the phone at her ear, feeling part dazed and awfully aroused. 'I'll ring you tomorrow,' she promised breathlessly.

'Don't.'

His sharp tone made her sit up. 'Why not?'

'I'll be writing.'

'God! Why did I ever suggest such a stupid thing?'

'I have no idea. Why did you? I know you hate it when I write.'

She sighed. 'I guess I wanted to keep you busy. You're far too good-looking to be left on your own for the whole weekend.'

He laughed. 'And what about you?'

'If you'd seen some of the men I spent this afternoon with I don't think you'd worry, whereas you're down there with a whole roomful of beautiful sexy women.'

'The only beautiful sexy woman I want is you, Gemma.'

She hugged the fierce emotion of his words to her heart. 'Oh, Nathan, I do so love you...'

'Enough to have my baby yet?'

Gemma's heart lurched then filled to overflowing. 'I'll stop taking my pills immediately,' she promised faithfully. Lord, how could she have ever thought he didn't love her, that his feelings encompassed nothing but lust?

'That would make me very happy,' he said with something like relief in his voice. 'I'll be waiting at the airport for you on Monday, darling. Don't miss your flight.'

'Wild horses wouldn't stop me getting on it.'

'Bye. Be good.'

'You too.'

Gemma had hung up before she realised she hadn't told Nathan about what that miner had suggested. She shrugged. It would wait till Monday. A lot better than she would.

Still, her heart was at peace as she snapped off the lamp and lay back down. A baby, she started thinking, a soft smile pulling at her mouth in the darkness.

CHAPTER FIFTEEN

AVA WOKE TO SUNSHINE streaming through the glass doors and on to the bed. For a few minutes she lay there, wondering what it would be like to wake up every morning like this, with Vince by her side and a feeling of utter peace coursing through her veins. Closing her eyes, she smiled her pleasure at such a scenario.

But that's just a fantasy, the new Ava reminded herself ruthlessly. Just a dream. Vince doesn't want anything more than what we shared together last night.

Sighing her resignation to the bittersweet reality of their relationship, Ava slipped out of the bed to make an essential visit to the connecting bathroom. On her return, she began picking up their clothes from where they were scattered on the floor, slipping Vince's brown silk shirt over her nakedness in lieu of a robe and placing the rest in a neat pile on the foot of the bed.

With a loving glance at Vince's still sleeping form, she padded out into the kitchen, which was quite finished and very well equipped, even to having food essentials in the cupboards. Five minutes later she was standing at the large plate-glass window in the main living area, sipping black coffee from a mug while she admired the panorama before her eyes. Sydney harbour had never looked so beautiful, she thought. Nor the sun so bright. Nor the sky so blue.

Was it perhaps that everything would look sharper to her from now on? Had the experience of love honed her senses to a level of sensitivity that she had previously dulled with her dreamlike fantasies? Ava knew she would settle for a few nights with Vince rather than a lifetime of such fantasies. Even the memory of the pleasure he had already given her was enough to set her nerves atingle and her heart racing.

Luckily, Ava glimpsed Vince's reflection in the glass as he approached or when he put his arms around her she might have spilt her coffee. As it was, she gave a small shudder as he pulled her back against his splendidly naked body.

'Your wearing my shirt does things to me that are positively indecent,' he whispered, slipping his hands underneath it.

'Vince, I'm going to spill this coffee,' she warned shakily.

'Put it down and come into the shower with me.'

'The shower?'

'Uh-huh. I'm afraid we'll have to be leaving soon. It's nearly ten and I'm due home for a family gathering today. Since I have to take you back to Belleview first, we'll have to shake a leg.'

Ava thought she hid her disappointment quite well, having hoped they might spend the day together. The prospect of Vince dropping her off with an 'I'll call you some time,' farewell sent her heart plummeting to the ground. 'I—er—don't think having a shower together's a very good idea.'

'Why not?'

'You don't behave in showers.'

'I promise not to lay a single hand on you.'

She gasped as his roving hands became very intimate. 'And what do you think you are doing at the moment?' she asked tautly.

'I said I wouldn't lay a *single* hand, not two hands.'

'Oh, God...stop it, Vince...'

'Are you coming into the shower with me or not?'

She groaned. 'You're wicked.'

'Tell me something new.'

It was ten-thirty before they were dressed and ready to

leave, Ava feeling somewhat alarmed at how quickly depression could follow physical ecstasy. Was this all she had to look forward to in future, see-sawing emotions plus an inability to control her own body?

'You're very quiet,' Vince commented on the way down in the lift.

'Oh?' Her swift smile had a decided edge to it. 'Maybe I'm exhausted.'

'In that case you won't want to go out with me tonight...'

Ava hated herself for the obvious joy that must have lit her face, till she became resigned to the fact that this was what being in love could be like. It could hurt like hell, but it could also be incredibly wonderful.

'You know I would,' she said eagerly, not bothering to think that she was being far too accommodating, as usual. Still, Vince seemed to like her that way. He was certainly looking at her with amused affection in his eyes.

'Where would you like to go?' he asked indulgently.

'You choose. I don't care.'

'In that case I'll take you out to dinner, then a movie, then back here for the night.'

Ava's eyes blinked wide. God, whatever would she tell Byron?

'Does that present a problem?'

'No,' she said, bolstering herself up with the thought that she was a grown-up woman of thirty. Why should she have to answer to her brother? 'No problem at all.'

They chatted together all the way back to Belleview, about all sorts of things. Ava had never thought of herself as a good conversationalist, but with Vince the words seemed just to flow. Neither did she ever feel that what she said was stupid, perhaps because he was a good listener, as well as an incorrigible flatterer.

'I can't get over how many movies you've seen,' he said at one set of lights, 'or how knowledgeable you are about them.'

Ava didn't enlighten him that watching movies had been the mainstay of her sanity over the years. She hugged his compliments to her heart and babbled on. It was only when they approached Belleview that Vince turned serious.

'Will your brother say anything about your not coming home last night?'

'No. He won't have gone home himself. He won't have come home this morning, either. He'll have gone straight to golf for the day.'

'I see. Is he serious about Catherine, do you think?'

'I hope not.'

'I hope not too, for *his* sake.'

Vince swung the Mazda into the driveway where Ava was startled to see the gates of Belleview already open, even though she hadn't pressed the remote control gizmo in her handbag.

'Oh, God,' she groaned. 'Byron must be home.' Her instant panic belied her belief that she had become a grown-up woman with the right to do as she believed. Suddenly, she was a bundle of nerves.

'Don't worry,' Vince said firmly. 'Leave this up to me.' And he shot through the gates, whipping around the semicircular driveway and grinding to a bone-crunching halt at the bottom of the steps. Immediately one of the front doors opened and Byron stepped out on to the patio, looking murderous.

Not only murderous but surprisingly unshaven. He was also still wearing the same clothes he'd been wearing at the party, a dark blue suit. His tie, however, was missing, and the top button of his shirt was undone. His hair looked greyer than usual and he didn't seem to have combed it.

Ava could not help staring at this most uncharacteristic sloppiness. Byorn was usually most particular over how he presented himself, even around the house. When Ava and Vince didn't get out of the car straight away he stormed down the steps and wrenched open the passenger door.

'You get yourself out of there immediately,' he roared at her.

'Stay right where you are, Ava,' Vince said in so cool, collected and commanding a voice that Ava was in no doubt whom she was going to obey. 'I would like to have a word with you, Mr Whitmore,' he added, already getting out of the car.

'You've got a bloody hide, Morelli, keeping my sister out all night then breezing in here like you've done nothing wrong.'

'I haven't done anything wrong. Unless you think making love to an adult woman who wants you to make love to her is wrong. In that case, look to yourself, Mr Whitmore. I doubt you've only been sipping coffee at night with Catherine Gateshead.'

An angry red slashed across Byron's cheekbones. 'You're nothing but a bloody gigolo, Morelli, taking advantage of lonely women who've had the misfortune to hire you to work around their homes.'

'Is that what Catherine told you? I'd take anything she says with a grain of salt, if I were you.'

'Once I've had you checked out, you won't be so cocky,' Byron threatened.

'You think not? Go ahead. Make my day.'

Byron's top lip curled. 'Very funny. You won't be cracking jokes when I can show my sister in black and white just what a cad she's got mixed up with. I've done a bit of checking up on you myself already and even your own mother told me you're engaged to a nice little Italian girl.'

Ava couldn't help it. She giggled.

Byron responded by grabbing her arm and hauling her out of the car, his face dark with fury. 'What in hell's happened to you?' he snarled. 'Has this bastard corrupted you so much that you've lost all sense of decency? Don't you care he's going to marry another woman, or that he's got the morals of an alley-cat? I hope you don't think he loves you. Men like him make silly women like you *pay* for the privilege of their professional expertise. It won't be long before he starts asking you for money, you mark my words!'

Byron never saw the blow coming. Vince's fist was like greased lightning and a second later Byron was a crumpled mess on the gravel. Ava gasped and dropped to her knees beside her brother, her hands frantic on his face. 'You've killed him,' she cried.

'Not quite,' Vince said, rubbing at his reddened knuckles as Byron made a moaning sound. 'But I'd have liked to. God, what a pompous puritanical pain your brother is. How you turned out so sensible and broad-minded, I have no idea. You must take after another branch of the family.

'But I like him,' he suddenly grinned, making Ava gasp with surprise. 'I would have done exactly the same if you'd been *my* sister. The ogre cares about you, Ava, and that speaks for a lot in my book. Here, help me get him up over my shoulder and I'll take him inside. He'll be coming round shortly. And stop worrying. He might have a sore jaw later and a bit of a headache but no lasting damage.

'Hell, but he's a big bloke,' he muttered as he carried Byron inside and laid him down on the very same leather sofa he'd put Ava on that first day. 'Perhaps you'd better get him some ice to put on his jaw, Ava. A couple of pain-killers and a drink of water might be in order too.'

When a groggy Byron started coming round a minute later and saw Vince sitting in a chair opposite him, he went to sit up, only to groan and slump back down on the pillows.

'Good idea,' Vince pronounced sternly. 'Now lie there and listen. First, let's get a few things straight. One…I did not make a pass at Catherine Gateshead; neither have I slept with any female except a discreet number of girlfriends who all knew the score. Secondly, I no longer mow lawns. Mowing Ava's lawn was a one-off thing. When she rang to hire someone for the following day there was no one free, but she sounded such a nice lady and so worried sick that her big ogre of a brother might start belly-aching over the bloody lawns, that I did her a special favour.'

Byron made a scoffing sound.

'Shut up and listen for once!' Vince commanded.

An impressed Ava used this short break in proceedings to hand Byron a tea-towel wrapped around some ice cubes. 'Put this on your chin,' she whispered. 'It's beginning to swell...'

His doing as she suggested in a rather dazed, almost bewildered fashion moved her to pity. Poor Byron, he really doesn't know what's hit him, either with Vince or her own changed self.

'That's how Ava and I met,' Vince explained, thankfully not mentioning her fall that day. 'We hit it off straight away. I did not seduce her. She did not proposition me. We became friends first. I recognised her artistic ability and introduced her to Giuseppe Belcomo, who's a master at recognising and fostering true talent. You can check him out too, if you like. Last night was the first time Ava and I made love. The *first* time,' he hit home. 'I respect and admire your sister very much, Byron. I'm sorry I slugged you but I could not stand by and have you belittle her. Or me for that matter, for when you belittle me, you belittle her.'

Ava squeezed her eyes tightly shut against the wave of emotion crashing through her. She had never had anyone stand up for her like this and it was...incredible.

'Finally, I do not need or want your sister's money. I have enough of my own and if you don't believe me, then by all means check up on that too. I'm a qualified engineer. I own and run Morelli Constructions, which specialises in building quality apartment blocks all over Sydney. We've been so busy and successful this past year that I haven't even been out with a woman in months!

'Last but not least, let me give you a word of warning about Catherine Gateshead. She is a coldly ambitious evil bitch who will do anything to get what she wants. But she is at her most dangerous when crossed. Her vicious lies after I knocked her back caused our family company to lose many clients. I'm not saying she isn't beautiful but, before you even think of marrying her, check out her other three husbands.'

'Three!' Byron gasped. 'I thought she'd only had the one.'

'There've been three. Believe me.'

'Good lord…' He appeared to mull over this information before decidedly sharper blue eyes snapped up again. 'What about your being engaged?'

Vince sighed. 'My mother has a problem with the way I conduct my private life. Lately, she's been telling any girl who rings me that I'm either engaged or about to become engaged to a nice little Italian girl. Obviously, she's started saying the same to their brothers.'

'I see…' He glanced over at Ava, who was perched on the arm of a chair near by, doing her best to remain composed under a whole range of emotions. 'I…I only ever had your best interests at heart, love, but I can see now I've been a very misguided brother as well as a highly inadequate guardian. I'm sorry. Forgive me?' he asked, his voice breaking.

Ava came forward and squatted down next to the sofa, smiling at him through suddenly blurred eyes. 'I always knew you loved me,' she said. 'We'll put the past behind us and go forward.'

A type of puzzlement filled Byron's eyes. 'You've changed so much. I can hardly believe it's my little Ava I'm talking to.'

'It's me all right.'

Vince tapped her on the shoulder. 'Ava, why don't you go and freshen up? Change into something a little more casual. I'd like to take you home with me. If you'd like to come, that is…'

Ava turned, eyes blinking with surprise. 'You want me to meet your family?'

'Yes, I do.'

She wanted to ask if he took home all the women who slept with him but decided not to push her luck. 'OK,' she said brightly. 'I'll go freshen up.'

Byron watched his sister leave, then frowned at this man who'd worked this miraculous transformation. 'She loves you. You do know that, don't you?'

'Yes.'

'And what are your feelings for her?'

Vince frowned and sat back down. 'Well, it's like this, Byron…'

AVA TRIPPED BACK DOWNSTAIRS, having happily found that her clever clothes for biggies were so clever that they looked good on not-so-biggies too. The elastic waists shrank to fit, the jackets even more slimming when they hung a little more loosely. But she was looking forward to buying herself a pair of jeans in the near future. And who knew? Maybe one day she'd squeeze into a bodysuit. But for now she was wearing the outfit Vince had first seen her in.

Vince and Byron were sitting together having coffee when she returned to the family-room, looking for all the world like the best of friends. Ava was astonished and must have looked as much when she entered, for Byron threw her a reassuring smile.

'Don't worry, love,' he said. 'No pistols at dawn. Vince and I have come to an understanding.'

Her laugh was slightly nervous. 'You mean I won't be told not to darken this doorstep again?'

'Of course not. You make me sound like an ogre!'

Ava was trying not to laugh while Vince guided her from the house and saw her into the passenger seat of the Mazda, though behind her suppressed humour was a type of shock.

'I think that knock on the jaw must have rattled Byron's

brain,' she commented as Vince climbed in behind the wheel. 'I just can't understand his attitude towards you. I mean...his accepting his little sister's lover so quickly and warmly is just not *Byron!*'

'Well, there is an explanation for that,' Vince said.

Ava frowned back at him. 'Would you mind sharing it with me?'

His glance carried an irony Ava found totally confusing.

'Remember last night when you said you would be my lover for as long as I wanted you?' he asked quietly.

'Yes...' Everything inside her squeezed tight. So this was it. He was going to say he didn't want her any more.

'Did you mean it?'

'What?'

He swivelled in the seat to face her, his own face surprisingly strained. 'Did you mean it?' he ground out.

'Of course I mean it! I don't say things I don't mean. What are you trying to say?'

'What I'm trying to say, Ava, is that I do want you...for forever...'

'For forever?' she repeated blankly.

'Yes. I want to marry you.'

Ava's stunned silence brought a frown after a short while.

'You don't want to marry me?' he said in a pained voice.

'Yes. No. I mean I...I—'

'Look, I know I said I didn't have the time for a commitment or even a real relationship,' he cut in forcefully, 'but that was before I realised I loved you.'

'You love me,' she whispered, her face on the verge of crumpling.

His eyes melted all over her. 'Madly.'

'Oh,' she squeaked, her whole vocal cords having seemed to seize up.

'I was worried all along that I was falling in love with you, but last night when Nathan was being appalling to you, and then this morning when Byron started on at you...well,

I just knew I loved you, Ava, because I wanted to kill him with my bare hands.'

'You love me,' she said again, still dazed and disbelieving.

'God, yes. How could I help but love you? You're so special. And your brand of loving is so special. I know I'll never find its equal anywhere in this world and if I let you go I'd be the biggest fool in this world. I thought of asking you to live with me, but I realised I was right the first time. You're the sort of woman a man has to marry because nothing less is worthy of the beautiful person you are.'

'But...but you said you didn't have the time...'

'I'll *make* time. To hell with being a multi-millionaire. I'll have to settle for being a simple millionaire. I'll build you a house, darling. Any house you want.'

'But I...I wouldn't mind living in the penthouse for a while.'

'Done! You can have *carte blanche* on the décor and the furnishings. You can even convert part of it to a studio, if you'd like. You can have anything you want!'

Ava bit both her lips in an effort not to cry. 'I've only ever really wanted you.' And she burst into tears.

Vince groaned and gathered her in, holding her and stroking her hair. 'Oh, God, darling, you make me feel so humble. I've been such a bloody fool. All those things I said to you. I'm not really wicked with women. Well, not lately...except with you, of course... You bring out the worst—and perhaps the best—in me.'

He kissed away her tears and Ava thought she would die from happiness.

'So you will marry me?' he murmured.

She nodded and he kissed her again.

'Shouldn't we go back inside and tell Byron?' Ava asked some time later. 'He might be relieved you're going to make an honest woman out of his sister.'

'He already knows,' Vince astonished her by saying.

'While you were upstairs, I asked him for your hand in marriage. He said to tell you that he wishes you every happiness and he'll pay for the wedding.'

'Oh, my goodness. Byron said that?'

'He did. Of course he didn't realise what he was agreeing to. Even a *half*-Italian wedding is enough to set the father of the bride—or substitute—back a pretty penny. I live in terror of my sister making a similar announcement.'

'Don't worry, Vince, Byron can afford it. He recently sold an opal for two million dollars.'

'No kidding! I didn't realise opals were that expensive.'

'This one was. It was called the Heart of Fire.'

'Aren't opals supposed to be unlucky?'

'That's an old wives' tale, though that particular one has a long history of scandals and secrets behind it.'

'You'll have to tell me the whole story one day, but as of now I think we should make tracks for the Morelli residence. You're about to make my mother's day.'

'Even though I'm not a nice little Italian girl?' Ava remarked a little nervously.

Vince's smile was so tender, Ava almost burst into tears again. 'My mother is going to adore you,' he murmured. 'My whole family is going to adore you, because you're simply adorable, don't you know that? Now let's get going. Our future awaits!'

SCANDALS & SECRETS

CHAPTER ONE

CELESTE was turning for her twentieth lap when a glimpse of male legs standing at the end of the pool brought her to a gasping halt, water-filled eyes snapping upwards.

'Good God, Damian,' she said irritably once she'd caught her breath and found her feet. 'You frightened the life out of me.'

Her brother laughed. 'Nothing and no one can frighten the life out of you, Celeste. What on earth did you think I was? A rapist?' He laughed again. 'I would pity any poor rapist who set his sights on you, sister, dear. I know who it'd be ending up on his back.'

Celeste flashed her brother a coolly reproachful glance as she stroked over to the wall, intuition telling her he was referring to her reputation as a man-eater, not complimenting her on her martial arts skills. Damian delighted in delivering sarcastic little barbs her way. In that respect he was very much like Irene.

Dismay and irritation mingled to rattle Celeste momentarily. If there was one person she didn't like thinking about it was her half-sister. Irene's death last year might have lessened the feelings of hostility and hatred Celeste had harboured against Irene all these years, but thinking about her inevitably led to thinking about another person, who was unfortunately very much alive.

'What do you want, Damian?' she snapped, her nerves suddenly on edge. 'It's not like you to surface on a Saturday till at least mid-afternoon. When you come home on a Friday night at *all*, that is.'

Her brother did not have a monopoly on sarcasm, Celeste realised with a twinge of conscience. Not that Damian was capable of being hurt by such remarks. If anything, he seemed to enjoy any allusion to his decadent lifestyle.

Damian was a lost cause in Celeste's opinion. Spoilt, selfish and lazy, he was also far too good-looking for his own good. When he'd been younger, she'd made excuses for his wild behaviour, hoping he might grow out of being reckless and irresponsible, especially when it came to the opposite sex. But twenty-nine saw him as a playboy of the worst kind. Celeste was appalled at how many happy marriages he had destroyed. What a pity the wives never saw the wickedness behind that boyish smile and those magnetic black eyes!

If Celeste had had her way, she would have tossed Damian to the four winds ages ago and forced him at least to fend for himself. That might have given him a bit of character. But he was the apple of their mother's eye, and Adele had ignored all her daughter's advice when it came to her 'baby'. She'd insisted Damian be given a position in the family company, for which he was paid a salary far and above his contribution to Campbell Jewels, a salary which never seemed to meet his ever-increasing needs. Only last week, he'd approached Celeste for a loan, which she'd given him on the condition it was the first and last time.

'I hope you haven't come here looking for more money,' she added tartly as she levered herself out of the pool and stripped her cap off. Long tawny blonde waves tumbled over her forehead and eyes. Celeste combed her hair back off her face with her fingers before walking over to pick up a towel and start drying herself. 'If you have, you're wasting your time.'

Damian lowered himself on to one of the cane loungers

and surveyed his sister with a curious mixture of dislike and admiration.

For a female rising forty, she was still a hot-looking bird. Of course she spent a fortune on her face and hair, and she worked the hell out of her body to keep it looking like that, without an ounce of extra flesh, every muscle toned and honed to perfection.

She was not to his taste, however, either physically or personality-wise. Celeste was as hard as her body. He liked his women soft, in all respects. And he preferred brunettes, especially one particular brunette with big innocent brown eyes, the most luscious body and the sweetest of smiles.

Damn, but he couldn't wait for the delectable Mrs Nathan Whitmore to fall into his hands. They said everything came to those who waited but he was getting sick and tired of waiting for Gemma to wake up to the sort of man that husband of hers was. Maybe he would have to think of some way he could give the situation a little push…

Meanwhile, he was about to relieve his boredom by giving his darling sister a different kind of push. Hell, but he was going to enjoy relaying the news he'd found out last night.

When Celeste saw Damian's mouth pull back into a wickedly smug smile, a prickle of alarm shivered down her damp spine.

'You'd like for me to have come crawling, wouldn't you?' he said silkily, linking his hands behind his head and crossing his ankles with an air of arrogant insolence. 'You like having men suck up to you. It makes you feel all-powerful. That's one of the reasons why you only screw around with younger men. Because they grovel better, and they're easier to control.'

Celeste's mouth dropped open for a second before it snapped shut. Underneath his nasty delivery and understandably inaccurate assumptions, Damian *was* right about her enjoying power over the male of the species. That was one of her rewards for staying alive, for picking herself up from the edge of insanity and suicide, and choosing to survive. It felt good to have men jumping to obey her every whim and want, having them bow and scrape. The days of her ever having to be afraid of a man, or in having them control any aspect of her life, were long over.

Or so she had believed. Till recently.

'What a delicate turn of phrase you have, Damian,' she said drily, needing a few moments to regain her composure after such a disturbing train of thought.

He laughed. 'Since when did you take offence at calling a spade a spade? You don't give a damn what people think of you, Celeste. You never have.'

Celeste frowned at this dig at the way she'd lived her life over the past decade or so, especially her uncaring attitude to scandal and gossip. It was true that she'd deliberately fuelled her reputation as a man-eater, publicly parading a long line of toy-boy companions for the gossip-mongers and tabloids to report.

What the general public did not know—or even her own brother—was that not once, during that time, had she actually been to bed with any of those young studs. Oh, yes, she'd flirted openly with them, especially when the cameras had been close. She'd allowed them to take her to highly publicised premieres, charity balls, the races and any other function where her photo was likely to be taken and printed, complete with partner.

Most of her supposed lovers had been independently wealthy playboy types from society families around Sydney. Some, however, had been employees—her personal assistant and chauffeurs were always young, male and handsome—whom she outwardly treated much more intimately than their position warranted. Amazing how quickly rumour escalated such relationships into tempestuous affairs.

Celeste suspected the men themselves lied about their conquests of the infamous female head of Campbell Jewels.

Perhaps their male egos prompted them to feed the gossip about her reputedly voracious sexuality, each one in turn thinking they were the only one not to succeed in getting her into bed.

Celeste had never been bothered by any of this before. She had revelled in it all, finding some kind of weird vengeance in the knowledge that there was one particular person whom her scandalous reputation might hopefully hurt. She used to like to picture his face when he read or heard the latest gossip about her. She would imagine him hating her, yet still wanting her at the same time.

Thinking about his ongoing unrequited desire evoked an inner satisfaction that soothed the savage beast lurking within her heart.

Or it had. Till she'd taken herself off to the Whitmore Opals ball a few weeks back and come face to face with that unrequited desire, only to find out that her own desire for Byron Whitmore was still there, just as unrequited as his, and just as strong as ever.

Celeste had been utterly thrown. She'd been so sure she would never feel any desire for any man ever again, let alone the man who'd been the instigation of all her pain and anguish. Suddenly, that night, her much vaunted control over her life had been in danger of slipping away.

Any imminent disintegration had been temporarily staved off, however, by the most unlikely circumstances: an attempted robbery.

The prize for the thieves was to have been the Heart of Fire, a magnificent uncut black opal, the auction of which had been advertised as the highlight of the ball.

When she'd first heard news of the auction on the grapevine, she'd tried dismissing the thought that this could be the same opal which had played such an unfortunate part in her life over twenty years before, but once she saw it for herself on display in the Regency store windows all sorts of tortuous thoughts and futile hopes had forced her to walk back into the lion's den and confront the past as she had never confronted it before. In the flesh.

The results had been horrendous. Not only was she shattered by the realisation that she still wanted Byron in a sexual sense, she had also stupidly forked out two million dollars for an opal she couldn't even bear to look at. She hadn't even been to elicit any real information about the circumstances of the Heart of Fire's reappearance, Byron having answered her query with some slick lie about it turning up in some old dead miner's things at Lightning Ridge and being returned to him. As if anyone would just hand over a two-million-dollar opal!

Celeste had been in a most uncharacteristic mental turmoil that night when the balaclavaed robbers made their unexpected appearance. When one grabbed her as hostage, she'd been momentarily at a loss, obeying his commands and weakly going with him like a lamb to the slaughter, till some brutal manhandling had snapped her out of her submissive fog, revitalising her bitter determination never to surrender any of her self to any man in any way ever again, either emotionally or physically.

Out of the blue, she'd struck back, using the self-defence skills she'd learnt many years before, felling her assailants with two quick kicks. With hindsight, she almost felt gratitude to those brutes for bringing back horrific memories which in turn had renewed her fighting spirit.

Suddenly, she'd felt strong again, strong enough to defy this unwanted weakness of still wanting Byron Whitmore in a sexual sense. When fate placed her in his insidious presence once again a few days after the ball, she had delighted in deliberately courting his disgust in an appalling display of over-the-top flirtation with her chauffeur.

Unfortunately, her outrageous behaviour had back-fired on her in a couple of ways. Firstly, the chauffeur had been inspired to take liberties later that evening and she'd had to fire him. But the second and more disastrous outcome was that this time Byron's obvious contempt had unaccountably *distressed*, instead of soothed her.

Celeste had eventually pulled herself together to the point where Byron ceased to fill her thoughts on a daily basis. But she certainly wasn't looking forward to confronting him again next Monday at the trial of the ringleader of the robbers, where they were both witnesses.

'Is this your version of the silent treatment?' Damian drawled in a derisive tone. 'If so, I find it incredibly boring.'

'Say what it is you have to say, Damian,' she answered sharply. 'I'm not in the mood for any of your sick little games.'

'*Moi*? Play sick games? Never!' His laughter grated on her already stretched nerves.

'Damian,' she rebuked. 'Get on with it!'

His hands dropped back to his sides and he sat up, a petulant expression on his too handsome face. 'You always spoil my fun.'

'Your idea of fun is not my idea of fun.'

'Really? I always thought it was. I like a bit of young stuff myself.'

Celeste's chin came up and she eyed her brother with distaste. 'I'm going over to the house. I have other things I'd rather do than stand here freezing to death.'

'What?'

'What do you mean, *what*?'

'I mean what else have you got to do? After all, you haven't found a new young stud to fill your leisure hours yet, have you? You know, Celeste, you never did tell me why you fired Gerry. I mean, I do realise it's rather cliché—and a tad tacky—for the rich lady employer to have her chauffeur perform extra services but he did seem well equipped for the job.'

Celeste was appalled at the fierce heat that raced up her neck and into her cheeks. Blushing had never been her style but her newly sensitised self was suddenly finding the picture she had painted of herself over the years not only embarrassing but almost obscene. When hadn't she seen what she was doing? Where had her pride disappeared to? Clearly, her hatred of Byron and men in general had warped her so much that she didn't care what *anyone* thought of her.

But suddenly, she did. Dear God, she did…

'Well, well, well,' Damian drawled. 'Whatever did Gerry do? I would have thought he was a very straight young fellow. Did he try something a little more…adventurous? Is that it?'

'Don't be disgusting, Damian,' she snapped. 'I simply decided I didn't need a chauffeur any longer.'

'I see. So you have another gorgeous young hunk to tease Byron Whitmore with, do you?'

Celeste gasped before she could stop herself.

'You thought I didn't know?' Damian's smile was pure malice as he stood up and walked towards her. 'Silly Celeste. Didn't you know Irene always told me everything? I know all about your encounters with our dear sister's husband. Whoops, *half*-sister. Though he wasn't her husband the first time, was he? Merely her boyfriend.'

'He was not,' Celeste choked out, her head whirling with Damian's disclosure. 'Irene and Byron were not going out when I first met him. I was on work experience at Whitmore's. She didn't start going out with Byron till after I went back to boarding-school. I didn't try to take Byron away from Irene. She took him away from me!'

'And what of later, Celeste?' Damian said in a low, smarmy voice. 'He was her husband then, wasn't he?'

Celeste closed her eyes and shuddered.

'Yet you made love to him, didn't you?' Damian taunted softly. 'You had to have him, no matter what…'

Celeste's eyes opened, huge and haunted. 'Yes,' she confessed brokenly. 'Yes…'

'You callous bitch,' he said with so much venom that Celeste was stunned.

She shook her head. 'You don't understand how it was.'

He laughed. 'Oh, I understand only too well. We're all tarred with the same brush. Irene… You… Me… We take after dear Papa, which makes us not good people to cross. We want what we want and God help anyone who gets in our way. You and Irene wanted the same man. A cat fight was inevitable, but the only one who came out on top was Byron. Literally.'

'You're disgusting!'

'That's the pot calling the kettle black, surely.'

'It wasn't like Irene said. I didn't set out to seduce Byron. I didn't set out to do *anything*!' Anger that she was having to defend her morals to Damian, of all people, had her whirling away and dragging on the towelling robe that she'd brought with her. Flicking her hair over her shoulder, she turned back to face her brother with a steely expression on her face. 'I do not wish to discuss what happened with Byron in the past. It's dead and gone as Irene is dead and gone.'

'Really, Celeste? Are you saying you don't feel a thing for Byron any more, that he hasn't been your silent sexual prey all along?'

Outrage at both Damian and her own stupid feelings rose in her breast. 'I detest Byron Whitmore!' she lashed out. 'I wouldn't let him touch me if he was the last man on earth!'

'No kidding. Then it won't bother you that he's about to be married again.'

Celeste could no more stop the blood from leaving her face than she could the daggers of dismay that stabbed into her heart. She clutched the robe around her and did her level best not to sway on her feet, or look anything other than coldly indifferent. With a supreme effort of will, she somehow found a wry smile and a semblance of composure. 'Is that so?' she drawled. 'And who's the unlucky lady?'

Damian seemed disconcerted by her quick recovery. Clearly, he'd wanted to distress her, wanted to twist those daggers. His black eyes were still watchful on her, waiting for her to betray her feelings, but this only hardened Celeste's resolve to keep them to herself. If she was stupid enough still to feel anything for that holier-than-thou hypocrite, then the last thing she was going to do was show it or admit it. That would betray everything that had sustained her all these years.

'Her name is Catherine Gateshead,' Damian informed her sourly.

'And how did you come across this priceless information?' Celeste thought her tone was perfect. Just a little sarcastic, and a lot bored.

'A friend of hers told a friend of mine they were going to announce their engagement at Byron's fiftieth birthday party last night. It seems they've been quite a hot item for quite some time.'

Celeste battled to control a whole host of reactions, not the least of which was shock at hearing Byron's age. Fifty! He didn't look fifty. Clearly, he wasn't acting as though he was fifty, either, she thought bitterly. Still, he'd always been a highly sexed man and Irene *had* been dead for nearly a year.

'And how old is this Catherine person?' she asked as nonchalantly as she could manage.

Damian's smirk suggested he'd picked up on her tension. 'A good few years younger than you, dear sister. And smashing-looking, I'm told.'

Celeste threw her brother a savage look and he laughed.

'Jealousy can be an ugly thing. Not that you've got anything to worry about, Celeste. No woman can hold a candle to you when you put your mind to it. I'll never forget the look on that bastard Whitmore's face when you swanned into the Regency ballroom recently in that dress. God, he couldn't keep his eyes off you. Not that I blame him. That was some dress.'

Celeste cringed at the memory of the aforesaid dress. She hadn't realised, till she was making her way down the centre of the ballroom and caught a glimpse of herself in one of the mirrored walls, how that dress looked from a distance. The skin-coloured material and tightly fitted style gave the illusion of nudity, the selected beading marking out a provocative outline around her nipples and crotch. Up close in the boutique, it had not looked so scandalously revealing. Still, under Byron's critical gaze, she'd had no alternative but to carry off the outrageous outfit with panache or be left looking a fool.

'It was perfectly obvious to anyone with a brain in their head,' Damian was raving on, 'that you've only got to click your fingers his way and he'd drop Catherine Whatsername as though she has a contagious disease. Alternatively, you could have some real fun and wait till he married the silly bitch, then move in for the ultimate kill. A married Byron seems to bring out your best hunting instincts.'

Celeste amazed herself by not reacting visibly to Damian's crude and inflammatory remarks. Her expression remained remarkably cool, as was her laugh. 'I think you're confusing me with yourself, brother dear. You're the one who's always running after married people. I prefer my bed partners both single and decidedly younger than fifty. I don't think Byron Whitmore fills the bill, do you?'

Retying the sash on her robe, Celeste picked up her towel and pushed past her brother, striding confidently towards the door. Damian scowled after her, irritated by his lack of success at stirring up trouble. What he didn't see was the grey pallor in his sister's face as she left the pool-house, or the haunted look in her eyes. Neither could he guess at the storm of emotion gathering in her heart, nor her lack of confidence in her ability to deal with any of it.

Celeste headed across the lawns and up the stone steps

to the back of the house, blinking madly as she went. I do not care about Byron Whitmore, she kept saying to herself. I do not care what he does or where he goes or whom he marries. I do not care!

Celeste swept into the huge kitchen and put on the kettle for a cup of coffee. By the time she was sipping its soothing warmth, she was almost her old self again.

Till she suddenly remembered the trial on Monday.

Her head dropped into her hands, her stomach instantly churning.

'Oh, God…'

CHAPTER TWO

THE taxi sped off, leaving Gemma standing on the pavement with her suitcase at her feet. She was smiling to herself.

Nathan was going to get the shock of his life when she walked in. He thought she was out in good old Lightning Ridge, patiently awaiting the Monday afternoon flight back to Sydney. Instead, here she was, home a day early, the lucky passenger on a private jet chartered by an American couple staying at her motel.

The McFaddens had dropped in on the opal-mining town as part of a whirlwind tour of the outback of Australia, and, not finding the dust, flies and heat to their liking, had decided to head for Sydney posthaste. When Gemma had told them over breakfast this morning in the dining-room that she wished she were back home in Sydney as well, they'd offered her a lift. Delighted, she'd accepted, and here she was!

A glance at her watch showed it had only just passed one in the afternoon.

For a few seconds, she regretted that her trip back to Lightning Ridge had been so unrewarding in the matter of finding anything out about her missing mother. Perhaps she should have stayed the extra day and come back on the Monday as originally planned.

In all honesty, she hadn't tried all that hard, had she? One short interview with Mr Gunther—her dead father's only friend in Lightning Ridge—and one afternoon spent talking to the miners who'd just happened to drop into the pub.

Neither would qualify as an in-depth investigation. Was it that underneath she was afraid of the truth? Or of finding out that Nathan was right? Some people's pasts were better off left there.

Still, the trip back to where she'd grown up had made Gemma appreciate the life she had made for herself now in Sydney. She had an interesting job selling opals to an exclusive clientele in Whitmore's glamorous store in the Regency Hotel. She was married to Sydney's most successful playwright who also just happened to be the most handsome, sexiest man who'd ever drawn breath. And soon she was going to start having the family she'd always wanted.

Her big brown eyes melted as she thought of her husband, and their phone conversation last Friday night. That had been less than two days ago, but it seemed like an eternity. She'd done exactly as he'd suggested and thrown away her pills. Then she'd done the second thing he'd wanted: come home.

Smiling a very female smile, she extracted her keys from her carry-all handbag, picked up her suitcase and walked over to the security door of the four-storey building that housed their apartment. On the top floor, their unit had a lovely view of Elizabeth Bay and, while Gemma called it home for now, she knew she wouldn't want to bring up a child, or children, in such a contained and restricted environment. She would want a house and a big back yard with a dog in it, a dog she would call Blue.

Gemma's heart squeezed tight as she thought of that moment out at the Ridge yesterday when she'd visited Blue's grave. He was buried not far from the dugout she'd been brought up in, on a small hillock he used to lie on sometimes. She hadn't been able to stop the sudden welling-up of emotion nor the flood of tears that had streamed from her eyes. Now, as she turned the key and let herself into the building, she felt those tears pricking at her eyes again.

She would have brought Blue to Sydney with her if she'd

had the chance. But some rotten swine had poisoned him while she'd been at her father's funeral. She'd been shattered when she found his body, seemingly more upset over her dog's death than her father's.

Gemma felt a stab of guilt at that memory, frowning as she carried her case inside the cool foyer and shut the door behind her. Going back to Lightning Ridge had dredged up memories she would rather have forgotten. Yes, Nathan *was* right. One's happiness lay in the future, not the past. Her future and her happiness lay in her marriage to Nathan, in their having a family together.

A determined expression momentarily thinned Gemma's full mouth. If Nathan thought she was going to stop at one baby, he was very much mistaken. She'd hated not having any brothers and sisters, hated not having a mother *and* a father. No child of hers was going to go through life feeling deprived and different, as she had done. Her children would have every advantage she could give them.

Gemma's mouth suddenly relaxed into a quietly rueful smile.

Just look at me, getting all carried away and serious. Thinking too far ahead was as bad as spending all one's energy worrying about the past. My first priority is being happy here and now—and in getting pregnant with my *first* baby. Still, if Nathan's mood on the phone the other night was anything to go by then the latter shouldn't take too long.

Gemma hurried over to press the lift button on the wall, her heart racing excitedly as she thought of what was in store for her upstairs.

The lift doors whooshed back and she stepped inside the empty compartment, pressing number four and waiting impatiently for them to shut again.

Actually, she and Nathan hadn't made love for ages. Not that Nathan hadn't wanted to. He *always* wanted to. But some recent and rather shocking allegations about Nathan's sexual history had played on her mind, and she'd begun making excuses not to make love with her husband. Even after being assured by an independent source that the most shocking of these allegations was untrue, she'd still found herself acting very negatively in the bedroom. Nathan had been remarkably patient with her, and she aimed to reward that patience in full tonight.

Maybe I'll fall pregnant straight away, Gemma thought excitedly as the doors shut and the lift began to rise.

Probably not, she conceded, but it felt wonderfully warming to think about the possibility. It would give added meaning to what had previously been little more than a physical intimacy between them. Gemma held high hopes that having a baby together would bring about the emotional bonding with Nathan that she'd always felt was missing in their relationship.

With spirits high and pulse galloping, she stepped out of the lift on the fourth floor, eager to have her husband's arms around her, to have him kiss her as he'd kissed her at the airport the other day. Too bad if he was deeply involved with his writing. She was going to insist he leave it and give her his full attention. No doubt he would be holed up in his study, his handsome face buried in the computer screen. But nothing was going to save him from being seduced today. Nothing!

Gemma's grin faded to a frown as she opened their apartment door. Nathan's raised voice was coming through the closed double doors that led into the living-room, sounding so impassioned that Gemma was shocked into stillness, her hand on the doorknob, her case still in the hallway outside. His next words came crystal-clear to her startled ears, and their content staggered her.

'So what if it was just sex last night?' Nathan scoffed angrily. 'And the night before. When has it ever been anything other than just sex between us?'

Gemma paled, her hand tightening over the knob as Lenore's voice flung a furious reply.

'When has it ever been anything else but just sex for you with *any* woman?'

Nathan laughed.

Despite her being already frozen with shock and horror, that cold laughter chilled Gemma to the bones.

'You think I didn't love you that night all those years,' Lenore swept on, 'when we made a baby together? You think that was only sex for me?'

'I *know* it was.' Scornfully.

'You bastard!'

'Nothing is to be achieved by calling names. Why don't you come over here and stop being a fool? Besides, you can hardly flounce out of here in a temper. You're not properly dressed.'

Gemma had to stuff a fist into her mouth to stop an anguished groan from escaping.

A muffled groan did find its way through those hideous doors, however, and Gemma thought she would die.

'I should never have let you talk me into coming here,' Lenore cried. 'I should never have let you touch me. You've always been bad news for women. God, but I hate you.'

'Shall we see how much?' he taunted.

'No, don't! Oh…oh, God, I'm hopeless…'

Gemma couldn't stand another second of such emotional torture, but the wild urge to burst in on them and create an embarrassing scene was superseded by feelings of pained pride. Why should she humiliate herself in front of two such shameless creatures? They wouldn't really care, except in how being caught out would affect their cruelly selfish and amoral lives.

But oh, God, the betrayal hurt as she'd never been hurt before. Nothing compared with the vice-like pain gripping her heart, nor the wintry emptiness within, as though her soul had been sucked dry by some huge emotional vacuum cleaner.

Gemma somehow managed to close the door, hoist her

carry-all up on to her shoulder and pick up her suitcase. She didn't take the lift. She went down the fire stairs, quite slowly, each shuddering step like a death-kneel, her mind disbelieving of how quickly her excited happiness had been changed to despair.

Tears filled her eyes and flooded over, running down her cheeks. She didn't stop to wipe them away. Neither did she stop going down those steps. If she did, she would surely sag down into a wretched impotent huddle, and once she did that she would not have the energy or the courage to do anything or go anywhere. Nathan might accidentally find her there and she couldn't bear to hear the lies he was sure to come up with to explain what she'd overheard.

Gemma exited the building and turned to walk up the streets and around the corner, no real destination in mind. She just wanted to get as far away from Nathan and Lenore as she could. The act of walking was a salvation in itself, for having to put one foot in front of the other had a kind of robotic comfort. Gradually, the breeze dried the tears on Gemma's cheeks and she felt the pieces of her shattered soul gradually reassemble into something that was capable of making decisions.

Not that she was whole again. Her heart would never be whole again, she recognised bleakly. It would remain broken, but a type of glueing together was taking place as she walked, her bewildered despair giving way to the human survival technique of cynicism and anger.

You shouldn't be surprised, Gemma, a bitter voice berated. You had plenty of clues that Nathan hadn't married you for love, no matter what he claimed. True love does not keep its emotional distance, nor harbour dark secrets. It is open and trusting and warm and wonderful. Nathan, on far too many occasions, was secretive and distrusting and cold and downright wicked. Look at the way he enslaved your senses, turned you into little more than a sexual puppet. If he's been patient with you lately, it was because he had other fish to fry. He didn't need to make love to you because he was having an affair with Lenore!

And you suspected as much. Go on, admit it, you stupid little idiot! Underneath you were worried about the time he was spending with Lenore but in the end you chose to ignore it, because you wanted to believe in his love, wanted to keep pretending.

As for Lenore…

Now that the initial shock was over and she was thinking more clearly, Gemma was stunned to find she didn't feel quite so angry with Nathan's ex-wife. In fact, she almost felt sorry for her. If Lenore hated Nathan, as she said, then that was because she was also still in love with him. Gemma could well understand a woman loving and hating Nathan at the same time. She certainly did right at this moment. But at least the hate part seemed to clear one's vision of the man he really was. Lenore didn't sound as though she was under any illusions. Neither was Gemma any more. Just to love Nathan was to become a fool, there was no doubt about that. A blind fool!

Gemma looked back over all the warnings she'd been given about Nathan, the warnings she had naïvely ignored. Instead, she'd stupidly gone into a marriage based on nothing but the physical. His wanting her to have a baby was the one thing that she didn't quite understand. There again, men had babies all the time with women they didn't love. Maybe it was a matter of ego, of wanting to replicate their genes, or of wanting to keep the women under their control.

Nathan had demonstrated a jealousy and possessiveness over her from the start, suggesting that, while he might not love her, he did like 'owning' her. Since their marriage, he'd moulded her into the sort of wife that suited him, a sexually submissive little doll whom he could dress as he fancied, parade in public on his arm, then bring home and make love to as he pleased.

Well, he wouldn't be 'making love' to her any more, she

vowed with an intense bitterness that kept the despair at bay. Their marriage was over as of this moment. She would never go back to him. Never ever!

Gemma strode on, around the next corner, heading towards she knew not what. But the ramifications of the decision she had just made were not long in sinking in. Would Byron give her the sack once he found out she'd left his precious adopted son? Even if he didn't, where was she going to live now? She had no real friends, no one she could turn to, except perhaps…

Damian had said she could rely on him if ever she needed a friend.

Gemma slowed her step. Why was she so loath to call Damian Campbell? Was it just pride that was stopping her, or something more complex than that? Nathan's own warnings about his enemy no longer held water, did they? One couldn't believe a thing he said. And yet…

Gemma sighed her confusion, halting completely on the pavement, putting the suitcase down. Momentarily, she closed her eyes, the events of the day threatening to overwhelm her. She felt so alone, so alone and so wretched. Tired too. Yes, suddenly, she felt dreadfully tired. Emotional exhaustion, she supposed.

Opening her eyes, she glanced around and there, on the next corner, stood an old hotel. What she needed was a quiet place to lie down. Somewhere she could simply sleep for a while. Nathan was not expecting her back in Sydney till the following afternoon. He was not expecting her to call tonight. This gave her over twenty-four hours to decide what action she was going to take. Wearily, Gemma picked up her suitcase again and began walking in the direction of the hotel.

What would have happened, she wondered grimly as she carefully crossed the street, if she had stayed in Lightning Ridge and come back as originally planned?

Gemma shuddered to think that she would have innocently gone back home to her husband's bed, unknowing of his treachery, unsuspecting of how callously he had betrayed her over the weekend, how he would go on betraying her.

Innocent.

Unknowing.

Unsuspecting.

Well, she wasn't innocent any longer and she would never be unknowing or unsuspecting again. From this moment on, Gemma Whitmore would place her trust in one person only.

Herself.

CHAPTER THREE

CELESTE surveyed her wardrobe with some concern on the Monday morning, moving outfit after outfit along the racks in her dressing-room, mulling over the effect each one would have on Byron Whitmore. What could she wear that wouldn't inspire contempt in his eyes?

Or lust.

At this last thought, Celeste brought herself up sharply. What on earth was the matter with her, caring what Byron thought, or felt? It was her own feelings she had to worry about. Her own lust. Or desire. Or whatever people called it these days.

She'd read somewhere recently that lust had a chemical basis, hormones or such sparking off endorphins in the brain which in turn impelled one's body to mate with the object of its desire without any reference to logic or common sense. A mindless animal thing, in other words.

A mindless animal thing was all she could possibly still feel for that man, she'd decided bitterly after her run-in with Damian at the weekend. Nothing else. Certainly not anything finer or deeper. She'd been silly even to consider such a possibility, let alone worry about it!

Since this was the case, she reasoned ruthlessly, then the person who needed protecting was *herself*, not Byron. How better to protect herself than to dress as provocatively as she always had, thereby ensuring his lust *and* contempt?

Celeste knew full well that the holier-than-thou Byron Whitmore would not contaminate himself by touching someone who epitomised everything he despised. She was safe, as long as she ran true to form. Whereas if she came out looking unexpectedly demure, shock might make him vulnerable to the primitive desires she knew still lurked in that staunchly high-principled soul of his. She'd seen the lust in his eyes the night of the ball as surely as she had felt her own.

A canary-yellow dress jumped out at her and she drew it from the rack, smiling. If that didn't put some fire in his veins and disgust into those beautiful blue eyes of his then her name wasn't Celeste Campbell.

Made of stretch jersey wool, the yellow sheath fitted her like a glove and finished mid-thigh. The high rolled neck and long tight sleeves practised reverse physiology by being more provocative than the lowest-cut, most revealing style. Perhaps this had something to do with the way it clung, projecting a subtle promise rather than overt promiscuity.

Subtle?

Celeste laughed. There was nothing subtle about that yellow dress if it was worn without a bra and only tights underneath—the ones with built-in panties which had not a single ridge to reveal their existence. She had worn it that way to the races one day and caused a minor sensation. Celeste remembered the occasion with wry affection because her photograph had been splashed across all the Sunday society pages and she felt confident Byron would have seen them. There was nothing that made her feel better than the knowledge she might have upset Byron's equilibrium.

It was not simply a matter of a woman scorned having her revenge, as her brother probably believed. It was a matter of justice. Byron had to be punished for what he had set in motion with his merciless ambition. She shouldn't have to be the only one to suffer.

The image of her lovely little baby girl swam before her eyes for a moment before she ruthlessly forced it down, down into the depths of darkness, hopefully never to surface again. She'd trained herself not to think about that any more, for what was the point? She'd done all that she could, had tried to find her baby. Tried and tried and tried. In the end, she had had to put the search side and go on with her life. Either that, or kill herself, or go mad.

Her decision to put the past behind her and go on living had been a brave one. Of course, that didn't mean she no longer suffered, or that she was totally successful in blocking those crippling memories. This was the second time this year she had lapsed. The first time had been when she'd seen that damned opal. How could she *not* have started thinking about the past when confronted by a piece of it? But confronting an inanimate object was nothing compared to confronting the man who'd set all the horrors in motion.

Celeste shuddered, then stiffened and straightened, using every ounce of her iron will to smooth the pained anguish from her face. Her tiger's eyes, which had mirrored intense distress for a second, now flashed with the type of coldly glittering lights that would have terrified any enemy.

Celeste only had one enemy within reach these days. Byron Whitmore.

If I wear the matching yellow sandals complete with three-inch heels, she decided with icy determination, I should meet him eye to eye.

Well, not quite, she conceded drily as she draped the yellow dress over her arm and picked up those same yellow sandals. Byron stretched the tape measure to six feet four. If that wasn't daunting enough, he had shoulders like axe-handles and legs any football player would kill for. Top that off with a classically handsome face which was ageing better than Cary Grant's and you had a man so damned attractive it was downright unfair!

What irked Celeste as well was that Byron's sex appeal was not dimmed by his possessing the sort of chauvinistic attitude to women that sent feminists into a right flap. Yet, for some weird and wonderful reason, most women responded to his strongly male stance very positively. They became coy in his presence. Coy and fluttering and feminine. She herself had been guilty of such a reaction in the old days, as had dear sweet Irene. Oh, yes, Irene had been putty in his hands, quite the reverse of the hard-edged sarcastic bitch everyone else had known her to be.

Thinking about the way she herself had blindly responded to Byron in the past rehardened Celeste's heart towards him in the present. Unfortunately, her emotional toughness did not seem to spill over into other areas. Her mind and body were running their own races, recalling things she would rather not recall.

Byron, kissing her in his office when she'd been only seventeen.

Byron, making love to her. Once again in his office.

Byron, making love to her yet again. Not in his office. On the billiard-table. At Belleview. Two years later…

For a few tormenting moments she could almost feel how it had felt when he made love to her. God, she would have done anything he wanted. She *had* done anything he wanted!

Celeste squeezed her eyes tightly shut, detesting herself for the wave of heat flooding her body. But when her nipples actually hardened, her eyes flung open wide in shock.

Furious with herself for her lack of control, Celeste swept back into her luxurious bedroom, dumping her clothes on the huge round bed before heading for her equally luxurious bathroom. Arousal quickly gave way to other more satisfying emotions, a vengeful smile curving her generous mouth as she slipped the silky robe from her shoulders and snapped on the shower taps. God, but she was going to enjoy making that bastard's loins itch today. It was the least she could do in the face of her own damnable desires.

CELESTE'S BITTER RESOLVE lasted right up till the moment her taxi pulled up in front of the court-house and she saw

Byron walking down the street towards her. Her immediate flutter of nerves mocked her determination to be ruthlessly seductive in his presence, her instantly churning stomach bringing with it both irritation and dismay.

What in God's name was the matter with her? This was Byron Whitmore here, the man who'd almost destroyed her. No mercy, Celeste. No mercy!

Damn, but he did look good in that black suit. Distinguished and handsome, yet incredibly sexy. She couldn't take her eyes off him.

The driver curtly announcing the fare snapped Celeste out of her emotional confusion. She handed him over a note, told him brusquely to keep the change, then began to alight from the back seat, just as Byron drew alongside. Their eyes met as she swung the door wide and presented her long legs to the spring sunshine.

Byron halted mid-stride to glare at her, his blue eyes soothingly derisive as they raked over her, taking in everything she'd wanted him to take in. This was familiar ground to Celeste and she indulged in a smug smile. With her self-confidence restored, she uncurled her tall athletic body with the sensuous grace of a Siamese cat, swinging the door shut behind her before turning to face her foe.

'Good morning, Byron,' she said huskily, that confidently sensual smile firmly in place.

Byron seemed to stiffen under its impact, which only made her sense of satisfaction increase. She revelled in the way his eyes followed her every movement as she smoothed the tight skirt down over her hips, then adjusted the brim of her wide straw hat.

'For God's sake, Celeste,' he snapped at last, blue eyes glittering. 'You're going to a trial, not the races.'

So! He *had* seen those photos of her in the paper.

Good.

'Looking at you,' she returned silkily while she idly

played with the gold rope necklace hanging between her breasts, 'one might have thought we were off to a funeral. Truly, Byron, you should never wear black. Grey's your colour. And you shouldn't scowl like that. It's bad for your health. Gives you high blood-pressure. A man your age has to worry about such things.'

The muscles in Byron's jaw convulsed as though he was clenching and unclenching his teeth. He seemed to be doing the same with his hands. His eyes, however, kept flicking back to her chest where she could feel her braless nipples growing more erect by the moment. Far from being disconcerted by this as she had been earlier on, Celeste found that her own arousal fuelled her to be even more outrageous.

'Did you know that owning a pet can lower your blood-pressure?' she purred. 'It has something to do with the stroking. You look like you could do with a pet, Byron. Not a dog, though. A cat. A nice soft sensual cat that enjoys a lot of stroking…'

Their eyes locked, Celeste lifting a saucy eyebrow at him while she awaited Byron's reaction to her provocative words.

Those beautiful blue eyes of his blazed for a second before they turned icily contemptuous. Celeste smiled her satisfaction with the way the encounter was going. Byron was so predictable.

'Thank you for the advice, Celeste,' he bit out, 'but I think I know what clothes suit me after all these years. As for my blood-pressure,' he went on drily, 'it's just fine. I have no need of a cat, nor any other artificial method of relaxation.'

'Really?' Her smile was a deliciously sarcastic curve. 'Oh, I *see*! Silly me. I did hear you were getting married again. I forgot. Yes, you're right, there's nothing to compare with mother nature's natural relaxant, is there?'

Byron's frozen stare unnerved Celeste for a moment.

'I am not getting married again,' he said coldly.

Celeste thought she hid her reaction very well. 'You're not?' she said airily. 'Well, there you are. People say you should only believe half of what you see and none of what you hear.'

'Where you're concerned, Celeste,' he returned frostily, 'I believe everything I see and add considerably to all that I hear.'

Her laughter was light and flirtatious. 'You're such a flatterer! Shouldn't we be going inside?'

Without waiting for his reply, she turned and began walking up the never-ending steps. He automatically fell into step beside her, Celeste suddenly finding his nearness claustrophobic, which was rather perverse. Hadn't she wanted to tease him, to inflame his unrequited desire for her?

'You came in a taxi,' he remarked on the way up. 'What happened to your Rolls?'

'Nothing. It's in the garage at home. It's simply minus one chauffeur.'

Byron slanted her a sardonic glance. 'What happened? Didn't he come up to expectations?'

'Obviously not. Didn't your fiancée?'

Byron ground to a halt. 'Catherine was never my fiancée.'

'Oh? What was she, then?' Celeste was unnerved by the pleasure she found in the word—*was*.

'A friend.'

'A *close* friend, from all reports. And quite a deal younger than you.'

Byron's handsome face darkened. 'At least she wasn't on my payroll!'

'You think women like that are free?' Celeste countered caustically. 'I'll bet she knew what you were worth, right down to your last dollar. And I'll bet she thought an affair was a down-payment on a more permanent contract.'

'Then she thought wrong.'

Celeste heard the harsh note in his voice. 'What happened, Byron?' she queried softly, moving closer and reaching out to touch him on the wrist. 'Did you find out she was a mercenary gold-digging bitch? You poor darling…' Her fingernail slid down his sleeve, over his cuff and onto bare flesh. 'Better to stick to the devil you know in future, don't you think?'

For a few excruciatingly tense seconds, Celeste thought he was actually going to drag her into his arms and kiss her. His eyes were like hot coals on her softly parted lips, his chest rising and falling with visibly unchecked passion.

But Byron did not let her down. He gathered himself superbly, giving her the coldest look while he lifted her hand from the back of his with obvious distaste.

'I'd appreciate it if you would keep your hands to yourself,' he drawled. 'I don't know where they've been.'

Celeste's heart contracted fiercely at this open insult. You'll keep, Byron, she thought savagely. You'll keep.

Outwardly, she delivered a silky smile. 'Shall we adjourn to courtroom six?'

'By all means,' he returned, just as smoothly.

Courtroom six, however, was not where they ended up. Instead, they were shuffled into a waiting-room where there was nothing to do but wait till they were called to the witness stand. The minutes ticked away with endless tedium. Celeste finding it difficult to remain in the same room with Byron without the soothing comfort of his ongoing contempt. A silently brooding Byron was far too attractive to her recently renewed desire for him.

Celeste contemplated starting a conversation about the night of the ball, and the robbery, and what he was going to say in the witness stand. But that would lead to talk about the Heart of Fire. And while she would have liked to question Byron again over how that rotten opal had come to turn up again, she couldn't bear dredging up any more memories today, certainly not *those* memories…

'Tell me, what's happening with your family?' she asked Byron so abruptly that he jumped in his seat.

He eyed her suspiciously. 'Why would you want to know about my family?'

Her shrug was nonchalant. 'Why not? They're my family too, in a roundabout sort of way. Besides, I'm fed up with that old feud nonsense between the Whitmores and the Campbells. We should let bygones be bygones.'

'Pardon me if I say I don't believe that for a moment,' he scoffed. 'You singlehandedly revived the old feud when you took over Campbell Jewels. Your mother might have been prepared to let bygones be bygones after your father died. But not, you, Celeste. Never you.'

'A woman can change her mind, can't she?'

Byron laughed. 'You mean you're going to drop all your unfair business tactics? You're not going to deliberately undercut our prices, even at your own expense? You're not going to bribe any more Japanese tour guides to bypass our stores in favour of yours?'

'That was not done with my sanction,' she said sharply.

'Then I suggest you get rid of your sales and marketing manager before he ruins you.'

'I have spoken to Damian.'

'*Spoken*? He should have been fired!'

'He's family,' she sighed. 'You must know what that's like. I feel responsible for him.'

Celeste was surprised to see understanding soften Byron's face. 'Yes,' he sighed as well. 'I do. But one makes a lot of mistakes in the name of family responsibility.'

Celeste nodded her agreement while Byron fell silent.

'Ava's getting married,' he resumed abruptly after a short interval.

'Good lord!' Celeste was genuinely surprised. 'Who to?'

'A very interesting man by the name of Vince Morelli.'

'An Italian?'

'An Australian-Italian. In his early thirties and handsome as the devil, though not in a typically Latin fashion. He has the colouring and the body of a Bondi lifesaver.'

'Well, I am surprised. I'm afraid I rather saw Ava going to her grave a spinster. Are you sure he's not after her money? As your only sister, she must have quite an inheritance.'

'He has more than enough money of his own. Runs a construction company that specialises in building blocks of units. My solicitor says he's rock-solid.'

She threw him a dry look. 'I see you had him checked out.'

'I didn't get where I am today by being trusting, Celeste. Still, you wouldn't have so many doubts if you saw Ava today. She's trimmed off a lot of weight and is looking positively glowing. Being in love suits her.'

Celeste flinched inside. 'How nice for her,' she said a little stiffly. 'Speaking of being in love, has Jade tied the knot yet with that hunk of a fiancé she was with at the ball?'

'Yes, and she's expecting a baby.'

Celeste had to fight hard this time not to show a thing on her face. 'Really,' she said with a falsely bright smile. 'Is she going to stay home and give up her career?'

'No such luck, Celeste. Kyle's the one who's retiring. Apparently, he fancies himself a house husband while Jade stays head of marketing at Whitmore's.'

'Just my luck,' she muttered. 'But let's not talk about business. What's this I hear about Nathan's marriage being on the rocks?'

'What rubbish!' Byron exclaimed hotly. 'Nathan and Gemma are extremely happy.'

'Well, there, you see what I mean? How can one believe what one hears? Nathan's blissfully happy with his child bride and you're not getting married again, either. I really must stop listening to gossip. Are you sure you're not getting married again? You're not just trying to keep it a secret, are you?'

'I have no intention of ever getting married again,' Byron bit out.

'Oh? Why's that? Wasn't your one experience with marriage a happy one?'

'You know damned well what my marriage was like, Celeste.'

'I'm not sure I do. Why don't you tell me?'

'I am not going to rake over old coals. Neither am I going to speak ill of the dead. Irene tried to be a good wife to me, and I did my best to be a good husband to her.'

'But you didn't love her.'

'Don't you dare talk to me about love,' he snarled. 'You have no concept of what love is.'

Celeste was startled by his sudden vehemence.

'Women like you are poison to all decent men,' he raved on in a low but highly emotional voice. 'You make them think you love them, but you don't. You play games with them. You turn them inside out. You fuel their desires, use their bodies, and when you've had enough you throw them away. Well, I called your bluff that last time, didn't I, Celeste? I used you and I threw you away. Watch out, darling, or I might do the same thing again. After all, we both know what you are, don't we? Not a cat. An alley-cat. I could have you just like that!' And he clicked his fingers.

It was ironic that at that precise moment Byron was called to the witness stand. He stood up, and, without a backward glance, strode proudly from the room.

Celeste stared after him, her heart pounding madly in her chest. Outrage at his insults warred with the astonishing realisation that Byron might really have loved her once. Why else would he still be so bitter towards her? Why else hate her so virulently?

Celeste had always suspected Irene had fed him a whole lot of lies about her after she'd gone back to school, lies that had made her look very bad. Even so, Byron had been very ready to believe those lies, had been very quick to write her a 'dear John' letter, dismissing their affair as a temporary infatuation which he deeply regretted. He'd stated quite coldly that he wanted nothing to do with her ever again.

Celeste had been crushed by this brutal and rather confusing rejection, then shattered when a few short months later he'd married Irene.

Recalling the distress she had felt at that time hardened Celeste's heart again. No, she decided staunchly, and clenched her teeth down hard in her jaw. Byron's fierce antagonism towards her just now was no proof of a past love. He was simply being the same hypocritical bastard he'd always been, pretending to be holier-than-thou, judging her on standards that he himself didn't live up to. He'd lied when he'd told her he loved her back then. Lied for the sole purpose of possessing her body. and when he'd had his fill and she'd gone back to school, he'd callously dumped her and moved on to Irene, who he'd obviously thought would bring him Campbell Jewels as well as her beautiful and undoubtedly willing body.

Men like Byron didn't love women, Celeste accepted with a bitter cynicism. They loved sex and money and success. They loved power and position in the community. Nothing was more important to Byron than his social standing, his so-called good name. Why else would he spend so much time and money working for charity? Why else would he have taken that degenerate boy off the streets and adopted him, for heaven's sake?

Because he wanted everyone to look up to him and say what a great man he was. How generous and good. How bloody wonderful!

But that shining reputation of his had been won at a cost. She'd been the one to pay. Yet he had the hide to tear strips off *her* character, as well as the gall to claim he could have her as easily as he could snap his fingers.

Like hell, she thought. Like bloody hell! There was no way she would ever let him touch her again. Never in a million years!

CHAPTER FOUR

GEMMA'S hand trembled as she dialled. It was the hardest thing she had ever had to do but she had to do it. Nathan would be leaving soon to go to the airport to pick her up, and even she didn't have the heart callously to let him worry when she didn't get off that plane.

The telephone in their apartment rang and rang and rang, but he didn't answer. It had not occurred to her that Nathan might not be home, that he might go straight from rehearsals at the theatre to Mascot Airport. But now it did, and she groaned her dismay. God, she just wasn't thinking straight.

With her heart thudding madly in her chest, she hung up hurriedly and looked up the theatre number in the telephone book. This time, someone answered immediately, and luckily Nathan was soon located. He came on the line, sounding worried.

'Gemma? What's wrong, darling? Did you miss the flight?'

'No, Nathan,' she replied, fighting to keep her voice steady. 'I didn't miss the flight.'

'Then where are you ringing from? You're supposed to be in the air. Oh, I see. The flight's been delayed. Never mind, darling. These things happen. So when will you be arriving?'

The two 'darlings' had really hurt, bringing the sense of outrage she needed. 'I won't be arriving, Nathan. I'm not coming home.'

'Not coming home?' he repeated in a stunned, almost blank tone.

'That's right. You told me once that if I ever wanted out of our marriage I was to say so up-front.' She paused long enough to drag in a much needed breath. 'I want out of our marriage, Nathan. My solicitor will be in touch.'

'Wait!' he cried, seemingly aware that she was about to hang up. 'You…you can't just leave me like this, Gemma. You must give me a reason. God-dammit, I have a right to know the reason!' he demanded, clearly shaken.

'The reason? The reason is you're a cheat and a liar. I'm sure it won't take too much intelligence to work out what I'm talking about. You took me for a fool, Nathan. And I'm not. I'm not…' Her voice broke and she struggled for control. 'Oh, God, how could you? I didn't deserve that. I…I…' She broke off and forcibly pulled herself together. 'Goodbye, Nathan. Don't bother trotting out to Lightning Ridge to find me. I'm not there.'

She hung up, then sank down on the side of the hotel bed, looking and feeling utterly drained. No tears came. She was all out of tears.

But dear God, whatever was she going to do? Where was she going to go?

Her overnight stay in the old hotel and many hours of thinking had provided no solutions except that she was going to divorce Nathan. No doubt some fancy solicitor could drive a hard bargain for her when it came to a financial settlement, but she automatically shrank from that and from what people would say about her. They'd only been married a few months, after all. She also shrank from having to tell Nathan's family the reason for her leaving him—that he'd been cheating on her with his ex-wife.

Not that they would necessarily believe her. Nathan would deny it, of course, and so would Lenore. Byron, Gemma realised, would be loath to believe such a thing of his golden-haired boy. Nathan could do no wrong in his eyes, being supposedly as old-fashioned in his moral principles as his adopted father. Ava was the only person Gemma could think of who would be on her side, but how could she put brother against sister? It wasn't right.

No, she would have to strike out on her own. She still had the money Byron had paid her as a reward for bringing back the Heart of Fire. That would cover her expenses for a while. And she could probably get a job easily enough with her mastery of oral Japanese.

Going back to work at Whitmore's was not an option. Even if Byron didn't fire her, Nathan would descend upon her there like an avenging angel, demanding further explanations when doing his best to whitewash his behaviour. He might even throw himself on her mercy and beg her forgiveness. She could not have borne that.

What she needed, more than anything, was to disappear for a while, out of reach of Nathan and any private detective he might hire to find her. Which meant not staying in any hotel, nor going to real estate agents nor applying for a job. That would leave a trail any decent detective would easily pick up on.

So where could she go?

Damian's offer, which had been hovering at the back of her mind all along, but which she had previously dismissed, jumped to the fore. Why not? she rationalised. He was in a position to help her. He had the money and the connections. He'd even promised her a job if she ever wanted one. Campbell Jewels had stores in other states. Maybe she could move to Brisbane or to Melbourne: get herself well away from Sydney and Nathan.

At three in the afternoon, Damian would probably be in his office. Gemma looked up the number of the head office of Campbell Jewels and, once again, dialled.

'Could I speak to Damian Campbell, please?' she requested of the girl who answered.

An extension was tried but no one answered.

'Mr Campbell doesn't seem to be in his office at the moment,' the receptionist said with brisk politeness. 'Would you like to leave a message and I'll get him to ring you back?'

Gemma sighed. 'Yes, all right.' And she relayed her name and the hotel number, adding that this was an emergency and she would appreciate every effort being made to get the message to Mr Campbell as soon as possible.

After she had hung up yet again, Gemma lay down in the dimly lit room and closed her eyes. Depression descended, as did exhaustion. She hadn't slept much the previous night. Now, she could not stop her mind from slipping into the blackness.

CELESTE LEFT the court-house in a highly agitated state. Her encounter with Byron was bad enough, but having to face that pig who had manhandled her so brutally the night of the robbery had upset her more than she'd thought it would. Still, she was sure he'd be put behind bars after her solid and unwavering testimony. Men who perpetrated violence against women should be incarcerated and the key thrown away, in her opinion.

She chose to walk back to the office. It was only a couple of blocks and the fresh air would do her mood good. On the way she made a brief stopover in a coffee lounge where she banished some hunger pangs with a roll and some coffee. By the time the lift carried her up to the tenth floor of the city office block that housed the head office of Campbell Jewels, Celeste felt much better.

Five minutes later she was seated behind her large modern desk, reading the monthly sales reports and chewing thoughtfully on a Biro. Shaking her head, she picked up her telephone and asked for Damian's extension, only to be told by his secretary that he wasn't back yet from lunch.

Striding out to Reception, she informed the startled receptionist that Mr Campbell was to be sent into her office the moment he reappeared, and not a second later. She was fuming by the time he walked in—without knocking—at five to four.

'You wanted to see me, Celeste?' he said with arrogant nonchalance, plonking himself down on the black leather chesterfield and drawing a packet of cigarettes from his pocket.

'I don't allow smoking in here, Damian,' she said coldly.

'Tough. If you don't like it, fire me.' And he lit up, drawing in deeply, then exhaling in her direction.

She glared at him through the haze of smoke. 'I just might do that.'

'No, you won't. Darling Mama holds the ultimate reins in this place and she wouldn't hear of it.'

'Darling Mama is in Europe for another few months,' came Celeste's dry reminder. 'Before she left, she gave me a free hand to do whatever I thought was best for the company. Not in one's wildest imagination could your performance as sales and marketing manager be labelled that. Our retail outlets are still suffering a backlash from the publicity we received over the tour-guide scandal. Our exports are down nearly twenty per cent. And the quality of the opals we've been using leaves a lot to be desired.'

'Shocking,' he murmured, clearly not at all concerned.

Celeste's eyes narrowed on him. 'Have you been drinking, Damian?'

His smirk was revealing. 'I may have had a tipple or two with lunch. Is that against the rules as well?'

'No. But having a three-hour lunch is. You were supposed to be back at your desk at two. It's after four.'

'Is it really?' he mocked. 'I must have lost track of time.'

'Damian,' she said sternly. 'You must realise I can't allow this to go on.'

'Why not? The family's so rich that Campbell Jewels could go bankrupt and we'd still be all right. Your obsession with trying to outdo Whitmore Opals all the time is such a bore and so unnecessary. You should be out there enjoying yourself, like I do.'

'Doing what?' she snapped. 'Drinking yourself silly and playing poker?'

'Tch tch. Such spleen. I take it your meeting with Mr Whitmore in court did not go to your liking? What went wrong? Didn't he succumb to the charms you so discreetly put on display today?' His black gaze encompassed her thoroughly, noting her high colour as well as her figure-hugging clothing.

'You don't know what you're talking about, Damian. And you're trying to change the subject.'

'Is that what I'm doing? I thought I was sitting here, smoking.'

'You really are quite drunk, aren't you?'

'Uh-huh.'

'That's it then. As of today, you're no longer the sales and marketing manager. I won't sack you completely. I wouldn't do that to Mother. But I'm moving you into some useless position where you can't do any harm. You can be director of public relations.'

'Director of public relations? We haven't *got* a director of public relations!'

'Exactly. It should be right up your alley. No one will notice or care if you came to work or not.'

Celeste watched Damian's annoyance disappearing as the practicality of his new position sank in. 'Sounds perfect,' he drawled. 'And who are you going to get to replace me?'

She made a dismissive gesture with the Biro. 'I'm sure there must be someone in this company who can do the job.'

Damian laughed. 'I'm sure there is. I can see him now. He'll be bright and young and handsome, not to mention prepared to be extremely grateful to the boss.'

Celeste had had just about enough. 'Damian, I'm warning you. I—'

A sharp tap on the door stopped her in mid-flow.

'Come in,' she said sharply, knowing her assistant would not interrupt like this unless it was very important.'

'Yes, Luke?' she asked when he popped his head in the door.

'Miss Landers says an urgent message came in for Mr Campbell a while back, but she only just found out he *had* returned from lunch and was in here.'

'What is it?' Damian asked, swivelling round.

'Here... She wrote down the name and number.' He handed over a piece of paper to Damian, who remained seated where he was. 'The lady said it was an emergency and you were to ring her back as soon as you came in.' Luke nodded towards Celeste, then left, shutting the door with discreet quiet behind him.

Celeste was shocked by the look of sly glee that came into Damian's eyes as he read the note. 'Fantastic,' he muttered, then jumped to his feet. 'I must go.'

'Wait a minute, Damian! Who is this woman? And what's the emergency?'

'That, my dear sister,' he said with dark passion in his voice, 'is none of your business.'

'I hope you're not getting tangled up with another married woman.'

He threw her a scornful look. 'I never get *tangled up* with a married woman, Celeste.'

'That's just playing with words. You know what I meant.'

'Yes, of course I do. And as I said before, mind your own damned business!'

There was nothing quiet or discreet about Damian's exit. He slammed the door after him, leaving Celeste feeling more worried about her brother than she'd been in years. Drinking. Gambling. Getting into debt. Having affairs with other men's wives. Where would it all end?

She shook her head and looked back down at the appalling sales reports. There was nothing she could do about

Damian, but there was something she could do about Campbell's dwindling profits. Reaching over, she pressed the intercom button.

'Yes, Ms Campbell?' Luke answered.

'I need to see you,' she rapped out. 'Straight away.'

'Coming...'

Luke presented himself immediately, adjusting his tie a little self-consciously as he came to attention in front of her desk. At thirty, he was older than her previous assistant, and not nearly as handsome. But he knew how to dress to make the most of his very good body and he knew how to follow orders. Above all, he was intelligent and ambitious. Ruthlessly so, she believed. Every now and then, a cool sharpness came into those bland grey eyes of his, giving him a totally different look. Celeste sometimes wondered what he would have done if her occasional public flirtation with him had been put to the acid test. To be honest, she had a feeling he would have turned her down, which was perhaps why she was about to give him the chance of a lifetime.

'As of this moment, Luke,' she said crisply, 'the position of sales and marketing manager is vacant. Mr Campbell is going to take over a new position in the company as director of public relations. I was wondering if you'd be interested in his old position.'

Celeste was gratified with Luke's reaction. He was suitably stunned for a split-second, but quickly assumed that cool and highly self-contained bearing she rather admired.

'I would indeed,' was all he said. There was no gushing, no grovelling.

Celeste smiled at him. Yes, she thought with great satisfaction. You'll do. You'll do splendidly.

CHAPTER FIVE

GEMMA was wrenched out of a deep sleep by someone shaking her. Her eyes sprang open to find Damian Campbell sitting on the hotel bed beside her, peering worriedly down into her face. There was another equally worried-looking man hovering behind him. It took her a few moments to recognise him as the desk clerk from downstairs.

'Are you all right, Gemma?' Damian was asking anxiously. 'You haven't done anything silly, have you?'

'Wh...what?' she stammered, her head still fuzzy from sleep. 'I...I...don't know what you mean.'

Damian smiled. 'She's fine,' he threw over his shoulder at the desk clerk. 'You can go now. Thanks for letting me in. False alarm.'

Gemma's mind slowly started working. She levered herself up on one elbow and watched the man leave. When he'd closed the door, her gaze returned to Damian. 'What on earth did you tell him? My God, you thought I might have tried to kill myself, didn't you?'

Damian shrugged. 'Who knows what you might have done? I didn't get your message for quite a while and you did say it was an emergency. When I rang the number and found out it was a hotel not far from the city, I decided to hot-foot it right over here instead of just ringing. Then when I knocked on your door, you didn't answer.'

'I was *asleep*!'

'I can see that now.'

His smile was so sweet, Gemma couldn't stay angry with

him. 'I...I've left Nathan,' she admitted unhappily, swinging her feet over the side of the bed and sitting up properly.

'I gathered that,' came Damian's gentle reply. He picked up her closest hand, stroking it soothingly with his other hand. After an initial instinctive resistance, Gemma soon found the action both relaxing and comforting. She closed her eyes and sighed.

'I always knew it was just a matter of time,' Damian said.

A sob caught in Gemma's throat. Damian dropped her hand to put one arm around her shoulder, the other stroking her head as he cradled it against his chest. Once again, she did not have the strength to resist him, and it did feel good to be held so tenderly.

'Poor darling,' he crooned. 'I can just imagine what it was like, married to that bastard. You did the right thing, leaving him before it was too late.'

'Maybe it is too late,' she muttered miserably. Gemma knew in her heart that she would never love another man. Nathan had vowed to make her his and she *was*, with every fibre of her being. Maybe that was why she felt so lost and so lonely. Because the very essence of her life had been taken from her.

Suddenly, and for the umpteenth time, she started to cry. Damian let her till the last sobs hiccuped their way to nothing. It was then that he made his suggestion, a suggestion she was too emotionally drained to turn down. She was only too glad to have somewhere to go, and someone to take her there.

CELESTE HAD to take a taxi home from work, for what else could she do? Damian had not returned to work after an apparently dramatic exit from his office, so he wasn't there to give her a lift home. She no longer had a chauffeur to take her everywhere in the Rolls and did not feel inclined to hire another. Yet she did not drive herself. She did actually have a licence, but when circumstances had prevented her driving for a number of years she had somehow never found the nerve to get behind the wheel again. Odd, really, when she had found the nerve to do plenty of other things.

With a sigh, she settled into the back seat of the taxi and prepared herself mentally for a hair-raising trip home. That was the one thing she deplored about taxis. The drivers! Thank the lord she didn't live far from the city.

The heavy traffic went some way to stopping the trip from reducing her to a nervous wreck, but she was still glad when the cab turned down her street.

Campbell Court—as the family home was called—had a very exclusive address in Point Piper, right at the end of a cool leafy street that ran along the shores of Sydney Harbour. The huge granite manor-style house stood grandly on a rise at the front of the large block amid superb grounds, rolling lawns sloping down behind the house, first to a terrace where the pool-house sat, then down to the waterline and a private jetty. Moored not far out from this jetty was the yacht which Celeste had personally inherited on her father's death.

It was called the *Celeste*, and Stewart Campbell had brought it for a song in the fifties, but it was now conservatively worth six million dollars and needed a crew of ten to man it. Celeste rarely, if ever, took it out, choosing to use it as an exclusive setting for business luncheons and dinner parties. It was a good getaway spot as well, especially when her mother was in residence at Campbell Court and was having one of her infernal musical soirées, full of pretentious people.

Much as she loved her mother—who really was a softie despite being a social snob—Celeste was always glad when her remaining parent went away on holiday. Perhaps it was the fact that her mother knew all her dark secrets that sometimes made Celeste ill at ease in her presence.

Not that Adele would ever betray her. She had never breathed an indiscreet word in all these years. But sometimes Celeste would catch her mother looking at her in a certain way, a sad understanding in her eyes. Invariably this was when Celeste was being outrageous, or ruthlessly tough, and Celeste would suddenly want to scream at her, It's not my fault. Can't you see? I have to be this way. It's how I survive!

Celeste's train of thought was broken when she spied a navy blue Mercedes in the driveway of her home, parked in front of the security gates. She didn't recognise the car. Who could it belong to? There was someone sitting behind the wheel, but it was getting dark at six-thirty and she couldn't even make out if it was a man or a woman.

'Pull in behind that car, would you?' she directed the taxi driver. He did so and as she paid him Celeste was stunned to see Nathan Whitmore alighting from the Mercedes.

'What on earth is he doing here?' she muttered under her breath, frowning as she herself climbed out of the taxi and swung the door shut. The taxi immediately accelerated away, leaving Celeste to walk over to where Nathan had remained standing beside his car.

Those cold grey eyes of his swept over her as she approached and Celeste found herself bristling.

There was something about Byron's adopted son that had always irritated her. He was too everything. Too handsome. Too smooth. Too controlled.

Not that she'd had much to do with him over the years. She'd run into him occasionally at various social functions, and found that, even from a distance, he could present a disturbing figure. He could look across the room at you without any visible expression on his face, but you would still want to shiver in your boots.

That was why she'd been taken aback at the ball when he'd almost lost his temper with her. It had been so unlike him. She'd also been taken back by his lovely young bride, whose air of virginal innocence seemed at odds with Nathan's man-of-the-world sophistication. Damian, for one, hadn't been able to take his eyes off her all that night. It had worried Celeste at the time that her brother might pursue the girl, especially when he'd remarked the following day that he'd heard the new Mrs Whitmore wasn't all that happy.

Celeste experienced a sudden awful feeling that she knew why Nathan was on her doorstep.

'Hello, Nathan,' she said crisply. 'To what do I owe this highly unexpected visit?'

He didn't answer her directly, his darkly puzzled frown as bewildering as his reply. 'So you really *weren't* home.'

'Pardon?'

'I was speaking to your housekeeper a while back on phone,' he went on agitatedly, 'and she told me no one was there except herself. I didn't believe her.'

Celeste blinked a couple of times. 'Would you mind telling me what you're talking about?'

He shook his head, the action flopping a wayward blond lock over his high forehead. He immediately raked it back with splayed fingers, shocking Celeste when she saw his hand was actually shaking.

'Gemma hasn't been in touch with you?' he asked, only adding to her confusion.

'Why would your wife be in touch with *me*?'

He stared into her face as though trying to see if she was lying. His steely grey eyes narrowed, and she just stopped herself from shivering. Men like Nathan always frightened her a little. They were so secretive, both with their thoughts and their actions, which they never explained. She hated that.

'If you've nothing else to add, Nathan,' she said curtly, 'it's been a long day, I'm tired and I would like to go inside.'

His hand shot out to enclose her arm. 'You swear to me that Gemma has not contacted you today, either in person or by telephone?'

'Take...your...hand...off...my...arm,' she enunciated very slowly and very clearly.

Perhaps Nathan recalled what had happened to that creep who had manhandled her at the ball. Whatever, his hand slipped from her arm and Celeste began to breathe again. Nathan didn't know how close he'd come to a karate chop to the neck.

'Well?' he prompted.

'I already told you. Your wife has not been in touch with me. What in God's name makes you think she would have been? We hardly know each other. In fact, we *don't* know each other. You're not making any sense.'

'Nothing makes sense now,' he muttered.

When his shoulders sagged, he looked so dejected and wretched that Celeste felt an unexpected sympathy for him. Damn, she hoped Damian had nothing to do with this. It was clear as the nose on her face that Nathan's wife had left him. It was also too much of a coincidence that Damian had received an urgent message from some lady-friend this afternoon and gone racing to her rescue like a knight in shining armour. Only Damian was no white knight. He was the devil incarnate when it came to sweet young things like Gemma Whitmore.

But there was no way she was going to relay any of these suspicions to Nathan. God knows what he might do if she said his wife might be with her brother.

'Am I to assume your wife has left you?' Celeste asked.

His steely grey eyes projected the most peculiar hate her way. 'If she has, I know who to thank for it.'

'My God, you're crazy, do you know that? I had nothing to do with any of this!'

He glared at her, before making a frustrated sound and shaking his head in a disconsolate fashion. 'If that wasn't what she meant, then what *did* she mean?'

Celeste was getting angry with his totally cryptic remarks.

'Nathan, I'm sorry, but I can't help you with this. It's none of my business.'

It *is* none of my business, Celeste kept telling herself. I don't want to get mixed up in any of it. Nathan means nothing to me and neither does his wife. Let them sort their own lives out.

So why was it that, when Nathan climbed into his car and drove away, she was left feeling hopelessly agitated? Was it that she suspected Damian had played a role in the break-up? That didn't make much sense. Damian had played a role in the break-up of several marriages and while she didn't condone his behaviour—was, in fact, disgusted with his morals—she hadn't been personally affected by any of his tacky affairs.

This time, however, she couldn't get Nathan Whitmore out of her mind. Or was it that lovely young wife of his she couldn't stop thinking about? Celeste was appalled to think Damian had spirited her away somewhere and might be, at this very moment, seducing her.

My God, she suddenly realised. Maybe they were inside Campbell Court! She hadn't thought of that.

Celeste hurried over to the small side security gate, using her key to let herself in then striding forth up the paved driveway to the house.

'Cora?' she called out to the housekeeper as she let herself in. 'Cora, where are you?'

'Back here, Celeste,' came the reply from the direction of the kitchen.

Celeste tossed her straw hat on to the hat stand in the corner of the entrance hall before striding down the black and white tiled hall, glancing in the various living-rooms as she went. They were empty.

'Is Damian home?' she asked on entering the kitchen.

Cora looked up from where she was doing the vegetables. A plain spare woman in her fifties, she was as sharp as a tack when it came to the family she'd been the housekeeper for for more than a decade. A widow, she lived in during the week, staying with her married sister at the weekends. Her shrewd gaze took in Celeste's agitation at once.

'No, he's not,' she said, then added exasperatedly, 'What's he been up to this time?'

'God only knows.' Celeste sagged on to a kitchen stool. 'Has he rung?'

'No.'

'Damn.' She bit her lip and wondered where he could possibly be. She had suspected for a while that he had a flat somewhere where he took women. Either that, or he had dubious friends who let him use their places for romantic rendezvous. Of course, they could also be holed up in some hotel or motel somewhere, assuming they were together. She *was* just assuming this, after all. Maybe Damian wasn't involved.

It was a slim hope and one she clung to for all of ten seconds.

'What am I going to do with him, Cora?' she muttered dispiritedly.

'There's nothing you can do, Celeste. He's ruined.'

Celeste squeezed her eyes shut while her heart flip-flopped. 'Yes, you're right. He is ruined. Totally. So why do I still care about him?'

'Why does any of us care about him? Because we love him, I suppose, no matter what he is or what he's done. He does have some good qualities, you know.'

'Name one.'

Cora was clearly at a loss, but Celeste knew what she meant. Damian had a way with women in general, not just the ones he wanted to seduce. He remembered things like birthdays and anniversaries. And he seemed to know just what to say sometimes to make you feel special. No doubt it was mostly only manipulative flattery and clever conning, but it worked.

'The problem is,' Celeste went on sadly, 'he's ruining other people's lives as well. He has to be stopped.'

'How?'

She shook her head, her heart heavy. 'I don't know.'

Both women fell silent, and it was into this depressed silence that the telephone rang.

'Maybe that's him now,' Cora suggested. 'He's usually fairly thoughtful when it comes to telling me if he's not going to be home for dinner.'

Nerves fluttered in Celeste's stomach as she made her way back to where an extension rested on a table in the front hall. If it was Damian, what could she possibly say to him? He'd already told her to mind her own business back in her office.

'Campbell Court,' she answered, trying to stay cool.

'It's Damian, Celeste. Just ringing to let Cora know I won't be home for dinner.'

'Oh? Aren't you coming home at all?'

'No.'

'Where are you staying, then?'

'With a friend.'

Celeste swallowed then decided to take the plunge. 'Damian, are you with Gemma Whitmore?'

There was no doubting his sharp intake of breath.

'Please don't lie to me,' she raced on. 'Nathan Whitmore was waiting here when I got home.'

'*Nathan*? At *Campbell Court*?'

Celeste could hear a female make a frightened gasping sound in the background. Who else but Nathan's wife would react like that to the sound of his name?

'Hold on there a moment, Celeste.'

There was some kind of muffled interchange before Damian came back on the line.

'What did Nathan want?' he asked.

'He didn't really say. He didn't make much sense. I don't

think he was himself. She is there with you, Damian, isn't she?'

'Yes.'

Celeste closed her eyes for a second on a silent groan. 'Have you been having an affair with her, Damian?' she asked, trying to keep the weary exasperation out of her voice.

'No,' he denied sulkily. 'I bloody well haven't.'

'Then why did she come to you?'

'She didn't know anybody else in Sydney.'

'What happened, then, to make her leave Nathan? He seemed genuinely perplexed about it all.'

'I have no doubt. He thought he was safe with Gemma out at Lightning Ridge.'

Celeste let out a frustrated sigh. 'Not you, too. Please try to make sense. What on earth has Lightning Ridge got to do with anything?' It vaguely crossed Celeste's mind that this was the second time Lightning Ridge had come into her life lately. Firstly, the Heart of Fire was supposed to have turned up again in Lightning Ridge, and now this. No doubt it would pop up again a third time, since things did seem to happen in threes.

'That's where Gemma grew up,' Damian informed her. 'She'd gone back for a visit and while she was away Nathan spent the weekend with Lenore. Gemma came back unexpectedly early and caught them together.'

Celeste contained her shock while she got the facts. 'Now wait a minute till I get this straight. If Gemma caught Nathan and his ex-wife together then why is he so confused over why she left him?'

'Because Gemma didn't make her presence known. She left without them seeing her.'

'I see...'

'She doesn't want to see him or talk to him ever again. She says he knows in his heart why she left him.'

'He was very upset.'

'Tough. So's Gemma.'

Celeste frowned. 'What is she to you, Damian?'

'Butt out, Celeste.'

'If you hurt her, you'll have me to answer to.'

There was dead silence on the other end.

'I want to speak to her,' Celeste demanded.

'No. She's too upset to talk.'

'Bring her home here, then, where she can be properly looked after.'

'Are you serious?'

'Yes, I am.' At least here at Campbell Court, she could keep an eye on things, could perhaps drop a few words of gentle warning about Damian.

'I'll think about it.'

'She'd be safe here,' Celeste argued with quiet logic. 'Nathan probably wouldn't think of looking here again, but we have good security if he does.'

'Yes…yes, I didn't think of that. Nathan's the sort of man who won't let go easily. But Gemma's too tired to go anywhere else tonight. The poor darling's wrung out. I'll bring her there tomorrow.'

'I think that would be wise.'

'Do you just? Goodbye, Celeste,' he said brusquely. 'I'll see you tomorrow some time.'

He hung up, leaving Celeste to stare down into the dead receiver. Damian's manner puzzled her. He sounded as if he was genuinely fond of the girl. Could it be that he had finally fallen in love? *Really* in love?

If he had, it would be the first time that she knew of. The only person Damian had previously been in love with had been himself.

Her thoughts turned to Nathan and his affair with his ex-wife. Much as she didn't like the man, this news had shocked her. He'd only been married for a few months, after all. Not that she should be surprised by the things men did when in the grip of lust.

Still, it was perfectly clear to Celeste that Nathan had no idea his wife was *au fait* with his adultery. Perhaps if he knew the reason why she'd left him then he'd let her go quietly, without any fuss. It worried Celeste that violence might erupt between Nathan and Damian, if and when he found out who Gemma was with. Men were violent creatures. That, she was sure of.

Telephoning Nathan directly was out of the question. He would quite rightly jump to the conclusion that his wife was with Damian. For how else would Celeste have gained such information? She wanted him to know Gemma knew about his being unfaithful, but she didn't want him to know where Gemma was. Obviously, what she needed was a go-between…

It didn't take Celeste too long to come up with the perfect person, the *only* person who she could trust to do the job tactfully and with discretion.

A rueful smile creased her mouth at her putting words such as trust and tact in the same sentence as Byron Whitmore. But her hatred for the man was not a blind hatred. She knew his good points as well as his bad.

Telephoning Byron, however, after what had happened today, was not something Celeste was keen about. In fact, she just couldn't face it on an empty stomach. What difference would an hour or two make? She would ring him after dinner, and after several glasses of wine.

'That was Damian,' she told Cora on re-entering the kitchen. 'You're right. He won't be home for dinner.' She headed straight for the refrigerator where she extracted a bottle of her favourite Chardonnay, then proceeded to open it. With the cork dumped into the bin, she selected a good-sized wine glass from the glass cupboard, picked up the bottle and headed for the door. 'I'm off to shower and change, Cora. I'll eat here with you in the kitchen. You won't mind if I'm in my nightwear, will you?'

'You could go to a ball in your nightwear,' Cora called after her.

Celeste laughed, for she did have a penchant for glamorous lingerie, but the word 'ball' quickly reminded her of Byron and what she had to do after dinner. Groaning, she stopped at the base of the staircase and poured some wine into the glass, gulping it all down before giving a wry chuckle and starting up the stairs. If only some of her business associates could see her now, having to get some Dutch courage out of a bottle.

She paused on the landing halfway up the stairs to have another deep swallow, lifting the glass to the stained-glass window in front of her. 'Here's to you, kid,' she toasted the angel who stared expressionlessly back down at her. 'Not much to say for yourself, have you?' she muttered. 'Still, I guess I'd get a damned shock if you ever did talk back to me. Good grief, I must be going potty talking to a window. Is that one step up from talking to the wall or one step down? See you later, window. I dare say by the time I pass this way again, I'll have sorted out that crucial question. If not, it certainly won't bother me any more.'

Celeste laughed, poured herself another glassful of wine and headed for the shower.

CHAPTER SIX

CELESTE liked the feel of satin against her bare skin. No other material was as cool, or as smooth or as soft. All her nightwear was made of satin, mostly in neutral or smoky colours that looked good at night and flattered her rather delicate colouring. Ivory, oyster, pearl, champagne and a silvery grey, they were her favourite colours. Occasionally, she would wear a dusky blue or pink. Never black. She didn't like to wear black, yet she wasn't sure why. Black looked well against her blonde hair, but she always shied away from it.

The nightie she put on after her shower was a silvery grey, full length and quite simple with a deep V neckline and tiny shoe-string straps. Her arms raised, it slithered down over her freshly washed and powdered skin, the top moulding around her small firm breasts, the rest falling in deep folds to the floor. Slipping her feet into low-heeled fluffy white mules, Celeste drew on the matching robe, which flowed and floated around her as she swanned back down the stairs, pausing briefly to send a mocking glance up at the angel.

'You still there?' she taunted. 'What do you think of this outfit? You don't like satin? Too bad. I do. What about my hair? It looks good caught up at the sides like this, doesn't it?'

Hell, I'm smashed, she thought as she sashayed down the rest of the stairs, still carrying the glass and wine-bottle, though both were now empty.

It had been years since she had drunk a whole bottle of wine—before dinner, that was—and it had really gone to her head. She had to get some food into her before she dissolved down on to the floor somewhere.

Cora, God bless her dear heart, said not a single critical word during the meal, despite Celeste dropping her cutlery, missing her mouth with a forkful of food, at which point she giggled uncontrollably for a while. Despite all this, the alcohol did not dull the distressing awareness that she had to contact the enemy after dinner and tell him something he wasn't going to want to hear.

Celeste went to help clear up afterwards, but the housekeeper waved her away. 'You pay me to do this, Celeste. You go have a swim or something.'

'Straight after dinner?'

'Since when did a little thing like a full stomach stop you going for a swim?' the housekeeper said drily. 'Besides, the exercise might sober you up a bit.'

Celeste laughed. 'What an awful thought. I'll be up in my bedroom if you want me.'

'And I'll be in my room if you want me. There's a movie on television tonight I've been looking forward to seeing.'

'In that case I'll answer the phone if it rings.'

Cora smiled her thanks. 'Everyone should have a boss like you.'

'You're the only one who thinks that, Cora. I'm nicknamed Attila the Hun around the traps.'

'Ah, yes, but they don't know the real you. You're a softie underneath.'

Celeste laughed her way out of the kitchen and along the hall. When she turned to walk up the stairs and encountered the glass-cold eyes of the angel looking down at her, she stopped laughing. 'So what are you turning your nose up at?' she snapped. 'Don't you agree that I'm a softie underneath?'

Lifting up her own nose, she careered back up the stairs

and into her bedroom where she flopped her tipsy self down on the bed and reached for the telephone before she lost her nerve. She was actually punching in Byron's number before it occurred to her that she knew his damned number off by heart, yet she hadn't dialled it in donkey's years.

But she'd looked it up plenty of times. Looked it up and stared at it and been tempted to call, call and tell him the awful truth, the crippling truth, the soul-destroying truth. Her courage had always failed her, as it was in danger of doing now. But she persisted, gripping the receiver more tightly with each successive unanswered ring. With a bit of luck, he wouldn't be home.

'Belleview,' Byron answered curtly on the sixth ring.

'It...it's Celeste here, Byron.'

Dead silence.

Celeste hoped and prayed his reaction was shock that she'd called him at all, and not because she'd sounded as rattled as she was sure she had. Pulling herself together, she continued in a much more controlled manner. 'Sorry to call you at home, or at *all* for that matter, but this was an emergency.'

More silence.

Damn the man! Now she was getting angry. Gritting her teeth, she launched forth again, quite bluntly.

'Nathan's wife has left him.'

'*What* did you say?' Byron stormed down the line so loudly that she flinched and held the receiver away from her ear.

It was a pleasure to keep her cool while he was losing his. 'There's no need to shout, Byron. I can hear you as well as I'm sure you can hear me. And you heard me correctly the first time, I'm sure. Gemma has left Nathan. When I arrived home this evening, he was waiting for me in the driveway, looking for her.'

'And he thought he might find her at *your* place?'

'Believe me, I found it as odd as you do. He seemed

pretty upset, I'm afraid, and not thinking straight. I gather he hasn't contacted you about any of this yet?' Celeste had already guessed that he wouldn't have. Men like Nathan solved their own problems, their own way. They didn't run to their fathers for help.

'No, he hasn't,' Byron growled. 'Where is he now, do you know?'

'Probably at home. I told him I couldn't help him and he went away.'

'So why have you rung me? Surely it's not merely to crow, is it? I wouldn't have even taken *you* for being that vicious!'

It irritated Celeste that Byron could still hurt her, but she staunchly ignored the jab of dismay and went on. 'I have since found out some information which you might like to relay to Nathan.'

'What kind of information?'

'When I spoke to him earlier, I gained the impression he had no idea why Gemma had left him. I have since found out the reason.'

'*You* found out the reason?'

'That's right. Gemma made a trip to Lightning Ridge this weekend, didn't she?'

'Yes. She flew there last Friday and was due home today. But what the hell does that have to do with anything? Nathan knew she was going there.'

'I realise that, but the thing is she flew home earlier than expected. When she arrived at wherever she and Nathan live, his ex-wife was there with him in compromising circumstances.'

'Lenore? In bed with Nathan? I don't believe that. I won't believe that.'

'*Don't*, then! But Gemma does and she's the one who's left Nathan. Apparently neither Nathan nor Lenore actually saw her and she simply left.'

'Who told you this? None of this makes sense. Or maybe

it does,' he muttered, Celeste almost able to hear his sharp mind ticking over. 'Nathan for some reason thought Gemma would be at Campbell Court... Since she wouldn't be going out there to see *you*, then that only leaves that snake of a brother of yours. Damian's behind all this, isn't he, Celeste?' Byron pounced. 'He's turned Gemma against Nathan somehow, twisted things, made things look bad for him.'

'That's not true!' Celeste defended.

'Bulldust! I saw the way he looked at her the night of the ball and I know his reputation for seducing other men's wives. Can you swear to me that Gemma's not with Damian at this very moment?'

'I'm not going to swear to anything! I was just trying to do the right thing by ringing and telling you this. I thought if Nathan understood that his wife had uncovered his adultery then he wouldn't go running around Sydney like a chook with his head cut off.'

'You mean you thought he wouldn't force his way into that fortified castle you call a house and strangle Damian with his bare hands. You're a fool, Celeste. A damned fool. I'll relay your message, but God help your brother. Nathan loves Gemma, *really* loves her. He would not be unfaithful to her. There is a reasonable explanation for what she saw, or thought she saw, and I aim to make sure she hears that explanation before your brother does something he's likely to get killed for!'

He slammed the phone down in her ear, so forcefully that she cried out. Celeste dropped the receiver back into place then slumped back on to her pillows.

Oh, God...

She should never have become involved, should never have stuck her big nose in where it wasn't wanted. She should definitely never have asked Damian to bring Gemma home tomorrow. Next thing, she would have a furious and possibly violent Nathan on her doorstep.

Celeste contemplated ringing Byron back again and begging him not to say a word but she knew that was useless. Byron wouldn't take any notice. He would possibly take delight in stirring up trouble for her.

Crossing her arms across her eyes, Celeste lay there, aware of her head still spinning and her heart racing. Was it just the wine, or had even talking to Byron done this to her?

God, but I hate that man, she told herself, sitting up abruptly and swinging her feet on to the thick pile carpet. Resisting the silly urge to actually go swimming, Celeste decided she might join Cora in watching that movie. Distraction was desperately needed.

But when she swayed violently on standing up, then almost banged into the bedroom door on the way out of the room, Celeste decided a strong cup of coffee might be better, by which time the movie would have started. Movies weren't much good when you'd missed the beginning. Perhaps she'd read a book.

Ten minutes later, she was browsing through their extensive library, a mug of steaming black coffee cupped in her hands. Nothing appealed, however. Really, a visit to a bookstore was in order. Classic novels were all very well but there were times when one just wanted to be entertained in a racy, pacy way.

Maybe some music, she decided, leaving the library and wandering along to the lounge-room where the CD and cassette players were located. Selecting a Michael Bolton tape, she slotted it in, pressed play then settled back to simply enjoy.

She was still simply enjoying when the doorbell buzzed, the doorbell connected to the front gates, *not* to the front door. Celeste shot upright from where she'd been lying on the lounge. Good God! Nathan Whitmore. Byron had told him Gemma was here and he'd come to storm the Bastille!

The bell buzzed again, then continuously, as it did when someone leant on it.

Clearly, he was not going to go away. Neither was Cora going to come to the rescue and answer it, because Cora was ensconced away in her room at the back of the house, watching a movie. She wouldn't even *hear* the buzzer.

Squaring her shoulders, Celeste stood up and walked out into the entrance hall where she flicked the button on the security intercom. 'Celeste Campbell speaking,' she said in her best authoritative voice. 'Who is this?'

'It's Byron Whitmore, and you'd better let me in right away or I'm going to huff and puff and blow your bloody house down.'

'Heavens to Betsy,' came her droll reply. 'I'm simply terrified.' Which she actually was, but be damned if she was going to show it!

'Celeste, I'm warning you, I...'

'Oh, do shut up, Byron. It's much too late at night for such twaddle. If you'd stayed on the line long enough before, you rude man, I would have been able to tell you that Damian and Gemma are not here. Neither do I know where they are.'

'Prove it! Let me in so that I can see for myself that they're not there.'

'Be my guest!' Celeste snapped, pressing the button that would open the gates. It was only when Byron drove in and actually presented himself at the front door that she remembered how she was dressed. And by then it was too late. If she didn't open the door immediately he would probably batter it down. Or break one of the glass sections.

Wrapping the négligé around her as modestly as she could, she went to the door and opened it. Byron strode straight in, looking devilishly attractive in a casual pair of grey trousers and a sky-blue crew-necked sweater. Looking at him, Celeste could not believe he was fifty. He looked many years younger. He also looked very, very angry.

His glittering blue gaze swept over her, turning mocking and sardonic by the time it reached her fluffy footwear. 'Did

I interrupt something? Or do you always go round the house dressed in stuff like that?'

'You interrupted something,' she couldn't resist saying, revelling in his reaction. His whole body stiffened, his nostrils flaring as his nose shot up.

'I was in the middle of being entertained by Michael Bolton,' she added in a low, husky voice. 'Surely you know Michael?'

When Byron remained frozen and silent, she gave a melodramatic sigh. 'I see you don't. Truly, Byron, there is more to music than opera and symphonies, you know. Michael Bolton is a singer. He specialises in love songs.'

Was that relief momentarily flashing across his eyes or had she merely imagined it? What would he have done, she wondered, if a half-naked man had wandered out to see where she was, a handsome, half-naked, very young man? God, she almost regretted firing Gerry, regretted turning down what he'd pressed for that night. It might have been worth it actually to take a real toy-boy lover if she'd known it would have provided such a superb revenge.

'One day, Celeste,' Byron ground out, 'you're going to goad me one time too many.'

'Oh? And what will you do, Byron? Sully your hands on the very thing you most despise? I doubt it. You're too *good* for that,' she spat at him. 'You came to see if Gemma and Damian were here? Come, then. This way for the grand tour. Shall we go upstairs first and check the bedrooms? Yes, I think so…'

She swooshed up the stairs, letting her robe flow free in an act of defiance which he knew was deadly dangerous. But his ongoing contempt for her had sparked an intensely compelling urge that refused to listen to common sense. She ached to push him to the limit, to make him break, one way or the other. And vows she had made about not letting him touch her again seemed irrelevant in the face of her desire to make him eat *his* words, to make him admit that he still wanted her, to make him reach out and try to take what he had once craved as badly as she had.

It was madness. Celeste accepted that. But then, she'd been mad about Byron from the first moment she'd met him. It had merely taken seeing him face to face a couple of times recently to bring it out in her again.

'I'll open the doors for you if you like,' she offered blithely, throwing each one open as she moved briskly along the upstairs hall. She didn't turn her head to find out if Byron actually looked into the rooms or not, but she could hear his footsteps behind her. 'Don't forget to look under the beds,' she called back over her shoulder. 'And in the bathrooms. They might be hiding in one of the showers together. That room's mine. Perhaps you shouldn't go in there if you don't want to contaminate yourself.'

Celeste cried out when Byron's hands suddenly closed over her shoulders, dragging her to a halt and back against him. 'Stop it,' he hissed, his mouth brushing the top of her hair. 'Just stop it.'

'Stop what?' she answered, but her voice was trembling and so was she. Oh, God…this wasn't at all what she'd been trying to do. *He* was supposed to end up the victim here, not her own silly self.

But dear heaven, she couldn't stop herself from melting back into him, couldn't stop her head from tipping back against his chest, or her eyes from closing on a ragged sigh of sheer desire.

Byron's tortured groan went some way to soothing her own dismay. Clearly, he couldn't resist the physical contact any more than she could.

'Damn you, Celeste,' he rasped. 'I should have known better than to come here.'

'Touch me, Byron,' she pleaded in a voice she scarcely recognised as her own. 'Touch me…'

Another groan escaped his lips as his hands slid from her shoulders down her arms, down past her out-stretched fingers and on to her satin-covered thighs. Her heartbeat went wild when his hands moved across her thighs and up over her stomach, massaging its muscular flatness through the slithery material then following the gentle curve of her rib-cage till they reached the undersides of her breasts.

When he hesitated at this point, she moaned her disappointment, her own hands lifting to urge his up over the exquisitely swollen curves. When his fingers brushed against the already erect nipples, she gasped, her hips automatically moving against his as everything inside her contracted.

'God, Celeste,' he muttered, his head dipping to suckle ravenously at the tender skin of her throat. His hands were rough on her breasts now, his lips harsh against her flesh. She began to yearn for him, yearn and burn. Her arm lifted to curve up over his shoulders, her hands finding his head, her fingers splaying passionately into the thick black waves. Her own head began to twist round, her mouth blindly searching for his.

'Kiss me,' she rasped.

He spun her round so quickly that her head whirled madly, though it whirled further when his mouth clamped hungrily over hers, when his tongue drove between her softly parted lips so deep that she almost choked. But then his tongue suddenly retreated, and her own followed, diving as boldly into his mouth as his had in hers. The erotic exchange went on for long tempestuous moments till at last he broke away, breathing hard as he glared down into her wildly flushed face.

'I must be crazy,' he grated out. 'But suddenly, I don't care. I want you, god-dammit, and I'm going to have you. I take it there's no objection?' he taunted, bending to scoop her up into his arms.

She stared up at him with wide eyes and he laughed.

'Don't say later you didn't have the chance to say no,' he growled.

She didn't say no. She didn't say anything as he carried her into her bedroom, even when he dumped her unceremoniously into the middle of the bed. If it had been any other man, she would have fought him, would have kicked out at him with deadly accuracy, felling him with one blow.

But this was Byron, the man she loved, the man she had always loved.

Oh, yes, she hated him too, but there was no room in her for hate tonight, not while her body was aflame with a fire it hadn't known in so long. Only Byron could quench that fire, she knew. And so she reached for him, twining her arms around his neck and drawing him down towards her with a tortured moan of sensuous surrender.

'Oh, my darling,' she whispered, with far too much emotion.

She felt his instinctive retreat, felt him fight the same futile fight that they'd both been fighting all day, and then he collapsed upon her, devouring her in an orgy of kissing and touching that might have frightened any other woman.

But Byron's passion had never frightened Celeste. It drove her wild, her hands running over him in the same frantic fashion as his were on her. Her flesh, however, was more accessible than his with what she was wearing, and soon the satin was bunched up over her hips and he was stroking bare thighs and buttocks, tangling his fingers in the damp curls between her legs, caressing the valley they guarded so ineffectually.

'Like silk,' he murmured while she bit her bottom lip in an effort to stop her moans. 'Or is it honey?'

Celeste gasped a feeble protest when he slid down her body and started to feed on that honey. But any resistance was token. She could still recall what it had felt like the first time Byron had done this to her, how her embarrassed shock had quickly changed to an avid willingness to have him do it as often as he liked. Once she'd even let him do it to her while she was sitting on his desk. There was nothing like it.

There was still nothing like it, her senses spinning out as his lips, and tongue moved over her. Desire flared wildly, then exploded.

'Oh, God,' she cried out, her back arching from the bed under a series of sharp, electric spasms.

The intensity of her pleasure, however, was mingled with dismay. She had not wanted it like this. She had wanted Byron inside her, had wanted to hold him close and pretend that he loved her. Instead, he seemed almost removed from her, his only touch a brutal grip on her thighs as he held her open for his rapacious mouth.

Oh, why didn't he stop? she groaned silently. It was over. Surely he could tell it was over!

But he didn't stop. He went on and on and, amazingly, it wasn't over. The build-up returned, more excruciating than ever, her sensitivity seemingly having moved up on to a higher plateau. Her blood grew hotter, her head lighter, her nerve-endings more stretched. There was another shattering release, and this time, there was no ebbing of desire. She wanted more. And more. Suddenly, Celeste began to worry he might go on like this forever. And for all its heady delights, it would not be enough, not till he came to her properly. Only that would truly satisfy her. Only that...

Tortured words came from her mouth as she struggled to express what she yearned, even as her body betrayed her a third time.

'No more...please...no more...'

His laughter was demonic as he lifted himself from her and stood to stare down at her body, spread-eagled in utter abandonment for his desire-filled gaze. 'I haven't got what *I* want yet, Celeste,' he growled, stripping his sweater over his head to reveal a bare chest underneath, a very male chest with broad shoulders and rippling muscles and a smattering of dark curls across the centre. 'I was just getting you in the right frame of mind.'

His shoes and trousers joined the sweater, followed by his briefs and socks till he stood before her, still the man she remembered. Nothing had changed. Nothing had wilted with the years.

She gave a small shuddering sigh, her eyes closing as she sat up and reefed her own clothing over her head, flinging it away before lowering herself back down on to the satin quilt, her smokily aroused eyes fluttering open with another sigh that was the very essence of female sensuality.

Byron's eyes narrowed upon her, his fists closing and unclosing by his side. 'God, but you're a beautiful bitch,' he muttered. 'A beautiful brazen bad bitch. But that's all right. Tonight I want you to be bad, Celeste. Nothing else will do.'

Celeste gasped when he moved abruptly on to the bed to straddle her body. For a few seconds, he knelt tall above her, dark and dangerous, but then he settled his weight across her stomach and hips, his knees sinking into the mattress as he leant forward to present himself perilously close to her face. When he actually pressed himself against her mouth, shock sent her jerking backwards and her lips falling slightly apart. But along with the shock came a wickedly compelling excitement. She had done this for him once before, but it had been only very briefly and only as part of foreplay leading to making love. This could hardly be put in the same category. And yet...

She licked suddenly dry lips, and Byron's gaze was riveted to the movements of her tongue as it moistened her mouth in what must have looked like a blatantly erotic tease. It was, however, the action of suddenly ambivalent emotions. She wanted to, yet she didn't want to. Maybe if she closed her eyes and pretended he still loved her...

'Just do it,' he urged, his hard words giving her nothing of pretence to cling to. This was dominant male demanding from submissive female, maybe even with an underlying intent to humiliate. It went against everything Celeste had vowed never to let happen to her again.

'No,' she choked out, and turned her face away to the side.

She didn't dare look up at him, a tremor of fear rippling through her at the position she realised she was in. Byron was a powerful man. With her body pinned to the bed like this, she had little hope of successfully using her martial art skills against him, not without endangering his life. And did she really want to do that?

She felt his weight tip backwards on to her pelvis, her eyes flinging open to find him sitting down on her and appearing to study the contours of her body, first with his eyes and then with his hands. His strokes were long and sweeping at first. Down and up her sides. Down and up her arms. Then his hands turned over and he started trailing the backs of his fingertips over her by now almost quivering flesh. When his nails trailed over a particularly sensitive spot, she couldn't help an involuntary shudder which brought a grunt of satisfaction from Byron.

Celeste found herself holding her breath when he started moving closer and closer to her breast, sucking in a sharp breath when he skimmed over her nipples. As though sensing she wanted more of this, he stopped doing it, moving his attention to her stomach which proved to have its own brand of erotic torture. Who would have dreamt that a lazy finger encircling one's navel could make all one's muscles clench inside, would make one yearn to take that finger and suck it deep into one's mouth?

But it was when he returned to her breasts in earnest that Celeste knew she was in danger of losing all control. Though only small, especially when she was lying down, her breasts seemed to have swollen to twice their normal size, her nipples almost doubling in length, stretching upwards in a type of pained supplication.

Byron was teasingly slow to oblige, her anticipation so great by the time his head bent to lick one that a violent tremor raced through her. His head lifted and a wickedly rueful smile tugged at his mouth. 'It's agony, isn't it, wanting something so much? Do you want me to do it again, Celeste? All you have to do is say so…'

Their eyes locked and she would have died rather than say it. Byron laughed and bent to torture her some more, first one breast, then the other. Her excitement soared, bringing with it a desire to *do*, rather than just receive. Her hands ran restlessly over his shoulders, her head lifting to kiss the top of his head. She would have moved her lower body if she could have, but only her legs were free to move. They shifted agitatedly on the bed, her knees lifting then falling wantonly apart. Again and again she found herself licking dry lips. If only he would kiss her. If only he would fill her mouth with his. Her lips fell softly apart on a raw moan.

And then he was there, and she was taking him in, and there was no thought of saying no again, no thought of stopping, no thought of anything except doing what he wanted, what *she* wanted.

Dimly she heard Byron's groan of dark triumph. And then she heard nothing, her senses whirling into the eye of an erotic storm which could only end one way.

CHAPTER SEVEN

CELESTE leant against the marble vanity-unit, then slowly lifted her face to the mirror. How could I have allowed that? she asked herself shakily. More to the point, how could I have *enjoyed* it?

She shook her head, dropping her eyes back into the basin and the water still swirling there. Snapping off the still running tap, Celeste turned away before she caught another glimpse of that humiliating reflection with its flushed cheeks and overbright eyes.

Pride battled with her ongoing desire. You can't go back out there, she lectured herself. You just can't! What must he think of you to demand such an intimacy without love? What must he think of you now that you have given it to him, seemingly without love?

Oh, God…

Celeste's head dropped into her hands, self-disgust beginning to override everything—till that old familiar tape clicked into play and she remembered everything that he had done to her, everything he had set in motion. Byron might still be her Achilles' heel in a sexual sense, but he didn't have to be in any other way. OK, so she loved him somewhere down deep in her psyche, but she hated him at the same time. He might think he could use her again, but she would prove him wrong there. If anyone was to be doing the using this time, it would be her.

Picking up a hairbrush, she took her hair down out of the combs that kept it back from her face and brushed it out till it tumbled in wild waves around her shoulders and halfway down her back. There seemed little point in putting lipstick on her pink puffy lips so she merely sprayed some perfume over her totally naked body, took a deep breath and opened the bathroom door.

A pair of wintry blue eyes surveyed her nakedness as she walked across the plush-pile carpet. Not that he could make any comment when he was lying in the nude on top of her bed, his arms linked nonchalantly behind his head.

'Are you planning on staying the night?' she asked as she bent over with seeming nonchalance and picked up the robe of the négligé set. She slid her arms into the silky sleeves and did her best to resist the urge to pull it tightly around her. 'For if you are, I'll go down and lock up.'

When he didn't say anything, she was forced to look over at him. Suddenly, the expression on his face infuriated her. How dared he lie there in judgement of her? How dared he look at her with that hard gleam of contempt in his eyes?

As always, her only satisfaction lay in apparent indifference to what he thought or felt about her. After all, she already knew he still wanted her as much as ever. She also doubted he would be able to resist the temptation to stay and taste whatever other delights he thought she offered all her lovers. That in itself was sweet vengeance.

A softly mocking smile teased her mouth as she drifted back towards the bed, the action of walking sending the robe floating back from its centre parting. She exulted in the way his eyes became riveted to her body, and the triangle of dark curls at the junction of her groin. She sat down on the bed, and crossed her legs, leaning over to place a provocative hand on his nearest thigh, then running it up over his body till it rested on his chest. His heart was hammering like mad beneath her hand and she knew he was hers, whenever she wanted him. He'd crossed a line tonight and she would never let him go back.

'I want you to stay,' she whispered huskily. 'Please, darling…'

His eyes flashed with the endearment, his hands whipping down to snatch her wrists and pull her up on to his body.

'You bitch,' he rasped. 'You'll pay for this. I don't know how, but you will.'

'Maybe I already have…'

He laughed. 'And what was the price?'

'I've never been able to assess it. What price do you put on one's sanity, or one's life?'

He frowned at this, his hands tightening around her wrists as he dragged her further up on to him. 'What the hell are you talking about?'

'That's what I'm talking about. Hell. A living hell.'

He laughed again. 'Yes, that's what you are all right, Celeste. A living, breathing hell. You've never been any different. Even when you were little more than a child, you were the devil's child, tempting me, corrupting me.'

'Corrupting *you*?' she scoffed. 'I was only seventeen, for pity's sake. You were twenty-seven. Who was the corrupter, I ask you?'

His face darkened with fury. 'Don't try to blame me, Celeste. You know damned well what you did. You found every excuse to come into my office those two weeks. You wore the most exotic perfume I've ever smelt on a female. You never wore a bra. Sometimes I wondered if you had *any* underwear on. You flicked those cat's eyes of yours my way all the time and you let me know with every movement of your lush, nubile young body that I could have you whenever I wanted you.'

An irritatingly guilty heat flamed in her cheeks. Yes, she had been provocative. She had to admit that. But she'd been in love, dammit. She'd adored the man. How else was she to get him to notice her when he could have any woman he wanted? She had to show them that *she* was a woman, or nearly one.

'I see you agree with me,' Byron snarled, seeing her betraying blush.

'I do not!' she snapped. 'I was a silly young girl, I admit, but only silly because I was in love. You took advantage of me, Byron. You made me think you loved me.'

'*I* made *you* think I loved you!' he exploded, rolling her over and spreading her arms wide on the pillows, his grip quite brutal on her flesh. Once again, she was pinned to the mattress, and once again, her skills of self-defence were useless. 'That's a laugh. I would have said the very opposite was true if it didn't make me look a fool. Not that you didn't make a fool of me back then, Celeste. It was only after you'd gone back to school and I found out what an experienced little seducer of older men you already were that I appreciated the extent of my stupidity. You say you were in love with me. Well, you seem to fall in love a lot, don't you, Celeste? Is it that you need to tell yourself you're in love to justify what you do with me?'

Celeste's eyes widened at his astonishing accusations, her heart racing. 'What do you mean, I was already an experienced seducer of men? You were my first lover.'

'Oh, for pity's sake, Celeste, even if Irene hadn't told me all about you, I still knew there'd been others before me. You were no virgin when I made love to you that day in the office.'

Celeste bit her lip as she realised that that awful incident when she'd been only fourteen would have destroyed her technical virginity. Even the doctor who examined her back then had waffled over the possible extent of her sexual activity. When she'd reported the teacher for attempted rape, he had claimed she'd been more than co-operative, then another teacher on the staff had backed him up by saying the same thing about her.

It had been a conspiracy, of course, for the first man to escape retribution for his vile act. The two men had been devils in arms and she had unfortunately left it a couple of weeks before reporting the frightening incident. By then any damage to her young body had healed and she was left with no evidence of forcible entry.

Her mother had believed her, however, taking her away from that school and putting her in another. She'd also put her on the Pill for safety, aware that Celeste had the sort of looks men found it hard to resist.

'What...what did Irene tell you?' she asked shakily, staring up into Byron's glittering blue eyes.

'The truth! That you'd slept with half the male staff at your school when you were only fourteen. That you were expelled and that your mother had to put you on the Pill because she was scared you'd be pregnant before you were fifteen, you were so sex-mad. From the way you acted with me, she did the wise thing.'

'And what if I said I didn't sleep with those teachers or any other men before you? What if I told you one of the teachers tried to rape me, that he actually had me on the ground before I kneed him in the groin and got away?'

'What would you say if I said your behaviour over the years hardly backs up that story?' he countered savagely. 'You're verging on being a nymphomaniac, Celeste. Admit it. You are sex-mad. Over the years you've craved younger and younger men because they can probably last longer and can do it more often. But let me assure you, sweetheart, I'm not done yet tonight. I'll give you what you crave.'

He used his massive legs to push hers apart, settling his weight between her thighs. Without letting her arms go he began to probe with his body. Celeste tried not to feel anything as his desire rubbed and pressed against hers, but she could not prevent the exciting sensations he was evoking or the way her blood began to pound in her head.

She sucked in a sharp breath when he finally achieved success, gasping when he drove his desire home to the hilt.

'This is what you want, isn't it, Celeste?' he said through gritted teeth, surging into her again and again. 'But it's not love. It's pure unadulterated lust. Say it like it is for once, Celeste. Tell the truth and shame the devil. You want this, and only this...'

Her body convulsing uncontrollably around his made him cry out with raw satisfaction. His back arched away, his hands pressing her wrists down in the pillows as his own arms straightened. And then he was pulling her up from the bed, keeping their spasming bodies fused together as he sat back on his heels. With a tortured groan, he released her wrists to wrap his arms around her, clasping her close and rocking her to and fro, his head dropping to bury his face in her hair. Reaching up her back, he grasped a clump of hair, pulling her head back so that he could feed on her throat like some ravenous animal.

Celeste was beside herself with the awful ambivalence of the sharpest emotional pain yet the fiercest of sexual satisfactions. To have the man you loved find such pleasure in your body, despite his despising you, had a kind of perverted triumph to it. Celeste chose to lock on to this bittersweet victory, rather than any crippling despair, for she'd long learnt that there was no future in harbouring hurt over Byron's opinion of her, just as there was no point in arguing with him over Irene's lies.

Byron would never believe her version of events, just as he would never believe the truth about the way she'd lived her life since. She'd been hoist by her own petard and she would just have to live with it.

At least there was some consolation in a new understanding of the events on that day in the billiard-room at Belleview, two years after he married Irene. Byron hadn't been quite the callous bastard she'd always believed him to be, merely a man torn apart by unwanted feelings for a girl he thought unworthy of anything but the basest treatment.

Which was how he'd treated her that day, taking what she had unconsciously offered him again, then scorning her afterwards when she broke down and told him how much she loved him. It was at that point that Irene had walked in, taken one look at their guilty faces then left the room, whereupon Byron had launched forth into a bitter tirade.

'I'll never forgive myself for hurting a good woman over a slut like you,' he'd flung at her. 'And you dare to speak of love. That wasn't love you gave me on the billiard-table just now, you little tramp. It was the same thing you give every man who looks sideways at you. I'm married, for pity's sake, to your own sister. Doesn't that mean anything to you? Haven't you any decency at all? God, you disgust me, almost as much as I disgust myself for being too weak to resist your insidious appeal. Go and screw up some other poor bastard's life, not mine! I don't want to set eyes on you again, do you hear me? Get out, out of this house and out of my life. I can't stand the sight of you any longer!'

Much as she had never forgotten those words, nor forgiven them, Celeste could now understand them a little better.

Besides, she thought with a black satisfaction, whose arms is he in now? Whose bed is he in? Whose body can't he keep his hands and eyes off?

Mine!

Celeste ran tantalising fingertips over his sweat-slicked back, squeezing her muscles tightly around him, teasing him back to arousal once again. With the quickening of his flesh, she began to lift her hips in tiny up and down movements, gripping and releasing him till he was fully erect again.

'Yes,' she insisted huskily when he groaned. She pushed him back on to the bed, holding his shoulders down while she straddled him as mercilessly as he had straddled her. This time she was on top and she aimed to keep it that way, riding him as relentlessly and ruthlessly as he had her, closing her eyes so that she didn't see his contempt.

'Yes,' she cried out in exultation when his body finally arched up and exploded into her. 'Yes,' she sobbed as her own body shattered into pieces and she collapsed in a spent heap across his chest.

Did they sleep? They must have, limbs tangled, bodies exhausted.

Celeste snapped awake to the sound of Cora calling out to her up the stairs.

'Are you still awake, Celeste? Shall I lock up for you?'

Celeste lifted her head and spoke in a stunningly calm voice, even though her heart was instantly pounding. Dear God, what if Cora had come up and found her like this? They'd left the bedroom door open, the bed in full view of anyone who even walked past.

'It's all right, Cora. I'll do it. I'll be down shortly to have a nightcap. You go to bed.'

'OK. The movie was pretty awful, by the way. Goodnight, then.'

'Goodnight.'

Celeste closed her eyes with a relieved sigh, opening them to find Byron looking up at her with that familiar mocking cynicism in his eyes. 'I see you have your housekeeper trained never to come upstairs, or to ask sticky questions. I dare say she's used to you having every Tom, Dick and Harry spend the night.'

'Don't you mean Luke, Gerry and Byron?' she retorted. Celeste had already made up her mind not to try to defend herself to Byron. It was a waste of time. Neither was she going to let him treat her like dirt, or ride roughshod over her emotions. 'Naturally, I don't have to answer to my housekeeper, Byron. Do you ever answer to yours?'

'I don't have a housekeeper any more, as you verv well know.'

'Ah, yes. The gorgeous Melanie flew off with that racing-car driver, didn't she?' Is that why you started running around with Catherine Whatsername? Because your live-in lady found alternative outlets for her—er—needs?'

With a low growl, Byron heaved Celeste from his body

and threw himself on to his feet, glaring down at her with fury in his face. 'Just because you have all your employees service you, Celeste, it doesn't mean everyone else does.' He snatched up his trousers and started dragging them on.

'Don't you think you should put your underpants on first?' Celeste suggested sweetly.

Byron told her not so sweetly what he thought of her suggestion, zipping up his trousers so angrily that she winced. He rammed the blue sweater roughly over his head, combing his hair back into place with splayed fingers before sitting down on the edge of the bed to put on his shoes and socks.

Celeste knelt up behind him, draping her arms around his shoulders and kissing him on the ear. 'Don't be angry, darling. I don't care what you did with Melanie.'

'I didn't do anything!'

'You must have thought about it. She was very beautiful.'

Celeste felt she had struck a nerve for he definitely stiffened. 'I have no intention of defending my thoughts. I never touched the woman.'

'Good for you. I'm glad to see you're still as virtuous as ever. When am I going to see you again?'

'Never, if I can help it.'

Her laughter was drily amused. 'Don't be silly, darling. You enjoyed yourself tonight as much as I did. Why, I haven't been this impressed since...since we were last together.'

'God, don't remind me of that. I've been trying to forget that day for the last twenty-one years.'

'You and me both,' she muttered under her breath, and shrank back on her heels.

Byron turned to stare at her. 'If I didn't know better, I'd think you regretted that day as much as I did.'

'Oh, yes, Byron, I still regret it. Bitterly.

He seemed surprised. 'You might be more human than I thought you were.'

Her smile was ironic, her pleasure warped as she wriggled on to his lap, snaking her arms around his chest and kissing him with tantalising softness on the mouth. 'I'm very human,' she whispered, and ran her tonguetip over his lips.

His groan thrilled her.

'When am I going to see you again?' she tempted a second time. 'If you don't come to me, I'll come to you. You do know that, don't you?'

'Yes,' he bit out.

'Take me out to dinner tomorrow night.'

'You have to be joking! I won't be seen in public with you. I'm not going to make a laughing-stock of myself for the sake of this.'

'For the sake of what?'

'This!' he snarled, and crushed her to him, taking her mouth in a savage kiss that branded his feelings for what they were: lust. Nothing more. They had never been anything more. He knew it and she knew it. But the realisation still had the power to bring pain.

Celeste pushed him away and scrambled off his lap to stand with her hands on her hips. 'Then to hell with you, Byron Whitmore! I'm not some cheap whore to be visited in the dead of night down some dark alley. Whatever you pretend in public, you're no better than me, are you? You're here and you wanted me as much as, if not more than, I wanted you.'

Byron's mouth twisted, his face hardening at her accusation. 'Yes,' he admitted with a healthy does of bitter remorse. 'But I'm not proud of it.'

'Why not?'

He threw her a disbelieving glance.

'You're a normal man, aren't you?' she taunted. 'Well, a normal man has normal male desires. Surely you're not going to tell me you've only been holding hands with Catherine Whatsername? No, I didn't think so. Your wife's dead, Byron, which means you're either going to be celibate for the rest of your life, marry again, have one-night stands or come to a sensible arrangement with some co-operative woman. Who better than me? As for the gossip-mongers… They'll have a field-day for a whole week, but if you don't react they'll forget you and me and move on elsewhere.'

'And what of my family?' he pointed out scornfully. 'You're not exactly well liked around Belleview. Nathan, for one, detests you. He… Oh, my God, *Nathan*! I forgot all about him and Gemma. Hell, I forgot everything!' He jumped to his feet and glared at her. 'I usually do whenever I go anywhere near you, don't I? What is it? Have you cast a spell on me? Sold your soul to the devil in exchange for mine? Damn you, cover yourself up! How can I have a sensible discussion with you when you stand there, flaunting yourself at me?

Celeste shrugged, but wrapped the robe more modestly around herself. 'You can't live your life by what others think, Byron.'

His laughter was rueful. 'You certainly don't.'

'No, I don't. People will believe whatever they want to anyway.'

'Are you referring to me?'

'Among others. You're no better than all those narrow-minded little people who gobble up everything they read in the tabloids without stopping to question a thing. They love reading dirt and believing dirt. It's so very easy to make the general public think very badly of you. So very, very easy.'

Byron was frowning at her. 'You make it sound like you deliberately set out to make that happen.'

'Maybe I have…'

'Why would you do that?' he jeered.

'Why not? Maybe it amused me. Good God, Byron, if I'd had as many lovers as the papers and magazines suggested I had, I wouldn't have had time to do any work. I'd have been flat on my back all the time.'

'Or on your knees,' he sneered.

Her hand flashed out to crack him a beauty around the face. 'Don't you ever say that to me again. I have never done that for any other man, do you hear me? Not a one!'

Immediately scepticism flittered across his eyes, quickly followed by a definite doubt, then finally a troubled acceptance of the truth. 'I see no reason for you to lie to me about that, so I apologise.'

'Apology accepted,' she choked out, blinking madly as her eyes filled with unexpected tears.

This only made his frown deepen. 'I've really upset you, haven't I?' he said with surprise in his voice.

'It doesn't matter.'

'Of course it does. I…I guess I forgot…'

'Forgot what?'

'That you are still a human being,' he said gently. 'With feelings.'

That almost did it.

Celeste's only salvation was to walk away so that he couldn't see the blurring in her eyes and the torment in her face. Gathering herself quickly as she walked, she was able to turn when she reached the open doorway, a cool mask in place. 'I think you'd better go.'

He sighed. 'Yes. I think I'd better.'

'You can tell Nathan with a clear conscience that Gemma is not here.'

'And you honestly don't know where she is?'

'No, I do not. To be honest I regret becoming involved at all. Gemma and Nathan are nothing to me.'

'Damian is your brother. If he's involved, then so will you be.'

'I don't see it that way. Damian's an adult. I'm not responsible for what he does. I think you would be wise to adopt a similar attitude with Nathan. His marriage is his marriage. He won't appreciate your interference.'

'You could be right. But since Gemma hasn't seen fit to

tell him what she thinks she saw, I have no option but to do so.'

'Maybe. But after that, it's up to Nathan to fight his own battles. But let me give you a bit of female advice. If he's been unfaithful to her, then I don't like his chances.'

'Not all wives throw out their husbands for one lapse,' he said pointedly.

Celeste smiled. It was not a nice smile. 'If you're referring to darling Irene, then not all women are as forgiving and Christian as my sweet half-sister, are they?'

'Are you being sarcastic, Celeste?'

'Of course I'm being bloody sarcastic, Byron!' she stormed. 'God, you were as blind about her as you were about everything else. Didn't you ever find out what a bitch she was? What an evil, manipulative, cruel bitch?'

Byron stared at her.

'Just ask Ava! Or Jade! Or anyone else other than your own stupid self. You married a monster, Byron. Oh, yes, she loved you, much more than she hated everyone else!'

Celeste laughed as he continued to stare at her. 'I suppose I shouldn't be too hard on you. You're just a man, after all. What man can resist having a woman who is willing to play any role to fit the occasion and flatter his ego? Blushing virgin fiancé, then adoring bride, and finally the understanding and ever-sacrificing wife. I wouldn't have believed any of it if I hadn't seen it for myself. But she couldn't keep it up, could she? In the end her dark side came to the fore, didn't it?'

'I don't want to hear this,' he muttered.

'I'm sure you don't. Who wants to hear the awful truth?'

'She was a sick woman. I know that. But I couldn't throw her away, could I? Not after I—'

'Done her wrong?' Celeste broke in scoffingly.

Byron's eyes narrowed. 'Yes,' he bit out. 'I should never have married her.'

'You didn't love her, did you?'

'No.'

Celeste's heart contracted, just before it swelled with a heart-wrenching emotion. 'I knew you didn't love her,' she said in a strangled voice. 'How could you? You loved *me*!'

'Loved *you*!' he spluttered. 'I never loved *you*. You were nothing but a...a sickness! One I don't seem to have developed an immunity for. But at least now my sickness doesn't have to hurt anyone else. I have that salve for my conscience. And who knows? Maybe if I have you often enough this time, this damnable fire that has tormented me all these years might burn itself out at long last!'

For a few agonising seconds this new but equally brutal rejection of her love almost did what his earlier rejections had not succeeded in doing. But at the last moment, Celeste gathered herself, a bitter little smile curving her mouth.

'Oh, I doubt that, Byron,' she drawled. 'I doubt that very much. However, I suggest you do go home now. I've had enough of you for tonight. But we'll never be finished. Not while there's breath in my body. Let yourself out. I'll lock up later.'

Her smile faded once she'd made it into the bathroom and shut the door. There, she surveyed herself in the mirror with narrowed eyes and clenched jaw. It had been imperative, of course, that she not break down again. If she had, nothing would have saved her. Not drugs, or doctors, or anything.

Of course she should never have slept with Byron again. It had opened a Pandora's box of emotions that were dangerously difficult to control.

But that didn't mean she wouldn't do her damnedest to control them. She might still love and desire the man, but she also hated and despised him. It was a volatile mixture, one which would need the most careful of handling if she was to survive unscarred for a second time.

And Celeste meant to survive. Oh, yes...she hadn't come

this far to go under now. If there was to be a victim this time, it wasn't going to be her!

After a few minutes, Celeste exited from the bathroom to find the bedroom blessedly empty. So was the rest of the house. Byron's car was no longer in the driveway.

She closed the front gates, locked up, then went back upstairs to have a relaxing shower and climb into bed, where she did her best to will herself into a calm, restful sleep.

But Celeste was to find that sleep was one thing she was powerless to control. So were her dreams. When sheer exhaustion finally claimed her in the early hours of the morning, her mind was filled with nightmares in which a face came back to haunt her from the past, a hard sculpted face with chilling blue eyes and a granite jaw and fists like iron.

CHAPTER EIGHT

CELESTE was in conference with Luke, briefing him further on his new position, when the red light on her desk winked on. With a tut-tut of irritation, she flicked the switch on her intercom system and leant forward.

'Yes, Ruth?' she asked the temp she'd had sent over this morning from an agency Campbell's always used.

'A Mr Whitmore to see you, Ms Campbell.'

Celeste's stomach clenched down hard. Byron hadn't waited long to inform Nathan, it seemed. And Nathan hadn't taken long in showing up. Dear God, the last thing she wanted today was to have to placate some irrational and potentially violent husband. Not only did she have serious business on her plate, but she felt emotionally fragile. Still, Nathan was unlikely to simply go away, and she didn't think it would be wise if she asked him to wait.

'Show Mr Whitmore in, Ruth.'

'Yes, Ms Campbell.'

'Sorry, Luke,' she apologised as she got to her feet. 'Here. Take these sales analyses and see for yourself where our weaknesses lie, then start formulating a plan to redress matters, both short-term and long-term.'

Luke took the huge pile of computer printouts and threw her one of his little-used smiles, one which quite transformed his face from ordinary to extremely attractive. The smile still lingered on his face as he turned and met Mr Whitmore on his way in.

Not Nathan Whitmore, Celeste saw to her intense dismay. Byron Whitmore.

She froze, the events of last night seeming not only more shocking in the cold light of day, but almost unreal. Looking at Byron standing there in his navy pin-striped suit, the very essence of dignified respectability, made it difficult to cope with the images that kept popping into her mind. Her salvation was the sardonic expression that slid into his bright blue eyes as they raked over the smiling Luke.

'Thank you, Ruth,' she said dismissively to the secretary. 'I'll see you later, Luke,' she added in deliberate defiance of Byron's presence. 'We'll have lunch together. Book somewhere near, would you?'

To give him credit, Luke accepted these sudden arrangements with casual aplomb. Celeste realised she had found a gem in that young man.

The office door closed behind the departing people and Celeste was left to stare across the room at the man she both loved and hated.

'I take it *that* Luke is the Luke you referred to last night?' he said with cool derision.

'Of course.'

'You're sleeping with him?'

'Actually, no. Not yet. Cats like to play with their mice for a while first.'

'I'm no mouse, Celeste,' he warned darkly. 'You play with me at your own risk.'

'Maybe risk turns me on, Byron,'

'What doesn't?' he sneered.

'Losing.'

Darting her a black look, he slid his hands into the pockets of his trousers and began to pace to and fro across the dark green carpet in front of her desk. 'I haven't come here to indulge in smart-arse repartee, Celeste. I've come for some answers.'

Celeste sighed and sat back down in her large black

leather swivel chair. 'I told you before, Byron. I do not know where Damian and Gemma are. You've wasted your time coming here. I cannot be browbeaten into confessing something I don't know.'

When Byron ground to a halt in front of her desk, his dark brows bunched together in a troubled frown, Celeste found herself staring at his firm male mouth and remembering the pleasure it had given her the previous evening. She squirmed on the leather chair, hating her vulnerability to this man almost as much as she found it exciting and irresistible.

'I haven't come here about Nathan,' he said curtly.

Celeste forced herself to sit still and think clearly. 'You haven't told him yet about why Gemma left him?'

'Yes, I told him.'

'And?'

'I let him think she'd contacted me and told me why she'd left,' he admitted grudgingly. 'I had to lie and say she hung up without telling me any real details and that I had no idea where she'd temporarily run off to.'

'And that satisfied him?'

'I wouldn't describe Nathan's reaction as satisfied. Frankly, I didn't understand his reaction at all! If I didn't know better I'd say he was relieved, which hardly makes sense.'

'No, it doesn't. What man would be relieved to find out his wife believes he's cheating on her? What other dark secrets does he have on his conscience, I wonder...?'

'God, not you too. Ava's been giving me curry over this as well. She heard me on the phone to Nathan. When I was forced to admit Gemma had left Nathan she ripped right into Nathan's character. Why does everyone speak so badly of him? What's he ever done to deserve such treatment?'

'Aside from his rather colourful background, Byron, he did divorce his wife and marry a girl almost young enough to be his daughter.'

'Lenore divorced him, god-dammit! She and Nathan only ever married in the first place because she was pregnant with Kirsty. As for Gemma…I can well understand his becoming besotted with someone young like her. She was innocent, you see, innocent and untouched. The complete opposite to that rotten mother of his, and that other old tart who got hold of him when he was only a boy. Good God, why can't people appreciate what a fantastic job he's done of turning his life around? The man's a credit to himself!'

'And to you?'

'No, not to me! I didn't do all that much. He did it all himself.'

'You gave him a home, Byron. And you loved him. Love can heal a lot of wounds.'

Byron didn't seem to hear the sad irony in her words, sweeping on with his usual insensitivity. 'Which is why I want you to get a message to Gemma if you can. That girl loves Nathan. I know she does. She would forgive him anything.'

'Even adultery?'

'He swore blind he'd not been having an affair with Lenore. Apparently, she *had* been at his flat on the Sunday, which was stupid of him, I suppose. But he says he was helping her rehearse a difficult section of the play which opens this Friday. He thinks Gemma might have jumped to conclusions because he was also with Lenore at my party last Friday night. He can see it must have looked bad but all he wants is a chance to explain.'

'I wonder if he'd give her the chance to explain if the situation was reversed?' Celeste mused aloud.

'Of course he would,' Byron stated pompously. 'Why wouldn't he?'

'Because men don't always want to hear women's explanations. They're princes at jumping to conclusions. A lot of girls who are merely silly are branded sluts without a trial, without even a hearing.'

'Are you referring to yourself, Celeste? To *me*?'

Celeste surveyed his blustering anger with a wry ruefulness. 'Of course not, Byron. Why would I do that? You didn't jump to conclusions about me, did you? You simply believed what the woman who loved you told you. What motive would she possibly have had to lie?'

'Why are you taking this stance after all these years?' he asked, throwing his hands up in the air with a frustrated groan. 'You can't honestly expect me to believe you were a total innocent that first time—or later. If that was so, then why have you led such a decadent life since then? All those young men! A few weeks ago it was your chauffeur. Now you've set your sights on that poor bastard who just left here. God, I pity him!'

'Why? I'm going to look after Luke very well. He's going places around here.'

'He sure is! Right into your bed!'

'Not for a while, Byron,' she informed him silkily.

'Why the delay? Why not invite him home tonight, with us? I'm sure it won't be the first time you've had more than one man at a time.'

A pained outrage sent colour to her cheeks and fury pulsing through her veins. But when she spoke, her words were laced with an icy venom that refused to deny his vile accusation. 'And if I have, what's it to you? You don't really care about me. All you've ever wanted from me is what you got last night, so don't give me any more of your holier-than-thou crap. I'm the only one who's ever cared in this relationship. I loved you, Byron Whitmore, and I've no intention of letting you off the hook by letting you believe otherwise!'

'Don't be so bloody ridiculous!' he rapped out. 'You never loved me, Celeste. You merely wanted me. But I became the one who got away, the one who wouldn't dance indefinitely to your tune. You've shown your true colours since then by surrounding yourself with a whole string of sexual puppets. But you've finally grown bored with them, haven't you? That's the answer I was looking for today, and the reason for last night. You need a real man again to satisfy you, a man who can control you, who can call all your bluffs and put you in your place.'

'And where is that?'

'Under *me*.'

'You're an arrogant, presumptuous pig!'

His laughter sent a chill running down her spine and excitement along her veins. 'I've got your measure, Celeste. You can't fool me any more. Don't even try.'

She flushed at the way he started looking her over. Despite the fact that she was dressed in a severely tailored business suit which hid her body well, his desire-filled gaze sent goose-bumps racing all over her skin. Her nipples peaked hard against the silk lining of the jacket and she felt the pull of her own desire between his thighs.

'You were right when you said last night that we haven't finished yet,' he said in a low, threatening voice. 'But you were wrong to assume you had the controlling hand in this. Your fires for me are as hot as mine for you. Maybe even hotter. If they weren't, you'd have thrown me out by now. After all, I'm well aware of your capabilities in throwing out a man. I saw you in action at the ball.'

'Something you'd be wise not to forget,' she countered, but rather shakily, she thought.

His smug smile confirmed it. 'You had plenty of opportunity to use your skills on me last night but you didn't. That's rather telling in itself, don't you think?'

When Byron started moving around the large desk, Celeste stiffened back in her chair, her eyes flinging wide. 'Don't you dare touch me,' she rasped.

He swung her chair round to face him, placing a hand on each armrest, effectively imprisoning her in her seat. 'You can always kick me in the groin,' he suggested drily. 'No?

Then I'll take your lack of retaliation for an open invitation.' And he bent to kiss her quivering mouth.

Celeste detested the way her heart leapt at this lightest of kisses, but she was quick to resign herself to the situation. Byron was right. Resistance to his sexual approaches was a waste of time. Humiliating too if she tried to fight them, only to surrender eventually like some wimpish victim.

Her lips pulled back into a sexy smile under his, her eyes glittering boldly as they stared right into his. 'Do you think you might wait till lunchtime?' she murmured seductively. 'I'll cancel my lunch with Luke and meet you somewhere.'

Her swift change of tack threw him somewhat, his head drawing back while his eyes narrowed with suspicion. 'Such as where?'

'Don't you have a company suite at the Regency?'

Byron stood up straight, his arms swinging back to his sides as he took a backward step. 'How do you know that?' he asked sharply.

'I know everything about Whitmore's.'

He gave a sarcastic snort. 'You never did fight fair, did you? Your coming into the billiard-room that day in that minuscule bikini was downright wicked. When you actually kissed me, I had no chance, did I?'

Celeste let out a ragged sigh. 'You might not believe this, Byron, but seduction was the last thing on my mind that day. I was trying to make up my mind about something. I kissed you because I wanted to find out if I was over you.'

He laughed. 'You got more then you bargained for, then, didn't you?'

'I certainly did,' she said bitterly. 'For someone who proclaimed that he didn't want to rake over old coals, you have a habit of doing so.'

'I guess I like to keep reminding myself of the type of woman I'm dealing with.'

'Oh? And what type is that?'

'Ruthless. Conscienceless. Vindictive.'

'Vindictive.'

'Do you think I don't know why you revived that old feud between the Campbells and the Whitmores? It had nothing to do with what happened between our fathers. It was because of you and me, Celeste. I rejected you and you couldn't take it. You were the classic woman scorned. You set out to make me pay any way you could. And you succeeded. You succeeded very well. You almost brought Whitmore's to its financial knees. You also worked damned hard to make sure I never forgot what you were like to make love to. You flaunted your sexuality for all the world to see, but you didn't want the world to see it, did you? You only wanted me to see it.'

A wry lop-sided smile curved her scarlet-glossed mouth as she rose from the chair. Byron stood his ground as she pressed herself against him, but Celeste had the immense satisfaction of feeling his shoulders square back, seeing the flash of near panic in his eyes. Oh, how easily she could turn the tables on him. How very easily.

'You could be right, darling,' she purred, snaking her arms up around his neck and standing up on tiptoe to run her tongue-tip over his stiffly held mouth. 'You see, I've never found a man who can do for me what you do. You're the best, Byron. The very best. I don't think I will ever get tired of making love to you...'

His groan as he crushed her to him echoed in his ears, his impassioned kiss going some way to blocking the unbearable pain he had unwittingly evoked again. When he finally tore his mouth away he sounded as if he'd run a very long, very hard race. She was merely in a daze. Their power over each other was getting worse, she realised. Where would it all end?

'Be there at one,' he muttered thickly into her hair.

He didn't wait for an answer. He gave her one last impassioned glance then strode from the room, leaving the door open behind him. She walked over and shut it, shuddering as she leant with her back against it. Her eyes went to the clock on the wall. Ten o'clock. One was three long hours away.

SHE LAY NAKED in his arms, her head lying in the crook of his left arm, his free hand lazily tracing patterns over her very relaxed body.

Celeste opened heavy eyes to glance idly around the hotel bedroom. Their clothes lay tidily folded up on adjacent chairs, the sight of them bringing a rueful smile to her lips.

She had insisted on undressing him herself, doing it slowly and methodically, then making him climb into the bed while she undressed herself. There had been no attempt at any erotic striptease. Celeste had been desperately trying to keep control over what was becoming more and more an uncontrollable situation for her. She hadn't been able to work all morning, her thoughts on nothing but being with Byron again.

By the time she had climbed into that bed with him she'd wanted him immediately. Fortunately, his need had been similar and they had come together without any preliminaries. Now they lay together, two spent forces, waiting for the wanting to begin again. Celeste didn't think it would be long.

'You haven't asked me to use anything,' Byron murmured as he stroked her. 'Is that wise?'

Celeste cringed at the implication he was making. It was a perfectly understandable question, considering her reputation, but she still reacted badly to it. 'For you or for me?' came her stiff reply.

'Just answer the question, Celeste. I always used protection with Catherine. Have you been practising safe sex as well?'

'Very safe,' she said drily, thinking that not doing it at all was the safest sex she knew of.

'I'm not talking about just being on the Pill,' he muttered.

'I'm not on the Pill.'

Every muscle in his body froze. 'Isn't that rather dangerous? I'm not too old to become a father, you know. Neither are you too old to become a mother.'

Celeste slipped out of Byron's arms and sat up. 'I can't have any...' She broke off before the word *more* slipped out. 'I can't have any children,' she said tautly, then stood up. 'I'm going to have a shower.'

She was under the hot jets of water when Byron slid back the glass door. 'How long have you known that?' he asked brusquely.

Not looking at him, she closed her eyes and tipped her face up into the water. 'Quite a while.' There was no way he could see her tears with the water beating into her eyes.

He swore, and when she finally opened her eyes he was gone. Five minutes later, she returned to the room, wrapped in a towel. Byron was lying under the sheet on the bed, looking pensive.

'Why didn't you tell me?'

'Why should I?' She dropped the towel and slipped under the sheet next to him. When he gathered her in close, she shivered.

'Because it explains so much,' he rasped. 'A woman who can't have children can do strange things. How did it happen, Celeste? Did you have an abortion and it went wrong? Was that it? Don't be afraid to tell me. I'll try to understand. Really I will.'

Something inside Celeste shattered. Against all common sense and everything she'd vowed, she started to weep.

'God, Celeste,' Byron groaned, and held her close, stroking her back. 'Don't. Please don't. I...I can't handle it. It's not like you to cry.'

Rolling her over, he cupped her face and began kissing the tears from her eyes and then her cheeks till, with a muffled moan, he took her mouth with his, drinking in her sobs, biting at her lips and sucking on her tongue with a wildness that stunned her. Clinging to him, she begged silently for his compassion, not passion, but instead he surged deep into her body, surged till she was forced to forget, to think of nothing but his flesh filling hers, till her cries were the cries of a pained release, her moans the moans of despair.

Afterwards, she refused to say any more on the subject of her barren state, no matter how often he asked, dressing quietly and going back to work. If Luke looked at her oddly a couple of times when they met later in the afternoon, at least he had the sense to say nothing.

At five, Celeste had been about to pack up for the day and call a taxi, when Byron telephoned.

'Have dinner with me tonight,' he urged.

Celeste's eyes squeezed tightly shut as her heart skipped a beat. 'Aren't you afraid of being seen with me in public?' she returned an edge in her voice.

'We could have Room Service up in the suite again.'

Like hell, she thought.

'I'm sorry, Byron, I can't,' she said crisply, almost as though she was turning down a business dinner and not another assignation with her lover.

'Why not?'

'I have things I have to do at home tonight,' she said firmly.

'What? Wash your hair? I'll wash it for you. I'll do anything you want. I'll even paint your toenails if they need painting.'

Celeste groaned silently. What a fool she'd been to surrender her body again to Byron. She should have known what would happen. The man had always been a predator. Now that he was a widower, there was nothing to stop him reverting to type. No guilt. No moral constraints. No nothing.

'I'm having friends for dinner at home,' she said thinking to herself that if Damian brought Gemma home as he said he would then it was close to the truth.

'When are they leaving? I'll come over after they've gone.'

Celeste gritted her teeth. 'Byron, I said no. If you wish to continue to see me then you have to learn to take no for an answer.'

'I'm better at yes,' he growled.

'Aren't we all?'

'When am I going to see you again?'

'I'll call you tomorrow at your office. We'll make plans then.'

'I don't trust you to call. I'll call you.'

'Whatever you like.'

'I'd like to come over later.'

'Byron, for pity's sake!'

'If you had any pity you'd let me come over. God, I think I'm going crazy, Celeste. I can't think of anything else but being with you. You've bewitched me, woman.'

'I'm glad to hear that, Byron. The boot's on the other foot at last.'

She heard his sucked-in breath. 'You're a real bitch, aren't you?'

'So people keep telling me.'

'Add me to the list!' he snarled, and hung up.

Celeste stared down into the dead receiver. Taking a deep, shuddering breath, she hung up herself, then lifted the receiver up again and dialled for a taxi to take her home.

CHAPTER NINE

DAMIAN opened the front door before Celeste could get her key out.

'Hi there, sis. I'm home.'

'So I see,' came her dry reply. 'I take it you're not alone?'

'Hey, why the attitude? You're the one who suggested I bring Gemma here.'

Celeste sighed. 'Maybe I've changed my mind.'

'Too late for that. When you meet her, you'll be glad I did. She's a sweetie.'

'That's what worries me.'

Damian laughed. 'I've been a perfect gentleman.'

'But for how long?'

Damian pulled a face at her, then took her hand and pulled her along to the main living-room where Mrs Nathan Whitmore was curled up in an armchair looking so forlorn that Celeste's heart went out to her.

'Celeste's home at last,' Damian said as they moved into the room.

Gemma jumped, her legs shooting out from under her.

'Don't get up,' Celeste told her, which brought a look of surprise.

Is it my ultra-conservative clothes, Celeste wondered drily, that are making her look at me with those startled doe eyes of hers?

Celeste conceded that with a smart business suit on and her hair up she was a far cry from the outrageously dressed siren who'd attended the Whitmore Opals ball. No doubt this girl thought her as disgraceful a person as her husband did. Not that Nathan could condemn anyone for their morals, or seeming lack of them.

'And how are you bearing up, my dear?' Celeste asked gently. 'I take it things have been a bit difficult for you lately.'

'I... Yes... You could say that.'

'Please feel free to stay as long as you like. We have plenty of room here.'

'You're most kind,' the girl murmured. 'Your brother's been very kind too. I...I don't know what I would have done without him.'

Celeste settled herself in a chair opposite. 'Yes, Damian is not all bad, despite his reputation.'

Now the girl looked even more startled, with Damian quickly coming to his own defence.

'With you for a sister, who needs enemies?' he mocked. 'Don't believe a word she says, Gemma. I'm a saint in wolf's clothing.' He came forward to perch on the arm of her chair, placing a comforting hand on her shoulder.

Gemma looked up at him with a slightly nervous smile, Celeste frowning as she took in how very lovely this child was. Those large velvet-brown eyes were captivating enough, but combined with that flawless olive skin, that sensual mouth and that gloriously thick dark brown hair, she was a stunner. Her attractions did not stop at her face, either. There was no hiding the lush fullness of her breasts beneath that soft green cashmere sweater, the slimline tan stirrup trousers she was wearing just as revealing of the rest of her shapely figure, including the tiny span of her waist and the swell of her quite womanly hips.

'Not to worry, Gemma,' Celeste said briskly. 'I'll keep him in line. And so will Cora. You've told Cora we have an extra for dinner, Damian?'

He gave her a droll look. 'Of course.'

'Maybe you could make yourself scarce for a minute. I have something to say to Gemma.'

'Such as what?'

'If I wanted to tell you, I wouldn't ask you to leave,' she said drily. 'Perhaps you could go select some wine to go with our meal tonight. Gemma looks as if she could do with some relaxing.'

Damian brightened at this suggestion, which only made Celeste more suspicious of his intentions. 'What a good idea! I'll go haunt the cellar. Do you prefer red or white, Gemma?'

'White, actually. Riesling if you have it. Though Nathan always said that…' She broke off, tears immediately flooding her eyes.

Celeste wanted to kill Nathan Whitmore at that moment. What a bastard! Taking this young girl, making her his then utterly destroying her. She knew exactly what that felt like. Byron had made her irrevocably his in two short weeks. This devil had had months of marriage to brainwash this child both emotionally and sexually.

What chance did she have of throwing off his dastardly influence, of ever being normal with any other man? Celeste recognised the type. This girl felt deeply, as she had felt deeply. No other man would ever do for her, just as no other man but Byron had ever done for Celeste. One only had to look at how she'd acted today, running to him when he'd snapped his fingers, giving him all he asked without asking for anything in return.

His unexpected sympathy today had got to her for a while but, in the end, he'd turned it to his own advantage, using her momentary vulnerability as a springboard to yet another sexual encounter. If ever Celeste needed a recent example of male selfishness, then that would suffice. Or she could gaze upon this crushed creature and her big bruised eyes.

Damn, but she wished she could help her, *really* help her. But she felt so helpless.

'Get lost, Damian,' she bit out, taking his place on the armrest of Gemma's chair and putting a sympathetic arm around her slender shoulders.

'Things might not be as bad as you think, love,' she said softly once Damian had departed. 'I was speaking to Byron today and it seems Nathan insists he's innocent of any wrong-doing with Lenore.'

'Then he's a liar!' the girl bit out heatedly. 'I…I heard him, with my own ears. He…he spent the night with her. And he said other things. Awful things.' She shuddered violently and Celeste wanted to kill Nathan anew. But she had to give this child some hope.

'Sometimes people say things they don't mean to say, Gemma. And they do things they don't mean to do. Men will be men, my dear. Nathan's spending the night with his ex-wife might not be as black and white as it seems. Have—er—things been all they should be between you two in the bedroom lately?'

Celeste could not misinterpret the guilty colour that flooded the girl's cheeks. So! Things hadn't been all hunky-dory between them.

'It had been a couple of weeks since we'd made love,' she admitted unhappily.

'You…you haven't been having an affair with Damian, have you?' she asked carefully.

'No!' There was no doubting the girl's horror at this suggestion. 'I would never do a thing like that. I love Nathan. I always will!' She burst into tears at that, weeping into the crumpled handkerchief in her hands.

'There, there…' Celeste patted her gently on the shoulder. 'Perhaps you should go upstairs, get yourself together, wash your face and then we'll have dinner. I'll walk up with you.'

Celeste kept a comforting arm around her waist as they walked slowly up the stairs together, surprised at the tug of emotion she was feeling for this sweet child. It was not just sympathy. It was a real empathy.

She's so like I was at her age, came the dismaying realisation. Basically innocent and naïve, yet extremely sexual and emotional. Falling in love meant giving of oneself utterly and totally. What a pity the men we fell in love with didn't return the same unfailing devotion.

Celeste resisted telling Gemma that men were not as simple and straightforward as women. She saw no point in making her as cynical and world-weary as she was, nor in explaining to her that a man could sleep with one woman, claiming he loved her, then marry another a few months later. Or that, while married to that woman, he could still lose himself in that first woman's body to such an extent that all reality had ceased to exist, only to turn on her a few minutes later, deriding her most cruelly and banishing her from his life.

Or maybe she should? Maybe it was time the girl heard some of the facts of life.

'How old are you, Gemma?' she asked as they turned at the landing and mounted the rest of the stairs.

'Twenty. I *think*.'

Celeste frowned. 'What do you mean, you think?'

The girl sighed. 'It's a long story. My birth certificate turned out to be full of lies and I'm not sure when my birthday is.'

'How awkward for you.'

Gemma shrugged a type of weary resignation.

'Would you be offended, Gemma,' Celeste asked carefully, 'if I told you that not many husbands go through life being faithful to their wives?'

Those big brown eyes slanted her way, shocking Celeste with their sudden coldness. 'I don't want to be married to that kind.'

Goodness, Celeste thought admiringly. She's not so softly sweet after all. Damian doesn't know what he's in for if he tries anything with this girl.

Celeste found herself feeling much better about that situation. 'I fully agree with you,' she said drily. 'That's why I've never married. What guest room did Damian put you in?'

'That one,' Gemma indicated, pointing ahead to the third door on the right.

'Have you got everything you need?'

'Yes, thank you.'

'Don't bother to change for dinner. You look delightful in what you're wearing. I'm going to slip into something more casual, however. I'll drop back at the door and collect you on my way downstairs.'

'Miss Campbell,' Gemma called after her as she walked away.

Celeste turned, wincing a little. 'Celeste, please. I keep 'Miss Campbell' for junior typists only.'

Gemma smiled, reminding Celeste forcibly of her stunning beauty. 'All right. Celeste. I just wanted to thank you again, and to say that you're not at all like I thought you'd be.'

Celeste smothered an amused smile. 'What did you think I'd be like?'

'I don't know. Not so nice. Oh, that sounds awful!'

'It sounds perfectly reasonable to me. I'm often not very nice, Gemma. But I don't think anyone could help being nice with you.'

Gemma looked disconcerted by this compliment. 'I'm not always so nice, either. Maybe I did push Nathan away from me. I...I'm not sure of anything any more.' Tears filled her eyes and she looked away.'

Celeste was appalled at the sudden pricking of tears behind her own eyes. Good God, she was going all mushy and sentimental in her old age. It was all Byron's fault, raking up old memories, making her say things she should never have said. Or maybe this unexpected vulnerability was because her own daughter would be about Gemma's age now. She might even look a little like her.

Celeste was not a natural blonde, her fair tresses achieved with considerable effort from her hairdresser. Her daughter was sure to be a brunette, like Gemma, and probably with similar brown eyes. Despite Celeste's own eyes being a light yellowish brown, dark eyes did run in the Campbell family. One only had to look at Damian. Since a blue-eyed father with a brown-eyed mother almost always produced a brown-eyed baby. Celeste's daughter would most likely have deep brown eyes something like Gemma's.

Celeste swallowed and dragged up a covering smile. 'Don't think about it any more tonight,' she advised the obviously confused and very distressed girl. 'I won't be long. I'm a quick dresser.'

Dinner did not prove to be as difficult as Celeste had begun to fear it might be. Damian was his usual charming self and Gemma, with the help of several glasses of wine, relaxed enough to talk a little about herself in a general sense. She explained how Byron had made her learn Japanese before letting her work in any of his stores, and that she'd become quite competent at it.

'You won't have any trouble getting a job, then,' Celeste said. 'There are openings all over the place if you can speak Japanese well.'

'That's what I'm hoping.'

'We could find her a job at Campbell's, couldn't we, Celeste?' Damian suggested casually.

'Any time,' she offered, and meant it. Gemma would be an asset behind any counter.

'I did originally hope that,' the girl admitted. 'But now I think I should strike out on my own. Maybe I'll move interstate.'

'Why in God's name would you do that?' Damian's voice was sharp.

'Because she wants to be independent, Damian,' Celeste explained somewhat caustically. 'A concept I realise you don't understand.'

'She should be near friends at a time like this.'

Gemma gave him an apologetic look. 'I'm sorry. Damian. You've been marvellous, but I really don't like imposing on you and your sister.'

'What rubbish!' they both answered at once, then simultaneously laughed.

'At least stay a week,' Celeste compromised, knowing decisions should not be made in the heat of the moment.

'Yes, give us a week of your delightful company at least,' Damian insisted.

'All right.' Gemma's sigh of acceptance sounded relieved, and Celeste felt another pull on her heart-strings. Damn, in another week she wouldn't want her to go any more than Damian. Despite the traumas surrounding Gemma's visit, it was surprisingly pleasant having her around. Celeste decided she must definitely be entering a sentimental phase in her life. Next thing she'd be getting herself a dog!

'I hear you're an outback girl,' she said by way of changing the subject.

'That's right. Born and bred in Lightning Ridge.'

'Damned awful place!' Damian scorned. 'Hot as hell and wall-to-wall flies. I only went there once. Celeste had this idea about my learning to become an opal buyer. I soon dissuaded her, didn't I?'

'I think I quickly realised that anything with physical discomfort involved was not your forte.'

Gemma laughed. 'Then you wouldn't have wanted to live where I lived. I not only had wall-to-wall flies but wall-to-wall dirt.'

'How's that?' he asked.

'Dad and I lived in a dugout. You know. A hole in the ground. Well, not in the ground exactly. It was dug out of the side of a hill.'

Damian shuddered. 'You poor thing.'

Gemma shrugged. 'I didn't know any differently. But you

can imagine what I thought when I came to Sydney and went to live in Belleview. I thought I'd died and gone to heaven.'

'How did that come about, Gemma?' Celeste asked. 'Your going to live at Belleview, that is? Or don't you like my asking that? You don't have to tell us if you don't want.'

'No, it's all right. I don't mind. My dad died, you see. There'd only been the two of us. My mother—er—my mother had died when I was born. I...I decided to come to Sydney to live. To be honest, I never did like the heat and the flies either,' she said with a quick smile Damian's way. 'I decided to sell up everything I inherited to get some money. Not that there was much. Dad was an opal miner, but not a very successful one, I'm afraid. All he had to his name was a battered old truck and a small hoard of second-rate opals. That's why I...why I...'

Her voice trailed away and Celeste suspected some memory was too painful to talk about, for the girl suddenly dropped her eyes to her food and frowned. When she looked up, she still looked troubled for a second then her expression cleared and she resumed her story.

'Anyway, I went to sell these opals to Byron. He goes up to the Ridge to buy opals all the time.'

'Yes, I know,' Celeste said, and threw Damian a reproachful look. 'Byron really knows his opals. So what happened? I hope he gave you a good deal.'

'Well, no, he didn't. I mean he *couldn't*, because he wasn't there. He was in hospital after some accident or other and he'd sent Nathan in his place.'

Celeste nodded thoughtfully. That would have been the boating accident when Irene was killed. 'I see,' she murmured.

And she did. Nathan had taken one look at this exquisite creature and had simply had to possess her.

'So what happened then?' she asked, impatient to see how Nathan had achieved his wicked purpose.

'I sold the opals to Nathan instead.'

'Yes, but how did you come to be living at Belleview?'

'Oh, that. Well, when I mentioned to Nathan that I was moving to Sydney, he gave me his business card and said if I ever needed a job to look him up, so I did.'

'And what job did he offer you that required you to live in at Belleview?' Damian asked, sounding sardonic.

Gemma flushed a little at his obvious innuendo. 'It's not what you're thinking. Nathan offered me a position as sales assistant at one of Whitmore's opal shops, but Byron insisted I learn Japanese first, so while I was doing that Nathan hired me as a type of minder for his daughter. Kirsty was staying with him at Belleview for a while, you see. She'd been giving her mother some trouble and Lenore had sent her to her father to straighten her out. Naturally, I—er—had to live in.'

Celeste almost repeated the *naturally*, but didn't. She did, however, catch Damian's eye across the table and her expression was similarly cynical. Not that he could cast any stones. She'd like a dollar for every devious line he'd thrown a woman.

'And that's when you both fell in love,' Celeste commented matter-of-factly.

'Yes,' Gemma muttered, looking and sounding miserable again.

'Let's talk about something else,' Damian said firmly. 'Some more wine, Gemma?'

She put her hand over the glass and shook her head. 'Any more and I'll be paralytic.'

'At least you'll sleep well.'

Cora came in then, wanting to know who wanted dessert.

'What is it?' Celeste asked.

'Lemon meringue pie with cream.'

Celeste groaned. 'You bad woman, tempting me like that.'

'You shouldn't worry. You can always punish yourself

with twenty laps of the pool afterwards.' Cora began stacking up the dinner plates. 'There are no refusals, I take it?'

'No!' they all chorused.

'Just as well,' the housekeeper said crisply. 'I don't like slaving over a hot stove for nothing.'

'She's so nice,' Gemma remarked once Cora was out of earshot.

Damian grinned a wickedly attractive grin. 'We're all nice, aren't we, Celeste?'

She looked at her brother and wished he weren't so handsome, or so charming. Her earlier confidence that Gemma would be able to resist him worried her anew. Women did stupid things on the rebound. Hadn't she gone from Byron to Stefan thinking she could lose herself in his Viking good looks, his supposedly gentlemanly consideration?

And what had happened?

She'd been drawn into a hell that no woman should have to endure but which many did. Celeste could well understand why battered women eventually struck back and did murder. She wished she had had the courage, or the strength. Then she might have kept her lovely baby.

Instead, she'd had her child stolen from her, had been left bleeding and broken on that cold stone floor. If a passing shepherd hadn't heard her pathetic cries for help, she would be dead now. Instead, she had lived to survive. But had her survival been worth it?

Maybe, she decided, looking at Gemma down the end of the table. She could still be of help to people occasionally. And she could still get pleasure out of life occasionally.

Her mind drifted to Byron and she shuddered. Oh, yes, she could still feel pleasure. But when would the pain stop? When would she be able to forget?

CHAPTER TEN

GEMMA sat on the edge of the bed, holding her temples. She shouldn't have drunk so much of that wine. The blood was pounding in her head and she felt a little nauseous. The wine had made her run off at the mouth a little over dinner as well, something she regretted now.

At least she'd stopped herself before she'd told them all about the Heart of Fire. Irrespective of her breakup with Nathan, Gemma felt she owed some loyalty to the Whitmores. Byron had always been good to her and she was sure he wouldn't like her blurting out Whitmore business to the Campbells. Celeste's buying the Heart of Fire at the ball had clearly annoyed Byron. He'd been reluctant to tell her any real details that night of how the opal had come back in Whitmore possession, so one didn't have to be too bright to conclude he wanted to keep that information a secret.

Gemma wasn't too sure why, but since her own father had clearly been involved in the original theft of the opal she didn't mind not telling all and sundry. Celeste and Damian had already been shocked by her less than genteel upbringing at Lightning Ridge. What would they think if she had revealed her father had not only been a drunk and a loser, but a criminal as well?

Not that Celeste Campbell had any right to judge others, Gemma reasoned quickly. Her reputation was hardly lily-white. And yet…

Gemma shook her head, frowning. The scandalous lady boss of Campbell Jewels was not at all as Gemma had imagined her to be. Though clearly an assertive and confident businesswoman who Gemma was sure could be very tough given the right occasion, she also had a surprisingly soft and warm side of her character that was very engaging. Gemma had found herself drawn to the woman. She had wanted to pour all her woes out to her, sensing a genuinely sympathetic ear.

But a lifetime of being a very private person with no mother, no brothers or sisters and few friends had made Gemma reluctant to open up to people. Not that Celeste Campbell could solve her problems. No one could solve her problems, for there was no solution. She'd fallen in love with the wrong man, had married him, made him her life, and now he'd snatched that life out from under her.

It would be a long, long time before she got over his betrayal. Maybe a lifetime would not be enough.

A tap on the door had her jumping to her feet. Lord, but she was a bundle of nerves.

'Yes?' she asked agitatedly through the door.

'I've brought you a nightcap,' Damian returned. 'I thought you might need one to help you sleep.'

With a sigh, Gemma went over and opened the door to find Damian standing there with a smile on his handsome face and what looked like a glass of port in his hands.

'I couldn't possibly drink any more alcohol, Damian,' she said apologetically. 'But thank you for the thought.'

'You're still dressed,' he chided. 'Look, why don't you have a relaxing shower, climb into bed and I'll bring you a mug of hot chocolate?'

'Really, there's no need.'

'There's every need,' he said firmly. 'You should see the dark rings under your eyes. You need a good night's sleep, Gemma.'

'All right,' she sighed, agreeing with him. If she didn't sleep tonight, she wasn't sure what she'd do.

Gemma was under the bedclothes, the sheet pulled well

up over her rather revealing ivory silk nightie—she didn't have any other kind—when Damian knocked.

Was it her being in bed that made her feel suddenly vulnerable when he came back in and closed the door behind him? Or was it the way his flashing black eyes narrowed on her near naked shoulders as he walked towards her?

Whatever, Gemma found her whole insides contracting, her stomach fluttering with a funny little feeling something like fear. She was not such a fool as to be unaware that Damian fancied her. She'd been rather expecting him to make a pass some time, but she didn't think he'd try something here, with his sister just down the hall.

Still, her eyes followed him somewhat worriedly when he put the drink down on the bedside chest and sat down on the side of the bed. 'Feeling better after your shower?' he asked, smiling.

She nodded, finding it hard to find her tongue all of a sudden.

'I'm an expert at hot-chocolate making,' he said, and picked up the mug again. 'Here… Drink up…'

When he actually held it to her lips instead of handing it to her, she automatically curved her own hands around his, lest the liquid spill on the bed. Appalled to find her fingers trembling, she gulped the drink down very quickly, all the while aware of Damian staring at her over the rim with those penetrating black eyes of his. She found herself staring back at him and seeing him in a totally different light.

Where before he'd presented himself as a darkly elegant and very handsome man with flashing black eyes, a boyish smile and an engagingly charming manner, she now noted a wicked gleam in those eyes and a decadent weakness in the slack set of his mouth. Dressed all in black as he was tonight, and with his straight black hair slicked back from his face, he gave off a menacing aura that was making her heart beat faster and her stomach churn. All she wanted was for him to leave her room as soon as possible.

'All gone,' she said with false brightness once she'd drunk all the hot chocolate and was able to take her hands away from his.

'Good girl. Sleep well, now.'

Gemma could not help her look of surprise when he simply stood up and began to walk towards the door.

She was still staring at him when he stopped with his hand on the doorknob and looked back over his shoulder. 'I suggest you sleep in as long as you can tomorrow morning. Unfortunately, I have to show my face in the office, but Cora will be here all day to look after you. Feel free to use the pool—it's heated—or anything else that appeals, and I'll see you when I get home tomorrow evening. OK?'

His smile was so warm and tender that she felt guilty at her earlier bad thoughts about him. Her imagination was definitely getting the better of her. Or maybe her opinion of men had been seriously damaged by what Nathan had done.

'I'll never forget how sweet you've been to me,' she said with genuine feeling. 'I don't know what I would have done without you.'

'Men can be good friends too, Gemma. Always remember that.'

'I will from now on.'

IT WAS AFTER two when Damian slipped back into her room. The sleeping tablets he'd crushed in her drink would be at their peak now. He'd tripled the normal dose, making sure of her unconscious state.

The room was in darkness, the curtains drawn at the windows. Making his way carefully over to them, he very slowly drew them back so that moonlight fell across the bed and the sleeping form within.

Standing next to the bed, he gazed down at her for ages then very slowly peeled the bedclothes back down. Shock riveted him to the spot when she moaned and rolled over on to her side, facing him. But her eyes remained shut, her lips softly apart as she breathed the deep, even breathing of the heavily drugged. His own eyes fell to where her movement had wrapped the nightie tightly around her body, the top awry on her full bosom.

His gut clenched down hard at the sight of half a rosy nipple peeping out at him, his desire flaring madly. The idea of touching her while she was asleep was so exciting that he actually shuddered.

He recalled how her hands had trembled on his earlier tonight. She'd been momentarily afraid of him till he'd managed to allay her fears with his wimpish retreat. But she had every reason to be afraid of him, though, didn't she? Every reason…

His own hands trembled as he reached out to draw the strap down off her shoulder and down her arm. He was about to expose her breast totally when he heard the sound of the doorknob turning. Reefing the strap back up, he dived under the bed and was hiding there, quivering, when he saw his sister's slippers appear beside the bed.

Holding his breath lest she hear his breathing, he listened to her rearranging the bedclothes, then watched her walk over to the windows where she drew the curtains, blessedly darkening that side of the room. His relief when she left the room was enormous, but for some rotten reason Celeste left the damned door ajar. And the light in the hall was on.

Clearly, his sister was having one of her sleepless nights, when she would wander the house at all hours. If he closed the door, she might see it.

Damian lay where he was for some time before slipping out from under the bed and returning to his room. Though furious, he put his frustration on hold with the thought that tomorrow was another day. He determined that it would not only be Gemma's drink he put the sleeping draught in the next time. Darling Celeste was going to have her insomnia fixed as well.

GEMMA WOKE with a terrible hangover. She groaned when she saw the time. Nearly noon. How could she have slept for so long?

Dragging herself out of bed, she visited the *en suite* then returned to draw on her only modest dressing-gown—a floor-length cream silk number whose coverage was adequate, although it wasn't the thickest of material. Still, only Cora would be left in the house at this late hour. Damian and Celeste would have gone to work.

Work…

Gemma felt guilty about how she'd let her own workmates down yesterday, ringing up at the last moment and claiming she was sick. She would have to ring again today and let them know the real situation, though maybe Byron had already done that. From what Celeste said last night, her father-in-law already knew everything.

Picking up her hairbrush, she began putting some order into her tangled hair. She really had had a restless night, despite sleeping so long. There was a vague memory of dreams which she was rather glad she could not remember. She was sure they hadn't been happy dreams. But they weren't likely to be, were they?

With her appearance in some semblance of order, she went in search of Cora and a cup of coffee. Maybe some aspirin as well. She really did not feel too good. Her head was terribly thick. Not exactly a headache but a woolly feeling.

Gemma glanced admiringly around on her way downstairs, especially at the elaborate stained-glass window rising above the landing halfway down. Her stark outback upbringing made her appreciate beautiful things but she was not naïve enough to think that riches brought happiness. Her own marriage to a wealthy successful man certainly proved the saying that money wasn't everything. It was *nothing* if not combined with love and true intimacy. Nathan had showered her with clothes and gifts, given her everything but himself in a real sense. She'd been worried all along by their lack of emotional bonding, worried Nathan's feelings for her didn't go deeper than lust and possessiveness, and she'd been proven right.

Gemma stepped off the staircase with a sigh and headed for the kitchen, looking in the other rooms on the way.

The kitchen was empty, and there, on the counter, propped against a bowl of fruit, was a note.

Gone to do the week's shopping. I've put a selection of cereals on the side. Coffee and tea next to them. There's milk and orange juice in the fridge, bread already in the toaster. Help yourself. Be back by three. Cora.

'Just coffee to start with, Cora,' Gemma told the absent housekeeper. 'Pity about the aspirin.'

She took the steaming mug back upstairs with her, sipping down most of it before stripping off and plunging into the shower, in the hope that the hot jets of water would clear her head. No such luck. She really needed a couple of painkillers.

Unfortunately, the wall cabinet in the guest *en suite* was empty apart from a spare toothbrush, some mouth-wash, and a couple of tubes of toothpaste. Gemma didn't think anyone would mind if she searched the other medicine cabinets for something to take, so she covered her nakedness with her robe and walked out of her bedroom into the next.

Clearly, it was a man's bedroom, the furniture dark, the brown and gold furnishings having not a single piece of feminine frippery about any of them. There was also an absence of the type of ornament and knick-knack women dotted around their rooms. The bed was made and the room tidy, but the black trousers and shirt Damian had worn the previous evening were draped across a chair in the corner.

Not wanting to linger, Gemma hurried across the room

and into the connecting bathroom. This time, the cabinet was full of a wide range of medicine and other items, including several packets of condoms. Gemma tried not to make judgement over this—at least he was practising safe sex—but seeing so many of them sitting there so openly and so casually sent a funny little shiver down her spine. Her eyes darted along the shelves and when she spied some headache tablets she snatched them up, extracted a couple and put the packet back, relieved to slide the glass door back into place. Popping them into her mouth, she turned on the tap, cupped her hands and drank from the pool of water that formed in them.

When she lifted her head from this action and automatically glanced in the mirror, she screamed.

For Nathan was standing in the open bedroom doorway, glaring over at her as though he wanted to kill her.

She whirled round, and her eyes had never felt bigger as they took in his unshaven face and his chillingly cold grey eyes. Dressed in washed-out grey jeans and a crumpled blue windcheater, he looked far removed from his usual elegant, well-groomed self. He looked far removed from his usual self all round. Dear God, he had never looked at her like that before, so full of hardness and hatred.

After an initial freezing, Gemma's heart jolted into an erratic beat, her headache forgotten in the face of other more frightening feelings.

'So I was right,' he said in a voice made all the more terrifying for its control. 'You were here all along. I just jumped to the wrong conclusion.'

Gemma pulled the robe defensively around her quivering nudity. 'How…how did you get in here? The gates are locked.'

'There's no lock on the jetty, Gemma. I came by boat.'

'I'm not alone, you know,' she bluffed, sensing his simmering violence. 'The housekeeper…'

'Won't be back till three,' he finished frostily, and produced Cora's note from his pocket. Crumpling it into a ball, he threw it in a corner. 'I came here,' he ground out, 'hoping and praying that somehow I'd be proven wrong about you, that all I had to do to set things right was say I was sorry for being so stupid as to have Lenore over. But I wasn't wrong about you, was I? You took the first flimsy excuse you could find to run to your lover. You blackened my name to my whole family while all the time you were letting that bastard Campbell screw you silly!'

Gemma hadn't realised till that moment what impression her presence in Damian's room would give, especially with her not being properly dressed. Any irony over Nathan's turning things around and making her the accused one was lost in the wake of her anxiety to make him see the truth.

'You've got it all wrong!' she defended. But in vain, she thought. There was no reasoning in Nathan's face. No capacity to listen. Yet she had to try. Having him believe such a thing of her was untenable. 'I...I only came in here to get some aspirin. Here...look!' She slid back the cabinet and pointed to the packet of tablets.

Nathan's chilling gaze moved from the aspirin to the other packets on the shelf, then returned to survey Gemma's swiftly flushing face with a chillingly mocking expression.

Oh, why do I have to look so guilty? Gemma agonised.

'I know what you're thinking but you're wrong!' she cried. 'There's nothing between Damian and myself. I'm staying here as a guest,' she explained desperately, 'and I have my own room. I'll show it to you. It has my things in it.'

When she hurried forward and went to brush past him, Nathan grabbed both her arms and swung them behind her, holding her wrists in an iron grip while he pushed her back into Damian's room. He slammed her face-down on to the bed, his breathing ragged behind her.

'You might have your own room but *this* is where you've been spending your nights, you lying, cheating bitch! I've known it from the moment that hotel clerk described to me the man who came to collect you. You've been seeing Damian Campbell ever since that night of the ball, haven't you?'

'No!' she cried, terrified now. 'I swear to you, I haven't. 'I...I did run into him one day, but we...we only had coffee.'

Nathan laughed. 'Damian doesn't just have coffee with women, Gemma. He doesn't *just* have anything. The man's well known for his perversions. One in particular.'

Gemma was horrified when she felt her robe being pushed up to her waist, exposing her bare buttocks.

'It seems you haven't progressed to that yet,' he muttered darkly. 'But you will. And he's welcome to you. You know, I sometimes wondered when you would change, when you would fall "out of love". I always knew you were far too young for true love. And far, far too beautiful. Extremely beautiful women rarely love. They're too bloody self-centered!'

'I do so love you,' she sobbed.

'Do you?' he jeered. 'Do you really? In that case you won't mind if I have a little of what you've been denying me these last couple of weeks.'

Gemma gasped when she felt him cruelly enclose her two wrists in one brutal grasp on the small of her back, when she heard the sound of his opening his trousers. He jammed a knee between her thighs, forcing them apart.

'Oh, God...no, don't...don't do this, Nathan!'

But it was already happening before she'd finished her plea. Disbelief brought a type of horrified submission, his harsh panting echoing in her ears. When he finally ejaculated and withdrew, she just lay there, stunned. Silent tears began to stream down her cheeks and she couldn't bear to turn over and look at him.

She vaguely heard him mutter something, heard him rearrange his clothing. Stiffly she closed her legs and buried her face in the quilt. When he laid a perversely gentle hand on her shoulder, she shuddered, and his hand retreated.

'I'm sorry,' he said in the most hollow-sounding voice. 'God…'

There was the sound of footsteps gradually receding and then there was an awful silence. It was ages before Gemma could bring herself to move, creeping back off the bed and running back to her bathroom where she turned on the shower and climbed in despite still having the robe on. The water gushed over her, soothing, cleaning water. But she couldn't seem to get herself clean. No matter what she did, she felt dirty and unclean and ugly.

In the end she had to get out of the shower before she turned red-raw. Fresh underwear and a soft flannel tracksuit went some way to making her feel better in a physical sense but she suspected that emotionally and mentally she was walking a razor's edge. If only she had a mother to confide in, someone who loved her unconditionally, who really cared what happened to her.

The image of Celeste's sympathetic face last night came to mind. While she was hardly a mother figure, she was a woman of the world. She would understand what had happened here today, would perhaps help her put it into perspective. One part of Gemma almost understood Nathan's reaction to finding her in Damian's bedroom. Another part was so outraged she couldn't bear to think about it. On top of everything else, she'd begun to doubt what she had heard with her own ears in their apartment the other day.

Nathan had acted the wronged husband with such vehemence! Could she be wrong? Had she misheard something? How could she have? What Lenore and Nathan had said to each other was crystal-clear, and so utterly, utterly damning. There could be no excuse. No explanation.

And yet…

Gemma forced herself to return to Damian's bedroom to check that she had left no evidence behind of what had transpired there. For a long moment, she stood in the doorway, staring at the indentation in the bed. Luckily, there was no stain, but still, she felt sick just looking at it. She would never forgive Nathan. Never!

She raced over and plumped up the mattress, straightening the quilt with sweeping strokes, her colour and emotions high.

How dared he speak so disparagingly of Damian? she thought agitatedly. Perverse, indeed! The man was a saint compared to Nathan. A misunderstood and genuinely kind man. The only pervert in this house today was her husband. No, *ex*-husband. She couldn't divorce him quickly enough. If she felt she could make the charge stick, she would have him charged with rape. Men should not be allowed to get away with treating their wives like that!

But Gemma was wise enough these days to know she had no hope of getting a conviction. It was a man's world all right, she thought bitterly.

As she turned to leave the room, Cora's crumpled note in the corner caught Gemma's eye. Swooping on it, she stuffed it in her pocket and hurriedly left the room. She couldn't stay here any longer, she decided. She would talk to Celeste when she got home tonight, ask her for a job at one of her interstate stores and make the move as soon as possible.

With this thought in mind, she went back into her room and packed, leaving nothing out but her night-wear and toiletries. She was coming back downstairs to put her soaked robe out on the clothes line when Cora came home.

Gemma schooled her face into a blank mask, surprising herself when she was able to conduct a normal conversation with Cora as the other woman went about preparing the evening meal. So it came as a considerable shock when Celeste and Damian came home, Gemma immediately found her iron composure crumbling. When Damian disappeared upstairs to change and Gemma found herself briefly alone with Celeste in the living-room, she promptly burst into tears.

CHAPTER ELEVEN

CELESTE was stunned.

Gemma had seemed happy enough when they'd arrived home, yet suddenly, here she was, in floods of tears. All she could think to do was to hold her. At first the action felt awkward, but when the girl dropped her head on to her shoulder with a shuddering sigh, the most amazing wave of maternal love swept through Celeste and she found herself embracing Gemma quite naturally and without embarrassment.

'You poor darling,' she murmured, holding her close and stroking her back. 'It's Nathan again, isn't it?'

'He...he was here today,' she choked out.

Celeste pulled back in shock. '*Here*? In this *house*?'

Gemma nodded, her misery obvious.

'But how? I mean...you must have let him in.'

She shook her head in vigorous denial. 'He said he came by boat. He...he just appeared upstairs. I nearly died.'

'Where was Cora?'

'Shopping.'

'Oh, yes, it's Wednesday. She always does the grocery shopping on Wednesday. So what did he do?'

Celeste was appalled when the girl looked stricken and then blushed. *Blushed*, mind you.

The awful reality came to Celeste in a rush and she almost vomited on the spot, gagging down her revulsion with great difficulty. 'He raped you, didn't he?' she said, her voice shaking.

The girl stared at her, making Celeste aware that she must

have been looking very peculiar. 'He…he didn't beat you, did he?'

The girl looked horrified. 'Oh, no! Nathan wouldn't do a thing like that!'

Celeste pulled herself together but she still couldn't quite get a grasp of the situation. Why was she defending this monster? He should be hung, drawn and quartered!

'He was upset because he found me in Damian's bathroom,' Gemma explained shakily. 'I'd just had a shower and had gone in there to find some aspirin. I…I only had a thin robe on. He thought Damian and I had been having an affair, even before I left him. He was…most upset.'

'Which gave him the right to *rape* you?' Celeste gaped in disbelief.

'Of course not,' Gemma countered. 'But I can see now that there were mitigating circumstances leading to the incident.'

'The incident,' Celeste repeated weakly. Dear God…

She stood there, incredibly shaken, till gradually her tottering emotions came together with a vengeance.

'He must pay,' she bit out. 'He can't be allowed to get away with this.'

Gemma shook her head. 'I thought that at first but my wish for revenge, or justice if you will, is beginning to weaken. No judge or jury would convict him anyway. Besides, there's nothing to be gained by locking Nathan up. He's not really a criminal. He's no danger to society or even to me. I'm sure he'll never do again what he did today. It's not as though he even hurt me physically. There's not a mark on me.'

'There is on your *mind*! Celeste protested.

'My mind is quite clear now,' Gemma insisted with such conviction that Celeste was staggered. 'It is Nathan's mind which will be affected by what transpired here today. I think it will live with him for a long, long time. He's not some brute or monster, Celeste. Underneath that cool façade he wears, he's a very vulnerable human being, but I think he's very mixed up when it comes to his concept of love. I don't think he knows what love is. I don't think he ever did...'

'My God, you still love him, don't you?' Celeste said.

Gemma's smile was so sad that Celeste almost burst into tears herself. 'I will always love him,' the girl admitted.

Celeste stood there, shaking her head and feeling hopelessly confused—till she remembered her own incredible weakness in still loving Byron. How could she sit in judgement when she was guilty of the same blind stupidity?

'I can't stay here any longer, Celeste,' Gemma said simply but firmly. 'I'm extremely grateful for all you and Damian have done for me but I think it best if I got right away, away from Nathan and Sydney. Much as I'm quite sure Nathan won't assault me again, he might make a nuisance of himself. I'm all packed,' she went on with a down-to-earth bravery Celeste could only admire. 'I'll call a taxi after dinner and go to the airport Hilton. I've already called them and booked a room. And I've booked a ticket on a flight back to Lightning Ridge tomorrow.'

'But you said you hated it there.'

'It's where my roots are. And there's something unfinished there that I have to finish to my satisfaction before I can even think of going on with my life.'

'What? What do you have to finish?'

'I'm sorry but I'd rather not discuss that. It's very private and quite painful to me. I think if I started talking about it tonight I'd really break down. So please, don't press me about it.'

'I wouldn't dream of it, my dear. I just wanted to help, that's all. You must know how very fond of you I've grown, even in this short time we've had you here.'

The girl's smile was so sweet that Celeste again struggled to contain her emotions. 'I've grown very fond of you too. And Damian's the best friend I've ever had. He had almost single-handedly restored my faith in the opposite sex.'

Celeste remained diplomatically silent on this score. If

there was one plus about Gemma moving out it would be that she wouldn't have to keep feeling uneasy about Damian's intentions. 'I—er—I think it might be wise to keep your immediate destination a secret from Damian though, don't you? The fewer people who know, the better.'

'What? Oh…all right. But what will I tell him?'

'Nothing. I'll tell him after you're gone that I've sent you away on a little holiday. A cruise, perhaps, so that he can't even *think* of following you.'

The girl looked startled, then slightly worried. 'You think he might try to follow me?'

'I think,' Celeste said drily, 'that Damian might want eventually to deepen your friendship into something else. You're a lovely-looking girl, Gemma, and not nearly as naïve as I originally thought. Don't disappoint me by underestimating your attractions, or Damian's weakness for beautiful women.'

Those big brown eyes widened before becoming steady and thoughtful. 'I won't, Celeste. Thank you for speaking plainly. I appreciate it.'

'I have a reputation for speaking plainly.' She smiled a wry, lop-sided smile. 'I have a reputation for a lot of things!'

'None of them deserved, I'm sure. You're a good person. I won't believe any of that horrible gossip about you any more.'

Celeste kept smiling even while her heart flipped over. 'A girl of rare judgement.'

'You can't fool someone from the bush. Or children. Or dogs. Dogs always know a good person when they see one.'

There was a rueful note in Gemma's voice that piqued Celeste's curiosity. But it didn't seem the right moment to question her. Maybe one day, they'd have the chance to have a real heart-to-heart. Celeste knew she would like that. Very much.

'What are you going to do after you settle whatever you have to settle in Lightning Ridge?'

'I'm not sure. That will depend on how things pan out.'

'Will you promise to keep in touch, let me know what you decide to do with your life when you do decide?'

'You really want me to?'

'Of course!'

Her smile was dazzling. 'Then I will be happy to.'

'Good. Now I must pop upstairs and get into my swimming costume. I've been very naughty this week, not keeping up my exercise routine. Care to join me in the pool?'

'I'll come with you and watch, if you like, but I don't feel much like swimming.'

'All right. Why don't you stay here and watch TV while I change and I'll pick you up on the way through?'

Celeste was hurrying along the hall and had one foot on the bottom step when the telephone rang. Instant intuition warned her to take the call.

'I'll get that, Cora!' she called out and bolted down the end of the hall to pick up the receiver. 'Yes?' she said rather breathlessly.

'Is that you, Celeste?'

Her breath caught. Byron. It was Byron, ringing her. She hadn't heard from him since he'd hung up the previous afternoon, and she'd had too much pride to contact him. But with the sound of his voice, her heart had stopped for a moment, only to pulse back to life with a galloping rate. Dear lord, this was definitely getting out of hand, but how was she to stop herself? Her feelings for Byron had never responded to logic or common sense or even pride. They had the impetus of a runaway roller-coaster and about as much stoppability.

'Yes,' she said, sounding like a schoolgirl who'd just been telephoned by the captain of the football team. 'It's me.'

'Would you be able to come over here this evening after dinner?' he asked abruptly.

'To Belleview?' she was shocked. She hadn't been invited into those hollowed walls since…

Any feelings of excitement or pleasurable anticipation

were immediately tainted by dark memories from the past. Belleview was the last place she would choose to be with Byron.

Still, if he wanted her to go there, if he wanted her as much as she was instantly wanting him, then she simply had to go.

'That's right,' he said curtly. 'And I want you to bring Gemma.'

These last words flicked a stinging rebuke across Celeste's silly heart. Her presumption that Byron had rung to organise a romantic rendezvous had been premature, and typically female. After witnessing Gemma's blind love for Nathan, she was extra-sensitive to her own stupidity regarding this man who had done nothing but hurt her.

'And why should I do that?' she lashed out. 'If you want to see Gemma, then come here.'

'That won't work, I'm afraid. I have no way of contacting Lenore back. And she's coming here.'

'What's Lenore got to do with this?' Celeste demanded, though she had a feeling she already knew. The bitch was going to deliver a whole lot of lies to whitewash Nathan.

'Lenore thinks she knows what Gemma overheard between Nathan and herself the other day. She said it would have sounded bad but is perfectly explainable.'

'Is that so?'

'She only just found out this afternoon what happened between Gemma and Nathan. Apparently, Nathan's totally shattered. Can't work. Can't do anything.'

'I'm so sorry for him,' Celeste's words dripped with an acid sarcasm.

Byron sighed. 'I do realise a man would never get your sympathy, Celeste, but we do have feelings too, you know.'

'Only below the waist.' It was on the tip of her tongue to tell Byron what that appalling boy he'd so nobly adopted had done to his wife this afternoon, but she bit her tongue. Gemma's amazing understanding of that bastard's vile actions meant she was sure to want to keep the 'incident' a secret. Celeste herself could not imagine such understanding, but she had to admire the girl for her stance and would not dream of betraying her trust simply to gain a petty victory over Byron.

'Well, are you coming or not?' Byron asked curtly. 'I would suggest you send Gemma over in a taxi but I don't have any faith in her turning up.'

'You honestly expect me to bring that poor child over to have a face-to-face meeting with a lying adulterous whore?'

'People in glass houses shouldn't throw stones, Celeste,' Byron bit out.

'I do not sleep with married men,' Celeste snapped before she realised what she'd said.

'You mean not any more, don't you?' came the inevitable remark, delivered in a bitterly cutting tone.

'That's right.'

'How very fortunate that I'm widowed, then. I wouldn't like to be the one to spoil your wonderful moral standards. But we digress,' he went on with crushing coolness. 'Will you bring Gemma here or not? I suppose I could always wait till Lenore arrives and bring her over there, but that's a lot of time wasted, isn't it?'

'When do you expect her?' Celeste asked sharply.

'Around nine.'

'I don't drive these days. I'll have to take a taxi.'

'Gemma can drive. And she knows the way. Do you have a car she can use?'

Celeste thought of Damian's Ferrari and dismissed it. And the Rolls was too big. 'We'll come in a taxi,' she decided aloud.

'Whatever you prefer. Just come. It's important.'

'Oh, I'll come, Byron. I wouldn't miss the chance of seeing you again.'

'There won't be any of that tonight, Celeste. And definitely not here.'

'We'll see, Byron. We'll see.'

Celeste hung up, aware that she was shaking. That man, she decided angrily, needed taking down a peg or two. He also needed a salutary lesson on who was running this affair. Did he honestly think he could control his desire for her any more than she could control hers for him? If she wanted Byron to make love to her tonight—at Belleview or any other damned place—then that was what was going to happen.

Muttering her frustrations to herself, she was about to flounce off back down the hall when the reason for Byron's call in the first place flooded back into her mind. Her groan was full of guilt and dismay. What was the matter with her? God, but she was a selfish bitch.

A severe mental lecture followed, after which she forced her thinking processes back on to the serious matter at hand: Gemma's happiness. What if Lenore could genuinely white-wash what Gemma had heard or seen that day? What then? Would she go back to that bastard? Celeste did not feel at all confident that she wouldn't.

But I suppose that's up to her, she realised with a resigned sigh. We all have to do what we have to do. And how can I sit in judgement? When it comes to matters of love, I've made the biggest mess of my life. I'm still making the biggest mess of my life!

Love, she thought savagely, has a lot to answer for!

Gathering herself, Celeste strode back down the hall and into the living-room, knowing in her heart that she wouldn't have much trouble convincing Gemma to go with her to Belleview. That girl was as much in love as *she* was. Which meant she was doomed to make stupid decisions and do stupid things!

CHAPTER TWELVE

'I REALLY will have to start driving again,' Celeste muttered under her breath when the taxi lurched into the adjacent lane and accelerated with hair-raising speed up the next hill, only to have to brake madly when the lights ahead changed to red.

It had begun to drizzle as they left Campbell Court and the roads were becoming dangerously slick. When the lights turned green and the driver screeched off, she leant forward and tapped him on the shoulder. 'We'd like to get where we're going in one piece, if you don't mind.'

'Sure thing, lady.' He grinned at her in the rear-view mirror, without changing his speed one iota.

Celeste sighed and sank backwards.

Gemma gave her a weak smile. 'We'll be there soon,' she whispered.

'And none too soon.'

In an attempt not to have her heart jump right into her mouth every few seconds, Celeste tipped her head back, closed her eyes and tried to think of other things.

Damian had not been too thrilled with her news that she was taking Gemma out to meet with Lenore after dinner. When she refused to explain further, he'd said some very rude things, then stormed out of the house and taken off in his Ferrari. Celeste felt a little badly about this—and so did Gemma—but at least it stopped any awkward questions over why Gemma had to take two suitcases with her just to see

Lenore. The conditional plan was for her to go on to the airport Hilton after Celeste had been dropped home.

'Did Byron give you any idea what Lenore's supposed explanation is?' Gemma asked as the taxi slowed to turn into Belleview.

Celeste opened her eyes and straightened. 'No. Sorry.' She was surprised at how agitated just seeing the house was making her. There were too many bad memories here. And yet it was a beautiful home. Elegant and graceful. Like one of those great Southern mansions.

Maybe it wasn't the house that was agitating her. Maybe it was the way she was dressed.

Celeste cringed a little when she imagined the expression on Byron's face when he saw her. But damn it all, she had to get something out of this meeting other than high blood-pressure and a sleepless night.

'That's Lenore's car,' Gemma informed her as the taxi pulled in behind a small sedan.

Celeste brushed aside Gemma's offer to pay for the taxi, relieved to be out of the potential coffin, even if she was no longer looking forward to the coming encounter with Byron.

'Put the luggage up there beside the door,' she ordered the driver, after which she gave him a generous note and happily dismissed him. The thought that she would have to take a taxi all that way home again in the rain did not sit well with her, but she decided to worry about that later. Her immediate concern was keeping her cool and her wits about her. Suddenly, she wasn't so sure what Byron's reaction to her appearance would be and she wanted to be ready for any outcome.

Both women mounted the steps that led up to the white-columned portico and the massive front doors. Celeste leant against the doorbell, throwing Gemma a reassuring look as they waited to be let in.

'You look fine,' she said when Gemma started nervously brushing down her clothes. The combination of a cream woolen trouser suit with a caramel silk shirt underneath was both sophisticated and flattering on her tall shapely figure, yet Celeste gained the impression that the girl did not feel confident in her clothes. Why was that? she wondered. The reflection Gemma saw when she looked in the mirror had to please her.

Her own reflection was something else. Celeste had poured herself into some scandalously tight jeans for the occasion. Add to these a black lace bodysuit, black ankle-height boots with stiletto heels, and a black leather battle jacket, and you had a dangerously provocative image. With her hair piled haphazardly on top of her head, gold gypsy hoops dangling from her lobes, she looked like a refugee from a bikers' meeting.

Or Cher gone blonde.

Byron answered the door, and his face betrayed not a single darned thing when those piercing blue eyes of his briefly raked over her. Gemma, however, received a warm greeting and a solicitous hand, while Celeste was totally ignored. When Byron drew Gemma inside she had no option but to trail after them or stay standing where she was like a shag on a rock.

'Aren't you coming in?' Byron was forced to ask when he went to shut the door.

'Not till you've said hello and invited me in.'

His smile sent a prickle running down her spine. My God, he hates me, she realised. Hates whatever power I have over him. Hates what I can make him feel.

Good, she thought savagely, and waited.

'Hello, Celeste,' he said with icy politeness. 'Do come in.'

By this time Gemma was looking perturbed behind Byron. Celeste decided not to make a scene, brushing past Byron to walk into the spider's parlour. But *she* would remain the spider, she decided fiercely. And *he* would stay the fly.

'Can I take your coat?' he asked with false gallantry.

'I'll keep it on, thanks,' she countered. 'It's chilly in here. Must be all the marble. Is Ava home? I'd like to see this miraculous transformation you told me about.'

'What transformation?' Gemma asked, frowning.

'Ava's lost a lot of weight lately,' Byron explained. 'Smartened herself up no end. Sorry, Celeste, but she's not home. She's out with her fiancé.'

'*Fiancé*!' Gemma gasped. 'Ava's *engaged*?'

'She is indeed. To a charming Italian man by the name of Vince Morelli.'

'Good heavens, when did all this happen?'

'Just this past weekend.'

Gemma's smile faded suddenly. 'A lot of things happened this past weekend...'

'Apparently,' Byron muttered. 'Which is why I asked Celeste to bring you here. We're about to sort one of them out. Lenore's waiting for us in the family-room. Shall we?' He waved the two women on ahead. When Gemma looked reluctant to move, Celeste took her elbow and guided her down the corridor past the grandfather clock.

Lenore was sitting on one of the huge leather sofas that dominated the large casually furnished room, looking so intimidatingly chic in black silk culottes and a crisp white blouse, her glorious red hair twisted into an elegant French roll, that Celeste had a sudden insight into Gemma's unexpected attack of insecurity outside the front door.

Nathan's first wife made her feel inadequate and inferior. It was the old *Rebecca* syndrome, understandable given the gap in their ages, not to mention the enormous gap in their relative life experiences. What a pity Gemma didn't understand that it was these very differences that had probably attracted Nathan to her in the first place.

'Hello, Lenore,' Gemma said stiffly.

Celeste watched Lenore like a hawk. There was no doubting she was giving a marvellous performance as the halting and embarrassed 'other woman' as she stood up, went to come forward, then stayed where she was.

'This is even worse than I thought it would be,' she said with just the right amount of dismay. 'I mean…I do see that I might have been insensitive to your feelings, Gemma, taking far too much of Nathan's time. But you have to believe me when I say there has been nothing of a sexual nature between us since our divorce.'

'That's a lie,' Gemma said in a low, shaking voice. 'Even if I somehow made a mistake on Sunday—though I don't see how—I saw you and Nathan kissing one night in this very house!'

Was that sincere astonishment on the woman's face? Celeste wondered. Or more brilliant acting!

'It was in the billiard-room,' Gemma added bitingly. 'The very first night I came to stay.'

Lenore seemed to recall something but her glance Gemma's way was full of pity. 'Dear girl, that was nothing.'

'Don't patronise me,' Gemma lashed out. 'The kiss I saw was not *nothing*!'

Lenore had the good grace to blush. 'Maybe not nothing,' she admitted unhappily, 'but it was nothing for you to worry about.'

'I hate to interupt,' Byron said carefully. 'But a kiss all those months ago is not what Lenore has graciously come here to explain. Please, Gemma, let's try to keep some perspective in all this. At that time, you hardly knew Nathan. Or am I wrong about that?' he queried softly.

Celeste blinked when Gemma sliced an icy look Byron's way. This girl could really take care of herself! For some unaccountable reason, she felt a fierce pride. It must be a sisterhood empathy, she reasoned after a momentary confusion. But truly, this girl kept evoking feelings in her that she'd never felt before.

'There was nothing between Nathan and myself when I came to live here,' she returned firmly.

'And there was nothing between Nathan and myself last weekend,' Lenore insisted.

'How can you possibly say that?' Gemma attacked, her face flushing with anger and outrage. 'I heard you myself and I could not misinterpret what I heard.'

'What exactly did you hear?' Lenore asked, looking not at all like a guilty party, merely a concerned one.

Celeste was totally perplexed.

Gemma was staring at Lenore as well. 'You want me to repeat it in front of others?'

'Word for word.'

'Word for word!'

'Yes.'

'Oh…I…I'm not sure I can remember it all word for word.'

'*Try*. What was the first thing you heard? Who was speaking?'

'It…it was Nathan. He said…he said… "So what if it was just sex between us last night? When has it ever been anything else?" And you said… "When has it ever been anything else but sex for you with any woman?" And then Nathan laughed.'

'What a bastard,' Celeste muttered.

'Shut up,' Byron hissed from where he'd moved to be standing right behind her shoulder.

'What next?' Lenore probed mercilessly and Gemma winced.

Celeste couldn't stand the pain in those lovely brown eyes any longer. 'For pity's sake, Byron,' she whispered, throwing him a desperate look.

'Patience,' he exhorted under his breath.

Gemma was clearly struggling to remember the exact words. 'I think you then said something about having been in love with him when you got pregnant with Kirsty…'

'Would the words have been… "You think I didn't love

you that night all those years ago, when we made a baby together? You think that was only sex for me?"'

Gemma was taken aback. 'Yes, that's it. That's it exactly! Nathan replied he knew it was only sex and you called him a bastard.'

With a shuddering sigh, Lenore bent and picked up a large plastic folder from the coffee-table in front of her. Opening it, she flipped over some of the printed pages within, then brought it over to show Gemma, pointing to a spot at the beginning of one of the pages. 'Read from here,' she instructed.

Celeste watched as all the blood drained from Gemma's face. When she finally did look up, her cheeks were ashen and there were tears in her eyes. 'It's all from Nathan's play,' she choked out. 'Everything I heard was words from Nathan's play...'

'It's a scene I've been having trouble with,' Lenore explained. 'Nathan kept saying I wasn't putting enough emotion into it. He...he was helping me with it on Sunday, playing the part of my leading man.'

'Oh, God,' Gemma groaned, swaying on her feet.

Celeste rushed forward and grabbed her, making her sit down. 'Some brandy, Byron,' she ordered. 'Or some whisky. *Quickly*!'

'Won't be a sec,' he bit out, and hurried from the room.

'Oh, Celeste,' Gemma cried brokenly. 'What have I done?'

'Surely things can be fixed up between you and Nathan now that you know the truth,' Lenore suggested, in total ignorance of what had transpired that afternoon.

Celeste shook her head. 'You don't understand.'

'I'll speak to Nathan myself,' Lenore offered.

Byron returned to give Celeste a glass with a hefty slug of brandy in it which she proceeded to force a distraught Gemma to drink.

'I think, Lenore,' Byron said, 'that it's best if *I* speak to Nathan. Do you know where he is tonight?'

'Not really. We were to have a full dress rehearsal for the play today but he didn't turn up. We went ahead anyway and he did make an appearance towards the end of it in the most deplorable condition. I managed to get out of him that Gemma had left him and she thought we'd been having an affair. He mumbled something about her coming home and finding us together last Sunday and jumping to the wrong conclusion. He said he was going to get blind drunk and left. It was only then that it suddenly hit me what might have happened and I rang you. I suppose he might be home by now at a pinch. You could try there.'

'I'll ring straight away. God, what a mess! You might as well go home, Lenore. There's nothing more you can do here.'

'But I feel so *awful*!' she wailed.

'Just go home,' Celeste bit out, thinking Gemma could only improve with her absence, no matter how innocent she was.

'Wait!' Gemma said and got shakily to her feet. She walked up to Lenore and embraced her. 'I'm sorry I thought all those dreadful things about you,' she cried. 'You've always been sweet to me and I've returned your kindnesses with jealousy and suspicion. I'm so sorry. None of this is your fault. I've been a fool.'

'Oh, Gemma, love,' Lenore said with a sad sigh. 'You've never been a fool. And what happened was not your fault. Any woman would have thought the same thing. And I haven't helped, running to Nathan with my problems all the time. But he loves you, Gemma. For all his faults, he really loves you. Don't throw him away. If you do, you'll destroy him.'

'I don't want to throw him away,' she said with a strangled sob. 'But I don't think he wants me back.'

'Then fight for him,' Lenore urged. 'You love him, don't you?'

'Yes.'

'It's a precious thing, love. It doesn't come your way too often.'

Celeste found her eyes drifting to Byron's but the gaze he returned was so hard that she flinched. He'll never believe how much I love him, she realised wretchedly. He'll never believe how much he's lost…

'I'll go now,' Lenore said, turning to Byron. 'Maybe if you talk to him, Byron. He obviously needs someone to talk to him. To be honest, I'm frightened what he might do.'

He's already done it,' Celeste thought bitterly.

'I will, Lenore,' Byron reassured her. 'Don't worry. Nathan's a reasonable man.'

Celeste only just stopped herself from laughing.

'Here,' Byron said, picking up the script from where it had fallen from Gemma's limp fingers to the floor. 'Take this with you. I think we've seen enough.'

'I don't know how I'm ever going to do that scene now,' Lenore said with a shudder.

'You're an actress, Lenore,' Byron told her with his usual lack of sensitivity. 'Act!'

Celeste returned Gemma to the sofa while Byron shepherded Lenore from Belleview. By the time he returned, Gemma had been persuaded to drink all the brandy and she was sitting there like a zombie.

'I didn't get any answer from Nathan's number,' Byron told them both. 'If he's been drinking he might be out to it. Or maybe he's not at home at all.' He threw Gemma a worried look. 'I think she'd better stay here for the night, Celeste. I'm sure I could find her something to sleep in.'

'She has her luggage with her,' Celeste told him, aware that Gemma seemed incapable of talking. She was almost catatonic, sitting there. 'She was going to go to the airport

Hilton tonight and catch a flight back to Lightning Ridge tomorrow.'

'But why? I didn't think she liked it there.'

'She didn't. It was something about unfinished business. Anyway, you go and get the suitcases. They're on the front porch. And then we'll take her upstairs and put her to bed.'

Amazingly, Gemma seemed to go to sleep as soon as her head hit the pillow. Celeste still sat with her for a while, then tucked her in, turned off the bedside lamp and was creeping out when she saw Byron still standing in the doorway, watching her. There was the most peculiar expression on his face which was something akin to pain.

'What?' she whispered. 'What is it?'

He shook his head, abruptly ushering her from the room and closing the door.

'Did you get on to Nathan?' she asked.

'No. He doesn't seem to be home. But I contacted the Hilton and cancelled Gemma's room as well as her flight to Lightning Ridge. She's not going anywhere tomorrow and that's final. She has things to patch up here first.'

'Mmm,' was all Celeste said.

'You don't think she can patch it up with Nathan?'

'We'll see,' she said non-committally.

Byron gave her a narrow-eyed look. 'What do you know that I don't know?'

'Have you got all night?'

'Very funny.'

'I'm tired, Byron,' she said and began striding away from him down the hall. 'I'm going to call a taxi and go home.'

'You don't look tired,' he called after her. 'You look fantastic.'

Celeste ground to a halt, whirling to stare at him standing there, his handsome face unbelievably arrogant as he began blatantly to look her over. Not a second look all night and now this...this blisteringly sexual appraisal.

'You're sex on two legs, Celeste,' he said in a desire-thickened voice, 'and you know it.'

She folded her arms and lifted her chin, but behind her outward cool was a madly beating heart and pounding blood vessels. 'Do you honestly think you can treat me as you treated me when I arrived, then think a couple of tossed-off compliments will get you back in my good books?'

'I'm not interested in being in your good books,' he said with chilling honesty. 'My interests lie elsewhere...'

'No kidding. But if our interests aren't mutual, Byron, then I'm afraid it's a no go.'

'But our interests *are* mutual, Celeste,' he drawled, and started walking slowly towards her. 'Why else would you have come here tonight dressed as you are if you didn't want me to look at you, if you didn't want me to want you, if you didn't want me to do this?'

Celeste was stunned when his hands shot out to drag her into his arms, taking her mouth in a savage kiss while he shoved her back against the wall so hard that all the breath was knocked out of her lungs. He must have crushed his hands in the process but he didn't seem to notice, all his concentration on what he was doing inside her lips.

One of his legs pushed between hers and before she knew what she was doing she had lifted her right leg and was sliding the inside of her thigh up and down on his. He groaned into her mouth, and almost immediately his hands were on the waistband of her jeans and the snap fastener gave way.

But he didn't proceed any further in that direction. Instead, his hands crept up under her leather jacket to mould over her lace-encased breasts, teasing her braless nipples into rock-hard pebbles till they felt they had to be bursting through the already tightly stretched material. He didn't stop kissing at any point and Celeste could feel her limbs gradually going to jelly. Her leg dropped limply back to the ground and she would have slid down the wall to the floor if he hadn't been holding her upright.

'Good lord!' a female voice gasped from somewhere.

Byron wrenched away, Celeste sagging downwards before propping her back against the wall and levering herself into a standing position. Her wide, glazed eyes encountered a strange woman standing there, gaping at them both. It was a few seconds before she recognised Ava. Once she did, Celeste's gaze jerked to Byron, who was raking his hair back from his flushed face in an agitated fashion and trying to calm his ragged breathing.

'You might as well know, Ava,' he said at last. 'Celeste and I have started seeing each other.'

'So I gathered,' his sister returned drily, astonishing Celeste with her quick composure, not to mention her appearance. Where had the overweight, awkward, timid Ava of old gone to? In her place stood an unbelievably attractive, shapely, confident woman who was looking at them both with a sardonically arched eyebrow.

'You don't have to answer to me for what you do in your private life, Byron,' she went on, her voice and face quite calm now. 'I was merely surprised, that's all. But it's nice to see that the old feud between the Campbells and the Whitmores has come to an—er—amicable…ending. Hello, Celeste.' She nodded politely her way. 'Nice to see you're looking so well. So, Byron, what do you think of the new carpet?'

'New carpet?'

'You didn't even notice it, did you?' his sister mocked, and pointed to the long strip of grey-blue carpet that ran along the middle of the hall. 'It's up the stairs as well. I *did* tell you about it.'

'I'm sure you did. It's—er—very nice.'

'I'm thinking of putting it along the downstairs corridor and through my studio as well. I'm tired of slippery floors.' Ava smothered a yawn, smiling an apology at Celeste. 'Do excuse me. I'm a little weary. I'm going to bed. Will I be expecting an extra for breakfast, Byron?'

Byron, who was not one to be caught at a disadvantage for long, smiled wryly at this unveiled sarcasm from his sister and wickedly said yes.

When Ava looked taken aback,' he added drily, 'Gemma's staying with us for a while. She's asleep in the same room she used to have.'

Ava was frowning now. 'You mean she's left Nathan for good, then?'

'Maybe. Maybe not. We'll talk about the situation in the morning. Go to bed, Ava.'

There was the tone of an order in these last words which Celeste could see Ava resented. Clearly, Byron wasn't ruling the roost around Belleview as he used to.

How times they were a-changing!

Ava shrugged, however, said goodnight and did as she was told. *Not*, Celeste believed, because Byron had ordered her to, but because she wanted to, anyway.

The interruption had given Celeste invaluable time to get herself together and see the situation as Ava had first seen it. Shocking. Disgusting. And deplorable. They'd been acting like two animals, uncaring of anything but their own base needs. Celeste's supposed love for Byron was no excuse for allowing him to use her like that. The least she deserved was a little respect.

Snapping her jeans up again, she surveyed Byron's flushed face with a bitter resentment. It was time this man didn't get his own way for once.

Spinning on the heels of her black boots, she started to march down the hall, quickly reaching the top of the wide marble staircase.

'And where the hell do you think you're going?' Byron called after her.

'Home, Byron. Like I told you.' She kept on going.

'But you can't!'

Her laughter rippled back up the stairwell. 'Just try and stop me.'

'Maybe I could at that,' he snarled, catching up with her as she reached the bottom of the stairs. When she continued across the foyer towards the telephone, he reached out and grabbed her arm.

This time, Celeste had no patience left with him. She grabbed back, flipping him over on to his back on to the marble floor, her boot solidly in the middle of his chest. Though not seriously hurt, he *was* winded. And undeniably shocked.

'Don't presume to touch me again, Byron,' she warned darkly. 'Not unless you're invited. Now I'm going to call a taxi. Stop me at your own peril.'

He didn't try to stop her, and she left five minutes later.

CHAPTER THIRTEEN

'WHAT a pickle!' Ava said over breakfast. 'But surely, Byron, once you explain it all to Nathan, he'll understand why Gemma did what she did.'

'Gemma doesn't seem to think so.'

Ava turned puzzled eyes towards Gemma, who had woken this morning with ambivalent feelings. She wanted very much to do what Lenore had urged her to do—fight tooth and nail to put her marriage right, irrespective of the events of yesterday. But there remained in her heart the feeling that Nathan would never believe she hadn't slept with Damian. He didn't trust her. He didn't trust women in general. His mother had left him with this crippling legacy and Gemma wasn't sure if the love he did hold for her was strong enough to balance the scales in her favour.

'He thinks I went from his bed to Damian Campbell's,' she said with a grim honesty. 'He couldn't conceive that Damian might just want to be my friend.'

'Well, you can't blame him for that, surely,' Byron muttered. 'The man's reputation is hardly lily-white.'

Gemma settled her steeliest gaze upon her father-in-law. 'I don't set much store by people's so-called reputations any more. Till I met Celeste, all I'd heard about her were bad things, but she's not like that at all! She's a warm, wonderful woman and I won't hear a word against her. I won't hear a word against Damian, either. He might not be a saint but he's been very good to me and he's never made a pass or done a single thing to offend me.'

Byron scowled at this while Ava leant over to pat her gently on the wrist. 'It's very creditable of you to defend your new-found friends, Gemma. I, for one, agree with you that one can't always believe what is said about others, but please…understand our concern as well. There's never been any love lost between the Campbells and the Whitmores. And you're a Whitmore. Common sense demands one has to view with suspicion whenever a Campbell makes friendly overtures towards a Whitmore, wouldn't you say, Byron?'

Gemma blinked at the savage look Byron sent his sister across the breakfast table. 'We all have to run our own races in the end, Ava. You, of all people, should appreciate that.'

Ava's returning smile was so self-assured that Gemma was stunned. The word 'transformation' was not an exaggeration when applied to Ava. She'd fairly blossomed in every way, not just her looks. There was a confidence about her person and even her movements that was a pleasure to see. Gemma had always liked her but had also always pitied her. No one was ever going to feel pity for this composed, assertive, attractive woman ever again.

'So what are you going to do, Gemma?' Ava asked.

Byron jumped in before Gemma could verbalise a plan. 'If she's in agreement, I'd like to drive her over to see Nathan first thing this morning. Maybe I could have a word with him first, pave the way, so to speak. Nathan's likely to still feel highly emotional, and maybe irrational, about the situation.'

Gemma closed her eyes. God, if Byron did that, Nathan might tell him what happened yesterday. She didn't want anyone else to know about it. OK, so Celeste knew, but she'd sworn her to secrecy. There was nothing to be gained by blackening Nathan's name to his family. Clearly he hadn't been himself yesterday. Something had snapped in him and he hadn't been able to see reason. Gemma could see that now.

'Is that what *you* want, Gemma?' Ava asked kindly, perhaps interpreting her shut eyes as an unwillingness to go along with Byron.

She lifted damp lashes to give Ava a small half-smile. 'Yes. The sooner I talk to him, the better. Only...I don't want you to talk to him first, Byron. Please. I feel this is something private and personal between Nathan and myself. I know you all want to help but I feel we have to work out our problems ourselves. *I* must talk to Nathan, and he must be made to talk to me. *Really* talk, probably for the first time in his life.'

Ava nodded wisely. 'You're quite right. That's always been Nathan's problem. He keeps things to himself too much. He doesn't know how to open up to people.'

'I hate to admit it,' Byron said with a weary sigh, 'but I think you could be right. Even when he was a young lad, he didn't say much. He let me do all the talking. I used to think he was listening, that he was really taking in the advice I was giving him, but how do I know if he ever did? Maybe I failed him. Maybe he wasn't even the essentially good boy I thought he was... Maybe he's not turned out as well as I'd hoped.'

Gemma suddenly remembered Damian's earlier claim that Nathan had had a sexual liaison with Byron's wife shortly after he came to live with them. How odd, she thought, that now, even after what Nathan had done, her faith in her husband's moral fibre was stronger than ever. Perverse as it might seem, she was sure that there had never been anything between Irene and Nathan. Not ever. Nathan might be capable of a lot of things, but not that kind of treachery.

'Nathan is not easy to understand, Byron,' she told her father-in-law, 'but in his heart he is a good man. You should feel pride in what you've achieved with him. He would surely have been lost if you hadn't taken him in and I know he loves you dearly. He would hate for you ever to think him unworthy as his son, which is another reason why I don't want you to confront him this morning. He might feel belittled somehow in your eyes. That would never do. No, I can't allow that...'

Byron and Ava were both staring at her as though they couldn't believe what they were hearing. Her smile was softly wry, tears pricking her eyes. 'My love is not blind any more,' she murmured, 'and it's stronger for not being so. Nathan is a man worth fighting for. I won't let misunderstandings come between us, and I won't let his past come between us.'

'He's a lucky man,' Byron muttered. 'It must be really something to have a woman love you like that.'

A hushed silence fell on the table. Ava eventually broke it by abruptly scraping back her chair. 'Anyone for more coffee?'

'I'M GOING TO WAIT outside here,' Byron stated firmly as he slid his Jaguar into the kerb. 'I don't care how long you take. I'll just sit here and read the newspaper till you come back down.'

'I might be ages!' Gemma protested. 'You should go on to your office.'

'And what if things don't work out?'

'But they will,' she insisted, refusing to think of any other outcome.

'I'll wait,' he repeated stubbornly.

'Oh, all right.' She dragged in a steadying breath, letting it out slowly. 'Are you sure Nathan will still be there? I mean...how do you know that after your call this morning he hasn't done a flit? He might not want to see me.'

'He doesn't know it's you who's coming to see him.'

Gemma's head whipped round to stare at him.

'I thought it best,' Byron said ruefully.

Gemma sighed. 'Yes, it probably was.' Still, she was not fond of deception. Suddenly, she was reluctant to make a move to get out, her stomach churning. 'How…how do I look?' she asked nervously.

She'd taken a lot of trouble with her make-up and clothes, choosing a dark green slimline dress which was one of Nathan's favourites. It had a wide self-covered belt that pulled her tiny waist in even further, emphasising her hour-glass figure. A gold chain necklace filled the deep V crossover bodice and gold drop earrings dangled from her ears. Red Door perfume wafted tantalisingly up from where she'd sprayed it between her breasts.

It did cross her mind that it would seem crazy to anyone else that she was making herself physically attractive for the same man who'd virtually raped her the day before. But understanding and love made her see Nathan's actions as an expression of extreme pain, not violence, a reaction to an imagined betrayal that he could not cope with. He had struck out at her in a horrible way, admittedly, and she had been devastated at the time, but there was no future in keeping those feelings of anger and vengeance going. Her future, she felt sure, lay with understanding her husband, and unconditionally loving him.

'I haven't overdone things, have I?'

'You look absolutely delicious,' Byron complimented with such a look Gemma was taken aback for a moment. She'd never thought of her father-in-law as a member of the opposite sex before. He was simply Nathan's adopted father. The formidable head of Whitmore's. An invincible, almost machine-like individual.

Now her woman's eyes took in his strongly handsome face, his penetrating blue eyes, his highly sensual mouth. He might be fifty years old but he didn't look it. In fact, he looked fit enough to go quite a few rounds, either in the ring or in bed.

She almost blushed under her forthright train of thought, but she frowned instead, her mind sliding back to how Celeste had dressed for her meeting with Byron last night. It had struck her as peculiar at the time—Celeste's provocative clothing quite at odds with the occasion. Was the answer sitting behind the wheel in this very car? Who knew? Maybe Byron was the answer to a lot of things Celeste did…

Gemma gave herself a mental shrug. What did Byron and Celeste have to do with what she was about to do?

Nothing!

'I suppose I can't put this off any longer,' she muttered, and opened the passenger door.

'Good luck.'

'Thanks. I think I'm going to need it.'

'Don't forget I'm waiting down here.'

'I won't,' she said and climbed out, striding purposefully over to the building.

Her outward decisiveness was a complete sham, something that struck her forcibly once she found herself in front of the door to their apartment. Should she knock, or let herself in with her own keys? If she knocked and Nathan slammed the door in her face, what could she do then?

Gemma inserted her key with shaking hands,, let herself in then shut the door behind her. Immediately, Nathan appeared outside the door of his study, glaring down the corridor at her. She simply stood there and stared back at him.

Dear God, but he looked appalling. Unshaven. Bloodshot eyes. His hair a mess. Wearing navy blue pyjama bottoms and nothing else.

He didn't say a word as he looked at her. Not a word.

But his eyes were dead.

'What are you doing here?' he asked at last in a voice so unlike his she was stunned. There was no anger. No emotion. No nothing.

'Byron brought me. He…he's waiting in the car for me downstairs,' Gemma explained shakily. 'Look, I'm sorry he lied to you but he was worried you might not stay if he said it was me who wanted to talk to you.'

'He'd be right. Why in God's name you would want to

talk to me at all mystifies me,' he said in that horrible, hollow-sounding voice. 'But it won't make any difference. It's over. We're over.'

When he went to turn away, Gemma blurted out, 'I saw Lenore last night. She explained to me that what I overheard you and Lenore saying to each other last Sunday was actually a section of your play.'

Nathan froze. He didn't turn round, but he waited for her to continue.

'She showed me the actual script,' Gemma went on hurriedly. 'It was exactly what I overheard, word for word. She said it's a scene she'd been having trouble with and you were helping her with it. It's where the leading man tells his leading lady that it was only sex between them the night before. You must know the scene I'm talking about...'

'Yes,' he agreed flatly. 'I know the one.'

'Then you must be able to see why I jumped to the wrong conclusion,' she implored. 'That was the only reason I left, I swear to you. And I didn't run straight to Damian. I didn't even contact him till the next day when I couldn't think where to go and what to do. I...I didn't want to go back to Belleview and I couldn't think of anyone else I knew. Please believe me when I tell you we have not been having an affair, not before I left you or after. I swear to you, Nathan. I'm not lying about this.'

He turned slowly to face her, his eyes totally devoid of expression. 'And you think that would make me feel better? If I allow myself to believe you, my darling Gemma, then I would have no option but to go and blow my brains out. And I'm not going to do that over any woman,' he muttered and disappeared into his study.

Gemma raced after him, arriving in the doorway in time to see him slump down into the armchair in the far corner and lift a half-empty bottle of vodka to his lips. He drank long and hard, eyeing her quite fiercely now over the bottle.

'What happened to all those people you work with?' he

challenged when he jerked the bottle away. 'Why couldn't you have gone to one of them?'

She shrugged helplessly. 'I don't know. I didn't think of them.'

'Instead, you thought of Damian Campbell, the last man on earth any husband would want his wife near.'

Gemma fell silent. She was not going to argue with Nathan on this score, but neither was she going to agree with him.

'It's all immaterial anyway,' he muttered darkly, then took another swallow from the bottle. 'As I said before, we're finished. You can have your divorce, and whatever else you want. You'll get no arguments from me.'

'But I don't want a divorce!' she protested wretchedly.

'Don't be so bloody ridiculous,' he scorned. 'No woman would stay married to a man who did what I did yesterday. I dare say you couldn't wait to tell everyone what a disgusting creature you married.'

Gemma flinched, then decided to lie. 'I've told no one, Nathan,' she said huskily. 'No one.'

His eyes narrowed till they were cold slits of steel. 'Byron doesn't know?'

'No.'

He actually shuddered, his obvious distress and self-disgust tearing Gemma's heart out. She rushed forward, dropping to her knees beside his chair, grabbing his free hand. 'Let's forget what happened yesterday, Nathan. You were upset. You didn't know what you were doing. But you do love me. I *know* you love me. I refuse to let one unfortunate incident spoil what we could still have together. I love you and I don't want any other man but you.'

He was staring at her as though she was mad, his eyes wide with disbelief and yes...*revulsion*. He reefed his hand out of hers and pushed her away as he hauled himself to his feet. Lurching across the room, he reached his desk, where he whirled to face her once more. 'What kind of woman are you? How can you dismiss what I did to you so easily? *I* can't. I can't dismiss it any more that I can dismiss in whose bedroom I found you.'

Gemma groaned and shook her head as she got slowly to her feet. 'You're wrong about that, Nathan. So wrong. And you were wrong to do what you did. But love can forgive, can't it?'

'That depends on what it has to forgive.'

Gemma wasn't sure now if he was referring to her forgiving him, or him forgiving her.

'Please, Nathan, let's just forgive each other *everything*! We both did things we regret. It was poor judgement for me to go to Damian for help, but it was also poor judgement for you to have so much to do with Lenore. Can't we just learn from our mistakes and go forward? We love each other. With a little more trust I think we can still have a good marriage.'

'Trust… Now that's a commodity I think will be in short supply between us from now on, my dear. As for our loving each other, you never really loved me. Not your fault, of course. You were very young and I rushed you into marriage before you could differentiate between lust and love. I'm doing you a favour by letting you go.'

'And what if I don't *want* to be let go?'

He threw her an impatient scowling look. 'Then I'll have to *make* you go.' Striding behind the desk, he reefed opened a drawer and extracted a large brown envelope. 'Remember this?' he asked, waving it at her. 'You asked me what it was one day and I told you it contained business documents. It doesn't. It's a report from the private detective I hired to find your mother.'

Gemma could feel the blood drain from her face. Luckily she was standing next to a chair. Her fingers felt for the armrest and she leant against it. 'What are you trying to say, Nathan?' she said in a raw whisper.

'I'm saying I lied to you. He found your mother. *I* made the decision to keep her identity from you.'

'But…but *why*, for pity's sake?' she cried, shattered by this news. He'd known what finding her mother meant to her. How could he have done this? This was far worse than what he did yesterday. Far, far worse!

'What does it matter what my reasons were now? I did it. Here…' He tossed the envelope on to the edge of the desk. 'Read it. As fate would have it, I doubt the news will come as a big shock to you as it did to me.'

Gemma stared at the envelope across the room as though it were a deadly snake. Why would the identity of her mother come as a shock? Was she a form of low-life? A prostitute, perhaps? Her father had always said she was a slut. It was the only explanation for why Nathan would keep this a secret…

'Do excuse me,' Nathan tossed off almost indifferently. 'Now that I've settled the matter of our divorce, I'm going to go and clean myself up. I will presume that once you've read that you'll want to be on your way as soon as possible.'

Gemma was left feeling sick and alone with his abrupt departure. Her mind was having difficulty in taking it all in. She'd wanted to find her mother for so long, and her identity was inside that envelope. All she had to do was look.

Approaching the desk with a madly beating heart, she almost dropped the thing when she first went to pick it up. With it clutched in her hands, she made her way round behind the desk where she slumped gratefully into the chair.

The flap wasn't sealed and it flipped out easily. Gemma drew the dreaded sheets of paper out of their hiding place, her eyes glazed as they skimmed over the printed report, searching for the name.

It jumped out at her as though it were in neon lights, making Gemma catch her breath with shock.

Oh, my God, I don't believe it, came her shaken thoughts. I simply don't believe it! It…it's impossible. It doesn't make sense. She can't be my mother. She simply can't be!

CHAPTER FOURTEEN

GEMMA pulled open the passenger door of Byron's Jaguar and climbed in.

'Good God, Gemma!' he exclaimed. 'You're as white as a sheet. What happened? Don't tell me he wouldn't listen to you. And what's that you've got?' he added, staring at the envelope clutched in her hands.

'Nothing. It…it's personal,' she said, still shaken by the contents.

Byron frowned down at the envelope for a moment, then shrugged. 'Well, what about Nathan? Did you talk to him?'

'Nathan?' Gemma's heart hardened against her husband in a way she never thought it would. 'Oh, yes, I talked to him, as much as one ever talks to Nathan. He wants a divorce, and, as far as I'm concerned, he can have it.'

'*What*? But didn't you explain about the mix-up over the play?'

'Yes, but he still doesn't believe me about Damian. Nathan doesn't believe I love him or that I've ever really loved him. Then there are other things as well…'

'What other things?'

'Private things, Byron. Things I can't tell you.'

His sigh was full of frustration. 'Is there any point *my* talking to him?'

'Certainly not today. Maybe not ever. He seemed quite determined to have done with our marriage.' So determined, Gemma realised bitterly, that he had made sure she found out the one thing she *could* not forgive.

All Byron could do was wearily shake his head and start the car. 'Where would you like me to take you? Back to Belleview?'

'No. I…I would appreciate it if you could drop me off outside Campbell's head office.'

Byron's head snapped round, his expression grim. 'I don't care how stubborn or stupid Nathan has been, Gemma, do not go running to Damian Campbell again, I beg of you. Come…let me take you home to Ava. A nice long chat with a sympathetic lady is what you need.'

'I don't want to go to Campbell's to see Damian,' she said shakily. 'I need to see Celeste.'

'*Celeste*?'

'Yes.' Gemma had no intention of offering Byron an explanation at this traumatic juncture and he had enough intelligence to quickly size up her fragile yet determined mood.

'All right. But promise you'll take a taxi home to Belleview when you're finished there.'

'I promise.'

It was only a short drive from Elizabeth Bay into the city and within no time Gemma was presenting herself at Reception at Campbell's, where she stood waiting while the receptionist took a couple of incoming calls. This didn't help her underlying agitation, or her growing sense of awe at the amazing set of circumstances that had led to this moment.

'May I help you?' the receptionist asked politely once she finished answering the telephone.

'I need to see Miss Campbell. I don't have an appointment but if you tell her it's Gemma Whitmore and it's very important, I'm sure she'll see me.'

The receptionist spoke briefly to someone on the telephone after which she looked up and flashed Gemma a bright smile. 'Miss Campbell will see you immediately. It's the last door down that corridor. Go straight on in and her secretary will take you to her.'

CELESTE WAS besieged with uncharacteristic butterflies from the moment her secretary came through with the message from Gemma. She waited impatiently for her to be shown in, wondering what could be so urgent. The sudden thought that Gemma might have gone to see Nathan and been assaulted again brought with it a sickening surge which sent her leaping to her feet the moment the door opened. Worried eyes searched the girl's face as she walked in and closed the door behind her. While she did not look overly distraught, an underlying agitation was evident in her pale face and slightly hesitant movements.

'What is it?' Celeste asked, thoroughly agitated herself now. 'What's happened?'

When Gemma couldn't seem to find her voice, simply standing there with unexpected tears filling her eyes, Celeste almost panicked. Her first instinct was to race around the desk and go to her, but something in Gemma's face kept her rooted to the spot.

'What *is* it?' she asked again, a nervously fluttering hand coming up to her throat. She watched, her nerves stretching, as the girl visibly battled for composure.

'I...I'm not sure how you're going to take this news,' Gemma said haltingly.

'What news?'

'Oh, God...I can't...I just can't. You...you'd better read this.' And she came forward to place a large brown envelope on her desk. 'You'd better sit down.'

Celeste blinked. Sit down? Good God, what was in this envelope?

But she did as she was told, sat down and drew out several pages of what looked like a typed report. From the moment she saw the faded photograph attached, her stomach clenched down hard.

Celeste read each page with a fearful, yet excited anticipation welling up within her. This couldn't be true, she kept saying to herself. And yet is was. It *was*!

Her eyes flew up, locking with Gemma's suddenly tearful ones.

'You *are* my mother, aren't you?' the girl said, hopefully, pleadingly.

Celeste choked up totally, her head swimming as the force of emotion hit. All she could manage was a weak nod.

Then Gemma smiled and Celeste's heart burst open, all the pain of the past years obliterated by that one beautifully loving gesture.

'Mother,' Gemma said softly, and held out her arms.

With a strangled sob Celeste ran to her daughter, falling into her arms in an embrace that held all the unused love in her heart. 'Oh, my darling child,' she wept. 'My daughter. Oh, God, I don't believe it…'

'Believe it, Mother. Believe it.'

Celeste pulled back, stunned by the composure of this lovely girl who was her own beautiful little baby grown up. Her shaking hand reached out to trace over her hair and face. 'I…thought you were lost to me forever,' she said shakily. 'You were stolen from me, you know, like the detective suggested might have happened in that report. I didn't give you away, I promise you. And I did try to find you. Not with any success, unfortunately. I thought… I…I…'

The tears took over again and she could not go on.

Gemma pulled her back into a bear-hug. 'I knew that if you were alive somewhere,' she said firmly, 'one day, *I* would find *you*.'

Mother and daughter hugged for a while till Celeste drew back with a still bewildered look on her face. 'I still can't believe it. You don't understand what this means to me. You could never understand.'

You are my only child, came the wrenchingly emotional thought. The only child I will ever have.

But it didn't seem the right moment to say that.

'You're so beautiful,' she said, once again tracing trembling fingers over her daughter's sweet face.

Gemma smiled that heart-stoppingly sweet smile of hers, making Celeste go to mush once more.

'I must take after my mother,' she said generously.

Celeste's groan was tortured. 'Are you sure you want someone like me as your mother?'

'I'm proud to have you as my mother,' Gemma insisted warmly.

'But…but what about my reputation?'

'Are you talking about the lovers you've had? Why should you be judged so harshly for that? You're not married and you're still a very beautiful woman. You have every right to be loved.'

'But…but…'

'Do you think I'm shocked because you've had relationships with younger men? Why should I be? Nathan is many years older than I am. Age has nothing to do with love.'

'Would you believe me if I told you none of those young men was my lover?'

There was no doubting Gemma was startled. But she quickly gathered herself to speak in a reassuringly firm voice. 'Of *course* I would believe you! Why would you lie? But my love isn't conditional on such things. You're my mother! I love you as I've always loved you, even without knowing you. And now that I know you didn't deliberately leave me with my father, I don't even feel angry with you any more.'

Celeste was jolted by this. She hadn't yet thought of what Gemma's life had been like with that ghastly man. Oh, the poor darling, the poor, poor darling…

Her expression was anguished as she reached out to her daughter again, though it was so good to just touch her, to gaze into her lovely eyes while she stroked her lovely hair. 'He didn't...mistreat you, did he? I don't think I could bear that...'

'He tried to be a good father,' Gemma said. 'I think he loved me, but he was a hard man to live with.'

'How...how did he die?'

'Fell down a mine shaft. Or was pushed. I...I've always felt guilty that I wasn't able to grieve for him as a daughter should. To be honest, he and I never saw eye to eye. Ma says we weren't at all alike.'

Celeste's heart contracted. Should she tell her the truth? Was there anything to be gained by giving her more shocks? Not only that, did she dare bring in another party, who might try to take from her what she had only just found?

'Who's Ma?' she asked, stalling for time as she pondered this dilemma.

'An old lady neighbour of mine at Lightning Ridge. Everyone calls her Ma. She was very kind to me.'

'Lightning Ridge again,' Celeste muttered to herself. 'And this Ma thought you had none of your father in you?'

'Not a scrap.'

Celeste made up her mind. She couldn't let this lovely girl go through life thinking that bastard was her father. Maybe if Gemma had loved Stefan then she would not have said a word. But she deserved better than that.

'That's because he wasn't your father,' she said tautly, and held her breath.

Did those big brown eyes light up with shock, or relief?

'Then who?' Gemma asked. 'W...who was my father?'

Celeste gulped in a deep breath, aware that her heart was racing madly. Much as she felt Byron had been greatly at fault in their own relationship, he was a father to be proud of. Lifting her chin, she spoke with a quiet dignity. 'Byron Whitmore.'

Gemma took a staggering step backwards. 'B-Byron? Byron is my *father*?'

Celeste nodded. 'Perhaps you should sit down this time, darling,' she suggested softly, 'and I'll tell you all about it.' She guided the stunned child over to the chesterfield and settled her down. 'Perhaps a little drink would be in order as well? Coffee perhaps, or something stronger?'

Gemma grabbed her hands to stop her from walking away, drawing her down beside her. 'No, nothing. I'm all right. It…it just took my breath away for a moment.'

Celeste's smile was gently wry. 'Your father has always done the same to me. Taken my breath away…'

'You…you loved him, then?'

'I've never loved any other man.'

'And does he know about me?'

She shook her head. 'No. He doesn't even know we had a child together.'

'You have to tell him, Celeste,' she urged.

'Let me tell you first. I want you to know it all, so that you can understand…'

Celeste hesitated, knowing that she didn't have to tell Gemma the basic background details of the man she'd believed was her father all these years. It was well documented in the report that his real name was Stefan Bergman, and he'd come to Australia from Sweden in the Sixties to go prospecting in the opal fields of Coober Pedy in South Australia. When he'd struck it rich there, he'd come to Sydney to sell his finds and live it up big. It was also in the report that he'd started dating the pretty daughter of Stewart Campbell and several weeks later they'd both caught a plane for Europe, choosing to stay in Spain once it became obvious she was having a baby.

What the report didn't include was why Celeste had chosen to go with him in the first place.

God, but it was hard to tell her own daughter that she'd committed adultery with her own half-sister's husband and become pregnant by him, and that she'd run off with Stefan on the rebound. It sounded so appalling in the telling. Yet there was nothing but sympathy for her in her daughter's soft brown eyes when she at last found the courage to look at her.

'You really loved Byron, didn't you?' Gemma murmured.

Celeste nodded. 'Madly. We'd been lovers briefly when I was only seventeen. I thought he was in love with me too but he broke it off, saying it was only a sexual thing. I was devastated when he married Irene a few months later.'

'I've heard some terrible things about her,' Gemma said frowning. 'Why did Byron marry her? Surely he couldn't have been in love with her?'

'I don't think he was, but she was very beautiful and madly in love with him. People always said he married her to get his hands on Campbell Jewels but my father left total control of the company in my mother's hands. Whatever, the marriage was not a happy one. To be honest, I think Byron might have married me if Irene hadn't told him some rather damning lies about me. She made Byron believe I was a little tramp who slept with anything in trousers. Which wasn't true, I assure you. Byron had been my only lover at that stage.'

Gemma was shaking her head. 'Why was she so mean?'

Celeste shrugged. 'I don't really know. She always resented my mother, even though her own mother died soon after she was born. My mother tried to be nice to her but truly I can't remember a time when Irene wasn't very difficult to live with.'

'Byron should have divorced her and married you,' Gemma said. 'He must have loved you. He wouldn't have made love to you while he was married if he didn't.'

Celeste's heart leapt before she got it back under control. Gemma was only twenty, and twenty-year-olds could be very idealistic. 'I don't know about that, Gemma. Men can fall prey to lust more easily than women. I was very wrong to kiss him that day. I wanted to see if I was over him. Clearly, I wasn't,' she finished drily.

'So what happened?' Gemma asked.

'Irene caught us together soon afterwards and guessed what had happened. She didn't say a word, simply looked at both of us then walked out of the room. Byron turned on me and called me all sorts of names.'

'Which is why you went off with my father.'

'You mean Stefan.'

'Oh...yes...I keep forgetting.'

Celeste fell silent, not wanting to tell Gemma about her eventual disillusionment over the man she'd thought such a gentleman. She especially did not want to see the horror in those innocent brown eyes if the whole truth was revealed.

Even so, Gemma was frowning. 'I presume he thought I was his,' she said.

'Yes,' came Celeste's reluctant admission.

'And you refused to marry him, I suppose. Is that why he stole me?'

'Something like that.'

'Yet you stayed with him till I was born. Why did you do that?'

'I...I wasn't in the best of health and he...he said he wanted to take care of me.'

Gemma's frown deepened. 'Doesn't sound like the man I knew. Still...I suppose he might have been a kind person once. Maybe he changed once he realised you didn't love him. Maybe he became bitter and twisted.'

'Yes, I think that's what must have happened,' Celeste was happy to let her daughter believe this. Better than the ghastly truth.

'But what about the opal? You know...the Heart of Fire.'

Celeste's heart missed a beat. 'The...the Heart of Fire?'

'Yes. I found it along with that photograph after Dad died. I...I mean...after the man I *thought* was my father died.'

'Good God,' Celeste murmured. 'I didn't realise... So

Byron was telling the truth all along. It *was* found in a dead miner's belongings out at Lightning Ridge.'

'It certainly was. I thought I was rich for a while till I found out it was stolen. What I'd like to know is...if...if Mr Bergman was rich back then, why did he steal it...and *how*?'

Celeste flushed. 'He didn't steal it initially. Though he did later. From me. I was the original thief.'

'*You*!'

'Byron was going to give it to Irene on their wedding-day to symbolise the healing of the rift between our two families. I...I took it that day, vowing never to let the rift heal between the Whitmores and the Campbells.

'Oh...'

'It was very wrong of me.'

'Understandable, though.'

'Do you really understand, Gemma?' Celeste said pleadingly.

Gemma clasped her mother's hands tightly in hers. 'Of course. Loving someone as much as you love my father can make one do insane things.'

'Yes.' Celeste muttered bleakly. 'Yes, it can...'

'You still love him, don't you?'

Celeste blinked her amazement at this intuitive guess.

'I suspected as much when I saw you together last night,' Gemma explained gently.

'He...he's all I've ever wanted,' Celeste confessed brokenly.

'Then go to him. Tell him everything you've just told me. Tell him the truth.'

The truth...

Dear God, this sweet child didn't know the half of it.

'Please, Mother,' Gemma begged. 'For me...'

Celeste melted. 'All right, my darling. For you...'

CHAPTER FIFTEEN

CELESTE was a nervous wreck by the time she knocked on the hotel suite door. Byron wrenched it open immediately, a smouldering scowl on his handsome face.

'You do pick your moments, Celeste,' he grumbled. 'What could be so urgent that you had to see me immediately? And why, if it's not my body you want, did you choose to meet me here of all places?'

A wry smile tugged at her lips. Same old Byron, always huffing and puffing when he was caught at a disadvantage. Well, he *was* at a disadvantage, there was no doubt about that. He was also about to get the shock of his life, if she was any judge. Would it be a welcome shock? Or would the thought of a woman like herself's having had his child turn his stomach?

She'd never had the courage to tell him, first because of his marriage to Irene and secondly because she'd been afraid of his reaction. She could not have borne to see the scorn and scepticism on his face. Even if she'd been able to find their baby—and my God, she had tried—there had been no DNA tests to prove paternity all those years ago. Byron would have scoffed at her claim that he was the father. He would have seen this as another evil attempt of hers to break up his marriage.

But now, his daughter was living in his own home. The truth was an easy matter to prove in the Nineties. Three simple blood-tests and Byron would not be able to deny his paternity.

Celeste hoped and prayed he wouldn't want to. Not for her sake, but for Gemma's. Celeste's heart turned over as she thought of her daughter. How lovely she was, and how loving. Gemma deserved everything good in life, which included a father who would open his heart to her and give her all the love and support she needed at this difficult time in her life. She was having a tough enough time as it was with that rotten husband of hers.

Fancy Nathan's deliberately keeping her mother's identity from her when he must have known what it meant to her! Then, on top of that and everything else he'd done, he still had the hide to insist on a divorce because of her supposed affair with Damian. The man was a raving nutcase! Truly, Gemma was better out of the marriage, a decision she'd thankfully come to herself. Celeste would never feel happy with her daughter staying married to anyone as unstable and abusive as Nathan had already proven to be.

But that didn't mean the girl was happy about the situation. She loved that man so much it was quite depressing. Love like that could be incredibly self-destructive…

'For pity's sake, Celeste,' Byron muttered impatiently. 'Are you going to stay standing in the doorway all afternoon, or are you going to come inside and tell me what this is all about?'

Celeste stared at him. Why do I love you so much, Byron? she asked herself for the umpteenth time. What have you ever done to deserve such undying devotion?

Shaking her head more at herself than him, she brushed past him, moving along the corridor and into the sitting area of the suite. Placing her bag on the large low table between the two sofas, she walked over to briefly admire the harbour view from the window before turning her back on it to face a frustrated-looking Byron.

'How about pouring me a whisky?' she said. 'And get yourself one, while you're at it.'

He threw her a disgruntled glare before shrugging and

walking over to open the cabinet that housed the mini-bar. 'I take it this is going to be bad news,' he said curtly. 'No doubt something to do with Gemma.'

Celeste caught her breath. 'Why do you say that?'

'A logical deduction. I was the one who dropped her off outside Campbell's after her unsuccessful reconciliation with Nathan this morning. I concluded she must have found in you a sympathetic woman's ear, something that has been very lacking in her life so far.' He turned and brought the two glasses over, handing her one and lifting his own to his mouth. 'So what's the problem?' he asked after a couple of sips. 'Does she want to live with you at Campbell Court instead of at Belleview?'

'We haven't discussed that yet,' Celeste hedged.

'But it's on the agenda?'

'Maybe...'

'I would never feel comfortable with her living under the same roof as Damian, Celeste,' he pronounced pompously. 'I'll advise her against it, most strongly. She'd be safer at Belleview with me and Ava.'

'I'm sure Damian will not be any danger to Gemma...once I tell him what I'm about to tell you.' Damian was going to be rocked to his socks when he found out he was Gemma's uncle! But no more than Byron was going to be.

Celeste swallowed. How did one say news like this? Really, there was no other way but to just say it but dear God, her tongue suddenly felt thick in her mouth and a trembling had started up deep inside.

'For pity's sake, Celeste, would you just spit it out?' Byron growled.

His impatience was just the impetus she needed.

'Gemma is my daughter,' she blurted out.

Celeste knew that for the rest of her life she would never again see such an expression on Byron's face. Stunned did not describe it. Clearly, he was so shocked and astonished that he was rendered speechless.

Or was his goldfish-mouth stare an expression of disbelief?

'It's true,' she insisted, and walked over to snap open her carry-all and draw out the brown envelope. 'Gemma left this with me so that I could show it to you. It's a report from a private investigator. There's a photo too which she found in her father's things after his death. She told me that's what prompted her desire to search for me in the first place and was the main reason she came to Sydney. Anyway, Nathan hired a detective agency on Gemma's behalf some time ago but the bastard told her they hadn't been able to find her mother. Only this morning did he produce this, possibly because he considered such an unforgivable deception would make Gemma agree to a divorce.'

Byron took the envelope, still in an obvious state of shock.

'Sit down and read it,' Celeste suggested, her voice sounding firm despite her insides being an utter mess. What would Byron do when he was told the rest? He already looked pole-axed.

Slumping down on to one of the sofas, he put his whisky down and shakily extracted the report from the envelope. Celeste filled the intervening minutes while he read the report by drinking her whisky, refilling her glass and drinking that as well. Slowly, the alcohol seeped into her system, bringing with it a false sense of calm.

Finally, Byron dropped the report into his lap, but kept staring down at the photograph for ages, running his fingers over it. Finally, he looked up at her, his face ashen.

'Gemma never showed me this,' he said in an uncharacteristically subdued voice. 'Maybe I would have recognised you. But probably not, with those sunglasses on. And your face is so thin and drawn. Not as I remembered you...'

He frowned down at the photograph again. 'I take it the baby you're carrying here was Gemma?'

'Yes,' she choked out.

'So you were able to have children back then, it seems,' he muttered, an angry colour seeping back into his face. 'Whatever happened to make you barren must have happened after this.' His eyes snapped up, hard and glittering and accusing. 'One doesn't have to be a genius to guess what you did. This hospital stay when you got back to Australia explains all. Clearly, babies did not fit into Celeste Campbell's lifestyle. One mistake was enough, so you made sure there wouldn't be another.'

'That's not true!' Celeste gasped. 'I would never do a thing like that.'

'No? From what I've heard and seen for myself, there isn't anything you wouldn't do, Celeste, to ensure your sex life fulfils all your very demanding expectations. An unwanted pregnancy would curtail your activities for far too long. So tell me about this man,' he went on savagely, jabbing at the photo with a furious finger. 'This Stefan you *gave* your child to. I don't believe that other rubbish. Where did you meet him? Why did you go to Europe with him? Why have a baby by him? Was it that he was simply so good in bed you got carried away one night and forgot to take precautions?'

Celeste stared at Byron, disbelief changing to dismay and despair. She should have known Byron would always believe the worst of her. It was par for the course. This time, however, something snapped inside Celeste and she couldn't even find a righteous anger to fight back with. Her normally rebellious spirit began draining from her and she swayed slightly on her feet. Fearful of actually collapsing, she turned and walked slowly towards the window, where she stood for a moment before turning to glance back over at a still scowling Byron.

'I did not give Stefan my baby,' she said in an empty voice. 'He stole her.'

'Bulldust!' Byron scoffed. 'No one could take anything from you, Celeste, unless you wanted them to.'

Celeste was too tired to stop the ghastly memories from rushing back, or in stopping the emotional devastation they always caused. 'I woke one day to find him packed and the baby's cradle already empty. He told me not to bother trying to find either him or the child because I never would.'

'And you didn't try to stop him?'

'Oh, yes…I tried.'

'And what happened?'

'He beat me to a pulp and left me there alone to die.'

There was no satisfaction in Byron's shocked gasp. Or any confidence that he now believed her. Neither did she really care any more.

'My mother can vouch for what I'm saying,' she continued in a dead, flat voice. 'She spoke to the Spanish doctors who treated me, and paid for the hospital bill in Barcelona.' Celeste felt the tears welling up and she turned her face away, clutching at the curtains for support. 'I was taken into emergency surgery where, among other things, I was given a hysterectomy. I nearly died,' she admitted hoarsely. 'Occasionally, over the past twenty years, I wished I had…'

Celeste's head and shoulders drooped in defeat. For even if Byron believed her now, it wouldn't be enough. Underneath, she had been wanting more than his belief. She had been wanting his understanding and sympathy.

The unexpected feel of Byron's arms closing over her shoulders in what seemed to be a gentle, comforting gesture broke what little was left of her control.

'Oh, God,' she sobbed, and, whirling, threw herself into his arms. 'I'm telling the truth,' she cried against the broad expanse of his chest, tears streaming down her face. 'I swear to you…I'm telling the truth!'

'Hush,' he soothed, his warm strong arms holding her

ightly but tenderly. 'I know you are. No one would make ıp a horror story like that, least of all you, Celeste. Least of all you…'

'I tried to find her,' she wept brokenly. 'I spent a fortune on private investigators, but he was far too clever…and in he end I had to stop or go mad!'

'There, there, don't distress yourself any further. You've ound her again, haven't you? And if I know Gemma, she vill have no feelings for you but love. She's a daughter to e so proud of, Celeste. One in a million.'

Celeste drew back, dashing away her tears and looking lmost imploringly into his eyes. 'I…I'm so glad you think hat, Byron. I was hoping you would, because you see…you ee…'

'What?' he asked, an instant wariness zooming into his yes. But as Celeste struggled to make that final shocking onfession, the penny dropped and his eyes flared with hock. 'No,' he rasped. 'No…'

'Yes!' she cried. 'It's true. Gemma's *your* daughter, Byon. Not Stefan's. She's yours!'

For a few seconds, his face far surpassed the way it had ooked before, till a dark fury filled his cheeks and a wild littering began blazing away in his bright blue eyes. '*My* aughter? Gemma's *my* daughter?'

Oh, God, Celeste agonised. He's not going to believe me. Yes!' she insisted fiercely. 'I was no longer on the Pill vhen we made love that last time. I didn't need to be. 'here'd been no one else but you.'

He pushed her away, marching across the room before pinning round and glaring at her. 'And you didn't tell me? 'ou let that mongrel bastard steal my daughter and you idn't tell me?'

This totally unjustified slap in the face revived some of eleste's old fighting spirit. 'Don't you take that tone with ne, Byron Whitmore. You know damned well you wouldn't ave believed me if I'd come to you and said I was expecting your baby. Not that I didn't think of doing it. My God, I probably still would have if I hadn't by then been overseas in the hands of a man so vicious and vile and cruel that I lived every day in fear of my life.'

'Then why go with him in the first place?'

'Because he wasn't like that at first, you stupid man! He seemed sweet and kind and gentlemanly, the complete op-posite to the man I was in love with but who wanted nothing to do with me!'

Byron groaned.

'He *said* he loved me,' Celeste swept on. 'Said I was his ideal woman. He asked me to marry him and on the rebound from my last encounter with you I agreed. We were on our way to Sweden to visit his family when he found out wasn't a virgin. I'd just realised I was pregnant with your child, you see, and in a panic I decided if I went to bed with Stefan he wouldn't know it wasn't *his* child. It was a stupid thing to do but I did it anyway. You do stupid things when you're nineteen and mixed-up and dreadfully un-happy.

'Anyway, Stefan went off his brain when he realised he wasn't the first. He beat me so badly that I had to stay in bed in the hotel room for two weeks. He didn't even call a doctor. I've never been so terrified in my life. Or so intim-idated. God, I know now why battered wives don't leave their abusive husbands. You become too frightened. And you lose all your confidence. After that, Stefan decided wasn't fit to be his wife, but by then he'd become sexually obsessed with me. Every night, I would have to submit to him or be beaten. I was so terrified I let him do whatever he liked, but even then sometimes he still hit me. It was as if I had to be punished for his wanting me all the time. Finally, when I could safely convince him it was his child I was carrying, I told him I was pregnant.'

'Did he believe you?'

She nodded. 'The beatings stopped then, although th

threat was always there. He took me to this remote mountain village in Spain to have the baby, and a week after she was born he stole her from me.'

'My God, if the bastard wasn't already dead,' Byron ground out, 'I'd go and kill him with my bare hands.'

Celeste's tormented eyes flew to Byron. 'You…you believe me now?' she choked out. 'You're not angry with me any more? You understand what happened?'

His shoulders sagged, his face full of anguish and remorse. 'Do you think so poorly of me, Celeste, that you imagine I have no feelings? No heart? No conscience? Of course I understand. Only too well. I drove you into the arms of a monster, but *I'm* the one who's the monster for turning my back on the only woman I ever really loved. I didn't have the courage to live what I see now could have been a beautiful dream, simply because I feared it was my worst nightmare.'

Celeste heard nothing except that she was the only woman he'd ever loved. Her heart swelled to bursting point and with it the tears flowed anew. Byron strode back to gather her in and if she hadn't known better she might have thought he cried too for a short while.

'I did fall in love with you,' he admitted huskily. 'So wildly and so passionately that it worried me sick. I always thought that kind of love was like a disease, an unhealthy thing that made men do wicked and reckless things which had the potential to destroy their own and other people's lives. I was a ready and willing victim for Irene's lies about you—oh, yes, I can see now that they were lies—and I sought refuge from my feelings by escaping into a marriage which could never make me feel the same earth-shattering madness I felt when I was with you. I know people said I married Irene for Campbell Jewels, but that's not true. I married her because I thought it would make me safe from the type of love my father had felt for my mother, the consequences of which have haunted me all my life.'

Surprise had Celeste pulling out of Byron's arms. 'But people always talked about your mother and father as being the perfect couple. What was wrong with their love for each other?'

'Didn't your father ever tell you, Celeste? You must have wondered what happened between Stewart Campbell and David Whitmore to start off such a vicious feud in the first place. After all, they'd been best mates ever since they met on the boat that brought them to Australia as emigrants from the UK. They did everything together. When times got tough and jobs were hard to come by, they went mining together. Didn't you ever wonder what could have happened to destroy such a strong bond? It wasn't some silly argument over that opal, I can assure you.'

'Of course I did. But Dad never talked about the old days. He always clammed up whenever I asked him. All I know is he was still best friends with your father when the war broke out because they joined up together.'

'They were best friends up till the time my father was wounded in 1943 and was sent home early.'

'But how would that have ruined their friendship?'

'Your father sent my father to his own home to recuperate. To his wife.'

'His *wife*?' Celeste was confused. 'But Dad didn't marry Irene's mother till after the war.'

'He was married to *my* mother first,' Byron said drily.

Celeste gasped her shock. 'You don't mean...'

'Yes, that's exactly what I mean. Can you imagine what your father felt when he came home on leave to find his beloved Lucy with *me* growing in her belly?'

'Oh, God, Byron. Knowing his pride and his ego, he would have been devastated. And so hurt! No wonder he hated your father with such a passion.'

'And no wonder he kept the real reason a secret. My own father did the same, but when I was about twelve your father came round to see my father. They had the most awful row.

It started about their business rivalry but soon all the old ugliness came out. I couldn't help but overhear every word and it made a big impression on me at the time. I was utterly appalled at my father, who'd always been so strong on morals, yet he himself was nothing but the worst kind of adulterer. All he could say to excuse himself was that he couldn't help himself. He'd fallen madly in love and that was it. He made it sound as though everything was totally out of his control. And he did something that shocked me even more. He started to cry, blubbering away that he was sorry. He begged your father to accept the Heart of Fire as a symbol of his sorrow and remorse—apparently he'd found it while your father was still at the front and this was the second time he'd offered it—but your father spat on him and stormed out.

'I decided that very day that that kind of love had to be the worst thing in the world. I vowed never to succumb to such a destructive disease. Never would a woman be able to make me do anything against my better judgement. Never! And I managed very well, till I was twenty-seven years old. Then, one day, this vision of loveliness walked into my office and I was a goner…' His expression was apologetic and rueful at the same time. 'So you see, Celeste, there are excuses for what we both did, don't you think? Can we perhaps forgive each other and start again? Or is it too late for that?'

'It's never too late to love one another, Byron.'

His relieved but joyous smile was rather wonderful, she thought. Suddenly, she glimpsed the real man behind the arrogant and sometimes impossible façade. Byron had more strength and passion in his little finger than most men had in their whole bodies.

As if to confirm this unspoken realisation, he swept her into his arms and kissed her with a hunger that was as catching as it was comforting.

'You know, Celeste…' he murmured some time later.

They were curled up on the sofa together, Celeste half on Byron's lap, her head on his chest, her arms around his waist. 'I knew last night you weren't the woman you'd projected all these years. I saw you with Gemma, being so kind and caring, and I said to myself...that's no hard-hearted, sex-mad bitch there. There's a good woman, a woman worth loving. Naturally, I panicked anew and set out to prove once again that there was nothing to my feelings but lust. Till you put me in my proper place,' he added with a dry chuckle.

'Oh, and where's that?'

'Under your heel?'

'I thought you once said it was in your bed.'

'And so it is. But only if that's where you want to be too.'

They looked at each other and Celeste felt an intense surge of desire. Maybe Byron was right. Maybe their love was a bit of a sickness. But if it was, it was a terminal one for both of them. It had survived all these years and remained as powerful as ever to this very day. The thrill of being in his arms was as strong as it had been the first time. 'I want to be there every night of my life,' she whispered.

His head dropped to kiss her very, very slowly. 'You do realise my family is going to be scandalised if I marry you,' he said softly against her tingling lips.

'*My* family is going to be scandalised if I marry *you*.'

'Looks as if there are going to be a lot of scandalised people around Sydney, then, aren't there? Because I am going to marry you, Celeste Campbell. I'm going to do what I should have done over twenty years ago. Make an honest woman out of you.'

'Don't ask for miracles, Byron,' she teased. 'Marriage won't necessarily make an honest woman out of me.'

His head jerked back, his face stern. 'If you look at another young man again,' he warned, 'there's going to be hell to pay.'

'There's nothing wrong with looking, Byron. After all, that's all I've ever done.'

His face was both disbelieving and shocked. 'Are you saying...?'

'It was all pretence. I never slept with any of them.'

'Not even that hunk of a chauffeur you batted your eyelashes at and flirted with like mad?'

'Why do you think I had to let him go? I pretended so well he thought he was on to a sure thing.'

'What about that smarmy-looking Luke in the office?'

'Luke is a very clever, ambitious young man who only has designs on Campbell Jewels, not the boss.'

'God, I'm glad to hear that.'

'Say you love me again,' she rasped as she drew him down on to the sofa with her.

'I love you,' he moaned. 'More than I can say.'

'Then don't say it, darling. Show me. Show me how much.'

'I LOVE YOU,' she told him afterwards for the umpteenth time, clasping her to him and refusing to let their bodies separate. 'I've always loved you.'

Byron gave a small groan. 'Don't make me feel guilty any more, Celeste. I can't bear it. When I think of what I put you through. I don't deserve your sweet forgiveness.'

'I put you through a few things myself,' she murmured, and snuggled into him. 'Have you guessed yet that it was me who stole the Heart of Fire?'

'Good God!' Byron rolled her on top of him so he could look up into her eyes. 'You little devil! But how did that Stefan creep get hold of it?' he frowned. 'You didn't give it to him, did you?'

'Never in a million years. He found it in my things and stole it as he stole my little girl. Maybe that's why he never sold it in the end, because he was afraid I would be able to trace the sale to him. Gemma told me all about finding it in his things and bringing it to you. Wasn't that an incredible coincidence? But you've no idea how upset I was when it turned up again. I was torn between setting out on another potentially fruitless search for my baby and trying to put it out of my mind. Of course I couldn't, not when the opal's presence in Australia meant my baby might be here somewhere as well. I went to that ball, determined to find out the circumstances of its return, but found myself buying the damned thing instead, then eventually launching myself into a mad affair with the one man I had vowed never to let touch me again!'

'*You* ought to talk. I've been going to the dogs ever since the night you turned up at that damned ball! I haven't been able to think straight for wanting to be with you. I did all sorts of stupid things to try to put you out of my mind!'

Celeste laughed. 'We're a right pair, aren't we?'

'Yes,' Byron said with sudden seriousness. 'We are a right pair. Right for each other. Right in every way. Maybe it's taken me over twenty years to realise it but now that I have I'm never going to let you go, my darling. You're going to be mine, "for better for worse, for richer for poorer, in sickness and in health...till death us do part".'

Celeste's eyes swam, her heart swelling with love. 'Ditto, my sweet,' she choked out. 'Ditto.'

CHAPTER SIXTEEN

'YOU'RE right about the sequence of events being quite incredible,' Byron remarked on their way to Belleview later that afternoon. 'Really, if it hadn't been for your stealing the Heart of Fire from me in the first place, that opal would never have got into Bergman's hands, which means it wouldn't have come into Gemma's possession at his death. Without it, she might never have come to us in Sydney at all. She would not have married Nathan and subsequently put the search for you into action. As I said...amazing!'

Celeste darted him a wary look. 'So, am I forgiven for being the original thief?'

'Of course. In your position, I probably would have done the same thing. God, Celeste, it should have been you I married that day. My marriage to Irene was a disaster from day one.'

'I often wondered how you stood it,' Celeste said truthfully. 'Though I could see Irene was a different person with you than she was with anyone else.'

'I put my head in the sand a lot where she was concerned. It was easier than admitting what a horrendous mistake I'd made. That's always been a great failing of mine, Celeste, not admitting my mistakes or going back on what I've always believed. But not any more, I hope. That boating accident where Irene was killed and I was badly hurt gave me a lot of time to re-evaluate my life and my beliefs. Then, something else happened to bring a different perspective into my life, and a lot of other people's lives around Belleview, I think.'

'What was that, Byron?'

He sent such a warm loving look her way, Celeste melted. 'A lovely young woman came to live with us,' he said softly, 'bringing with her so much simple joy and caring that we all began to wake up to ourselves. The more I think about it, the more I realise how much like you Gemma is, when you were her age. There is a strength and vitality about her that is so endearing. And a sensuality that can be very disturbing. It's almost a relief to find out she's my daughter. Now I can stop having wicked thoughts about her.'

'Byron!'

He laughed. 'Only teasing, darling. But it is a relief to know that that sinful brother of yours has been relegated to the role of her uncle.'

'Yes, I thought of that myself. But I think he'll be thrilled. I'm sure he genuinely likes Gemma as a person, not just as a female.'

'Well, I'll have to take your word for that,' came his dry comment. 'You wouldn't be able to talk him into going and seeing Nathan, would you? If he could convince him that there was nothing between him and Gemma, then everything would be perfect. Gemma and Nathan would get back together again.'

Celeste stiffened. 'I'm not sure that would be so perfect for Gemma. If Nathan didn't believe her when she swore she'd been faithful, do you honestly think he'd believe anything Damian said?'

Byron's sigh was resigned. 'No, I guess not. I'll have a talk to Nathan myself once he's calmed down a bit.'

'I don't like your chances, either. The man has no trust in him. Gemma tells me he's always treated her like a child, or a possession, that he never confides in her or talks to her about things that matter. She still loves the man but she was terribly hurt by his keeping my identity from her. I'm not sure she'll ever forgive him for that.'

'Time has a way of lessening such hurts, Celeste,' Byron said with the wisdom of age. 'I'm sure there were times when you thought you would never forgive me. Yet here you are, sitting in my car, going home to have dinner at Belleview.'

Celeste slowly nodded her head up and down. 'Yes, you're absolutely right. I shouldn't make harsh judgements of other people and their relationships. We're about to make history, I would say, when we announce our intention to marry. I'm sure a few people are going to faint dead away, my own mother included. I'm just thankful she's overseas at the moment. My God, the things I said to her about you. Still, it was my love turned to hate that kept me going when things were so tough. If I hadn't had my vows of vengeance I think I might have killed myself.'

'Oh, no, Celeste. You would never have killed yourself. You're a fighter, and fighters don't know any other way then to come out of their corners with all guns blazing. You sure blazed a path through my life over the years, madam. Whitmore's almost went to the wall because of you.'

Celeste had the grace to colour guiltily. 'I might have overstepped the mark occasionally.'

'That's putting it mildly. But I forgive you,' he grinned, 'provided you agree to some treaty terms.'

'Treaty terms? What do you think this is, Little Big Horn? And which side are you on? Colonel Custer's or the Indians'?'

'Whatever side won. Now on to the rules of truce.' He slanted her a quick glance. 'I suppose it would be too much to hope that you would hand over control of Campbell's to an impartial manager and retire to graceful living as my wife and social hostess.'

'You wish!' she laughed.

'Just as I thought. In that case I have to insist you stop

using unfair and illegal business practices. If I find that Damian has—'

'Damian has been sacked from his position as sales and marketing manager,' she interrupted firmly. 'There will be no more shady goings-on at that level, I can assure you.'

'That's all I wanted to hear. Right! Now on to problem number two. Where are we going to live?'

'Certainly not in that imitation Southern mansion of yours!'

'Surely you don't expect me to reside in that crumbling castle *you* call home!'

They both looked at each other and laughed.

'We'll buy a brand-new place together,' Byron suggested, smiling.

'Only if I pay half,' Celeste argued.

'Agreed! It'll have to have a gym.'

'*And* a pool,' she put in.

'And I'd like to be by the sea for a change.'

'Good idea. It'll give me somewhere to put my boat.'

Byron scowled. 'I'd forgotten about that monstrosity. I'll bet it costs a fortune to run.'

'Mmm, it certainly does. Perhaps I should sell it. What do you think?'

'It's up to you.'

Celeste gave him a surprised look. 'You certainly have changed, haven't you? That's a most unByron-like answer.'

'You're going to be a most unByron-like wife,' he drawled. 'Maybe I should buy you a chastity-belt for a wedding present.'

She laughed. 'That cuts both ways, lover. Maybe I'll get *you* one.'

'After having you in my bed every night, I'll be lucky to make it to the office, let alone have the energy to consider extra-curricular activities.'

'From memory, you can be a very bad boy in offices.'

He groaned. 'Don't remind me. I still can't believe the sort of things we got up to that last week.'

'*We* got up to? Everything was *your* idea, might I remind you. You led and I simply followed.'

'There are followers and followers, Celeste,' he said drily. 'Your brand of following is something else. It's one of the reasons I thought you were more experienced than you were.'

'I loved you, Byron. I wanted to please you.'

'Hey, why the past tense? Don't you still love me and want to please me?'

'Silly man…' A lump filled her throat as their eyes locked for a moment.

'It's been a long time, hasn't it?' he said softly, but with a catch in his voice. 'But you've been worth the wait, my love. I hope you feel the same way about me.'

Celeste was incapable of answering. She let her blurred gaze do the talking and Byron's hand reached out for hers across the gear-stick. When she entwined her trembling fingers with his and he gave them a squeeze, her heart squeezed tight with them. It had indeed been a long hard journey, but at long last they were together. They were where they had always belonged. Her vows of vengeance would soon become a different kind of vow, one that would promise to love this man for the rest of her life.

When his hand had to leave hers to negotiate a corner she settled back into the seat with a happy sigh. Aside from her own personal happiness, it felt great to be going to give Gemma good news. Hopefully, their daughter would be pleased that her parents were going to be married. Maybe it would make up a little for her distress over the break-up of her own marriage. Celeste certainly hoped so.

'I STILL CAN'T believe it!' Ava said for the umpteenth time over dinner. 'It was enough of a shock when Gemma came home earlier and announced that you two were her parents, but now that I've heard the whole fantastic story I'm...I'm speechless!'

'For a person who's speechless, Ava,' Byron said drily, 'you've been saying one heck of a lot.' He suspected she might not be so chatty if she'd heard the whole unvarnished truth. But he and Celeste had decided that nothing would be gained by revealing the brutal treatment Celeste had suffered at the hands of that madman. It was to be thanked that he hadn't mistreated Gemma over the years. Clearly, he had loved the girl. But who wouldn't? It was impossible not to love such a loving creature. Not a word of criticism had she uttered against him and his treatment of her mother. He'd been accepted as unconditionally as Celeste had been.

'Very funny, Byron,' Ava retorted archly. 'You know what I mean. By the way, have you told Jade?'

Everyone at the table stopped eating, their mouths dropping open.

'She *has* just acquired a sister, hasn't she?'

'My God, so she has!' Byron said in a stunned voice.

Gemma's stomach had flipped over. A sister! She'd always wanted a sister. Not only that, Jade was expecting a baby, which meant she was going to become an aunt soon as well.

'I'll go and call her straight away,' Byron said, scraping his chair back and standing up. 'Maybe she and Kyle would like to drive over later and we can break open a bottle of champagne or two.'

'What a good idea,' Celeste said, then added mischievously, 'I wouldn't mind seeing that gorgeous hunk of a husband of hers at close range again.'

Byron glared down at her. 'I can see I'll be purchasing that CB before long,' he muttered darkly.

'CB?' Ava looked puzzled. 'What's a CB?'

'I have no idea,' Celeste said with mock bewilderment. 'What's a CB, Byron?'

Byron made an exasperated sound and strode from the room.

Ava shook her head after him. 'You have my admiration, Celeste, for having anything at all to do with that man! There are times when I'd like nothing better than to give him a swift kick up the backside.'

'I'll keep that in mind, Ava. So tell me all about that gorgeous hunk *you* seem to have snaffled for yourself. Have you met him, Gemma?'

Gemma, who'd been wondering how Jade would take the news, snapped back to the present. 'What was that?'

'Have you met Ava's fiancé?'

'No, I haven't yet. But he's dropping by later, isn't he, Ava?'

'Yes, I see him just about every night.'

Celeste noted the tinge of pink that immediately came to Ava's cheeks and she only just stopped her eyebrows from lifting. Apparently, therefore, it would be wise not to barge into Ava's room during any of this Vince's nightly visits.

'And when are you getting married?' Celeste asked.

'We've put the arrangements in Vince's mother's hands, and she's having a field-day. At the moment, we've made a tentative date for February next year. It seems it takes a while to organise an Italian wedding.'

'I can imagine.'

Byron strode back into the dining-room, a broad smile on his face. 'Jade's over the moon, Gemma. Frankly, I'm surprised I'm not deaf, she carried on so much. But I let her scream and cry and do all the things Jade likes doing. Anyway, she said she'd be over straight away.'

'Not alone, I hope,' Celeste quipped.

When Byron's blue eyes narrowed, she laughed, and leant over to kiss him on the cheek. 'You can't expect me to give up teasing you altogether, can you? You do jealousy better than any man I know.'

Would you believe Vince gets jealous of *me*?' Ava said,

sounding almost surprised. 'I think jealousy must be an infallible symptom of a man's love. If he doesn't get jealous at all then he probably doesn't care.'

'In that case, I must care for Celeste one hell of a lot,' Byron drawled. 'When another man even *looks* her way, I want to punch his lights out.'

'Must be the beast in you, darling,' Celeste murmured, and looked adoringly at him.

'Any man worth his salt has a bit of beast in him,' Byron returned. What woman wants a wimp, especially these days? He has to stand up and be counted, I say.'

'Hear, hear!' Celeste clapped.

'Vince can be a beast when necessary, can't he, Byron?' Ava said smilingly.

He gave his sister a rueful look and rubbed his jaw. 'He's certainly not a man to be toyed with.'

'Unless Ava's doing the toying,' Celeste murmured, bringing a startled look from Byron and a coy half-smile from Ava.

Gemma listened to this exchange, her thoughts whirling as the conversation reconfirmed what, in her heart, she already knew. Nathan did love her. Madly. Obsessively. He'd been thrown by her inexplicably leaving him, then distraught when he thought she'd run to Damian. Crazed by jealousy, he had done what others would decry as an unthinkable act, but she'd already accepted that the assault had been a momentary aberration, a temporary insanity which he had immediately regretted.

But Gemma's belief that her husband really loved her did not change the fact that he did not believe she loved him. He'd said so, told her she was too young for such depth of emotion, confessing that he'd selfishly rushed her into marriage on her response to a strong sexual attraction. This was the reason he'd treated her as he had, buying her gifts all the time, cosseting and smothering her as an insecure older lover might do to a Lolita-style mistress, fearful all the time that she would grow bored and leave him. He'd deliberately kept the focus of the relationship on sex because that was the area he was most confident in, his role becoming a mixture of father and Svengali.

It was in the father role that he made decisions for her all the time, especially the one not to tell her who her mother was, probably because he felt a mother like Celeste would be like his own mother, and consequently not worth knowing. The Svengali role was that of seducer and enslaver, taking her desire for him and exploiting it to the full, attuning her body to his needs so finely that she had seemed to lose some of her will power in that regard. He could sometimes make her respond even when she didn't feel she wanted to.

Who knew? Maybe Nathan had thought the other day that she would even respond to his forced act of intercourse. Of course she hadn't, and when he'd finally seen that, she gained the impression that he was filled with remorse and self-disgust.

But all this thinking left her where? Nathan insisted he didn't want her back as his wife, obviously because of her supposed adultery. How he could believe she'd go from him to Damian so soon after their very loving phone call on the previous Friday night was beyond her.

How happy she had been after that phone call. And how optimistic for the future. She hadn't been able to wait to throw away her pills, to come home to Nathan and to…

Gemma froze as the possibility struck. Dear God, she had never thought of that. The idea that she might have conceived a child that awful afternoon seemed a wicked twist of fate, but it was a distinct possibility, maybe even a probability!

Gemma blinked as the idea took hold. Why wasn't she appalled by the thought? Or disgusted? Or revolted?

Because she wasn't, that was why. Any child resulting from that unfortunate union would still be the offspring of two people who loved one another, however misguided one of them was.

'Gemma?' Celeste asked. 'Are you all right?'

Lord, but she was finding it hard not to actually feel excited by this, which was crazy! Looking up, she struggled for composure. 'Yes. I'm fine. Why?

'You...you looked strange for a moment.'

I not only look strange, Mother, I *am* strange, Gemma decided. Any other woman would be horrified. But not silly old optimistic me. Because even if I'm *not* pregnant, this has shown me what having a child of Nathan's means to me, what *Nathan* means to me.

It looks as if I'm going to have to win him back, came the astonishing realisation. By fair means or foul, if necessary. He's not going to get away from me, she decided with a surge of steely spirit. I'm not going to do what Celeste did with Byron. Nathan is the man for me and he's the man for me *here and now*, not in twenty years' time.

I have a weapon or two in my favour, Gemma planned with quite amazing calm. My body for one. Nathan does have an addiction for it. On top of that, he actually loves me. Lust plus love is a pretty powerful and potentially weakening combination. If I'm not pregnant this time, I'm certainly going to become so in the not too distant future.

And then...*then*...

Gemma grimaced at this point in her train of thought. She couldn't think that far ahead. She'd have to take this plan one day at a time.

'Gemma?' Celeste asked again.

She looked up to find everyone looking at her with concerned expressions on their faces. 'Sorry, I was daydreaming, making plans for the future.'

Now everyone looked even more taken aback.

'I can keep my job at the store, can't I, Byron?' she asked.

'Of course!'

'And I...I'd like to stay living here, if I could.' Nathan

was more likely to come to Belleview than Campbell Court, she reasoned. 'I hope you're not offended, Mother. I'll visit you as well.'

'You do what you think best, Gemma, love. You're a grown woman.'

'Then I think it best I stay here. Damian won't be annoyed, will he?'

'Your *uncle* Damian will understand,' Celeste said firmly.

'My goodness, so he is! I didn't think of that.'

'You've also acquired a grandmother,' Celeste added, 'who's going to come home like a shot once she finds out.'

'A grandmother too!' Gemma gasped. 'Gosh, it's hard to take it all in.'

'It's been quite a day, I have to admit,' Byron intoned drily just as the doorbell rang. 'And it hasn't finished yet. Come on, Gemma, I need moral support to let that mad sister of yours in.'

'Gemma laughed and stood up. 'I never thought I'd see the day when you'd become a scaredy-cat.'

'Well, take a good look, daughter, dear, because come tomorrow I'm going to revert to normal.'

And come tomorrow, she promised herself as she linked arms with her father and walked from the room, I'm going to set about getting my Nathan back!

MARRIAGE & MIRACLES

CHAPTER ONE

THE première of a new play by Nathan Whitmore had become quite an event in Sydney over the past few years. It was nothing to see the Prime Minister of Australia as well as other heads of state roll up with their wives, not to mention a good supply of the sort of socialites and celebrities who graced the pages of the tabloids and women's magazines every other week.

Gemma surveyed the famous faces in the crowd gathered in the foyer with a sincere lack of interest or awe. Fame as such did not impress her. Why should it? There was a time—not very long ago—when she would not have recognised a single famous face here tonight, and her life had not been any the less for it.

'Smile, Mrs Whitmore,' one of the plethora of photographers directed her way. 'And you too, Ms Campbell.'

'Smile, Gemma,' Celeste hissed under her breath. 'This was your idea, remember? I did warn you not to come, but now that you're here, you must grin and bear it.'

Both women smiled and Gemma wondered what the photographer would say if he knew he was not just taking a photograph of Ms Celeste Campbell and Mrs Nathan Whitmore, but mother and daughter.

There was no doubt that the news would set Sydney's social set on its ear, especially if it were also publicly revealed that Gemma's father-in-law, Byron Whitmore, was Gemma's biological father as well.

The long-standing feud between the glamorous lady boss

of Campbell Jewels and the handsome head of Whitmore Opals had fuelled many a discussion over the years. An affair gone sour had been whispered at occasionally, but no one could have guessed at the extraordinary set of circumstances which had brought about Gemma's birth, her subsequent stealing as a baby by a man who thought he was her father, but who wasn't, and her final return into the lives of her real parents twenty years later.

It had only been three days since Gemma had found out the truth, yet already she had forged a bond with her father and mother that was astonishingly close and full of love. They were both tremendous people, in her opinion. Not saints, of course, either of them, but basically good souls with deeply caring natures who only wanted the best for their long-lost daughter. The added news that they were finally going to get married had made Gemma very happy.

Her own marriage was another matter…

Gemma's stomach began churning. Her plan to get Nathan back had seemed a good one in theory. In practice, it was dangerous and risky and nerve-racking. But what alternative did she have? She loved Nathan more than life itself and felt sure that he loved her back, despite everything. She couldn't let cruel twists of fate and unfortunate misunderstandings destroy their marriage. Certainly not now, when she might possibly be pregnant.

'What's taking Byron so long?' she said worriedly after the photographer had scuttled away. 'I hope he's not trying to play peace-maker between Nathan and me. I asked him not to meddle.'

'Please give Byron more credit for intelligence than that, Gemma. He realises any influence he has over Nathan is at a low ebb at the moment. Nathan was far from impressed to find out Byron had slept with me while he was still a married man. Then when he added that we were going to get married…' Celeste's eyes rolled expressively. 'He said Nathan stared at him as though he were mad.'

Gemma sighed. 'Poor Byron. He deserves better than that from Nathan.'

'Yes, he does. Frankly, Gemma, everyone deserves better than they're getting from Nathan. Why you still love him after what he's done amazes me. Keeping my identity from you was despicable enough, but when I think how he...he—'

'You promised not to speak of that again,' Gemma broke in sharply. 'You know that Nathan was out of his head when he did that. If I can forgive and forget, why can't you?'

Celeste pursed disapproving lips. 'I'm sorry, but I can't abide a man perpetrating any violence against a woman, no matter what the provocation. Still, I won't mention it again. It's your life and I can see you're determined to try to save your marriage.'

'And you promised to help me any way you could.'

'God knows why,' Celeste muttered.

Gemma reached out and gently touched her mother on the wrist. 'Because you love me?' she said softly.

Celeste was stunned by the rush of maternal love that flooded her heart, tears pricking her eyes. Blinking madly, she nodded acknowledgement of this, squeezing her daughter's hands before finding her voice. 'I suppose I'll just have to take your word for it that Nathan is worth fighting for and not the coldest, most cynical bastard I've ever laid eyes on.'

'Lenore thinks he's worth it,' Gemma argued with a quiet intensity. 'And she was married to him for twelve years.'

Celeste sighed. 'Whatever his faults, he certainly knows how to inspire loyalty in his wives.'

'He's only had two!' Gemma protested.

'So far. If he divorces you as he says he's going to, that leaves the field clear for number three.'

'Nathan and I won't be getting a divorce,' Gemma said with a stubborn set of her mouth. 'And there won't be any number three!'

'Oh? And how do you intend to change his mind?'

'By whatever means are at my disposal.'

'Mmm...' Celeste gave Gemma the once-over, a sardonic gleam coming into her eyes as they carefully assessed her appearance. 'I was at a loss earlier on to understand what you hoped to achieve coming here tonight. Now I see it's not your attending the play you had in mind but the party afterwards.'

Gemma felt a guilty heat seep into her cheeks but she refused to succumb to embarrassment over her appearance, or shame over her plan. Nathan was her husband, after all! Besides, she wasn't nearly as provocatively dressed as she'd seen Celeste on occasions. OK, so her red crêpe dress was very form-fitting, the wide beaded belt emphasising her hour-glass figure. And yes, the deep V neckline showed clearly that she wasn't wearing a bra. But that was hardly a crime these days, was it?

'I only want to talk to him,' she lied outrageously. 'I can't achieve anything unless I talk to him, can I?'

'People who play with fire often get burnt,' Celeste warned softly. 'I should know. I've been there, done that.'

'And you ended up with the man you love, I noticed,' Gemma said. 'I aim to do the same.'

Celeste blinked in surprise at the hard edge in her daughter's voice, till it came to her that Gemma was a chip off the old block. Both her parents were pigheaded people who didn't know when to quit. She almost felt sorry for Nathan.

'Ah...here's Byron now.' Celeste smiled and linked arms with him. 'We thought you'd got lost, darling. How are things backstage?'

'Everyone's a bundle of nerves. Except Nathan, of course. That man had nerves of steel.'

And a heart of steel, Celeste thought, but declined to say so.

'What did he say about me?' Gemma asked nervously.

'Not a word.'

Gemma looked and felt crestfallen. 'Does...does he know I'm here, and that I'm going to the party afterwards?'

'I did mention it in passing, but he didn't seem to care one way or the other. To be honest, I'm a little shocked at Nathan's stand over this divorce business. I've never known him to be so inflexible, or so unfeeling. It's as though he's retreated behind some hard shell that nothing can penetrate.'

'That's just a façade he hides behind,' Gemma stated, and did her best to believe it. Because if she didn't, what then?

'It's time we went inside, isn't it?' Celeste jumped in, deciding a change of subject was called for when she saw a stricken look momentarily flash across her daughter's eyes. God, if that bastard hurt her again, she was going to kill him with her bare hands, something she was capable of. All those years of martial arts training had to be good for something!

'The bell hasn't gone,' Byron replied. 'But yes,' he added quickly on seeing Celeste's withering glance, 'I think we might go in.'

A photographer snapped the three of them as they walked into the theatre, Celeste and Byron flashing him a quick smile. Gemma's face, however, reflected an inner misery that she could not hide. Her faith in her plan was already crumbling, as was her faith in Nathan's love for her.

Their seats were in the middle of the fifth row from the front, the best seats in the house. As the play's producer, Byron had access to this whole row if he wanted. He'd offered seats to both Jade and Ava, but they had declined to come in protest over Nathan's unreasonable behaviour towards Gemma. Both women had declared they would never speak to him again till he came to his senses.

Gemma sat down and began flicking through the programme booklet Byron had bought her on arrival, anything to still the butterflies in her stomach. The sight of her husband's face staring out at her jolted her for a second.

The black and white photograph brought a hardness to

his looks that she had never noticed before. He'd always looked like a golden god to her, with hair the colour of wheat, skin like bronze satin, a classically handsome face, a highly sensual mouth and the most beautiful grey eyes. Now, those eyes stared out at her with all the warmth of a winter's dawn, a slight arching of his left eyebrow adding a cynical edge to their cold expression, as did the twisted curve of his half-smile.

Oh, how she'd always hated it when he smiled at her like that, as though he knew things about the world that she was not yet privy to. Nathan had always declared the world a rotten place full of rotten people. He was cynical through and through about the human race, and the female sex in particular, probably because of the wicked, even depraved women who had played vital roles during his growing-up years.

First there had been his mother, a spoiled rich bitch who had left home as a teenager to live a life of debauchery, drugs and total self-indulgence. Nathan had been illegitimate, his father unknown to him and possibly to his mother, who had spent her entire life going from lover to lover, orgy to orgy, trip to trip.

Gemma had heard about Nathan's mother from several sources—though not Nathan himself. He never talked about the past. Apparently, she had put him in his first boarding-school at the age of eight, dragging him out whenever her latest lover left her or vice versa, then putting him back in school once a new man came on the scene. After she died of a drug overdose when Nathan was sixteen, he had become a street kid up at King's Cross. When Byron had come across him several months later Nathan had actually been living with some woman old enough to be his mother, and there was nothing platonic about the relationship. Byron had befriended the boy and, later, adopted him.

Gemma shuddered to think what might have happened to Nathan if Byron hadn't come along.

Not that Nathan's life as Byron's adopted son had ever been without its problems, especially when it came to the opposite sex. His relationship with the female members of his adoptive family seemed dicey from what she'd gathered, and his shotgun marriage to Lenore had not been a raving success, even if his plays were. By the time Gemma had met Nathan early this year when he was out at Lightning Ridge on an opal-buying trip, he'd become a rather world-weary thirty-five, divorced from Lenore and about to resign from Whitmore Opals to write full-time.

From the first moment they met, Gemma had been totally smitten by his mature handsomeness, his city glamour and smooth sophistication, while Nathan had seemed equally bowled over by her youthful beauty, countrified innocence and obvious inexperience with men. Gemma had initially been very wary of having anything to do with a divorced man so many years older than herself, but within a few short weeks of her coming to Sydney Nathan had seduced and married her.

Gemma had gone off on her honeymoon with many warnings about Nathan ringing in her ears. Not too many people had been confident that their marriage would work out, their view being that Nathan had only married her for the sex.

They'd been right and they'd been wrong. Sex had played a big part in their relationship so far. This did not bother Gemma as much as Nathan's jealous possessiveness, plus his tendency to treat her as a naïve child. His extreme cynicism was another bone of contention between them, along with his obvious inability to communicate with women on any other level than the physical.

But none of that meant he didn't really love her, Gemma kept believing staunchly. He just didn't know how to express that love any other way, or how to trust in it. Gemma believed that time would bring about the real intimacy and bonding she was looking for with Nathan. Time and love.

She had no intention of giving up on her marriage at the first hurdle.

OK, so it was a pretty stiff hurdle. Not many wives would forgive their husbands falsely accusing them of unfaithfulness and then virtually raping them. But Gemma had, after all, been the first to point the finger in the matter of unfaithfulness. As for the rape…she understood why and how that had happened, and with the understanding had come forgiveness.

Nathan had gone crazy when he'd found her in Damian Campbell's bedroom. Fury had turned to a violent passion which had spun out of control before he could stop himself. Maybe if she had struggled instead of lying there in stunned horror, Nathan might have stopped. As it was, his remorse afterwards had been a palpable thing, and while Gemma had been shocked and appalled at first, in the end she'd been able to put the unfortunate incident into perspective.

Which was just as well, since it was possible Nathan had started a baby in her that afternoon. He'd obviously forgotten that he'd asked her to throw away her pills the previous weekend. But throw them away she had.

Most women might have revolted at a rape making them pregnant. But once Gemma had found it in her heart to forgive Nathan, she'd been consumed by an amazing feeling of rightness. It had also given her a way of getting her husband back. Hadn't he married Lenore—a woman he hadn't loved—on the strength of a pregnancy? Surely he'd come back to a wife he already loved if she was having his baby.

Which was why she was going to the post-première party tonight, hoping for an opportunity to seduce her husband, thereby increasing her chance of pregnancy, and at the same time freeing Nathan from having to accept that any baby she might have already conceived had been started on that awful afternoon. Gemma might have forgiven Nathan for the rape but it was clear to her that he hadn't forgiven himself. She was sure this was one of the reasons he was insisting on a divorce, because of his own self-disgust and guilt.

'It's not a very good photo of Lenore, is it?' Celeste suddenly commented, looking over Gemma's shoulder at the page across from the one she'd been staring blankly at.

Gemma refocused on the booklet in her lap and examined the photograph of the woman who was not only Nathan's ex-wife but also the leading lady in his new play.

Celeste was quite right. It was not a particularly flattering photo, though once again the black and white print did not do justice to Lenore's vivid beauty. In colour and in the flesh, Lenore was strikingly lovely, her bright red hair and flashing green eyes projecting a 'look-at-me' quality which no doubt served her well as a stage actress. Gemma imagined that from the moment Lenore walked on stage, all eyes would turn to her as though magnetised.

Though going on thirty-five, Lenore looked much younger, her figure still as spectacular as her face, its model-slim tallness and elegance adding to her already captivating package. Gemma had always felt gauche by comparison. No matter how many people complimented her pretty face and eyes, no matter how many men ogled her voluptuous curves, Gemma only had to look at Nathan's wife to feel inadequate and inferior.

Lenore's stunning sex appeal was the main reason Gemma had been so quick to believe what she had believed last Sunday, which was that Nathan had spent the weekend with his ex-wife while she'd been out at Lightning Ridge trying to find some clues to her till-then missing mother's identity. When Gemma had come back unexpectedly early and found Lenore in their flat with Nathan, she'd been right and ready to misunderstand tragically the seemingly shocking conversation she had overheard.

If she'd had a little more faith in her husband's love, she would have stayed and found out that they'd been rehearsing a section of their play, not discussing their previous night's dalliance. Instead, Gemma had fled, eventually to the Campbell house, thereby putting into motion the awful circumstances that had led to Nathan assaulting her.

The only good thing to come out of the horrors of the past week was that she not only found out her mother's identity, but had discovered, with a degree of relief, that the man who she had thought had been her father all her life and whom she had never been able to love was not her father after all!

'Byron tells me Lenore is having an affair with Zachary Marsden,' Celeste whispered. 'Apparently, they intend to marry next year after he's divorced his wife.'

'Yes, I know.'

'She's no danger to your marriage, Gemma.'

'Yes, I know that too. *Now*.'

'Better late than never.'

Gemma smiled across at her mother. 'Is that how you feel about marrying Byron?'

Celeste grinned. 'You'd better believe it. I can't wait to hog-tie him to me forever.'

'When's the big day?'

'As soon as we can arrange it. No long white dresses or anything. Just a simple ceremony. I have no patience with frippery at my age. All I want is Byron's ring on my finger.'

'And all I want is my Nathan back again.'

Celeste sighed. 'Are you sure your love for this man is not blind, Gemma? Do you know what you're dealing with? You were very young when you married him. Just twenty. You're only a few months older now.'

'You were only seventeen when you fell in love with Byron.'

Celeste shook her head. 'That's different.'

'How?'

'Will you two women stop whispering together?' Byron hissed down the line. 'The curtain's about to go up.'

Celeste patted his arm. 'Keep your shirt on, darling.'

'It's my shirt I'm worried about,' he grumbled back. 'I've ut a hell of a lot of money into this play.'

'Don't worry, if it bombs I'll sell my yacht and give you he proceeds.'

'I just might keep you to that!'

'Sssh,' someone in the row behind them said as the lights immed and the curtain rose.

It wasn't long before everyone was silent and totally en-rossed in what was going on on stage.

Gemma soon realised why the play was called *The Voman in Black*. The heroine, played by Lenore, was a idow in her mid-thirties, whose elderly husband had just ied. Her wickedly handsome black-sheep stepson showed p at the funeral and immediately created an atmosphere of ngling suspense and sexual tension. It quickly became ob-ious that he had once had an affair with his stepmother nd the affair had resulted in the birth of a son who the dead usband believed was his and who was now heir to the bulk f his estate.

Towards the end of the first half of the play the widow as once again in danger of being seduced by her evil step-n. He came to her bedroom the night after the funeral, here by some very devious and seductive manoeuvres he cceeded in binding her hand and foot to the bed. He was out to cut her nightwear off with a pair of scissors when e curtain came down.

'Good God,' Celeste let out on a shuddering sigh as the ghts came on. Slowly, she turned wide eyes towards emma. 'And the man who wrote that is the man you *love*?'

Gemma flushed fiercely. 'It's only a play, Celeste. It's t real!'

'Still…'

'My God, I'm on a winner!' Byron exclaimed excitedly. ust look at the audience. They can't stop talking about it. knew when I first read the darned thing that it was a powerfully emotional and erotic drama, but to see it enacted...' He shook his head in disbelief and admiration. 'Lenore's quite brilliant, isn't she? And that chap they've got playing the hero is simply incredible!'

'He's hardly a hero, Byron,' Celeste remarked drily.

'You know what I mean. Besides, I'll bet there isn't a woman in this theatre who'd say no to him if he put his slippers under her bed.'

'You could be right,' she said, revelling in the look of instant jealousy that burnt in his intense blue eyes.

'In that case, I'm not taking *you* to the party afterwards. That devil will be there. Gemma can go alone!'

'I doubt she'll mind that,' Celeste muttered, thinking Gemma might not want her father to see what she was up to. Despite Byron's passionate nature, he was basically a man of old-fashioned principles. It was the man's place to do the chasing, in his opinion, not the woman's. Seduction was not supposed to be a woman's domain. He was still coming to terms with Celeste's liberated views and would not condone his daughter doing her darnedest to get her husband back in her bed by the methods she obviously meant to employ later tonight. Celeste decided it might be wise to coax Byron away from the party afterwards as early as possible.

She didn't think she would have any trouble.

Her hand came to rest with seeming innocence on his thigh. 'Don't be silly, Byron,' she said, her eyes locking on his. 'You'll be expected to attend. At least for a little while,' she added, dropping her voice to a husky whisper, her hand moving ever so slightly up his leg. 'But I see no reason why we can't slip away early. If Gemma wants to stay and talk to Nathan she can go home to Belleview in a taxi.'

'You're wicked,' he groaned, but did not remove her hand.

She simply smiled. The things a mother did for her children, Celeste thought with a stab of perverse amusement.

Byron cleared his throat. 'Can I—er—get you two ladies a drink?' he offered, his voice a little shaky.

'That would be nice, darling,' Celeste returned smoothly. 'Champagne, I think. Celebrations are obviously in order.'

'Champagne it is.'

'What are we celebrating?' Gemma asked after Byron left them. Clearly, she hadn't been listening to their ongoing conversation.

'The success of the play.'

Gemma grimaced. 'I suppose I should be happy for Nathan, but I'll never like that play. How can I when it was responsible for breaking up our marriage?'

'The play wasn't responsible for breaking up your marriage. Nathan was, when he refused to listen to you, when he closed his eyes and ears to your love.'

Gemma frowned as the reality of what Celeste was saying sank in. Why had Nathan turned his back on her love? Why? His blunt confession to having kept her in the dark about Celeste being her mother had been a deliberate act to drive her away and make her agree to a divorce. Would a man genuinely in love do that?

Her highly practical and logical brain reached for an answer but her heart didn't like the one it came up with. Nathan couldn't love her, in that case. Maybe he never had. Maybe everyone else was right and he'd only married her out of lust. Maybe he'd even found someone else…the number three Celeste had mentioned.

Panic began to set in till Gemma remembered the baby she might be carrying. Could she afford to think negative thoughts, even if they were logical ones? Love wasn't logical, she reminded herself frantically. Love had never been logical. Perhaps it was shame and guilt that had impelled him to push her away with the only weapon he could find. That report. He *did* love her. He must! For if he didn't…

God, if he *didn't*!

Black thoughts swirled in her head.

'You don't *have* to go to the party afterwards,' Celeste said quietly.

Gemma blinked, her confusion clearing as she realised that if there was even the smallest chance Nathan loved her she had to take it.

'Oh, yes, I do,' she said, her nerves calming a little in the face of having no alternative. 'I don't have any choice.'

Celeste almost argued with her daughter, till she recalled all the stupid, crazy things she had done in the name of love. Could anyone have dissuaded her at the time? She doubted it.

So she remained silent, and eventually Byron returned with the champagne. Eventually, too, the play resumed, the second half as compelling and shocking as the first. And eventually, the three of them left the theatre to go to the post-première party.

CHAPTER TWO

'WHY didn't you hold this party at Belleview?' Celeste asked Byron as he drove up the ramp of the underground car park. 'Not that I'm complaining, mind. Double Bay is a lot closer than St Ives.'

'Which is precisely the answer to your question. The cast and crew have two performances tomorrow, it being a Saturday, and most of them live close to the city. So when Cliff offered his place as the venue I jumped at it.'

'Who's Cliff? One of your business cronies?'

'He'd like to be. He's an American movie producer who wants to buy the rights to Nathan's play. A colleague of his snapped one up earlier in the year. When Cliff read it, he hot-footed it over here as if he was shot out of a cannon. He's as slick as they come and thinks we Aussies have all come down in the last shower when it comes to the movie business. Which we have, in a way,' Byron finished drily.

'Don't let him have the rights to this play for less than two million, Byron,' Celeste advised. 'I've heard that's what a top screenplay commands these days.'

'Two million, eh? You're sure that's not excessive?'

'Not at all. That play will be a big hit, be it on stage or screen.'

'You're right!' Byron pronounced firmly. 'It's easily worth two million. I'll ask for three.'

'That's the spirit,' Celeste laughed.

Gemma sat silently in the back of Byron's Jaguar, grateful for her parents' lively conversation. It took her mind off the evening ahead, and her mission impossible. She wondered idly what kind of place this American movie mogul had rented. A large harbour-side apartment, she supposed. A penthouse, even.

When Byron turned down a quiet Double Bay street and pulled into the kerb outside an outlandishly huge Mediterranean-style white-stuccoed mansion, her eyes almost popped out of her head. She would not have believed that any home could make Belleview pale by comparison, but she was wrong. This particular place dwarfed Byron's home in size, outdid it for opulence, and made her realise that, while money could not buy everything, it could buy a hell of a lot!

Celeste must have been having similar thoughts.

'If he can afford a place like this, Byron,' she said as they climbed out of the car, 'then three million will be just a drop in the ocean.'

A security guard checked their identities at the gates, then let them inside.

Gemma was all eyes as they made their way through the lushly tropical front garden—complete with fountain—up some statue-lined steps and on to an arched portico that was at least twenty feet wide and God knew how long. It disappeared into the dim distance as did the ranch-style building itself. The ceramic pots lining the covered veranda at regular intervals were enormous and alone would have cost a small fortune.

Byron moved over to ring the front doorbell while Gemma turned to admire the gushing fountain from the top of the steps.

'If only Ma could see this place,' she muttered.

'Have you told Ma about me yet?' Celeste asked her daughter on hearing her mention her old neighbour out at Lightning Ridge.

Gemma nodded. 'I wrote to her last night. She's going to

be tickled pink when she finds out Byron is my father. I think she always rather fancied him.'

'Did she, now?' Celeste said archly. 'I think I'll have to put a stop to all those opal-buying trips dear Byron goes on. I've never subscribed to the theory that absence makes the heart grow fonder. I'm more inclined to believe out of sight out of mind, especially where the male sex is concerned!'

Gemma laughed. 'Ma's about seventy, Celeste. I don't think you have to worry on that score.'

'Worry?' Byron butted in. 'What are you worried about, Gemma? Look, I'm sure Nathan will come round eventually. Give the boy some time and he'll see sense.'

Byron's reminder of why she had come to this party brought a resurgence of nerves to Gemma's stomach. Her confidence slipped another notch and it took all of her courage not to turn and run away.

'Nathan is not a boy, Byron,' Celeste advised tartly. 'And we weren't talking about him, anyway. Did you ring the doorbell?'

Right at that moment, the heavy front door was flung open and a big, barrel-chested man with a ruddy face and thick white hair appeared, a glass of whisky in one hand and a cigar in the other.

'Byron, my man!' he boomed in a broad American accent. 'I've been waiting for you to show up. Everyone else has been here for a while. What kept you?'

'The Press.'

Cliff laughed. 'I saw them swarming all over you afterwards. I gather they were keen on the play?'

'Very keen.'

'How could they not be?' the American enthused. 'The damned thing was brilliant! If you don't sell me the rights, I'll have to throw myself off your Gap.'

Gemma was startled by this mention of a rather notorious Sydney suicide spot since she hadn't really been tuned into the interchange. Her mind had been elsewhere.

Byron merely laughed. 'That's a bit drastic. I'm sure we could be persuaded to sell at the right price. Have you a spare three million or so?'

'Three million! Why, you Aussie rogue, you! But let's not talk money matters on the front doorstep. I'm much better at negotiation after a pint or two of Southern Comfort. And with a bit of luck, you won't be,' he chuckled.

'Come in, ladies, come in,' Cliff continued expansively, and threw an appreciative glance first at Celeste, then at Gemma. '*Two* women, Byron?' he joked as he ushered the threesome into the spacious terracotta-tiled foyer. 'I thought you were a conservative widower. Is this a side to you I haven't seen before?'

Byron gave him a look of mock horror. 'Good lord, Cliff, one woman is enough for me to handle, especially one like this.' He linked arms with Celeste and drew her forward. 'Let me introduce my fiancée, Celeste Campbell. Celeste, this is Cliff Overton.'

Celeste shook his hand and smiled with mischievous seductiveness.

Cliff whistled. 'I see what you mean, Byron. And who's this gorgeous young thing?' he said on turning to Gemma. 'I don't recall seeing you on stage tonight, honey, yet someone as lovely-looking as you are must surely be an actress. I could set up a screen test for you, if you like,' he whispered conspiratorially.

'Back off, Cliff,' Byron said, putting a protective arm around Gemma's shoulder. 'Gemma doesn't want to be an actress, do you, love?'

'Gemma! What a fantastic stage name!' Cliff gushed on before Gemma could get a word in edgeways. 'And so individual. All it needs is the right surname. I can see it in lights now. GEMMA STONE.'

Celeste and Gemma rolled their eyes at each other while Byron's mouth thinned. 'Gemma is Nathan's wife,' he informed drily. 'I doubt he would like to see her name in lights.'

The American's broad grin faded to a puzzled frown. 'She *is*? But I thought Nathan was divorced. I mean, he—er—well, never mind,' he shrugged. 'I must have got it wrong. Nice to meet you, Gemma. You must be very proud of that genius husband of yours. That is *some* play he's written. Not to mention directed. I wonder if he'd consider coming to Hollywood to direct the movie. What do you think, Byron?'

'You'll have to ask Nathan that. He's his own man. I presume he's here?'

Their host looked oddly disconcerted again. 'Er—yes… yes, he is. Somewhere…'

'Perhaps we could go and find him, then?' Byron suggested, and Gemma's stomach clenched down hard. Suddenly, she didn't want to see Nathan. Not here. Not with a lot of other people around. She'd been stupid to come.

Her spirits sinking with each step, she followed the others down the wide tiled corridor to find herself eventually standing in an archway that overlooked a huge sunken living area full of laughing, talking, drinking, smoking partygoers. Music played in the background though only one couple was dancing. Lively conversation and thin cigarette haze filled the air.

The first person Gemma spotted was Lenore, who was standing, arm in arm with her leading man, surrounded by a rather large group of people. Everyone was drinking champagne and generally looking very happy and excited. When Lenore spotted Gemma too, her first reaction was a worried frown and a darting glance down the other end of the room. Gemma's eyes followed, and what she saw made her breath catch in her throat and her insides flip right over.

Nathan was sitting on a large padded leather sofa. And the beautiful blonde curled up next to him was hardly acting like a platonic acquaintance. She was all over him like a rash and Nathan wasn't warding her off.

Gemma's mouth went dry as she watched her husband bend forward to pick up a drink from the table in front of them, laughing and smiling with his companion as they shared the glass. When he brushed his companion's hair with his lips Gemma was almost sick on the spot. Suddenly, he looked up over the blonde's head, straight at the archway then straight into Gemma's appalled face. Without acknowledging her, he looked away and started talking to the couple seated on an adjacent sofa, his arm still firmly around the blonde's shoulder.

'Who the hell is that with Nathan?' Celeste snapped from where she was standing between Gemma and Byron.

'Her name is Jody Something-or-other,' Byron grated out. 'She's one of the understudies.'

'I'd hoped I got the wrong idea earlier,' Cliff muttered on the other side of Byron. 'Clearly I hadn't.'

'Gemma, darling,' Celeste said abruptly, grabbing her daughter by the shoulders and dragging her back out of sight. 'Why don't I take you home? You can see for yourself Nathan doesn't want a reconciliation. Don't belittle yourself by trying. *Please.*'

Having snapped out of her shocked reaction, Gemma's logical brain jolted into gear. What she'd seen with her eyes didn't make sense. Nathan loved *her*, not some strange woman. In that case, what was he doing, draped all over her like that and doing something as intimate as sharing a drink, not to mention kissing her hair?

Every instinct told her to flee. But she'd run away once before when things looked bad and look what had happened!

'I…I *have* to talk to him.'

'Not in there, for pity's sake,' Celeste said, nodding towards the crowded and quite noisy room. She turned to her host, her voice assertive. 'Cliff, you must have a quiet room near by where Gemma could speak privately with Nathan.'

'Yes, of course!'

Gemma was ushered back down the corridor and through a door into a darkly furnished study-cum-library, where she waited with Celeste while Byron went to get Nathan. A lingering nausea continued to swim in her stomach as she tried desperately to get a grasp on the situation. But it was beyond her.

Nathan came in the room alone, looking elegantly cool in his black dinner suit, not the slightest bit perturbed at having to face his estranged wife.

'You wanted to see me, Gemma?' he drawled with an indifference that stunned her.

'You unfeeling bastard,' Celeste bit out. 'We saw you just now with that little tramp.'

Icy grey eyes turned her way. 'Watch your mouth, Celeste. Jody is no tramp. And I should know. I've seen plenty of the real thing. I'm looking at one right now.'

'Nathan!' Gemma gasped, appalled by such open rudeness.

'It's all right, Gemma,' Celeste said sharply. 'I can take care of myself. Now you listen to me, you creep! For some weird and wonderful reason which eludes me, Gemma here still loves you, and believes you still love her. Or she did till she saw that lovely little scenario out there with that blonde! But you and I know what you are, don't we? You're not fit to be the husband of a lovely young girl like this. Why don't you do her a favour? Get the hell out of her life and stay out of it!'

'Celeste, please,' Gemma groaned, clasping her hands to the sides of her head.

'I'd like to do exactly that, Celeste,' Nathan snarled. 'Your precious daughter just isn't getting the message. Why in God's name you allowed her to come here tonight is beyond me. I don't want her back. I want a divorce. What more is there to be said?'

'There's plenty more to be said!' Gemma suddenly burst out. 'And I want it said to *me*! I'm here in this room, Nathan. Don't talk around me.'

He turned slowly to face her, the cold fury in his eyes making her flinch away. 'I have nothing more to say to you.'

Gemma almost crumbled at that point, but she knew if she walked out of here right now without asking him critical questions, she would never be able to live with herself, or the doubts that would remain. 'But I have things I want to say to *you*, Nathan,' she said with more steel than she was actually feeling.

His shrug was indifferent. 'Please yourself.'

Gemma turned to her mother. 'Celeste? Will you leave me alone with Nathan?'

Celeste grimaced. 'I don't like this, but I suppose I have no alternative. It is your life, after all. I'll join Byron for a while. But I won't be far away.'

Giving Nathan a warning glance, Celeste strode from the room, banging the door shut behind her. A strained silence descended, with Gemma eventually moving a little nervously away from Nathan.

'You don't have to do that,' he snapped. 'I'm not going to attack you again.'

'Good God, Nathan,' she groaned, 'is that what all this is really about? Do you think that I can't possibly have forgiven you for what you did that day? I can and I do, because I understand the pressures you were under when you did it.'

'You misunderstand me, Gemma,' he returned coldly. 'I do not care if you forgive me or not. And it's immaterial to me now whether you slept with Campbell or not.'

'But I didn't! I swear to you, I didn't. I won't deny that he fancied me and that he might have wanted something to develop between us. But nothing did. And now that he's found out he's my uncle, there's no risk of that.'

Nathan's laughter sent a chill running through her soul. 'As if something as trivial as a little incest would stop a man like that. God, but you still haven't grown up, have you? I would have thought some time spent in the bosom of the Campbells would have opened up those innocent eyes of yours.'

Gemma closed those eyes with a pained sigh before opening them again, her expression sad as she surveyed her cynical husband. 'You always believe the worst of people, don't you? Not everyone is wicked, Nathan.'

He laughed, then moved slowly towards her, making Gemma stiffen inside with an odd mixture of excitement and apprehension. When he reached out, to tip her chin upwards with a single finger, her eyes were wide and fearful.

'If they aren't, my darling,' he said in a dark silky voice, 'then it's only a question of time and opportunity. Even the best person can be corrupted, given the right weapons. Just look at Byron. All he needed was a woman like Celeste to come into his life and his morals went right out of the window. With some people it's sex. With others it's drugs. Or money. Or power. Total innocents can be corrupted even against their will, if they fall into the wrong hands.'

The awfulness of Nathan's words seemed to get lost under the spell of his physical closeness, and that finger which had slid under her chin and was even now tracing an erotic circle around her quivering mouth. Smoky grey eyes locked on to hers and Gemma found herself unable to tear her gaze away from his.

'I could have really corrupted you if I'd wanted to,' he murmured thickly.

Gemma moaned softly when that tantalising finger retreated from those tortuous circles. Dazed, she just stood there for a moment till she realised he was staring down at her braless breasts, which were at that moment rising and falling with a betrayingly increased heartbeat.

'Maybe I already have,' he rasped, startling her when he slipped his hands into the deep neckline and slid the dress off her shoulders, dragging the material down her arms, till her breasts were totally exposed.

'Why else would you have dressed like this tonight?' he taunted, his thumbs rubbing her rapidly hardening nipples. 'Unless you wanted me to see that your breasts were within easy reach. Unless you wanted me to touch them like this, maybe touch you far more intimately...'

She whimpered as desire shot through her, her heart leaping when his eyes locked on to hers and she saw an answering desire flare madly within his glittering gaze.

'If I did,' she whispered breathlessly, 'it's because I love you. And because I know you still love me.'

Her words brought a stunned look to his face, quickly followed by a darkening fury.

'Then you're a bloody fool!' he exclaimed, angrily yanking her dress back into place. 'I do not love you and neither do you love me. God, there I was, thinking you might have grown up a little, that you might have learnt to call our feelings for each other by its correct name. It's called lust, Gemma. L-U-S-T. Only romantic-minded little fools talk of love when they mean sex. Now get out of here before I do something we're both going to regret afterwards.'

Gemma stared up at him with her mouth agape and her head whirling.

'Didn't you hear me, you silly little bitch?' he snarled. 'Get out! And take your naïveté with you. I have no patience with it any more. I should never have damned well married you in the first place and nothing you or anyone else can say will stop me divorcing you!'

Gemma stumbled over to the door where she gripped on to the knob with a white-knuckled intensity. But she did not turn that knob. She dragged some deep, steadying breaths and, when she felt enough in control, slowly turned to face her husband once more.

'Just tell me one thing before I go,' she said.

'What?' he snapped, scowling over at her.

'If you never loved me, and didn't believe I loved you, then why *did* you marry me? You could have had me without marrying me. You *did* have me without marrying me!'

His sardonic laugh increased her confusion, and her pain. 'So I did. And you were enchanting, my dear. So enchanting that I thought I wanted you in my bed for forever and exclusively. I was even prepared to let you have a child to keep you there. Foolish of me, I realise. But even a mature man can be made a fool of when in the grip of a sexual obsession. Frankly, I was still quite enamoured of your charms when fate stepped in and sent you racing off to Campbell Court, which is why I reacted so poorly to finding you in Damian Campbell's bedroom.'

'But I wasn't sleeping in there!' she cried. 'How many times do I have to tell you that I never went to bed with Damian?'

'As I said before, dear heart,' Nathan drawled, 'I no longer care whether you did or not. My maniacal appetite for youth and innocence seems to have been cured somewhere along the line. Perhaps you saw the cure yourself with me earlier? She's thirty-three, blonde and very, very inventive.'

Gemma stared at him before shaking her head in a blank and bleak disbelief. 'I never really knew you, did I?' she said dazedly. 'Damian did. He said you were bad. I should have believed him.'

Angry grey eyes snapped back to hers. 'Why didn't you, then?'

'Because I stupidly believed you loved me,' she countered, her agony switching to outrage. 'I stupidly believed in *you*!'

'Yes, that was stupid, I'll grant you that.'

Gemma could only keep shaking her head at him. 'You don't have any conscience at all where women are concerned, do you? You're like that hero in your play. Sex and lust are all there is for you. You probably *did* sleep with Irene as Damian said you did.'

Nathan smiled a smile that sent a shiver down Gemma's spine.

'You know, some day that bastard is going to get his just deserts.'

'I suppose you're going to say he's lying about that as well,' she said bitterly.

'Not if agreeing I went to bed with Irene will get you out of that door and out of my life.'

Gemma blinked her shock.

'Oh, for God's sake,' he swept on irritably. 'Of course I didn't sleep with that pathetic bitch. Give me some credit for taste! But I dare say you won't believe me. If you did, that would mean your precious uncle must have lied to you.'

'I...I suppose Irene could have lied to him about it,' Gemma said hesitatingly.

'Good thinking, Gemma,' he praised, but in a mocking tone. 'Amazing how one and one doesn't always make two, isn't it? Sometimes you have to look outside the dots.'

Gemma frowned. 'And should I look outside the dots with you, Nathan? Could you be driving me away because you think it's for my own good, that you're no good for me?'

His laughter was dark but not without humour. 'That's so splendidly noble, I wish I could embrace it! But that *would* be lying, my darling,' he said, walking towards her with such a wicked glitter in his eyes that she shrank back against the wall next to the door.

'Don't touch me,' she whispered.

Nathan's raised eyebrows were pure sarcasm. 'Don't touch you? A few minutes ago you were dying for me to touch you. What's happened to change that, I wonder? Are you beginning to doubt my sense of honour? Are you afraid that at any moment I might change into the animal of the other day?'

'I'm not afraid of you, Nathan,' she lied bravely.

'Then you should be,' he warned in a raw whisper. 'Because if you stay here any longer, Gemma, my sweet, I might set about really corrupting you, just for the hell of it!'

Gemma stared at him, appalled at this dark stranger who had been her husband but whom she did not know.

'Too late,' he mocked. 'I withdraw the offer. Besides, I just remembered I promised Jody a night of indefatigable energy. If I use some of it up on you, darling, I just won't have enough to go around.'

Gemma's hand came up and slapped him. His head jerked back and a red mark immediately stained his cheek, but he made no move to retaliate, merely rubbed his cheek and smiled a faintly wry smile. 'Feel better now?' he taunted softly.

'I hate and despise you, Nathan Whitmore,' Gemma rasped, her voice shaking. 'How you can look yourself in the mirror in the morning, I have no idea. I came here to this party tonight hoping that we could get back together again. I was prepared to forgive you everything because I thought you loved me, and because I loved you. But I don't love you any more. I refuse to love someone so unworthy of being loved.'

'You've no idea how pleased I am to hear that, Gemma. Because I don't want your love. It's the last thing I want from you.'

Gemma could no longer deny the harsh sincerity behind the chillingly delivered words. But oh, dear God…what was going to become of her…without Nathan…without her dreams…? What point was there in going on?

'So why are you still standing there?' he jeered. 'What more is there to be said? You're free, Gemma. Free of our marriage. Free of loving me. Free of *me*. I'd say you're one lucky girl, wouldn't you? Now leave me be,' he bit out savagely, and turned his back on her.

Gemma somehow made it out of the room and back to Celeste, who took one look at her and called for Byron to take them both home.

CHAPTER THREE

LIFE went on.

Gemma would not have believed it could after her traumatic meeting with Nathan. Surely she must die from the pain and the hurt that was consuming every fibre of her being? Nathan didn't love her; had never loved her. All her dreams and hopes for the future were obliterated by that one cruel admission. As for the past…it was almost as painful to look back as it was to look bleakly forward. Her marriage had been a mockery, doomed from the start. Why hadn't she heeded the signs? Why had she stubbornly refused to see what others saw?

Because you *are* a naïve silly bitch, that's why, an angry inner voice kept telling her. Or you *were*!

It was this angry inner voice that sustained her through the following day, refusing to let her break down totally, although there were frequent bouts of weeping, as well as long hours of deep depression. But in the end anger, plus a healthy dose of burgeoning bitterness, stopped Gemma from succumbing to total despair.

When she woke on Sunday to the news that Nathan had delivered her car during the night—complete with the rest of her belongings—leaving again without speaking to anyone, her sense of outrage knew no bounds. What had happened to the man she had first met and fallen in love with? Where was this wicked stranger coming from? Had he always been there, hiding behind that cool conservative façade, that seemingly decent persona? He must have been, she supposed, her bewilderment almost as great as her disillusionment.

Still, she wasn't the only one to be fooled. Byron had clearly been taken in, as had Lenore. Ava and Melanie, however, had clearly had their misgivings about him all along. Jade had been ambivalent, warning her off Nathan at first before unexpectedly coming round to believe in his love for Gemma almost as much as she had.

But he hadn't been able to sustain the act indefinitely, had he? His dark side had finally surfaced, and surfaced with a vengeance. She now felt utterly mortified at having forgiven him for the rape. He had probably enjoyed every perverse moment, his supposed feelings of betrayed love being nothing but a bruised ego that his sexual possession might have dared turn to another man.

By Sunday evening, Gemma found solace in a bitter determination not to fall apart over the bastard's black treachery. He wasn't worth it. So on the Monday morning she gritted her teeth and went back to work.

From the first moment she walked into the shop, Gemma realised that the news of her separation from Nathan must have got around, because all the girls were extraordinarily nice to her, which was something new.

When Byron had given her a job as a sales assistant in the more exclusive of his two city stores, Gemma had gradually noticed an underlying resentment from the rest of the staff. She supposed they thought her employment smacked of nepotism, even though she had quickly proved herself a very competent salesperson, her Japanese better than anyone else's. Gemma believed she might have overcome her workmates' underlying hostility if Nathan hadn't vetoed her going out with them on social occasions.

In the circumstances, she didn't blame them for thinking she was a snob, so she was quite touched by their kindness to her that morning, and found it hard not to dissolve into tears. With a stiff upper lip and a lot of false smiles, she made it through the morning, but as one o'clock approached Gemma couldn't wait to spend an hour sitting by herself in a park somewhere.

At a couple of minutes past one she was walking through the hotel arcade, heading for the main exit, her eyes on the black and white tiled floor, when a man's voice suddenly spoke from just behind her right shoulder. 'Going my way, sweetheart?'

Gemma ground to a halt and spun round, her startled brown eyes quickly filling with reproach. 'Damian, you bad man. You shouldn't sneak up on a girl like that.'

'Sometimes it's the only way,' he returned drily. 'Some girls don't answer telephone calls.'

Gemma coloured guiltily. 'I'm sorry. I was going to ring you back, but I forgot. Truly. I...I was a bit of a mess over the weekend.'

'I can imagine. Celeste filled me in on what happened last Friday night. Which is why I was so startled when Ava told me on the phone this morning that you'd gone to work.'

'It seemed the best thing to do.'

'I couldn't agree more. I'm delighted to see you're determined not to be down-in-the-mouth and dreary. Life's too short to waste it mooning over bastards like Nathan Whitmore.'

Gemma's reaction was instant and quite absurd. She wanted to scream at Damian that he had no right to judge Nathan, that he knew nothing about him at all! Just in time, she controlled the quite irrational urge, recognising it as a hangover from what she had so very recently and stupidly believed in her husband and his love for her. 'Yes, well, I'd rather not talk about Nathan, if you don't mind,' she said instead.

'Your wish is my command.' Damian took her arm. 'What would you like to talk about over lunch?'

Gemma felt a reluctant smile pull at her mouth as she

was masterfully propelled towards the street. 'Who said I was having lunch with you?'

'You don't *want* to have lunch with your poor old uncle?' he replied teasingly.

She laughed at this description of himself. Damian was only twenty-nine. He was also the epitome of 'tall dark and handsome', with the added elegance and style that being very wealthy provided. Most men would have looked good in the suit Damian was wearing. He looked fantastic. And he knew it.

'Lunch is fine,' she agreed. 'But as I said, a mutual tongue-lashing of Nathan is out. I also don't want to hear any sarcasm about Byron and Celeste being my parents.'

'Hey!' Damian put up his hands in mock defeat. 'What do you think I am, an unfeeling monster? All I want is to have lunch with my very beautiful niece who, by the way, looks gorgeous with her hair up. You must wear it that way to the party this Friday night.'

'P...party? What kind of party?' Damian's sweet flattery had been unacceptable. His inviting her to a party made her uncomfortable for some unaccountable reason. Were Nathan's vile accusations about Damian still lingering at the back of her mind? It seemed the only reasonable explanation for her sudden unease. Or maybe her trust in the male sex in general had received such an incredible blow that it would be a long time before she could trust another man.

'Just a dance party, Gemma,' Damian explained with an indulgent smile. 'They're very popular with young people. A lot of my friends go to them. I thought it might make you feel better to get out and about, dance a little and meet some new people.'

It did sound innocent enough. And Damian *was* her uncle. Why was she hesitating?

'I...I'm not sure.'

'Hey, no sweat. You don't have to do anything you don't want to do any more. You're your own boss now, remember? Just think about it and if you decide you need some cheering up come Friday night give me a call.' Smiling, he linked arms with her again. 'Now let's go to lunch before your hour is up and we haven't had a thing to eat!'

GEMMA DID NEED cheering up by Friday night. Frankly, she needed cheering up a lot earlier than that.

Work occupied her mind during the day, but come night time, Belleview was hardly a hive of distracting activity and conversation. Byron, quite rightly, was spending a lot of time with Celeste, courting her as he should have courted her all those years ago. And Ava, God love her, either disappeared into her studio with Vince or went out with him. Knowing Ava's history, Gemma did not have the heart to spoil her fun at this glorious time in her life.

So Gemma pretended to be quite happy staying home alone watching television, saying she was tired after being on her feet all day. Yet all the while she was getting more and more depressed. By the time Damian telephoned her on the Thursday night, it didn't take much persuasion for her to say yes.

DAMIAN HUNG UP, not bothering to hide his devilish glee. No one could see him. Celeste had just left with dear old Byron, and Cora was out in the kitchen, clearing up after dinner.

'At last,' he muttered, and let his mind run free over how Friday night should pan out.

Sweet little Gemma would have no resistance at all to the drugs he would slip into her drinks. In the end, she would have no resistance to *him.*

Damian actually trembled with the anticipated pleasure of finally having her in his power. God, but he had waited months for this moment. Never had a woman possessed his brain and his body as much as Gemma had.

From the first moment he'd seen her at that ball he'd

wanted her, wanted her with a want that had gradually become an obsession. Her being his niece didn't change a thing. If anything, it would add a delightfully perverse edge to the experience.

Damian made his way slowly back upstairs while his thoughts raced feverishly on.

He was going to have to be very careful the first time. He would have to seem to give her everything she was looking for, and obviously needing. Tenderness. Comfort. Love…

Later, when she was totally addicted to the mindless ecstasy that the drugs and he could give her, he would introduce her to more refined pleasures. It was amazing the pain a woman could endure—and even welcome—when she was high on the right cocktail.

He would have to video-tape everything, of course, once it got to that stage. Otherwise she might be tempted to tell someone after the drugs wore off. He couldn't have that.

Damian smiled. He might even make some money out of her. It wouldn't be the first time. Amazing how much women were prepared to pay rather than have tapes of their sexual exploits posted to their husbands or their families. They never breathed a word, either. Damian considered it was ironic that it was Nathan himself who had first given him the idea of taping sexual encounters to blackmail women. Poor old Irene…

In a way, it was a form of justice that Nathan's own wife be similarly blackmailed.

Not that justice ever really interested Damian. He had only one aim in life.

Pleasure.

Sheer unadulterated pleasure.

He could hardly wait for tomorrow night to come.

BYRON DIDN'T COME home for dinner on the Friday night. He'd organised to meet Celeste after work for dinner in town and a night at the theatre. Ava and Vince went out for dinner as well, over to Vince's family. Which meant Gemma would be alone at Belleview when Damian came to pick her up at nine o'clock. She hadn't told anyone yet about the dance party, and now that she didn't have to she was relieved.

Gemma hadn't been looking forward to facing the frowns of disapproval. All the Whitmores thought very badly of Damian, yet in all honesty she had never seen any evidence to support his reputation as a wild and dissolute playboy. Any concerns she had ever had over the man had come from everyone around Belleview bad-mouthing him, as they had bad-mouthed Celeste. He was probably as innocent of any real wrongdoing as his sister had proved to be.

Nathan had been the chief castigator of both Campbells, yet it was Nathan who had proven to be the wicked one.

Still, it worried Gemma that she hadn't told Ava some white lie about going out somewhere. What if Ava came home before Gemma and found her bed empty? The poor darling would worry and Gemma didn't want that.

In the end, she decided to leave a note propped up on her pillow saying a friend from work had rung and she'd gone out to a party, and not to worry if she got home late. Byron had given her a set of keys to the house, as well as a remote control for the gates, so there was no trouble with letting herself in.

With that problem solved, Gemma set about having a relaxing bath, then getting herself ready. She had plenty of time—apparently these parties didn't start early. Neither were they dressy affairs. Damian had suggested she wear something casual. Jeans or a skirt and top would be fine.

Gemma's wardrobe was full of mostly classic or tailored garments but she did have a reddish-brown leather skirt which, when teamed with a simple cream silk shirt looked fairly casual. The colour also suited the auburn highlights the hairdresser regularly put into her shoulder-length brown hair. Remembering the compliment Damian had given her earlier in the week, she put it up as she had that day in a loose knot, with lots of wispy bits left around her face and neck. She put gold loops in her ears and a couple of gold chains round her neck. As it was night time, she wore a reasonable amount of make-up, high heels and perfume.

Gemma was ready and waiting, the gates open and her cream clutch bag in hand, when Damian drove in shortly before nine. His low wolf whistle when she opened the door unnerved her slightly, as did his words.

'God, you look great. I'll have to beat the men off with broomsticks.'

When Gemma frowned her immediate unease, Damian smiled reassuringly at her. 'Don't worry, love, you're with me. If we don't tell anyone I'm your uncle, they won't come anywhere near you. Damian's bird always has a hands-off sign on her.'

Gemma wasn't entirely reassured by this idea, and neither did she like others thinking they were boyfriend and girl-friend, but she could see the sense of it if she didn't want to ward off unwanted advances all night. The thought of dancing with perfectly strange men was suddenly anathema to her. Why had she ever agreed to come? She was not ready for this in any way, shape or form.

'Even if I went around telling everyone I was your uncle,' Damian added with an amused gleam in his eye, 'no one would believe me.'

He was right, Gemma conceded as she looked him over. He looked younger than his twenty-nine years, especially when dressed all in black, as he was tonight. Absolutely everything he had on was black, from his high-necked shirt and casual woollen trousers down to his socks and shoes. There was even an ebony ring flashing on one finger and a black-faced watch on his wrist. At least no one would stare at them together as they had often done at her and Nathan.

A jab of intense dismay made her stiffen for a moment.

Why do I keep thinking of him? Why can't I forget him as he has obviously forgotten me?

You know why, taunted a dark inner voice, and Gemma's hand instinctively moved across her stomach. God, what if she *was* pregnant? She didn't want to be. Not now. Not any more. She wanted to forget Nathan, to put him right out of her mind for the rest of her life.

'Are you feeling all right, Gemma?' Damian asked with such a warm concern she felt terribly guilty. Her worry was probably all for nothing anyway. Her period would be along any day, once her cycle got back to normal.

'I'm fine,' she said with a quick smile. 'And you're quite right, Damian. We make a handsome couple.'

He smiled, radiating that dazzling charm which no doubt sent all the women's hearts fluttering. But Gemma knew her heart was unlikely to flutter again for a long time. Not that it had ever fluttered for Damian. Nathan's jealousy had been way off the mark, and quite wasted.

A sharp bitterness shot through Gemma as she thought of all she had suffered at Nathan's hands because of what his sick mind imagined was going on between her and Damian. In a weird kind of way, she almost wished there had been something between them to justify the treatment she had endured. There was nothing worse than being accused of something you hadn't done, nothing worse than being punished when you were innocent.

'Stop thinking about that bastard,' Damian said abruptly, sending her thoughts scattering when he curled his hand around her empty one and pulled her down the front steps.

Gemma found herself belted into the passenger seat of Damian's red Ferrari before she could say boo.

'Wait!' she cried out when he zoomed through the open gates and would have taken off before she had a chance to close them. He screeched on the brakes, darting her a frustrated look.

'I have to close the gates,' she explained patiently, whereupon he gave her a sighing smile.

'For a second there, I thought you'd changed your mind about coming.'

'Never,' she said, determined to dismiss Nathan from her mind for tonight. He didn't deserve thinking about. 'Where is this dance party, by the way?'

'At a pub in North Sydney. You won't know it. It's in the back streets and not the newest establishment around, but the music's great and the drinks are cheap.'

Gemma laughed. 'I wouldn't think you'd care much if the drinks were cheap or not.'

Damian flashed her a wicked grin. 'Watch the pennies and the pounds will look after themselves,' he quipped. 'Light me a cigarette, would you? They're on the dash there, and there's a lighter in my left trouser pocket. Can't get it myself. Must concentrate on the road. This traffic's hell.'

The traffic on the Pacific highway was indeed bad. Every man and his dog seemed to be heading for the city. Nevertheless, Gemma felt very uncomfortable doing something as intimate as fishing around in Damian's trouser pocket. Luckily, she found the lighter quickly and was soon placing a glowing cigarette between Damian's lips. Their eyes met briefly as she did so and Gemma quickly looked away. For there had been nothing platonic in the look Damian had just given her. It had been oddly intense.

Either that, or her imagination was getting the better of her. The latter seemed the most likely.

Damian had always been a perfect gentleman in her company. Always. Nathan's wicked warnings had put the fear of the devil into her, Gemma decided. Listening to scurrilous gossip about people was wrong. And listening to unfounded fears was wrong too. She resolved not to do it any more.

With this in mind Gemma turned a smiling face back

towards Damian. 'It's really sweet of you to take me out like this. I really needed it. I was feeling awfully down.'

'I know, honey, I know,' he said kindly. 'Leave it to dear old Uncle Damian. He knows exactly what you need to cheer you up…'

CHAPTER FOUR

LUKE wouldn't normally have been seen dead at a dance party. At thirty, he considered himself too old for such goings-on. He'd briefly gone through a stage for a couple of years after finishing uni where he haunted clubs, pubs and discos every Friday and Saturday night, but those days were long gone. His life was Campbell Jewels now.

He'd only come here tonight as a favour to his mother. Apparently his kid sister, Mandy, had been coming here nearly every Friday night lately and his mother wanted him to check the place out. Luke thought she was being overprotective, since Mandy was twenty and a very sensible girl, but he'd promised to drop in and see for himself if there was anything to worry about.

He stood in a corner of the room, shaking his head at what was before his eyes. How had he ever enjoyed this kind of thing? The screechingly loud music was enough to give anyone an instant migraine. Add to this the garish lights flashing on and off, the heavy pall of smoke and the crush of a hundred sweaty gyrating bodies in an area where possibly fifty might comfortably have fitted, and you had a scene he found quite repulsive.

Still, Luke wasn't too old that he couldn't appreciate Mandy would quite like such an atmosphere, but he was perturbed by how open the drug use was. Nobody bothered to hide the pill-popping and marijuana-smoking. Luke had also seen a couple of suspicious-looking packages changing hands and quite a few empty syringes in the bins in the toilet block.

He began to worry if Mandy made a habit of coming to this place she might end up not being so sensible.

So Luke stayed in the dimly lit corner and waited, hoping she would show up and he could have a brotherly word in her ear. But after a further half-hour's peering through the smoke haze Mandy still hadn't turned up. He was about to leave when his attention was suddenly captured by a man dressed in black, an exceptionally handsome man with slick black hair, wicked black eyes and flashing white teeth.

Luke was not at all surprised to see Damian Campbell in a place like this. Everyone around Campbell's knew of his reputation for decadent living. He liked to mix with a young fast crowd. He liked his women beautiful, and he didn't care if they were married.

The girl with Damian was certainly beautiful, and very married.

Luke recognised Gemma Whitmore from the photograph in last Sunday's paper of her attending the première to Nathan's Whitmore's latest play. She'd been snapped alongside Celeste and Nathan's adoptive father, Byron Whitmore.

Now Luke was an astute man. He'd long known about the feud between the Campbells and the Whitmores. But one didn't have to be too astute to have noticed that something was afoot between the two families. Celeste Campbell and Byron Whitmore were suddenly as thick as thieves. Yet while that old feud business seemed to have gone out of the window, Luke still didn't think this extended to Damian draping himself all over Nathan Whitmore's wife.

Luke smelled a rat. And there wasn't a bigger rat around Sydney than Damian Campbell.

Luke watched his antics with distaste. The man was a real sleaze-bag. Under the guise of dancing, he was touching Mrs Whitmore wherever he could, finally putting her arms around his neck then curving his hands over her buttocks, pulling her hard against him.

Suddenly, the girl wrenched away from him, swaying violently on her feet. The look on her face was one of total confusion. It was then that Luke realised she was under the influence of some drug or other. Alcohol was unlikely to produce that type of bewilderment. He decided to edge closer and see if he could pick up some of their conversation.

'I...I don't think I like it here, Damian,' the girl was saying in a very slurred voice. Her hand fluttered up to her forehead. 'I...I feel hot, and sort of funny. You'd better take me home.'

'I'll get you a cool drink first,' Damian offered, and led her over to a wall where he virtually propped her against it. 'Stay here. I won't be long.'

Luke didn't know what to do. He didn't want to tangle with Damian Campbell, especially not after just being given the job as sales and marketing manager at Campbell's. But Gemma Whitmore's reactions bothered him. Clearly, she wasn't sure what was going on. Luke suspected she hadn't knowingly taken drugs. If she had, she wouldn't be acting so confused over her condition.

With this thought in mind, Luke followed Damian to the bar and watched while the bastard slipped some powder into the orange juice, mixing it very well while his eyes darted slyly around. Damn, he was right! He was drugging that girl without her knowledge.

Yet it wasn't any of his business, was it?

For a full ten minutes Luke argued with his conscience, then, with a resigned sigh, went in search of trouble. But Damian and the girl were no longer on the dance-floor or anywhere in the room. Swearing at himself, Luke raced outside to the car park where he spotted Damian leaning Mrs Whitmore against a car and kissing her. The girl's arms were dangling limply by her sides, like a rag doll.

Luke felt fury well up inside him. He didn't stop to think any longer, didn't stop to count the cost of his actions, just charged across the car park, whirled Campbell away from the girl and socked him one right on the jaw.

No one was more surprised than Luke when Damian crumpled immediately, falling blessedly unconscious to the concrete. Luke didn't think he'd even seen what hit him. Or who.

'Hey!' some bloke called out from a few cars away. 'What's going on there?'

Luke didn't stay around for any explanations. He swooped up the girl from where she had slid down to sit blank-eyed on the ground, and virtually carried her over to where his own car was parked. Stuffing her into the passenger seat, he raced around to get in and screeched away before anyone could collar him. He wasn't sure what he was going to do, especially after a glimpse in the rear-view mirror showed Damian Campbell getting groggily to his feet.

It was only after he'd driven several blocks and felt secure that no one was following that he pulled over to the kerb and tried to assess the situation. Mrs Whitmore was slumped down in the passenger seat, moaning softly. Hell, what had the bastard fed her? Clearly too much of something. She was almost out of it.

There was nothing for it, really, but to take her home, to her husband. A glance at his watch showed eleven thirty-five. Would Nathan Whitmore be home? Luke had read about his hit play, the one he'd written and was directing. What time did plays end? And where was home, anyway? Mrs Whitmore was hardly in a position to tell him and she didn't have any ID on her.

Spying a public telephone box on the next corner Luke decided to try calling him. If his number was in the book, that was. Damn, but this was becoming complicated. Luke almost regretted getting involved in the first place till he took another look at Gemma Whitmore's sweetly innocent face. How could he have left her with that devil?

Luke had a change of luck. Nathan Whitmore's number was in the book and he was home, answering quite quickly.

Luke kept his voice crisp and businesslike, hoping like hell that Nathan Whitmore was a sensible and reasonable man. He'd heard he was a cool customer, but men were not always cool when it came to their wives, especially beautiful young ones like his.

'Mr Whitmore, this is Luke Barton. Sorry to bother you at this hour, but it was an emergency.'

'Do I know you, Mr Barton?' came a rather tired query.

'Not personally. You may have heard of me. I'm an executive at Campbell Jewels. I was recently promoted to sales and marketing manager.'

'Then haven't you rung the wrong person? Any emergency at Campbell Jewels is hardly a concern of mine. Though maybe you could try my father,' he added caustically.

'This has nothing to do with business. It concerns your wife...'

Luke heard the sharp intake of breath on the other end. 'What about my wife?' he demanded with abrupt harshness.

'God, this is awkward.'

'You're beginning to worry me, Mr Barton. Has something happened to Gemma? Is she all right?'

'I think so.'

'You *think* so. God-dammit, man, what do you mean by that?'

'If you'll just let me explain,' Luke complained.

'Explain, then. But be quick!'

'Look, I'll have to start at the beginning. Earlier tonight I dropped into this disco in a pub at North Sydney—looking for my sister, actually—and while I was there I couldn't help noticing Damian Campbell dancing with a woman I soon recognised as your wife.'

Nathan muttered something highly uncomplimentary about his wife's choice of companion.

'I quite agree with you, Mr Whitmore,' Luke said drily, 'which is why I started watching them, and it soon became obvious to me that your wife was under the influence of some kind of narcotic. This place is rather a haunt for drug users, I think. Anyway, when I saw Campbell slip something into her drink without her knowing I realised she wasn't a willing party to what was going on, if you get my drift.'

'I get your drift only too well, Mr Barton,' he said bitterly. 'Can you tell me where exactly this place is? Is my wife still there?'

'No need to worry, Mr Whitmore. When I saw the lie of the land, I took it upon myself to get your wife away from the bastard. I have her with me in my car. She's—er—fallen asleep.'

Luke sensed a wealth of emotion vibrating in the taut silence that followed.

'If you'd give me your address, Mr Whitmore,' Luke offered, 'I'll drive her straight home.'

'Are you sure she's all right? Will she need a doctor?'

'I think all she needs is a good night's sleep, though she's going to have one heck of a hangover in the morning. But yes, Mr Whitmore, I'm pretty sure she's all right.'

Luke committed the address and Nathan Whitmore's directions to memory, grateful that he didn't live at Palm Beach or somewhere as distant as that. Elizabeth Bay wasn't more than a hop, skip and jump from North Sydney.

Nathan Whitmore was pacing up and down the pavement when Luke guided his car into the kerb. He immediately strode over and wrenched open the passenger door. As soon as he unclipped the seatbelt, his unconscious wife slumped sideways out of the car and into her husband's arms. Nathan scooped her up, his face grim.

'I should have killed that bastard the first time he came near her,' he muttered, Luke having no doubt whom he meant.

'She's only asleep, Mr Whitmore,' he reassured. 'I checked her pulse. It's fine.'

'Do you have any idea what he gave her?'

Luke shook his head.

Gemma stirred in his arms. 'Is that you, Nathan?' she said in a tiny, child-like voice.

'Yes, Gemma. It's me.'

She sighed her satisfaction then drifted back into her blessedly unconscious state.

'Help me get her upstairs?' Nathan asked Luke.

Some considerable time later, Luke was perched on the edge of a sofa in an elegantly furnished sitting-room while Nathan Whitmore was supposedly putting his wife to bed. Nathan had asked Luke to wait so he had. But he was certainly taking his time. He'd been away ages.

Frankly, Luke was beginning to feel concerned over what had happened back in that car park, despite Damian Campbell not having been badly hurt. It was a question of how much he'd seen. Hopefully, he hadn't had time to recognise him, or take down the number-plate of his attacker's vehicle. If he had, Luke could kiss his job at Campbell's goodbye.

'Can I get you a drink, Mr Barton?' Nathan asked on returning to the room. 'I certainly can do with one, but I can make you coffee or tea if you'd prefer.'

'I think a small Scotch wouldn't go amiss,' Luke said.

'I don't think I'll be making mine too small,' his host muttered, and, after handing Luke a conservative amount, poured himself a hefty slug.

There ensued a short, tense conversation where Nathan tried to elicit more details from Luke.

'So you actually hit him.'

'Had to. He's all right, though. I saw him beginning to get to his feet, but I hope to hell he didn't recognise me.'

'He won't be getting to his feet by the time I get through with him,' Nathan said darkly.

Luke frowned. 'Do you think that's a wise idea?'

'No. But the time for caution has passed. The man's a blot on society. He has to be stopped.'

'Stopped?' Luke repeated. 'What do you mean, stopped? Good God, man, you don't mean to...to...?'

Luke watched, appalled, as Nathan Whitmore's face became a stony mask. Those cool grey eyes of his turned icy cold before they met Luke's over the rim of the glass. 'Don't let your imagination get the better of you, Mr Barton,' he said with a silky smoothness that sent a shiver running down Luke's spine. 'There are many ways to stop a monster other than murder.'

An uneasy silence descended on the room. Luke finished his drink and was standing up to go when a telephone rang somewhere. His host excused himself and left the room, closing the door behind him. Luke could hear his muffled voice but couldn't work out what he was saying. When he finally returned, Luke also couldn't work out the expression on his face. It was most peculiar.

'That was my father,' he explained. 'It seems both our problems have been solved, Mr Barton.'

'Both our problems?'

'With Damian Campbell.'

'Oh? How's that?'

'Our esteemed Mr Campbell has been in a car accident. Wrapped his Ferrari around a telegraph pole a little over an hour ago. Witnesses say he sped out of a hotel car park in North Sydney like a maniac and immediately lost control of the car.' Nathan walked over and poured himself another drink, turning to raise the glass in a mock toast. 'He was killed instantly.'

Luke said nothing as Nathan Whitmore smiled a coldly satisfied smile, then drank.

THE FIRST FLUTTERINGS of consciousness were accompanied by a dull throbbing in Gemma's temples. She moaned softly and pulled the bedclothes up around her neck, squeezing her eyes shut against the pain. The throbbing increased as she surfaced further and another moan fell from her lips.

The mattress dipped beside her and a hand stroked some strands of hair back from her face. 'How are you feeling?' a familiar voice enquired.

'I've got a terrible headache,' she mumbled. Sighing a

deep shuddering sigh, she rolled over on to her back where slowly and quite painfully she opened her eyes.

Nathan was sitting on the side of the bed, looking down at her with those beautiful grey eyes of his. Only they didn't look so beautiful at that moment. They looked awful. Dull and sunken, with huge dark rings around them.

Any shock at his appearance was suddenly overridden by Gemma's shock at realising where she was and who she was looking up at. For one mad moment, she wondered if the past fortnight had been some ghastly nightmare and she'd woken to find everything was back as it once had been, and she and Nathan would live happily ever after.

But of course, that wasn't the case. She could tell that just by looking into Nathan's face. Yet what was she doing here? How had she got here? The last thing she remembered was dancing at that disco with Damian and feeling very peculiar.

Her face screwed up with the pain of her throbbing head and the effort to put the pieces together of the night before. Short flashes of memory kept jumping into her head, then skittering away before they came clear. Someone had kissed her, she thought. And held her very tightly. Had that been Nathan? She seemed to recall speaking to Nathan at some stage during the night. Had he shown up at the disco and taken her away from Damian? No, that didn't feel right. There had been some other man…

Gemma's head throbbed ever harder as she tried to remember. God, she must have been blind drunk. Yet she'd only had a couple of glasses of wine earlier in the evening before switching to orange juice. Could someone have spiked her juice with gin, or vodka perhaps?

More flashes of memory started to return, sketchy and quite alarming. She recalled being carried somewhere and then hands undressing her. Her eyes flung wide as that particular memory seemed to be accompanied by an intense wave of sensual pleasure. Dear God, Nathan hadn't, had he?

With a fearful gasp, she lifted the bedclothes to take a

quick anxious look at herself, and while she wasn't naked she only had a skimpy bra and bikini pants on. A frantic glance around the room saw her clothes draped over a nearby chair and her jewellery on the bedside table.

'No need to panic,' Nathan said drily. 'I didn't touch you, except in the course of undressing you and putting you to bed. Not that you didn't *want* me to. You were all for it. Fact is, I had the devil of a time getting away from you with my virtue intact. I could have done anything to you I wanted and you would not have objected. It was lucky for me that you eventually passed out again.'

Gemma stared at him. 'I don't believe you!' she exclaimed, horrified by the inner suspicion that what he was saying was true.

'There's no need to be so appalled at yourself, Gemma. It wasn't your fault. Anyone can become wildly uninhibited and promiscuous while under the influence of certain drugs.'

'*Drugs*!' she gasped, her head reeling.

'That's right. Your dear uncle Damian had been slipping something into your drinks all night.'

She just stared at him.

He shook his head, his eyes reproachful. 'Why did you go out with him, Gemma? I did warn you his being your uncle wouldn't stop him. Men like him don't have any qualms, or morals, or conscience.'

These last words outraged her so much she was propelled from her frozen horror into a somewhat shaky tirade. 'Isn't that the p...pot calling the kettle black? I've already told you a thousand times, Damian has never been anything but a perfect gentleman with me, so why shouldn't I go to a harmless disco with him? Besides, I only have your say-so that he was the one who put drugs in my drinks. Maybe it was someone else,' she argued, already knowing in her heart that she was clutching at straws.

'I don't blame you for not taking my word for anything,' Nathan returned ruefully, 'but I have an independent witness who saw everything. A Mr Luke Barton. He's an executive at Campbell's. He noticed what was happening between you and Campbell and didn't like the look of things. The man's reputation *has* preceded him. When Damian coerced you into the car park outside and started mauling you, he stepped in.'

'S…stepped in? What do you mean?'

'Rescued you, dear heart. Dragged Damian off you, popped him on the chin and took off with you in his car. The fact that you went with him without a whimper might underline my earlier claim that you were not in a fit state to say no to any man. You're damned lucky that Luke is a decent fellow. He could easily have taken over where Damian left off but instead he called me, then brought you home.'

Gemma closed her eyes against the horrors Nathan had just described to her. She didn't want to believe him, for to do so was to accept that everything he had ever said about Damian was true. And everything he had said about *her* was true. She *was* a naïve silly little bitch to have been taken in by someone as deeply evil as Damian obviously was.

The extent of her uncle's wickedness hit her like a punch in the stomach. Good God, the man was vile! But how had he hoped to get away with doing something so…so gross? Drugging her, then…then…

Nausea and an overwhelming feeling of betrayal sent a bitter taste into her mouth and she lashed out at the person closest to her, the one whose own betrayal cut even deeper than Damian's. Her eyes opened in a way they had never opened before, raking over Nathan with a type of coldly cynical gaze which had previously been his sole provence.

'Why didn't you tell this Luke person we were separated?' she asked, her voice hard and bitter. 'Why didn't you have him take me home to Belleview instead of here?'

Nathan seemed startled by her accusatory tone, which infuriated her further. 'You couldn't resist having the opportunity to say, "I told you so", could you? You had to lord it over me, make me feel small and stupid. You had to show me that you had known best all along and that if I'd listened to you this wouldn't have happened.'

Nathan sighed a weary sigh. 'That's not true, Gemma. When Luke rang, all I thought about was your welfare. I had to see for myself that you were all right.'

'You're a liar!' she flung at him wildly, hating the way her heart had turned over at his pretend concern. 'You don't care about me! You've only ever cared about yourself!'

Gemma threw back the bedclothes and climbed out of the bed, snatching up her clothes from the chair and whirling to glare down at a stony-faced Nathan.

'Don't go thinking you're any better than Damian, because you're not! You're both bastards. I hate and despise the pair of you. When I think that I spent this last night in the same bed that you've probably been busy screwing Jody in all week, I want to be sick.'

Nathan stood up, his face ashen. 'Jody hasn't been in this bed. Not once.'

'And I'm supposed to believe that?' she said scoffingly.

His eyes turned sardonic, a wry smile twisting his mouth. 'If you did, I'd probably call you a fool. But it's true, nevertheless.'

'Are you saying you didn't bring her home here the night after the party?'

'No, that's not what I'm saying.'

Her top lip curled with contempt. 'So! You're just playing with words. No doubt she was very happy to accommodate you in all those interesting places and ways your innocent and silly young wife used to shrink from, or be embarrassed over.'

'I never wanted you to do anything you weren't comfortable with, Gemma,' he said stiffly.

She laughed. 'Then why throw me over for an older, more experienced model? Didn't straightforward love-making satisfy you any more? Maybe I should have asked Lenore what she did for you that kept you in her bed for twelve years.

Obviously my country-bumpkin technique was a little lacking.'

'That's not true,' Nathan said rather bleakly. 'You know I enjoyed making love to you.'

'How kind of you to say so,' she retorted bitterly. 'I'm so gratified. Of course, there is only so much youth and innocence a man like you can take before he needs a change. Still, all that's water under the bridge now, isn't it? We're over, as you so rightly pointed out to me the last time we met. If I loved you once, I certainly don't any more, so if you're having second thoughts about getting rid of your regular lay then think again. I wouldn't have you back if you crawled on your hands and knees from here to Burke and back. Now, I'm going to have a shower and get dressed, after which I'm going to call Belleview and let them know where I am. I can only hope that they haven't noticed yet that I'm missing.'

'I've already spoken with Byron,' Nathan said, his expression totally unreadable now, his voice low and irritatingly calm. 'He knows where you are.'

'I hope you haven't given him any false hopes,' she warned darkly. 'We both know he wants us to get back together again. But I won't be manipulated. Not any more.'

'I won't deny he seemed pleased to hear you were with me.'

'My God, you really have changed your mind, haven't you? You want me back for some reason. Why, for pity's sake? Has the cost been too high?' she scorned. 'Is Byron's opinion of you so important that you would be prepared to put up with this naïve silly little bitch in your bed every night?'

Nathan flinched at this last remark. 'Please don't keep calling yourself that.'

'Why not? It seems very appropriate, especially after last night, wouldn't you say? I'd have to win the prize for shmuck of the century, wouldn't I? Everyone else knew the sort of person Damian was, even Celeste. But not good old Gemma from Timbuctoo! She thought he was a perfect gentleman—instead he was the worst kind of pervert. I sometimes wonder if there's something about me that attracts that kind of man,' she finished, glaring straight at Nathan.

He visibly blanched and for some unaccountable reason she felt guilty. Lord knew why. He deserved everything she could throw at him, surely!

'Let's not pursue this conversation further,' she suddenly snapped. 'Because there's nothing you could say or do to make me resume our marriage.'

Gemma brushed past Nathan's seemingly frozen body and strode angrily into the bathroom. It felt good to slam the door shut, felt good to snap the taps on, hard and strong. But by the time she had rid herself of her underwear and stepped under the steaming jets of water, tears were running down her face, tears for her lost innocence and her lost love, tears for all the dreams which she had once had and which would never now come true.

There was no evidence of tears, however, by the time she walked into the kitchen to find Nathan sitting up at the breakfast bar, drinking coffee. Gemma was fully composed, if a little fragile. Her headache was only marginally better, and there was a lingering of nausea in her empty stomach.

The clock on the wall said eleven-fifteen.

'I'm going to call a taxi now,' she told him crisply.

He looked up, his eyes betraying nothing as he looked her up and down. 'I think you'd better sit down a while, Gemma. I have something to tell you…'

CHAPTER FIVE

GEMMA sat on top of the mullock heap, idly swatting flies and fossicking through the dirt and rocks around her. The likelihood of finding any opal or gemstone of value in Ma's leavings was remote, but Gemma found the mindless activity soothing. She found life back at Lightning Ridge soothing all round.

When she'd stepped off the plane a little over six weeks ago she'd been a quivering wreck.

Twenty-four hours previously she had attended Damian's funeral, staunchly standing by her mother's and grandmother's sides, pretending for their sakes that she still loved her uncle, still held him in high esteem. It had been Byron who had asked this mammoth effort from her, explaining that it would have been totally cruel to blacken the memory of their son and brother. Cruel and unnecessary. What would be gained by exposing what Damian had tried to do the night he died? Byron had argued.

Gemma had already been in too weakened an emotional state to fight her father's wishes. She'd begun to fall apart from the moment Nathan had told her of Damian's fatal car accident. Nathan had tried to be kind in the telling, she supposed, but had clearly been at a loss to understand her tears. Disbelief had eventually changed to a cold anger, when he thought she was grieving for the man.

But it wasn't that at all. She was grieving for the pathetic mess people made of their lives when there was no need. Why couldn't everyone be decent and kind, loving and caring for each other instead of being consumed by their own selfish and self-destructive desires?

Nathan hadn't said a single word to her during the drive back to Belleview later that day. Gemma suspected he'd once thought there had been something more than a platonic relationship between herself and Damian at some stage, and she'd been too emotionally and physically exhausted to try to convince him otherwise. She'd sat in the passenger seat, huddled up and shivering despite it being a reasonably warm spring day.

If it hadn't been for Ava, Gemma believed she might have gone totally over some dark edge that day. But dear sweet Ava had enfolded her against her womanly bosom, fed her and fussed over her then put her to bed with a couple of sleeping pills. By the time Gemma woke late the next morning, the sun had been shining brightly and any serious breakdown had been averted.

Still, by the time the funeral was over a few days later it had been imperative that she get away. Gemma had somehow found just enough courage and spirit left to make that decision, and to follow it through. Both Celeste and Byron had argued with her, saying they wanted to look after her. Even Ava had argued with her, trying reverse psychology in claiming she needed Gemma's company around Belleview.

Gemma had smiled indulgently at this—Ava's days of wishy-washy dependence were well and truly over—then ignored it. She'd ignored all their wishes and booked her flight to Lightning Ridge. All she had promised was that she would write. She'd refused to agree to any return date, simply saying that she would come back when the time was right. She'd apologised to Byron for quitting her job again, but this time, she'd told him, it was for good. If and when she returned to Sydney, she was determined to get her own job, under her own steam.

But would she ever return to Sydney? Gemma wondered,

tipping back the brim of the old felt Akruba hat she was wearing and staring around her. There had been a time when she had found nothing pleasing to the eye in the dry, stark landscape around Lightning Ridge. And the lifestyle had bored her to tears.

Yet now, she could see a kind of raw beauty in the rocky ridges and the harsh blue sky. And she had welcomed the peace and quiet which came with the territory. The heat was the only thing she was taking some time getting used to again. Gemma pulled a handkerchief from the pocket of her denim cut-offs and wiped a fine layer of sweat from her forehead. She certainly hadn't sweated like this back in Sydney.

'What on earth are you doin' sittin' out here in the sun?' Ma growled at her. 'It's nearly midday, for heaven's sake. Only ''mad dogs and Englishmen go out in the midday sun''!'

'Is it really that late?' Gemma replied, scrambling down off the mullock heap and giving Ma a sheepish look. She had developed the habit of daydreaming since returning to the Ridge. Many a time she would just sit, and her mind would start wandering, or simply to blank for ages. The first time she had done it, she'd got a touch of the sun. Not burnt, mind. Gemma's skin wasn't the kind to burn. But she'd developed the most dreadful headache which had lasted for days.

'Just look at you,' Ma went on accusingly. 'You're getting as brown as a berry. Haven't you been usin' your sunscreen?'

'Yes, I have,' Gemma defended. 'Truly. I just have a lot of natural melanin in my skin.'

'A lot of what?'

'Melanin. It's a pigment.'

'It's an excuse, that's what it is. You don't want to be gettin' as many skin cancers as I've got when you're my age, do you? Why don't you make yourself useful,' Ma suggested, 'by gettin' us a good drink while I get the shoppin' out of the truck?'

Ma's idea of a cool drink was always a beer, but Gemma didn't object. She liked a cool beer herself when the temperature got up to thirty-five as it was today. And it was only November! By Christmas they'd be steaming. Ma thought the old dugout was cool compared to the caravan she used to live in. And it probably was, but hardly a patch on the air-conditioning at Belleview. Gemma missed her creature comforts sometimes.

She missed other things too.

Yet it had been good to come back to where she'd been brought up, good for her to get back to basic living. She'd been spoilt down in Sydney. It had made her soft. When troubles had come, she'd started succumbing to self-pity and that was a sorry way to live.

But a few weeks of being around Ma and looking after herself with little or no pampering had done her the world of good. So had not having any television or video to watch. They talked into the night most evenings, and Gemma had at last begun to put her marriage into perspective. Ma had a way of putting things sometimes that made everything seem so clear and simple.

'It was just sex, love,' she'd said about Gemma's feelings for Nathan and his for her. 'Happens all the time. Fact is, most marriages start that way but then kiddies come along and that either makes or breaks things. Bein' a parent makes one grow up, you see. Doesn't always happen like that, of course, specially with the men. Some men never grow up, love. That's the truth of it and there's no use breakin' your heart over that kind.'

Gemma didn't really think Nathan was that kind. He was a far more complex individual with deep dark hang-ups from a past that someone as simple as Ma would never guess at. But it was still good to hear her homespun philosophies which indeed gave Gemma plenty to think about.

'You don't think I ever really loved Nathan either, do you?' she'd remarked late one night.

'Nah. He bowled you over with his good looks and his know-how, that's all. How could you really love him? You didn't even get to know him. Except in the biblical sense,' Ma had cackled, leaning over to dig Gemma in the ribs.

Although Gemma had laughed too at the time, she was still a long way from getting over Nathan. And she was long way from forgetting what it was like when he made love to her. Many a night she would lie in the narrow, uncomfortable single bed she'd slept in as a child, her body encased in a simple cotton nightshirt, and think of her experiences as the wife of a man who had done to her what he had once vowed to do. He had made her body attuned to his, had made her respond even when she hadn't wanted to, had made her want him with a want that had nothing to do with love and everything to do with lust. In that respect, Ma was probably right.

Sometimes her skin would actually crawl with desire, and she would toss and turn, aching to have him there in bed with her to drive the madness away. She wanted to cling to him, move with him, dig her nails into him. She wanted... oh, she just wanted. There was no rhyme or reason to her frustrations, she knew that. She'd become a mindless victim to a devilishly sexy man who had taken her blank virgin body and programmed it with responses that only he could trigger, and needs that only he could soothe.

Which was why it would be a long time before she would forget him. Maybe she never would if what she suspected turned out to be true.

But that didn't mean she had to fall apart over him. Hell, no. She was made of tougher stuff than that, she hoped.

Gemma walked into the relative cool of the dugout and was bending down to extract a couple of cans of beer from the small gas fridge in the corner when the dizziness struck. Instinctively, she sank down to the ground and put her head between her knees, which was how Ma found her when she walked in.

'Good God!' Ma threw the shopping bags on the kitchen table and raced over to squat down beside Gemma. 'What is it? What's wrong?'

Gemma slowly raised her head. The black dots had gone from in front of her eyes but she still felt cold and clammy. 'I…I nearly fainted.'

'See what happens when you don't do as you're told? You've probably got sunstroke again.'

'I don't think it's sunstroke,' she said quietly, slumping down on the floor. 'I think I'm pregnant.'

Ma's eyebrows shot up. 'Good lord! Have you been to see the doc?'

'No.'

'Then how can you be sure?'

'I haven't had a period in ages, my breasts are sore and I've been feeling like throwing up the last few mornings.'

'And you didn't tell me?'

'I…I was trying to pretend it wasn't true.'

Ma sat down on the floor beside her with a thud, a troubled frown making more wrinkles on her already deeply wrinkled face. 'Don't you want this baby, love?'

Gemma sighed. 'In any other circumstances, I would be over the moon, but it's hardly the right time, is it? I always vowed that no child of mine would have the disadvantages I had, being brought up by a single parent with no brothers or sisters.'

'You're not plannin' on doin' away with it, are you?'

'Good lord, no!'

'Didn't think so.' Ma gnawed on her bottom lip for a while then looked over at Gemma. 'I'll help you any way I can but this is hardly the ideal place to bring up a baby. You better than anyone should know that.'

Gemma glanced around her at the primitive surroundings. 'Yes, I know.'

'What do you think you might do?'

'I haven't thought that far ahead yet.'

'How far are you gone, do you know?'

'A little over two months,' she said, deliberately adding a week to the truth. She'd told Ma just about everything that had happened between herself and Nathan since her last visit to Lightning Ridge, except the rape. She had substituted a fierce argument for that incident.

Ma gave her a sharp look. 'It *is* your husband's, isn't it?'

Gemma's dismay was acute. 'Oh, Ma…not you too. Of course it's Nathan's. I've never been to bed with any other man. I know you don't believe I loved Nathan any more than he loved me but you're wrong. I did. I would never be unfaithful to him.'

Ma reached out to curve a comforting hand over Gemma's shoulder. 'I believe you, love. But I had to ask. Come on, let's get you up off this floor and have that cool drink. Unless you think you should lie down.'

'I'm all right now. Really. I'll just sit at the table with you.'

'I'll get you a lemonade. No more beer for you, young woman. Ladies havin' babies don't drink beer.'

Gemma didn't think a can or two of light beer would do any harm but she wasn't going to argue.

'Do you still love him?' Ma asked as she handed Gemma a can of lemonade and sat down with her beer.

Gemma's stomach contracted. Did she? To be honest, she wasn't sure. Her shrug was full of confusion. 'Maybe. Probably. I don't really know. I still think about him a lot. He's a hard man to forget.'

'I'll have to meet this devil one day, see just what it is that gets the women in so badly.'

Gemma sighed. 'I doubt you'll ever get to meet him. He's not likely to drop in out here for morning tea, is he?'

'Oh, I don't know, love. Once you tell him about the

baby, I wouldn't mind bettin' he hotfoots it out here like a shot out of a gun.'

'I'm not going to tell him about the baby.'

Ma almost had apoplexy. 'Not tell him about the baby? Good God, whyever not, you stupid girl?'

Gemma bristled. 'He doesn't want me any more and he certainly won't want this baby,' she said firmly.

'Rubbish! He married that other woman cause she was havin' his baby, and he never fancied her nearly as much as he obviously fancied you. As for his not wantin' you any more, I can't believe you believe that nonsense. The man was crazy about you at one stage, so crazy that he married you after sayin' he would never marry again! OK, so he went off his head with jealousy when he thought you were having an affair and did some crazy things. But a lot of men do crazy things when they're insanely jealous. I'll bet he's already sorry he chucked you out.'

Gemma recalled that brief moment the morning after Damian's death, when she'd accused Nathan of wanting her back again. He certainly hadn't responded to that, nor had he done anything later to persuade her to resume their marriage. Yet he'd had plenty of opportunity, especially with her in such an emotionally vulnerable state.

'I don't deny Nathan was jealous,' she said with a sigh. 'But he doesn't love me, and it's perfectly clear he doesn't want me back. If he did, he'd have called, or written, or come up here personally. No, I won't use this baby to get back a man who doesn't love me.'

'Then you're a silly little fool. What if he finds out anyway then tries to take the baby away from you?'

Gemma stared at Ma, wide-eyed.

'He's a rich man, isn't he? You said he inherited a fortune from his grandparents on top of all the money those plays of his bring in.'

Gemma nodded.

'Amazing what money can buy,' was Ma's dry comment.

'Nathan wouldn't do that!' Gemma gasped.

'How do you know? You yourself said you didn't really know him. What if he's always wanted a son and you have a boy? What if he becomes as mad for the child as he once was for you? The man has *legal* rights as well. He might not need to bribe anyone to get custody of his child. All he needs is a sympathetic judge.'

Gemma was shaking her head. 'Nathan would never do something like that.'

'For pity's sake, don't start puttin' your head in the sand, love. You might be sorry one day if you do. It's time to be a realist, not a fluffy-headed romantic. You have to think of your own welfare as well. Bringin' a baby up all alone is one hell of a job in this day and age. It takes a lot of time and money for one thing.'

'I have time and money,' Gemma countered irritably, sorry now that she had told Ma. 'If I want more money, I can get myself a smart solicitor, divorce Nathan and take him to the cleaners.'

'Oh, lovely. Is that what city life has done to you? Turned you into a money-grubbin', hard-hearted little bitch?'

Shock at Ma's harsh words sent Gemma's eyes rounding.

'Don't look at me like that,' Ma scorned with a flick of her hand. 'You're no babe-in-the-woods any more. You're a married woman and you're going to have your husband's child. This is no time for a divorce!'

'You don't understand,' Gemma wailed. 'Nathan won't want this child!'

'Why won't he want it? I bet he'd be tickled pink.'

Gemma was about to blurt out the truth when something kept her mouth shut. Instead, she dropped her eyes and shook her head. 'He probably won't believe the baby's his,' she muttered.

'Rubbish! There's tests for that sort of thing these days. You could prove it.'

'Ma, stop it,' Gemma groaned. 'Please. I…I don't want to tell Nathan about the baby.'

'You're being a stubborn fool!'

'Maybe. But it's my life and my baby.'

'That's a very naïve thing to say, Gemma.'

'I am not naïve!' she cried.

'Then put your actions where your mouth is and tell him about the baby. Make him put his uninterest along with his intention to divorce you both in writin'.'

Gemma threw up her hands in defeat. 'All right!' she bit out, the 'naïve' accusation still stinging. 'I'll go to Sydney and tell him.'

'No, you won't. We'll ring him and get him to come out here. I want to see this devil for meself. And I want to see how he takes your news about the baby.'

'How on earth are we going to get him to come all this way without telling him about the baby first?'

'I'll think of something, love. Never you fear.'

CHAPTER SIX

HE WAS coming.

Gemma still could not believe it. Ma had gone back into town the previous afternoon and brought back a pregnancy testing kit from the chemist. When it had returned a resoundingly positive result, she'd driven back into town and rung Nathan at home, getting on to him immediately.

Apparently, he was flying up this morning, then hiring a car, refusing Ma's offer to pick him up at the airport. Gemma estimated that if the plane was on time he should arrive around eleven. Since it was just before ten, she still had over an hour to wait, yet already she was highly agitated.

'I want to know what you told Nathan to make him come,' she asked Ma again as he paced up and down. 'You told him about the baby, didn't you?'

'Nope.'

'Why won't you tell me what you said?'

'Because.'

Gemma stamped her foot in frustration. 'That's no answer!'

'It's the only one you're going to get,' Ma retorted firmly. 'Now go make yourself pretty for your husband. And put on some fresh clothes.'

'I will not! I look perfectly all right in these shorts and top which were put on fresh this morning. It's what I always wear and I'm not changing it for anyone, least of all *him*.'

Ma shrugged and had to battle to stop a smile from pulling at her lips. Little did Gemma know that in her present rigout she would hold more attractions for a jaded city man than the most dolled-up glamour-puss.

There was so much for him to feast his eyes upon.

Gemma's long shapely legs would have made a dancer proud, and every inch of their firm tanned expanse was on display, her short shorts only barely covering her buttocks. If she bent over, they didn't even do that. Then there was her singlet top which might have been reasonably modest on a less well-endowed girl. But Gemma's pregnancy had made her already full bust more than memorable, her darkening and distended nipples clearly outlined against the thin white material.

'I'm not putting any make-up on either,' Gemma pouted. 'Neither am I going to do anything fancy with my hair!'

Now Gemma's face had never really needed make-up, with her clear olive skin and thickly lashed brown eyes, her high cheekbones that flushed prettily when her blood was up, and her generous lips, which did likewise. As for her hair...at the moment it was falling around her face with that slightly dishevelled and tousled look which could sometimes be sexier than all the sleek coiffures in the world.

Ma had no doubt that when Nathan Whitmore arrived he would not be able to take his eyes off his lovely young wife, nor would he be able to stop himself from wanting her back in his bed, as he had obviously wanted her from the first moment he'd set eyes upon her.

'The least you can do is put some lipstick on,' Ma complained.

'What for? I don't think you've been listening to me these past few weeks, Ma. Nathan doesn't want me any more. And I certainly don't want him. God help you if you've been telling him I do. You...you haven't, have you?' she asked in a panic.

'Certainly not! Look, if you must know, all I told him was that you hadn't been very well.'

Gemma's expression was sceptical. 'Oh, come now, Ma, that wouldn't have got Nathan charging up here. He'd have simply told you to take me to a doctor.'

'Er—we don't have that kind of doctor up here.'

'What kind of doctor? Are you talking about a gynaecologist?'

'No, a psychiatrist.'

Gemma's mouth fell open then snapped shut. 'You told him I was mad as a hatter?'

'Something like that.'

'Ma, how could you?'

Ma shrugged, the action making her huge body jiggle like jelly. 'It was real easy.'

Gemma groaned. 'Nathan's the one who's going to be mad as a hatter when he finds out you lied to him.'

'Couldn't you pretend to be a bit loony?' Ma asked hopefully.

Gemma pulled a face at her. 'Very funny.'

'Look, it got him up here, didn't it? I'll straighten things out as soon as he arrives, then when you tell him the real reason you wanted to see him he'll soon forget my little white lie.'

'You've never said a truer word, Ma,' was Gemma's dry remark, her stomach turning over as she tried to imagine what Nathan's reaction to her pregnancy would be. 'God, this is going to be a disaster!' she grimaced.

'No, it isn't. It'll settle a lot of things in your mind, and it'll give the two of you a chance to come to some agreement where the baby is concerned. As I said before, Gemma, the man has rights. Best you see what part he wants to play in the child's life right from the start. Maybe he'll only want to give you financial support, but I have a feelin' in me water that he'll want more than that. Now, I'm going to make us a nice cup of tea then we'll talk about somethin' else for the next hour, OK?'

Gemma sighed her defeat. 'OK.'

Ma turned away to walk over to the primitive kitchenette, filling the kettle from the old tap which connected to the tank outside and lighting the small gas primus stove. She wasn't sure how things would turn out today with Nathan and Gemma, but she was one of the old school who believed marriage was a very serious business. It was not to be entered into lightly.

It was not to be thrown away lightly, either. Gemma had married this man and she was having his baby. They both had a responsibility to try again, especially since it seemed that what had broken them up had been a series of unfortunate mishaps, plus a healthy dose of male jealousy.

OK, so they didn't seem to have much going for them at the moment except sex, but that was not to be scoffed at, in Ma's opinion. Many a couple deeply in love had broken up because of problems in the bedroom. With a bit of luck, this baby might make Mr Nathan Whitmore see his wife as more than a sex object. Maybe he would begin to appreciate her generous and genuinely loving soul, and maybe, with a bit of luck, some of that capacity for love might rub off on to his own obviously lacking and selfish male heart.

Whatever, Ma believed she had done the right thing in organising this meeting. No matter what happened, Gemma had to tell the man about his baby. After that, it was up to them.

GEMMA WAS IN A state by the time eleven came and went without Nathan showing up. Her feelings swung between disappointment and relief. She kept walking outside and staring down the dusty track, squinting her eyes against the glare of the sun. A couple of times a cloud of dust in the distance sent her heart racing and a squirming feeling into her stomach, but no car materialised their way. The third time it happened, the butterflies stayed away. But then a car suddenly came into view, and everything inside Gemma flipped over. She raced back inside, pale and shaking.

'He's coming,' she whispered.

Ma stood up, a formidable figure despite being dressed in an old blue floral dress that should have been consigned to a charity clothes bin years ago. She put a steadying hand on Gemma's shoulders and looked her straight in the eye. 'Calm yourself, love. He's just a man.'

Gemma swallowed, knowing Ma was saying it as she saw it, but she didn't have all the facts. Gemma was worried sick over how Nathan was going to react to the news that a baby had been conceived that awful afternoon. It was ironic that she had first accepted such a possibility with such optimism, thinking a pregnancy could be used as a weapon to get Nathan back. She knew better now. Only Ma's argument that Nathan could cause her problems later if she didn't tell him about the baby up front had made her agree to this course of action. Still, that didn't mean she had to look forward to relaying the news.

'Don't skulk away in here,' Ma reprimanded. 'Come outside and meet him with your head held high and some starch in your backbone. Don't let him think you're afraid of him.'

'I'm not afraid of him,' she said stiffly. She was afraid of herself. She'd always been afraid of herself where Nathan was concerned.

Gemma walked out into the sunlight with Ma just as a blue Corolla pulled up where the track ended, twenty or so metres away. She lifted a hand to shade her eyes from the sunlight, but it was shaking so much she put it down again.

Nathan climbed out from behind the wheel of the dusty car, looking as though he'd just stepped out of an air-conditioned city office. He was dressed in a pale grey business suit, a crisp white shirt and dark grey tie. Ma, who had never seen Nathan before, sucked in a startled breath as he started walking towards them, the sun dancing on his blond hair as the elegantly lazy stride of his long legs covered the ground with surprising speed.

'Hell, girl,' she muttered under her breath. 'You didn't tell me he was *that* good-looking.'

'He's just a man, Ma,' Gemma countered with perverse humour, but her heart was pounding in her chest at the sight of her handsome husband, in much the same way as it had always done.

His beautiful grey eyes flicked from Ma to Gemma as he approached, disconcerting her when they travelled slowly down her body then up again. God, but she despised herself for the way her pulse-rate was going haywire. But at least she wasn't fool enough to mistake her reactions for love any more. She knew good old lust when she felt it these days. And much as she didn't want still to lust after Nathan, it was clear that she did.

'You look surprisingly well,' he said curtly, 'for someone's who's having a nervous breakdown.'

'Before any more is said,' Ma intervened swiftly, 'Gemma is perfectly well, as you've so rightly noticed. I lied to get you out here, Mr Whitmore. I'm not sorry I did, either.'

Nathan's glare was withering as his eyes shifted to Ma but she didn't flinch an inch.

'I hope you have a very good reason,' he grated out. 'If Gemma's face is anything to go by, she doesn't seem to agree with you, Mrs—er…'

'Call me Ma. The truth is, Mr Whitmore, that Gemma has something important to tell you and I wanted to be with her when she did.'

'Why?' he returned with a slicing edge to his voice. 'What did you think I would do to her? What has she been telling you about me?'

'Nothing I haven't seen for myself these few short moments, Mr Whitmore,' Ma returned, blood-pressure making her face go all red. 'My, but you're a cold bastard, aren't you? My Gemma will be well out of being married to you!'

'I dare say there are others who agree with you, madam,'

he said drily. 'As for my being cold…' He peeled off his suit jacket and loosened his tie, undoing the top button on his shirt. 'I feel far from cold at the moment. But surely you haven't dragged me all the way out here just to ask for a divorce, Gemma. A telephone call to Zachary would have sufficed.'

'This isn't about our divorce, Nathan,' she snapped, annoyed with herself for having stared so when he started to undress. 'I will leave the legalities of that up to you, since you were the one who was so anxious to get rid of me. Another little problem had cropped up that Ma felt you should know about.'

Nathan arched his left eyebrow, a steely glance slanting Ma's way.

She drew herself up as tall as her five feet and very rotund figure allowed. 'I think we should go inside,' she said quite haughtily.

'Amen to that,' Nathan drawled, ducking as he went ahead through the low, roughly framed door.

'Arrogant bastard,' Ma hissed at Gemma. 'But sexy as all hell. I can see why you're having trouble forgetting him.'

Gemma smothered a silent groan. God, the moment he'd climbed out of that car and looked her over with that lazily sensual gaze of his her wits had been in danger of becoming scrambled. As for her body…that didn't bear thinking about. It wasn't fair that any man should have that kind of power, but even Ma was feeling it. What chance did *she* have when she'd already spent so much time in his bed, when he'd successfully taught her to respond to as little as a glance, or a seemingly innocent touch?

Nathan stood behind one of the chairs at the large wooden table that dominated the single-room dugout, not bothering to hide his feelings as he glanced around. One could almost see his lips curl with distaste at such primitive living conditions.

'Do sit down, Nathan,' Gemma said sharply. 'The chairs

might be pretty rough but they're solid. Would you like a cool drink?'

'No, thank you. I'd like you to get on with telling me why I'm here,' he said, not a ruffle in his cool demeanour as he pulled out a chair and sat down.

Gemma swallowed, then plunged in before she could think better of it. 'I won't beat around the bush,' she said swiftly. 'The fact is, Nathan, I'm pregnant. And before you say another word, let me assure you that it is yours. If you don't believe me I'm quite prepared to have the appropriate tests once the child is born.'

Was she imagining it or did all the blood drain from his face?

She must have imagined it because the next thing she knew he was laughing. Both Ma and Gemma stared at him with their mouths open.

'If ever I was to believe in a just God,' Nathan said after one last harsh bark of laughter, 'then this would be the moment.'

Gemma had no idea what he was talking about. All she knew was that she found his laughter a hurtful and hateful thing. Finally, his eyes dropped from hers, his shoulders sagging a little. Gemma despised herself for feeling an unaccountable pity for him. But when he looked up again, any pity died in the face of his implacable expression.

'Don't you mean *unjust*?' she snapped. 'You don't think I *want* this baby, do you?'

Their eyes locked, hers projecting all the anger and bitterness that had festered in her heart over his treatment of her.

'I wish to speak to my wife alone,' he ground out, throwing Ma an uncompromising glance.

Ma looked uncertainly at Gemma, who nodded, not trusting herself to speak at that moment. She was too flustered.

Sighing, Ma stood up. 'I won't be far away,' she warned Nathan as she reluctantly left the dugout.

Gemma glared at Nathan across the table, finding solace in the righteous fury bubbling up inside her. It was better than looking at him and thinking how damned attractive he was or what she might do if he had the gall to suggest their getting back together again. God, but she had to be sick even to consider such a thing. The man had never loved her. He had used her and abused her. She had to fight this weakness within her, had to fight it to the death!

'Well?' she snapped. 'What is it you have to say to me that couldn't be said in front of Ma?'

His eyes darkened to slate as they raked over her angry face, seemingly assessing how she felt about the situation. Even so, she wasn't ready for what he was about to say. Yet she should have been, shouldn't she? She should have known, all along, what he would consider the ideal solution to her having conceived that awful afternoon.

'I presume you want an abortion,' he said tautly. 'And I presume you expect me to pay for it. In the circumstances, I can appreciate your—'

'No,' she cut in coldly. 'I won't want an abortion. I am going to have this baby, come hell or high water.'

His pained bewilderment seemed very real. 'But *why*, for pity's sake? Every time you look at the child you will remember how it was conceived. You'll end up hating it as you obviously hate me.'

Her look changed quickly from shock to scorn. 'How little you know about me, Nathan. But I don't have to explain my motivations to you. Or my feelings. I have informed you of the baby's existence, and my intention to have it. I would like to know what your intentions are. Do you wish merely to be its father in name only? Or do you wish to play some role in its upbringing? Either way, I can assure you that you *are* going to pay, and pay dearly.'

Nathan glared at her. 'So that's the bottom line, is it? Money. You're going to have the baby because it will squeeze a bigger divorce settlement out of me.'

Gemma was almost numb with outrage. But be damned if she was going to let him have the last word. 'And why not?' she taunted. 'If that's what I want. This silly little naïve bitch has finally grown up, Nathan. I'm going to screw you like you screwed me. Without mercy. And totally without love.'

Now the blood really did drain from his face, and for a horrible moment Gemma was filled with remorse. What had possessed her to say such wicked words? Was it because of the desire that kept pricking at her flesh? Did she hope to wipe away all her feelings for this man by wallowing in hate and revenge?

'So how much money *do* you want, Gemma?' he ground out at long last. 'Spit it out.'

'You think all I want is money?' she flung at him.

'Then what *is* it that you want?' he said, a weary exasperation in his voice. 'Tell me, and if it's possible I'll give it to you.'

She gave a small, hysterical little laugh. Tears pricked at her eyes and she looked down at the table. 'What if I told you that I want you back, as my husband and the father of my baby? What if I told you I want your love? Can you give me that, Nathan?'

He didn't say a word.

'Just as I thought,' she said bitterly, blinking back the tears. When she looked up again, her eyes were bright and hard. 'In that case, I'll settle for you being a real father to this baby, not just a cheque-book one.'

'I've never shrunk from my responsibilities as a father.'

'How noble of you.'

'I think we've already established that I'm not noble, Gemma. But I do have my own peculiar brand of honour. If you're prepared to overlook my obvious shortcomings as a husband, I'm prepared to have another go at our marriage. What do you say?'

Gemma shot to her feet, instant indignation firing up her

blood. 'I say to hell with you, Nathan Whitmore! I don't want some sacrificial lamb as a husband. Neither do I want a husband who doesn't love me. Who in hell do you think you are, making me an offer like that? Take your guilt and shove it, buster! Go back to Sydney and your precious Jody. I'm sure you won't have to feel guilty about screwing the likes of her! And if she gets pregnant I'm sure she'll rush off and have an abortion before you can say Jack Robinson!'

'What's going on in here?' Ma raced in, all bothered and breathless. 'What's all the shouting about?'

Gemma was almost beside herself. '*He's* what the shouting's all about,' she cried, pointing at an ashen-faced Nathan with a shaking hand. 'First, he wanted me to have an abortion and then when I said no to that he magnanimously suggested I come back to Sydney with him and play happy families!'

'Well, what's wrong with that?' Ma said, clearly flummoxed by Gemma's attitude. 'Sounds like common sense to me. Surely you're not thinkin' of havin' a baby all by yourself out here and bringin' it up alone, are you, when you have a perfectly good husband who wants to take care of you both?'

Gemma could not believe what she was hearing. Ma, whom she trusted and relied upon, turning against her! 'But I won't be alone,' she argued fiercely. 'I'll have *you*!'

'For how long, love? I'm old and getting older every day. I'd love to have you and the baby here, but it's not practical. Just look at this place. It's a dump. Surely you want more for your son or daughter than this.' She came forward and took Gemma's trembling hands in her large gnarled ones. 'Give it a go, love. If it doesn't work out then at least you won't reproach yourself for never trying.'

'How can it work out when we don't love each other?' Gemma groaned.

'But you will both love the child,' Ma insisted, 'and out of that love you might learn to love each other.'

'Who says we will both love the child?' Gemma muttered, knowing in her heart that Nathan, for one, wouldn't. *He* was the one who didn't want a constant reminder of what he had done, not her.

'If you come with me, Gemma,' Nathan said in a low, intense voice, 'I promise I will do my best to make reparation for what I have done. You won't believe me, I know, but I never meant to hurt you.'

'But you did.'

'Yes…yes, I did,' he confessed. 'I have had plenty of time lately to think about what I've done and regret it deeply. If you're generous enough to give me a second chance, I won't let you down again. And I won't let our child down, either. And who knows? Maybe Ma is right. Maybe we can learn to love each other properly this time. I, for one, would like to think it was possible…'

Gemma stared at him. God, but he was clever. Who would have thought that a few minutes ago he had coldly been discussing an abortion? What lay behind his offer? she puzzled cynically. Did he want her back in his bed? Or was it once again a matter of getting back into Byron's good books?

Gemma didn't understand how much his father's good opinion mattered to him, and Byron would be less than impressed when he learnt she was having Nathan's baby, but Nathan was still divorcing her.

'Now, Gemma,' Ma said by her side. 'The man can't do more than that, can he? Go with him, love. Give him a second chance.'

Gemma had no intention of blithely going back to Nathan, baby or no baby. She had not forgotten, nor forgiven what he had done to her. He could think again if he thought his probably insincere and highly manipulative apology just now would set the record straight.

'I will come back to Sydney with you,' she told him. 'But

I won't be living with you. I want a house of my own. And a decent allowance.'

'Now, Gemma,' Ma started. 'Don't be so stubborn. You—'

'No, Ma,' Gemma cut in firmly. 'I won't be swayed on this. I've made up my mind.'

'You can have the house up at Avoca if you like,' Nathan offered in such a silky-smooth voice that Gemma was immediately suspicious. 'And ten thousand a month. Is that enough?'

'That's more than generous, love,' Ma said.

'It certainly is,' Gemma bit out, her eyes locking with her husband's. His returning gaze was disconcertingly bland. Gemma knew that Nathan had a habit of wiping his face of all emotion when his mind was at its most active. It wasn't like him to fall meekly in with her demands like that. What devious plan was he hatching to get her to come back to him? Did he hope to use sex again to bend her to his will?

She almost laughed at this thought. For he didn't need a devious plan, did he? He'd put in the ground work long ago. All he had to do was press the right buttons again and she would probably be his for the taking.

Gemma decided it was fortunate he didn't seem to realise that. Or did he?

Damn, but she was a fool to put herself anywhere near the man, especially now when she was still obviously suffering withdrawal symptoms from being in his bed. Maybe if she waited a few months, till her body was large and clumsy with her pregnancy, there would be no danger of his being able—or even *wanting*—to seduce her.

Nathan glanced at his watch. 'I hate to hurry you but if we're to catch this afternoon's flight you should change and pack.'

'I see no reason for any hurry,' Gemma countered. 'Frankly, I would like to spend Christmas up here with Ma. I'll fly down some time in the new year.'

Nathan's face darkened at this. Even Ma frowned.

'I don't like you staying here in this heat and under these conditions,' he argued.

'She's been feeling the heat,' Ma put in, which brought an exasperated glare from Gemma.

'Well, you *have*,' Ma insisted. 'And she's been having a bit of morning sickness. Hasn't been to see a doctor yet either, though the test from the chemist said she was pregnant enough for two babies. I think your husband's right, Gemma. The sooner you get back to Sydney, the better. I'll pack for you if you like.'

Gemma knew when she was beaten. 'No,' she sighed. 'I'll do it myself. Are you sure there'll be a spare seat on the plane for me?' she asked Nathan, despite already knowing that it was rare for the flights to be full at this time of the year.

'I've already booked you one.'

This presumption irritated her. 'Why on earth would you do that? You didn't know I was pregnant when you arrived.'

'I thought I might have to take you back to Sydney with me to see a shrink, remember?'

'Oh…yes…I forgot about that.'

'I'll take Mr Whitmore for a walk while you change, love,' Ma generously offered. 'Maybe he'd like to see an old-fashioned opal mine in the raw.'

Gemma watched wryly as Ma took Nathan's arm and escorted him outside. She was chatting happily away to him before they even hit the sunshine.

Another female conquest, Gemma thought bitterly. And so easily done too. Handsome men had it too easy, especially when they were rich as well.

But Nathan wasn't going to have it easy this time, Gemma decided with a further hardening of her heart. It would take a lot for him to ever win her trust or her love again. Frankly, it would take a darned miracle!

CHAPTER SEVEN

'CAN we talk, Gemma?'

The plane had just taken off from Lightning Ridge, and Gemma was in the process of uncurling her nervous grip from the armrests when Nathan spoke. She slanted cool eyes his way.

'Talk, Nathan? That's a new one for you, isn't it?'

'Drop the sarcasm, Gemma. It doesn't become you.'

'I don't give a fig if it becomes me or not. I'm not going to pretend to be happy about this situation. I didn't appreciate being coerced into coming back to Sydney today. And I don't appreciate your arrogantly assuming that I will do what you wish. My days of doing what you wish are well and truly over, Nathan.'

'I realise that. But there are more people's wishes to consider than mine. The child you're carrying will be Kirsty's brother or sister, something she's always wanted. Could we try to come to a more amicable arrangement for *her* sake, perhaps?'

Kirsty…

Gemma hadn't thought of Kirsty.

Her heart turned over. The poor love had had a rough deal the past few years, what with her parents divorcing and then her father marrying a girl only a few years older than herself, someone Kirsty had looked upon more as *her* friend than her father's. Kirsty had only just recently come to terms with Gemma's marriage to her father. To announce she was expecting Nathan's baby in the same breath as she was divorcing him would distress the teenager terribly.

'Poor Kirsty,' Gemma murmured.

'We could at least put off the divorce for a while,' Nathan suggested. 'She doesn't know about our separation. Since she began boarding at St Brigit's, she's been so much happier, and Lenore didn't want to say or do anything to upset her again.'

Gemma knew he was referring to the incident where Kirsty had walked in on her mother kissing Zachary Marsden. Gemma herself had been shocked when first told of the affair till she was informed that Zachary was in the process of divorcing his wife, who had been the first to say that their marriage should end. She had also fallen in love with someone else. They had been waiting till their younger son finished his high-school exams at the end of the year before dropping the bombshell that his parents no longer loved each other.

Gemma could understand how such things happened but she still found divorce a terribly sad thing, especially where children were concerned. It turned her mind to her own child, doomed before it was even born to eventually having divorced parents. Unless that miracle happened...

She turned to look at Nathan's coolly composed face and knew that miracle would never happen. He would never love her as she wanted to be loved because he didn't have it in him to love a woman like that. Lenore had once told her not to throw Nathan away, because to do so would be to destroy him.

Lenore was wrong. He'd already been destroyed years before Lenore had even met him. His mother had been the destroyer. His mother and that other evil old bitch he'd lived with when he'd been little more than a boy.

Gemma felt so sure of this that she would have sworn to it on a stack of bibles. And while this appreciation of the forces that had shaped Nathan's personality brought a message of understanding for the man sitting beside her, it did not change the facts. Gemma could not risk putting herself in his hands again, for where women were concerned they were warped hands.

But neither could she deliberately destroy other people. Kirsty could not cope with another divorce just now.

'I don't want to be the cause of making Kirsty miserable,' she said with a ragged sigh. 'I'm prepared to delay our divorce indefinitely, if that will help. I can't see myself ever wanting to marry again, anyway.'

'I've made you bitter,' he said, so bleakly that Gemma was startled.

'Bitter?' she repeated. 'I wouldn't say bitter. I've simply become a realist instead of a romantic. You should be pleased, Nathan. I now look at the world in much the same light you do.'

'And you think that would please me?' he said grimly.

'Well, it certainly didn't please you when I was an innocent little thing with rose-coloured glasses.'

'You pleased me well enough,' he grated out, a muscle twitching in his jaw.

'For a while, maybe.'

'Can we talk of other things?' he snapped.

'Like what?'

'Did you know that your parents married two weeks ago?'

'Yes, of course. They wrote to me about it.'

'Yet you didn't come back to attend,' he said, almost accusingly, she thought.

'No. They understood why I didn't. I sent them a card and a gift with my best wishes. Don't tell me *you* went?'

'Byron wanted me to be his best man, so I could hardly refuse.'

'Despite despising the woman he was marrying?' Gemma said archly.

'Celeste's not as bad as I thought she was,' came the grudging admission.

'Good God, I don't believe it,' Gemma mocked. 'Next thing you'll be telling me you believe I didn't have an affair with Damian.'

'I know you didn't.'

Gemma gasped her shock.

'If you had,' Nathan went on, 'you would not have taken the stance you took today. I recognise righteous indignation when I see it, Gemma. And I recognise an embittered heart. You wouldn't hate me as much as you obviously do unless you were totally innocent of any wrongdoing. I'm only sorry that my view of the world and the people in it was so jaundiced that I couldn't trust what was obvious to everyone else.'

'What is this, Nathan? All this apologising is making me nervous. I keep wondering what you want.'

He darted her a wry look. 'You really have grown up a lot, haven't you?'

'It happens. So out with it? What *do* you want?'

He shrugged. 'No more than what I said in front of Ma. want you to give our marriage—and me—a second chance.'

'Why should I? I don't love you any more.'

'A marriage can survive without romantic love. I didn't ove Lenore, and we were reasonably happy for twelve ears. We also gave Kirsty a secure and stable home life, omething a child has a right to, don't you think?'

'Might I remind you that your marriage to Lenore eventually ended in divorce right at a time in Kirsty's life when he was at her most vulnerable—her teenage years? Might also remind you that Lenore obviously pleased you a lot nore in bed than I did? No, Nathan, I will not put myself ack in a position where I will worry over my performance ll the time, and where I will wonder whose bed you are in ehind my back. I could perhaps bear your not loving me, ut I could not bear your being unfaithful. Which reminds ne, how's Jody these days?'

'I am not having an affair with Jody,' Nathan bit out. 'My only relationship with her nowadays is strictly professional.'

'No kidding. What are you doing for sex, then? I can't believe you're doing without. Not you, Nathan.'

His scowl carried frustration. 'Would you believe anything I said? I doubt it. Yes, you're quite right,' he swept on savagely. 'I've been bonking everything in sight. Does that make you happy?'

'Yes.' Her voice was very hard, and very, very bitter. 'And I want you to *keep* bonking everything in sight, because if you ever come near me again, God help me, Nathan, I might do you damage.'

'Maybe the day will come when you *want* me to come near you,' he snarled.

She laughed. 'I can't see that day coming too quickly.'

'I wouldn't be too sure of that.'

Her eyes snapped round to glare at him. 'I'm warning you, Nathan.'

His eyes narrowed as he glared right back at her. 'No, I'm warning you, Gemma. Don't push me too far. I'm doing my best here to do the right thing by you and this baby. But that doesn't mean I'll be your whipping boy. OK, so you won't have me back in your bed. I can understand that. But that doesn't mean I have to like it, because, even if you don't want me any more, I still want you, my darling. That hasn't changed. That's *never* changed. Neither am I entirely convinced I don't do anything for you any more in a sexual sense. Your eyes have always betrayed your feelings, and the way you were looking at me out at Lightning Ridge reminded me of how you used to look at me when we first met.'

'I won't deny I still find you physically attractive, Nathan,' she bit out brusquely. 'But lust without love has never appealed to me. Oh, I know you think I never really loved you, but that's your problem, not mine! *You're* the one who can't really love, not me. You obviously find sex an end in itself but I, for one, would find it repulsive.'

'Is that so?' Nathan said with seeming indifference. With equally seeming indifference, he reached out and picked up her nearest hand, turning it over and drawing it slowly up to his lips, his eyes narrowing as they locked on to her own wide, startled ones. 'In that case you'll find this repulsive,' he rasped, and sent his tongue-tip across the sensitive skin of her palm.

A shiver of sensation rippled up her arm and down through her body.

'And this…' He pressed the palm hard against his hot open mouth, exerting an inward sucking pressure as his tongue continued to go round and round on her wet, tingling flesh.

Everything inside Gemma clenched down hard.

God!

She kept telling herself to tear her eyes away, to tear her hand away. Instead, she remained frozen while those wicked eyes told her without words what he'd really like to be doing to her. Her mouth went dry as her memory provided her with plenty of arousing images. He was so good with his mouth. So very, very good. As for his tongue…there wasn't an inch of her body that it hadn't explored, making her shudder with pleasure.

She shuddered now.

'Come home with me,' he muttered into her hand, his voice thick with arousal. 'You won't regret it. I promise…'

He'd chosen the wrong word with 'regret'. For she would regret it. Bitterly. Her pride would suffer, and so would her self-esteem. She would be back on that merry-go-round to nowhere, back to being Nathan's sexual puppet, back to dancing to the strings he pulled. As much as she wanted to go with him, oh, so desperately, she could not. She *would* not!

Slowly, with her heart and body aching, she shook her

head, till he stopped doing what he was doing and lifted his mouth from her hands. His expression was oddly bewildered.

'Why not?' he growled. 'You want to. I know you do.'

'Oh, yes,' she agreed. 'I want to, so badly it's almost painful.'

'I could make you,' he warned darkly, the glittering of raw desire in his eyes.

'No, you couldn't,' she said with surprising confidence. 'Not any more. Not without being as evil as Damian was. And you don't want to be like that, Nathan. I know you don't. Basically, you're a good man.'

He stared at her for a moment, clearly taken aback by her unexpected conviction. '*Am* I? I wonder... Would a good man do what I once did to you?' he said, squeezing her hands so tightly that she almost cried out. 'Would a good man ask you to get rid of his baby? Would a good man be trying to seduce you knowing that underneath you hate and despise him?'

Gemma didn't know what to say to that, her eyes wide upon his tormented face. Suddenly he released her hands, throwing them back into her lap with disgust in his gesture. 'You're still too trusting,' he snapped. 'Don't trust me, Gemma. Don't ever trust me. I'm not fit to be trusted.'

'You're frightening me, Nathan,' she whispered shakily.

'Good,' he snarled. 'Fear will keep you on your toes and on your guard.'

Now she was hopelessly confused, for along with the fire he'd managed to kindle in her veins was a feeling so much like love that it terrified the life out of her. She wanted to reach out to him and comfort him, to draw his tortured face down on to her breast and tell him she forgave him for everything.

Which showed that he was right. She *was* still too trusting. But at least he'd given her fair warning that his lust for her remained intact, and that he wouldn't hesitate to try to slake that lust when and if she gave him the chance. She would heed that warning and take the necessary steps not to be alone with him any more than was essential.

'In that case I don't want you dropping in on me unexpectedly up at Avoca,' she said crisply, her cool composure a total sham. But he didn't know that.

'Fine,' he said curtly.

'And I don't want you offering to drive me up there. I'll drive my own car.'

'Sensible.'

'I suppose I'll have to let you drive me home to Belleview tonight,' she muttered. 'It would look odd if you didn't. I dare say I'll have to stay there for a day or two before moving on. Ava will be angry with me if I don't.'

'No, she won't. She's not there. Belleview's deserted.'

'*What?*'

'I presume you know Byron and Celeste will be away for another two weeks cruising the Whitsunday Islands.'

'Yes, they wrote to me about it. They also said they were planning on selling the yacht up in Queensland at the end of their holiday then flying back. But I presumed Ava would be holding the fort at Belleview while they were away.'

'Well, she isn't. She got fed up with being in such a big house by herself and has moved into some luxury penthouse with Vince till Byron and Celeste return. Actually, Byron told me he was thinking of selling Belleview in the New Year. Celeste doesn't want to live permanently in the same house he lived in with Irene, and come February Ava will be married, which rather leaves the old place strapped for inhabitants.'

'What a shame,' Gemma said rather sadly. 'It's such a lovely house. It should stay in the family. What about Jade and Kyle? Maybe they'd like to live in it. They can't stay living in that houseboat after their baby is born, surely.'

'Byron offered it to them but Kyle recently bought a house in Castlecrag, overlooking the harbour. After living right on the water like that, they said they couldn't bear not to be near it. In truth, I don't think Belleview held too many happy memories for Jade but she didn't like to hurt her father by saying so.'

Gemma frowned. 'You seem well acquainted with the family's comings and goings. Have you been welcomed back into the fold?'

'Oh, I wouldn't say that exactly, but Byron keeps me informed. I haven't had that much to do with them, really, other than at Celeste and Byron's small wedding party.'

'What does everyone think is the situation between us?'

'Aah, now, you'll have to ask the individuals that yourself. It's not a matter I have discussed with anyone. I think Ava hopes we'll get back together again. She actually smiled at me. Once.'

'And what about Jade?'

'Jade, the dear romantic girl, has always thought we belonged together.'

'She also thinks you *love* me,' Gemma reminded him bluntly. 'And that I love you,' she added with a catch in her throat.

'Yes, well, Jade always was inclined to optimism,' Nathan drawled. 'I gained the impression she believes that given time you'd forgive me. Once she finds out you're pregnant, she'll be doubly sure.'

'Does...does everyone have to know that I'm pregnant?'

His sidewards glance was sharp. 'Why shouldn't they know? Are you reconsidering having an abortion?'

'Of course not!'

'Then there's no point in keeping it a secret. You having a baby will also put your returning to me into perspective as well.'

'I'm not really returning to you.'

'You know what I mean. Everyone will think you have. I'll tell them you're staying up in Avoca for the peace and quiet because you haven't been all that well, and that I visit you all the time. They won't know if it's true or not. Of course, I'm sure to have to bring Kirsty up to visit you on the occasional weekend, especially with summer on our doorstep. You know how much she loves the beach.'

'Oh, no, you don't! I recall what happened the last time the three of us were up there together. You dispatched Kirsty to an all-night movie session so that you could… could…'

'Have my wicked way with you?' he suggested drily.

'Yes,' she hissed, her mind filling with images she would rather have forgotten.

Nathan sighed a wistful sigh, as though he too were remembering. But any regret he was feeling was that he could not have a re-run this very night. 'I have to admit you've always been one hell of a temptation for me, Gemma.'

She didn't say anything to that. She didn't dare. What woman didn't want to be one hell of a temptation for a man? He couldn't have said anything more seductive if he tried. Oh, God, any minute now she would throw herself into his arms and beg him to take her home to bed.

'I can see you think I'm a right bastard,' he ground out. 'The kind only a mother could love.'

At this he laughed, the sound so dark and diabolical that the most horrible thought entered Gemma's mind. No, she denied quickly. Surely not! She couldn't have been that wicked. *Could* she? Gemma had read of such things but it was mostly a case of a father with his daughter, or perhaps a brother with a sister.

Yet she supposed it was possible for a mother to sexually abuse her son. It would explain Nathan's problem with really loving and trusting a woman, his focusing all his relationships on sex, as well as his reluctance to ever open up to anyone, especially about his past.

Oh, God, if it was true…

Gemma's tender heart filled with emotion, torn by feelings of sympathy and sadness which she had difficulty handling at this vulnerable time in her life. The more she thought about this idea the more she became convinced it was the answer to the puzzle that was Nathan Whitmore. Had Lenore had similar thoughts? Was that why she'd told Gemma that to throw Nathan away would be to destroy him? Maybe she should talk to Lenore, try to find out more about this enigma of a man she had married.

'You know, Nathan,' she said, trying to sound nonchalant, 'you've never really told me much about yourself. Irrespective of whether we eventually divorce or not, you're the father of my baby and I think it's time you told me a little more about your growing-up years.'

Slowly she turned a seemingly innocent face to his, but his answering frown suggested he was wondering what the hell had brought this subject up. 'I don't think this is the time and place for a D and M, Gemma,' he drawled.

'A D and M?' she repeated blankly.

'It stands for "deep and meaningful",' he volunteered drily.

'Oh, I see. But why not? We've a couple of hours to go and flying makes me nervous. I thought you might like to take my mind off things by telling me some childhood anecdotes.'

'I doubt anecdotes about *my* childhood would make soothing chit-chat,' he returned caustically, reinforcing Gemma's suspicions. 'I suggest you settle back and try to have a sleep. Once we hit Mascot we have a long drive through peak-hour traffic to Belleview. Unless, of course, you've changed your mind about coming home with me,' he added, flicking her a wicked smile.

She hadn't, her returning smirk making his smile turn wry. 'I didn't think so. Trust me to marry a girl with character and class. Still, our son or daughter will be grateful for his mother's excellent qualities since he or she has the disadvantage of having me as a father.'

'You've been a good father to Kirsty, Nathan, and you know it.'

'Perhaps, but we all change, Gemma. I'm not the same man who married Lenore. I'm not even the same man who married you.'

Gemma could not disagree with that. Once before, she'd thought of him as a dark stranger. And yet, if what she thought was true, many things might be explained, and understood, and forgiven. If only she could get him to open up to her, to tell her what had happened to him as a boy. If only he could learn to trust her, maybe he could also learn to love her. He still wanted her. She could see that. Maybe if they lived together again, if she let him make love to her…

No!

Her reaction was automatic and instinctive. Nathan had always used sex as a way to avoid true intimacy. By always keeping his relationships superficial and lustful, he never had to reveal anything of himself but his beautiful body and his undoubtedly masterful technique. If she slept with him again, she would never find out a single damned thing. Only by keeping their relationship platonic did she have a hope of drawing him out. Look how much he'd spoken to her even just now, on this plane. Would he have done so if she had melted at his first touch, if she had stupidly agreed to move back in with him?

No way. He'd even now be seducing her with his eyes and his words, keeping her body so aroused all the time that she wouldn't be able to think straight. It was his *modus operandi* for women who threatened to get under his skin. Keep them trembling with desire and wide-eyed with wonder lest they find out that a real human being with real feelings and real failings lay beneath the super-suave, super-slick, super-smooth façade.

Still, it wasn't easy to pass up what he could deliver. Gemma had been quite correct when she'd said she found the thought of lust without love repulsive. But that wouldn't be the case with Nathan, would it? If this flight had proved anything, it was that she still loved the man as much as she ever had.

It was extremely painful for her to put him in a position where he would undoubtedly continue to be unfaithful. If there was one thing she knew and understood about her husband, it was that he could not tolerate celibacy, unless he was writing, which he wasn't at the moment.

But she would do it! It might kill her but she would make the sacrifice if it meant she might ultimately bring about the miracle. Miracles, Gemma suspected, sometimes needed a little human help.

'And what does that look mean?' Nathan said.

'Look? What look?'

'Don't play dumb with me, Gemma. You know damned well what look. It's the sort of look you see a lot in a dentist's waiting-room.'

'Oh, that look.'

'Yes, *that* look,' he repeated drily.

'I was just thinking I would have to stay the night at Belleview alone.'

'If you want company, I'll stay with you,' he offered silkily.

'I'll just bet you would, but no, thanks, Nathan. I'm sure you're needed back at the theatre. The show must go on, you know.'

'Actually, I've organised someone to look after things for me tonight, so I'm quite free. I couldn't possibly let you stay in that great barn all alone, considering it's already been empty a couple of nights. Empty houses are ready targets for burglars. No, don't bother to argue with me. I insist.'

Gemma bit her bottom lip. Damn the man! But what could she do?

'Very well,' she agreed curtly. 'Just don't try anything, Nathan.'

'I wouldn't dream of it. Not within Belleview's hallowed walls. Actually, do you realise we have never—er—done anything there?'

Gemma blushed. She might not have actually done anything with Nathan at Belleview but she'd thought about it a heck of a lot when she'd been living there before their marriage. She would never forget the first night he'd brought her there, especially when he'd been teaching her to play billiards and he had leant over her from behind and curved his startlingly aroused body around hers. If Lenore hadn't come in when she had, God knew what might have happened.

God knew what might happen tonight as well, if Nathan had any say in the matter. He'd warned her not to trust him an inch. And she didn't.

'We won't be changing the status quo either,' she told him sharply.

'Spoil-sport.'

Gemma threw Nathan a disbelieving look. 'What on earth's got into you, Nathan? It's not like you to be so… so…'

'Crass?'

'Yes,' she snapped.

'It's called frustration, darling. I took one look at you in those short shorts and that skimpy top today, and my recently flagging libido went into overdrive.'

'Nothing about your libido, Nathan,' she pointed out ruefully, 'has ever been flagging.'

'Certainly not with you.'

'Do you think we could get off this subject?'

'If you insist.'

'I insist.'

'Very well, but I must have the last word. If you ever change your mind, darling wife of mine, then do please give me the nod. I'll be ready and waiting. Now lie back, close your eyes and relax. We've still got an hour to go before we arrive in Sydney.'

Gemma indulged in a silent groan. Relax! When every nerve-ending in her body was sizzling with sexual awareness? And what of tonight, when she would be so temptingly alone with Nathan in that great empty house with so many beds to choose from?

God, but this was a stupid idea of mine all round, she thought. How am I ever going to keep to my vow to keep our relationship platonic? How?

CHAPTER EIGHT

IT WAS nearly seven-thirty by the time Nathan's dark blue Mercedes turned into Belleview, gliding through the gates and smoothly following the semicircular driveway around the large lily pond before stopping at the bottom of the wide stone steps.

Gemma glanced up at the impressively faąded house with its white-columned portico and air of gentle Southern grandeur, a wave of sadness sweeping through her to think that this beautiful home would soon be passing out of the family.

'It seems a shame Byron's going to sell this place,' she said with a wistful sigh.

Nathan slanted her a thoughtful glance before a wry smile tugged at his lips. 'Do you remember when you first saw it, you thought it was like something out of a fairy-tale?'

'Well, I don't think that any more,' she returned, a little sharply. 'But I still think it's one of the most beautiful houses I've ever seen. The time I spent living here was very happy.'

'As opposed to the time you spent as my wife.'

Gemma dragged in a deep breath, letting it out slowly as she twisted to face Nathan across the car. 'I could have been *very* happy as your wife,' she said, 'if only you'd treated me like a real wife, instead of an expensive mistress.'

'Most women would have given their eye-teeth to be treated as I treated you, Gemma.'

Her sigh was rather sad. 'Then obviously I'm not most women. I've always thought of marriage as a partnership, where husband and wife were best friends as well as lovers, best friends who shared everything and had no secrets from each other.'

'You kept secrets from me,' he reminded her coldly. 'You were seeing Damian Campbell on the sly. I don't mean you were sleeping with him,' he quickly amended when her face flamed with indignation, 'but you were meeting him and not telling me.'

'I was not *meeting* him,' she denied. 'He spoke to me briefly at the ball, and I ran into him once in the street during my lunch-hour. Look, I'm not going to be drawn into defending myself over Damian. Clearly, I wasn't equipped to deal with so devious a devil as he proved to be, but I also did nothing with him that I'm ashamed of. If I didn't tell you about those two early meetings, it's because you were such a possessive and jealous husband that I didn't dare. Which is another thing I found hard to handle—your extreme jealousy. Husbands and wives have to trust each other, Nathan. Without trust, any marriage is doomed.'

'Tell me, Gemma,' he said quietly, 'did I do anything *right* during our time together?'

'You...you made love very well...'

His laugh was very dry. 'Clearly that wasn't enough.'

'No.'

'And it wouldn't be enough the second time round either, would it?'

'No.'

He said nothing for a few moments, staring deep into her eyes till she was forced to swallow. Only at the last second did she stop herself from licking suddenly dry lips, but they did fall a little apart, and her damned pulse-rate took off like a racing car revving on the starting line.

'We'll see, Gemma,' he said at long last. 'We'll see...'

She almost groaned aloud by the time he finally tore those merciless eyes away, unsnapping his seatbelt and climbing out of the car. There was no doubt this was going to be a long and difficult night. But she was not going to waver from her resolves. Making love was out! No matter what he said or did. He could climb stark naked into her bed and she would simply turn the other cheek.

Gemma started to giggle at this last thought, and was still giggling when Nathan wrenched open her door. 'I must have missed the joke,' he said testily. 'Care to share it with me, since you're so large on sharing?'

Gemma pulled a face at him as she climbed out. 'Sarcasm doesn't become you, Nathan.'

'Neither does celibacy.'

'I haven't condemned you to celibacy. There are plenty of other fish in the sea.'

'So there are, my love. So there are. But fishing is such a tedious occupation.'

'Then go to a fish shop,' she countered caustically.

Nathan gave her a disbelieving look. 'Are you suggesting that I frequent a brothel?'

'I'm not suggesting anything,' she snapped. 'Your sex life is *your* problem, not mine. Now would you kindly get my luggage out of the boot? I'm tired and I'm hungry and I'd like to go inside.'

He blinked at her autocratic tone, not to mention her uncompromising stance. 'Is this the same sweet, accommodating girl I married?'

'You'd better believe it, buster,' she told him, feeling more in control of her life than she had in a long time. She had successfully deflected Nathan's sexual overtures with a suitable amount of style and sophistication, and was even capable of ordering him around without quivering afterwards. Her miracle still seemed a long way off, but she had a funny feeling she was on the right track. Turning, she marched up the steps to wait for Nathan near the front door.

'I don't think your stay out at Lightning Ridge has done you any good,' he grumbled as he did indeed extract her suitcase from the boot of the car and carried it up the steps, placing it at Gemma's feet while he unlocked the door. 'That Ma is a tough old bird, if ever I saw one. She threatened me that if I did the wrong thing by you again she was going to personally come down and flay every inch of flesh from my body with a bull whip, starting on my appendages.'

Gemma laughed. 'Good for Ma. There again, she might have to stand in line. After me I think maybe Celeste and Kirsty and Lenore might like to have a go at you. I wouldn't think Ava or Jade would be too forgiving, either, if you start blotting your copybook again. Maybe I should even call Melanie in England and ask her what a suitable punishment might be.'

Nathan adopted an expression of feigned terror. 'God, don't do that. That woman used to frighten the life out of me! I can only admire Royce for taking her on. There again, any fool who would drive Formula One cars for a living has no appreciation of danger.'

'Melanie was a very warm and misunderstood lady,' Gemma insisted, brushing past Nathan to go inside, clicking on the light switch as she went. Immediately, the huge crystal chandelier hanging from the vaulted ceiling flooded the spacious foyer with light.

'I've heard the same said about Lucrezia Borgia,' Nathan drawled. 'Er…' He hesitated, throwing her a hopeful glance. 'What bedroom do you want me to put your case in?'

'Very funny, Nathan. The bedroom I've always slept in when I stay here, and it isn't yours.'

'Can't blame a guy for trying,' he muttered, and trudged on up the stairs. 'Put some coffee on, will you?' he called back over his shoulder. 'And see what food you can rustle up for us?'

When she didn't answer he stopped, turned and smiled down at her with a sheepish look on his face. '*Please*?'

Gemma sniffed. 'I suppose, since I have to eat myself, I could cook for two as well as one.'

'Thank God for that,' he muttered and moved on up the stairs.

Gemma stayed where she was a moment longer, smiling softly to herself, then frowning. Where had all her anger gone to? And her anxiety over what Nathan's intentions were? Was she being naïve and trusting again, thinking he really meant to try to win her back, that he sincerely wanted to change? Was he genuinely sorry for all the pain he had put her through? What about Jody, and the other women he had obviously been with while she was away? Was he going to put them aside and show her by his abstinence that he cared enough for her to do without if he couldn't have *her*, his wife?

Gemma had no faith in this last part. Nathan was not a man to embrace celibacy, as he had already indicated. She had long suspected sex was an emotional as well as a physical release for him. That was why, when he was writing, he didn't need it as much, because then he was pouring all his emotions in his characters.

Gemma made her way towards the kitchen, switching on lights as she went, wondering how she might get Nathan to start writing again. It would perhaps solve her worry over refusing him sexually, yet not wanting him to go to other women. She was moving through the family-room, pondering this dilemma, when she heard a noise which sparked some kind of recognition in her, but didn't register properly till she heard it again.

It was a dog, whining piteously.

She glanced around, but could see nothing.

The sound came again, thin and heart-rending. Gemma moved swiftly across the family-room, pulling the cord that shot the heavy curtains back from the French doors that led out on the terrace. A huge dog, which looked like no breed she had ever seen before, shrank back for a second before coming forward and pressing its black nose against the glass. His large brown eyes looked up into hers and it whined again.

'Oh, you poor darling,' Gemma groaned. A very large ugly dog, it was also as thin as an escapee from a concentration camp. It looked like it had some Great Dane in it, but she suspected it was a crossbreed. Naturally, there was no collar around its neck. What person would want to lay claim to such a neglected animal? Clearly, it had been dumped, and had come in here, looking for food.

'Wait there,' she told the pathetic, sad-eyed creature, and raced for the stairs.

'Nathan! Nathan! Where are you? Come quickly!'

He rocketed along the upstairs hallway to virtually collide with her, his eyes panicky. 'What is it? What's wrong?'

'I need the keys. There's a dog outside, a poor starving thing. I have to let it in and find it something to eat.'

Nathan grabbed her firmly by the shoulders, his expression exasperated. 'A *dog?* You came screaming up here about some stray dog? I thought something dreadful had happened.'

'Something dreadful has happened,' she informed him breathlessly. 'Some awful person has dumped the poor thing, probably he grew bigger than they thought he would. You should see him, Nathan. He's so thin, and his fur's all scraggy, and…and…'

'And he's probably full of fleas,' Nathan finished drily. 'As for letting it in and feeding it, you're not going to do any such thing. If you do, it'll never go away. And then it *will* starve, since you're going up to Avoca tomorrow.'

She stared at him, eyes wide and disbelieving. 'But…but…I can't not do something. I just *can't*!'

'Yes, you can,' he said with a callousness that made her shudder. 'People do it all the time. If you ignore it, it'll simply move on.'

Ignore that pitiable whining? Turn her back on those sad

suffering eyes? What kind of inhuman creature did he think he was? What kind of inhuman creature was *he*?

'Well, other people might do it all the time,' she huffed, 'but I *don't*!' Angrily, she shook his hands off her shoulders. 'I'm not asking your permission to do this, Nathan. Just give me the keys, please.' She held out her hand stiffly, her mouth pouting her reproach. 'As for going up to Avoca tomorrow, I'll simply take the dog with me.'

Nathan shook his head in total exasperation. 'Why do I have to be married to a woman who's not like most *people*, let alone most other women?' he grumbled, then sighed resignedly. 'OK, Florence, lead on and I'll follow with keys to the ready. I'll be interested to see this poor pitiful creature for myself…

'Good God, it's a horse!' he exclaimed on sighting the dog on the terrace. 'And just look at those teeth!' On seeing Nathan the dog bared his teeth at him, probably in fear.

'Oh, for pity's sake,' Gemma exclaimed, snatching the keys out of Nathan's hand and walking over to unlock the sliding glass door nearest the dog. 'If you're so frightened of him,' she snapped over her shoulder, 'then by all means stay where you are. I don't need any help. I've handled dogs a damned sight fiercer than this one!'

The door unlocked, Gemma wrenched it open, then wished she hadn't done it so abruptly, for the sharp movement had made the dog immediately skitter away into the shadows at the edge of the terrace.

'See?' Nathan said. 'He doesn't want to come in.'

She shot him a withering glance. 'What is it with you? Didn't you have a dog when you were a boy?' Immediately, she wished she hadn't said that. Of course he hadn't had a dog as a boy. When was he home long enough to have a pet as demanding and time-consuming as a dog?

'Can't say that I did,' Nathan admitted, thankfully not looking too annoyed at the question. 'I had some goldfish once but one of my mother's friends used to flick his cigarette ash in the tank and they soon departed to the great goldfish bowl in the sky.'

Gemma filed away that little piece of information into her 'Nathan' file for future reference. Really he'd told her more today than he had in nearly six months of marriage. 'What about Kirsty?' she asked. 'Didn't she ever want a puppy for Christmas?'

'Nope. She was quite happy with her pet rock.'

'A pet *rock*? I've never heard of such a silly idea.'

Nathan's smile carried a dry amusement. 'They were rather big around Sydney for a while. And very popular with parents. Pet rocks don't have big teeth and they don't require feeding.' He frowned over at her. 'What are you doing just standing there in the doorway? Aren't you going to go over and grab the damned thing?'

'I'm letting "the damned thing" get used to me first, and even then I won't be doing any grabbing.'

By this time the dog had sunk down on its haunches at a respectable distance, its soulful brown eyes darting warily from Gemma to Nathan then back again. Gemma decided to sit down on the doorstep, knowing this building up of trust could take a while.

'You go and start seeing to some food, Nathan,' she called over to him. 'I know Ava always keeps steak in the freezer and the microwave will defrost it in no time.'

'God, yes, I could do with a steak.'

'I didn't mean *you*, silly.'

Nathan's expression was rueful. 'I had a feeling you didn't but it was worth a try. Maybe I'll be able to find enough for us humans as well as Jaws there.'

Jaws growled ominously at the mention of what Gemma decided wasn't a bad name for him…considering. In all honesty, she had never seen teeth like it. His choppers put Blue's to shame.

Thinking of Blue brought a soft smile to her lips. Putting her elbows on her knees, she supported her head in her hands and adopted a highly relaxed pose. If she had learnt one thing in handling Blue it was not to make any sudden movements. Nor to expect Rome to be built in a day.

'I think someone might have frightened you,' she said conversationally. 'Still, you probably frightened the dickens out of them if you just showed up on their doorstep. But you're really just a lamb in wolf's clothing, aren't you?'

The dog crawled slowly towards her as she talked, his tongue lolling out of one side of his huge mouth. Gemma slowly lifted her head and let her hands flop down her shins so that the dog could sniff them if and when he got close enough. It took a while but soon he was nudging his nose against her fingers.

'You sure he won't bite?'

Nathan's sudden and rather snappy query from just behind her ear sent the dog into immediate retreat, snarling up at Nathan as he scuttled away. Gemma rolled her eyes as she twisted her head to glare up at her husband. 'Did you have to frighten him like that?'

'Is it my fault that underneath his killer equipment the dog's basically a scaredy-cat?'

'Takes one to know one,' she mocked.

Nathan smiled, and Gemma's heart flip-flopped. He was so endearing when he smiled like that. And so damned attractive. She looked away then stood up. 'No point my staying here with you hovering,' she said a little brusquely. 'Did you find any steak in the freezer?'

'Only rump and fillet.'

'That'll do. Jaws won't know the difference.'

'Rump and fillet steak? For a *dog?* Good God, I—' He broke off suddenly, a frown bunching his brows together. '*Jaws*?'

'That's his name. You gave it to him.'

'I *did?*'

'Uh-huh. Don't you think it's appropriate?'

'It sounds depressingly permanent. You still mean to take him up to Avoca with you, don't you?'

'Of course. He'll make a good guard dog in time.'

'Yes, I suppose so,' Nathan murmured. 'I didn't think of that. All right.' He brightened. 'You can take him.'

'Gee whizz, thanks.'

'How do you know he doesn't belong to someone?' he went on, ignoring her sarcasm.

'Does he look as if he belongs to someone?' she retorted. 'If he does, that someone isn't going to get him back, believe me.'

'You'll have to get him checked over by a vet.'

'No trouble.'

'And he'll need a collar and lead.'

'We could get one tomorrow when the shops open.'

'You're as stubborn as Ma says you are,' Nathan growled.

'And you'll be as cold a bastard as she originally thought *you* were if you don't go along with me on this.'

Nathan smiled his defeat, though it was a wry smile. 'Do you think Jaws would like his steak diced, or in strips?'

Gemma threw her arms around his neck and kissed him before she could appreciate the stupidity of her action. Immediately, his arms snaked around her waist, pulling her hard against him, his mouth taking hers in a kiss that was nothing at all like the spontaneous and grateful peck she had given him. As the pressure of his lips increased, her head retreated. So did her arms from around his neck till her hands were pushing against his chest.

But Nathan had always been much stronger than he looked, and with one outspread palm centred firmly in the small of her back he was able to use his other hand to cup the back of her head and keep her mouth captured beneath his. Before Gemma knew it, he had pried her lips open, and his tongue was sliding, hot and wet, into her mouth.

At this point, Gemma's struggle became more internal than physical as she battled to find all those good reasons she had formed in her mind for why she should not allow Nathan to make love to her. With the pleasurable sensations bombarding her at that moment, they now seemed not only irrelevant but masochistic. Why shouldn't she just melt against the man she loved and let him take her away into that wonderful erotic world that he had always been able to weave for her? All she had to do was close her eyes and allow him free reign to her body. He needed no verbal permission, no instructions. Her body language could tell him what he needed to know, which was she wanted this as much as he did.

Already her mind was racing ahead to that moment when she would lie naked beneath him, when the lips which were at present imprisoning hers would seek out all those sensitive places where the mere brush of them would make her breath catch in her throat. Her breasts, the inner flesh of her thighs, the very essence of her womanhood…

Her moan of surrender brought an answering groan from deep within Nathan's throat. Her hands were sliding up around his neck again, her thoughts having spun out into nothingness, when the cavalry came to her rescue in the form of a very large, very scruffy dog, who launched his trembling form through the open doorway and snapped his formidable teeth at the leg of the bad man attacking his nice new friend.

CHAPTER NINE

GEMMA'S arm flopped over the edge of the sofa where she had spent the night, her fingertips encountering something warm and furry. That something warm and furry also had a tongue like sandpaper.

'Yuk,' she shuddered, but refrained from whipping her hand away from the licking. Instead she opened her eyes and looked straight into a pair of beseeching brown eyes. 'Well, Jaws?' she said, rolling over on to her side and scratching him behind the ears with her other hand, the distraction stopping that icky licking. 'I suppose I should be grateful to you. So how come I'm not, eh? How come I'd like to get hold of your scrawny neck and wring it?'

Gemma said all this in a calmly smiling voice so that the end result was that Jaws lay there on the rug next to the sofa, happily thumping his tail from side to side. She'd always known it was the tone of voice, not the content of the words, that dogs responded to.

'Just as well you didn't really damage Nathan,' she told the adoring animal, 'or you wouldn't be here now. He'd have called the dog-catcher in so fast, you wouldn't have known what hit you.'

Jaws had fortunately only got a mouthful of trousers before Nathan wrenched away from Gemma and shouted at the dog, whereupon the poor creature, whose bravery was exceeded far and away by his cowardice, bolted back out on to the terrace. Nathan had scowled, slammed the door and turned back to Gemma. But the moment had been broken—thank God—and he'd quickly realised it, much to his frustration and fury.

'Not that you're popular,' Gemma told the happily panting dog. 'I think you've been consigned to the Siberia of Nathan's mind. And believe me, that's a chilly place.'

The dog suddenly stiffened, then a low ominous growl rumbled in his throat. Gemma levered herself up on to her elbow and glanced over the back of the sofa. The doorknob leading out into the hallway was turning, and soon Nathan popped his head into the family-room. Jaws immediately leapt to his feet, quivering with outrage and fear.

'Would you kindly put that beast outside?' Nathan demanded curtly. 'I'd like to have some breakfast.'

Gemma smothered a smile. 'Wait a sec. I have to put my dressing-gown on first.' No way was she going to swan around in her nightie, which was hardly neck-to-knee. She hadn't owned that kind of nightwear since she married Nathan, who had showered her with gifts of highly erotic lingerie from the very first day of their marriage.

She had, however, bought a simple cotton housecoat while staying with Ma, and it was this she drew modestly over the white silk and lace number which she'd slept in and which left little to the imagination. Once decently covered, she shepherded the dog outside, closing the door on her return.

'You can come in now,' she called out.

Nathan came into the room, blue jeans and a white T-shirt on, blond hair still wet from a shower. He looked much more coolly composed than he had been when he'd stormed out of this same room the night before, Gemma thought as she followed him out to the kitchen, but just as lethally sexy. The sooner she got herself up to Avoca alone, the better.

'Sleep well?' she asked, deciding trite conversation was better than the tense silence that seemed to have suddenly enveloped the kitchen.

'Don't ask stupid bloody questions,' he snapped over the electric kettle. 'Of course I didn't damned well sleep well!'

'Oh...'

He glared at her, then down at the small hint of white lace that was in evidence across the base of the V neckline of the housecoat. 'I was going to make the magnanimous offer to drive up to Avoca in front of you today, since you're not familiar with the way, but after last night's fiasco I've decided against that idea.'

'Oh...' Gemma did her best to hide her disappointment but couldn't. Annoyed with herself, she looked down, wryly accepting that after last night her own resolve to keep their relationship platonic was wavering.

When she looked up again, Nathan's eyes had narrowed and he was searching her face with a ruthless scrutiny that unnerved her. 'If you want me to come up with you, then say so. If you want me to stay...I can easily do that too. The play's running like clockwork and I have an assistant director who can handle things for a while.'

'Whatever gave you the idea I would want you to stay?' she said, doing her best to sound surprised. 'Don't misinterpret what happened last night, Nathan. You kissed me and I momentarily kissed you back. I would have stopped it myself any moment if Jaws hadn't.'

He made a scoffing sound. 'You expect me to believe that?'

'Believe what you damned well like,' she retorted haughtily. 'I have no intention of going back on what I said. We only have a pretend marriage for now. There will be no sex!'

'I see,' he bit out. 'Well, in that case, I have no alternative but to take the necessary steps to see that I don't go stark raving mad!'

Gemma paled, but she lifted her chin bravely. 'I've already told you I don't expect you to live the life of a monk, but I...I hope you'll be...discreet.'

He stared at her. '*Discreet*? Is that all you care about, that I'm *discreet*?'

Gemma felt as if he was backing her into an emotional corner where any moment she would blurt out the truth, that of course that wasn't the only thing she cared about. She cared about *him*. She *loved* him. But her ultimate goal in all this was to win his love, not just his lust. She wanted the whole miracle and this was the only way she could think of to secure it. If that meant she had to risk his going with another woman for sex, then so be it. But that didn't mean she had to like it!

'For God's sake, what do you want from me?' she lashed out. 'You hurt me, Nathan. You hurt me badly. I can't just take you back into my bed like that. I need time. I need for you to prove that you care about me. I'm not just a body. I have feelings, in here.' And she thumped her chest. 'And I have a baby growing, in here.' Her hands dropped down to cross over her still flat stomach. 'This baby needs a father who respects its mother, who thinks of her as more than a bed partner.'

'I don't just think of you as a bed partner,' he said stiffly.

'Is that so? Then pardon me if I say your actions don't back up that statement. You've always given me the impression that all you've ever wanted from me was sex, even now, after all we've been through and with my having your baby. Oh, I know you find it a wonderfully safe topic and a wonderfully safe activity. And I think I understand why. It's such a marvellous escape. From everything. From the past, and the present and the future. When it's good, it can create a world where reality recedes. And when it's great, it can begin to become an end in itself, an obsession. Believe me when I tell you I could easily become as obsessed by what you could do for me sexually as you once were with me. But I can't afford that kind of escape or obsession any more, Nathan. I'm having a baby. I'm going to be a mother. I have other priorities now, such as stability and security.

Prove to me that I can rely on your still being my husband and a good father to our baby till death us do part, and I'll give you all the sex you want.'

He said nothing for quite a while, simply stared at her with one of those closed-book faces he could wear and which always made her want to scream with frustration. 'That was some speech,' he said at long last, his voice low and coolly controlled. 'Just tell me one thing before I get the hell out of this house. Do you still love me?'

Gemma groaned silently. What could she say to that? She didn't want to lie but she didn't want to admit such a thing, either. It might negate all she was trying to achieve.

'You once told me you didn't believe I ever really loved you,' she hedged. 'So how can I *still* love you?'

He smiled. It was not a very nice smile. 'Don't play games with me, Gemma. I want the truth and I want it now.'

Gemma thought of something Ma had said and decided it was better than lying. 'How can you love someone you don't even know?' she successfully evaded again.

Nathan scowled at her. 'What in hell does that mean?'

'It means just that, Nathan. I don't know you, not the inner you, the real you. I don't know your secret hopes and wants and dreams. I don't know what has hurt you in the past, or why you do the things you do sometimes, or react the way you do. All I know is the superficial you, the flesh that covers your bones. Oh, it's very nicely arranged flesh and you certainly know what to do with it in bed. Maybe I'm still "in love" with that flesh, but do I love you, Nathan? I'm just not sure about that.'

And oddly, having said so, Gemma could see that what she said could possibly be true. Maybe her instinctive responses to Nathan were still bound up in the extremely strong physical attraction they shared. Maybe she didn't really love him. Oh, God, she felt so confused.

'Maybe I shouldn't have asked,' Nathan muttered, then lanced her with a piercing look. 'Are you sure you want this baby, Gemma? I can't stand to think of an innocent child suffering for something I did. I've never told you how dreadfully sorry I am for what happened that day. I have no excuse. What I did was unforgivable, but you…'

'Nathan, stop,' she said shakily. 'I *have* forgiven you for that. How many times do I have to tell you? If I gave you the impression out at the Ridge that I didn't want this baby, then I apologise. What I didn't want was for my baby's parents to be divorced, nor to have to bring up my child alone as a single parent. I know what that's like, as I'm sure you do, and it's hardly an ideal situation. But I would never make our child suffer for the way he or she was conceived. If I thought for a moment I might do that, I would have considered an abortion. But I never did. Not for a moment.'

'Thank you for that,' he said quietly. 'I really appreciate it. I was rather worried about that.'

'Then why didn't you say so before?'

'What?'

'Why didn't you tell me you were worried? It's what husbands and wives do, you know. Tell each other their worries.'

He seemed disconcerted by the idea.

Gemma decided they'd had enough heavy conversation for one morning. Nathan's system looked in danger of overload. 'Are you making coffee, or just standing there inspecting the kettle?' she quipped with a bright smile.

His eyes showed even more bewilderment, but after a bemused shake of his head he plugged in the kettle and set about getting out the coffee and the mugs.

'After breakfast,' she went on airily, 'I'll get you to draw me a map. And then I'm going to send you up the road for some dog supplies. After that I…'

Gemma kept him busy right up to the moment when he waved her and Jaws off. Actually, she felt quite nervous over the prospect of finding her way north up the highway to Avoca all alone—a distance of some eighty kilometres or so—but she didn't let Nathan see that. It was important to her that he see she could cope very well alone, that she was not some wishy-washy weak female who would go to mush at the first little problem.

Nevertheless, when it came right down to it, he'd still been loath to let her go, saying he was concerned over her living all alone, vowing to be up first thing the following Saturday with Kirsty in tow. Since it was already Wednesday that wasn't all that far away, but as Belleview and Nathan receded into the distance behind her it suddenly seemed like an eternity to Gemma.

The drive turned out to be very tedious, what with Jaws refusing to lie down on the back seat, spending the whole time standing up with his huge head hanging over her seat, dripping saliva down her back. Clearly, he had never been taken in a car before, the excessive panting a sign of extreme nervousness. And while Gemma tried to be patient with him, it was very distracting and tiring.

On top of that she got lost a couple of times. Well, not exactly lost, but she sailed past two turnings she was supposed to take before realising it, having to then negotiate difficult U-turns and double back before getting herself on to the right roads. She was very relieved finally to roll into Avoca and know she was only a couple of minutes away from the beach house.

Gemma glanced over to the ocean on her left as she drove slowly along the narrow main road that wound through the small seaside town. It being a Wednesday in the last week of November, with school holidays still a couple of weeks off, it wasn't very busy. But that would all change soon, she realised. The Central Coast was a popular holiday haunt for Sydneysiders, sun, surf and sand drawing them like magnets. Avoca was only one of a host of beach towns up this way, but it was one of the most popular, boasting plenty of white sand, good board-riding waves and a relaxed, laid-back life-style which beckoned stressed office and factory workers, especially over the Christmas break.

Gemma had not been up this way at Christmas, having only come to Sydney from Lightning Ridge last February, but she'd spent Easter up here and if that was anything to go by Avoca was about to become a hive of activity. In a way, she wasn't looking forward to it, her stint back up at the Ridge having made her appreciate peace and quiet. Still, she didn't have to leave the house if she didn't want to. It was spacious, with its own pool and a huge front balcony with a magnificent view of the Pacific Ocean.

The old picture theatre that was the pride and joy of Avoca came into view, signalling to Gemma that she was now only seconds away from home. God, but she would be glad to put her feet up and have a nice cool drink.

'And I'll be glad to get you off my back, dog,' she told Jaws, who responded by giving her another one of those huge icky licks on the face. 'Don't do that!' she said sharply, then immediately felt sorry when the dog slunk back. 'I'm sorry, Jaws, come back and lick me all you like. Yes, that's right. Good dog, good dog. No you're not a good dog,' she went in the same soothing voice, smiling through gritted teeth while he slobbered all over her. 'You're a smelly, skinny, flea-bitten excuse for a dog who'll probably be more trouble than you're worth but I guess I'm stuck with you now, even if you are the ugliest, most oversized, undernourished, scrawny, scraggy pooch I have ever set eyes upon.'

Jaws responded to her well disguised lambasting with a resounding 'Woof woof' which almost blew her ear drums.

'Good God,' she muttered as she swung the car into the steep driveway that led up the side of the house and into a car-port. 'I suggest you keep that bark for emergencies, Jaws. If the neighbours get a load of it too often, I'll be arrested for noise pollution.'

Getting the dog out of the car was almost as difficult as

it had been getting him in. But once actually on terra firma again, he stopped dragging back on his lead. Gemma was happy to deposit him in the thankfully fully fenced back yard, leaving him with a good supply of dry dog-food and a big bowl of water before she got on with opening up the house. It clearly hadn't been used for some time and smelt a little musty.

Apparently, whenever Nathan wanted to use it, he would contact a local cleaning lady who came round and aired the house, putting a duster and vacuum cleaner through the place before he arrived as well as stocking up the kitchen cupboards and refrigerator with essentials. But Gemma had vetoed his doing that this time. She would have little enough to do if someone started doing the housework and shopping for her. She'd also told Nathan she would make it her business to contact a pool-cleaning service and get the pool into swimming condition. Apparently, it hadn't been used this summer as yet and was green with algae.

Gemma had barely unlocked the front door and let herself in, thinking the unloading of the car could wait till she'd been to the toilet and had that cool drink, when the telephone started ringing. She just knew it was Nathan before she'd heard a single word.

'Yes, Nathan, I'm here safely,' she said straight away.

'How did you know it was me?'

'Extra-sensory perception?' She couldn't help a little teasing. 'Come on, Nathan, who else could it have possibly been? Who else knows I'm even back from Lightning Ridge, let alone up here at Avoca?'

'I could have rung Ava and Jade and told them.'

'Did you?'

'No, because then I'd have to explain why you were up there and not down here with me.'

'I thought you were going to say I hadn't been well…'

'Lord, can you imagine what reception that would get? I'd be accused of all sorts of negligent behaviour then given the cold-shoulder treatment again. No, Gemma, if you don't mind, I think I'll keep your presence up there a secret for a while yet.'

'You won't be able to keep it a secret from Kirsty if you're going to bring her up with you on Saturday.'

'I was rather hoping you might change your mind about that and let me come up alone. I promise on my word of honour that I'll be a good boy.'

The road to hell was paved with good intentions, Gemma thought drily. And Nathan wasn't the only one who might lapse. She recognised her own weaknesses where he was concerned only too well.

'Gemma?'

Her sigh was resigned. How could she refuse him entirely when he'd been so sweet, when it was obvious that he cared about her and was worried about her? But that didn't mean she had to do something as stupid as sleep alone with him in the same house he had first seduced her in. The vibes would be against her from the start.

'All right, Nathan. But I don't want you to stay the night. What if you come up just for the Sunday? I'll cook you a nice Sunday roast.'

Gemma could tell by his silence that he was disappointed with her answer but she wasn't going to budge.

'Thank you for the generous offer,' he said a touch testily, 'but if I'm only going to have your company for one day, I don't want you cooking. I'll book us somewhere nice for lunch up there.'

Better and better, she thought. A public place was infinitely safer than a private kitchen. Nathan had done things in the kitchen of their apartment in Elizabeth Bay which showed he needed neither a bed nor night time to put his desires into action.

'How's Jaws?' he asked abruptly. 'He didn't look too settled as you drove off.'

'He was a right pain in the neck all the way,' she admitted. 'But he's fine now.'

'You should have let me take him to the RSPCA,' he grumbled.

'Now, Nathan, you know no one would choose a dog like him. He's too darned big and too darned ugly. He'd have ended up being put down.'

'I suppose so,' he sighed. 'Well, I'd better get myself down to the theatre and see what's been going on in my absence. No doubt there'll be some minor calamity.'

'I thought you said your assistant director could handle things.'

'I lied.'

She laughed.

'I'll ring you tomorrow,' he insisted, 'see how you're faring.'

'Don't worry if I'm not in. I have vets to see and shopping to do.'

'And you have to go to a proper doctor, don't forget, get yourself a referral to a obstetrician up that way.'

'I'll do that, Nathan. Don't fuss.'

'I'm not fussing.'

'You are so too. Now say goodbye and hang up, will you? I have heaps to do.'

'You sure know how to make a man feel wanted,' he muttered.

Gemma was glad he couldn't see her face. Dear lord, she wanted him like mad. Thinking about those kitchen antics they had got up to on occasions had not had a good effect on her. Sunday, she already suspected, was going to be hell!

'Hang up, Nathan,' she ordered in a monotone as she clenched her teeth.

'All right, damn you, I will!'

CHAPTER TEN

GEMMA found the next few days living totally alone—except for Jaws—a real surprise. She'd always thought of herself as a bit of a loner, having never had a close girlfriend during her school years, having in fact spent many, many long hours of her young life by herself.

So she really hadn't expected to find living alone any great trial, or for it to require any major adjustments.

But she soon realised that she had never spent twenty-four hours, straight, alone, and never at night. By Friday night, she'd brought Jaws into the house, even allowing him to sleep on the end of her bed.

Yet for all the dog's company she still felt lonely for human contact. She found herself talking for longer than strictly necessary to the vet, to the doctor, to shop assistants, even a bank teller. Nathan's telephone calls were real lifelines and she tried to keep him talking, but he was not a chatterer. Once he had reassured himself that she was all right, he would ring off. In that respect he hadn't changed.

So by Saturday she was really looking forward to the next day and Nathan's visit. Any risk to her sexual resolves were secondary to her desperate need to see someone she knew, and who knew her. Gemma also finally accepted that she was bored, and would have to find things to do to fill the long lonely hours. Because if she didn't, she would surely weaken and move back to Sydney to live with Nathan.

Nine o'clock on Saturday morning saw her driving to Erina Fair, the largest shopping centre on the Central Coast and only ten minutes from Avoca. Gemma spent a lovely few hours finding and buying something attractive and summery to wear to lunch the next day, then splurging out totally on a new sewing-machine, some maternity patterns and some material. On top of that, she bought a selection of blockbuster novels. Then, on the way home, she dropped into the local video shop and joined up, brought home a couple of comedies to watch that night. Laughter was good medicine for loneliness and boredom. Or so she'd read somewhere.

When she arrived home, Jaws went off his brain with excitement, barking that great woofing bark of his as he leapt up and down at the side gate as if he were on a pogo stick. Gemma hoped he hadn't been doing much of that while she was away or the neighbours would soon be complaining, although the high wooden side fences plus the thickly foliaged trees which grew along each boundary provided a good sound barrier.

To make up for her absence, she made a big fuss of the dog, opening a tin of special dog-food, after which she let him into the house, where he soon settled down on the rug in front of the television in the main living-room. Gemma spent the next couple of hours setting up the sewing-machine on the dining-room table and learning its various intricacies. She'd taken textiles and design as a subject at school and was a good sewer, but had made little use of her talent since marrying Nathan. He'd chosen most of her clothes, dressing her in designer labels, seeming to know what looked best on her hour-glass figure. Once, he'd even gone as far as to have a balldress specially made for her from his own design.

Gemma cringed a little as she thought of that dress. Because thinking of that dress inevitably made her think of the ball, which had been the occasion of her first meeting with Damian. She really hadn't come to terms with Damian yet. Was he born bad, or had he become bad? Had he perhaps been corrupted by someone at a crucial point in his young life?

Gemma began to wonder what his relationship had been with his half-sister, Irene. She had undoubtedly been a twisted personality with a great capacity for hate and revenge. Had she got hold of Damian as a youngster and warped his mind to her own wickedly selfish way of looking at life?

Gemma's thoughts slipped from Damian to Irene without missing a beat. What had really happened between Byron's wife and Nathan? She no longer believed Nathan had slept with her. But he must have done something to make Irene lie so viciously about him. Maybe she had made a play for him out of some kind of revenge for Byron having had an affair with Celeste, and he'd scorned her advances. That seemed to fit in with what she knew of both of them. Maybe she would ask Nathan about it tomorrow…

If she dared.

Gemma rose from the dining-table with a frown on her face. Thinking about people like Damian and Irene always agitated her, maybe because she was afraid that in some small way Nathan was like them. Gemma was a simple, straightforward person, happy to say openly what she thought and felt. Dealing with dark and complex personalities such as Nathan's was not easy for her. She hated the feeling of not knowing exactly what she was dealing with, of being unsure.

Yes, she would ask him about Irene tomorrow. And she might ask him about other things as well. His mother, for instance…

Gemma gulped. Well, maybe not.

Six that night found her sitting in front of her television watching the news and devouring a home-made hamburger and chips. Any guilt over the cholesterol content was justified by saying she was eating for two. In truth, her recent stay in the heat of the outback had steamed a few pounds off the body. She was very streamlined, except for her breasts, which had gone from her normal B-cup to a C. The doctor she had visited this week had assured her this was perfectly normal and that she was lucky to have good-sized nipples, as a lot of fuller-breasted women sometimes had surprisingly small nipples, which made breast-feeding a problem.

Well, there was nothing flat about *her*, she thought drily. She would probably have enough milk to feed quads! Some girls at school had envied her her bust but quite frankly she'd always thought her breasts an embarrassment and a nuisance.

Still, Nathan seemed to like them. A lot.

Gemma thought of the outfit she had bought for her lunch date with him tomorrow and experienced a stab of guilt. If she wasn't prepared to sleep with the man, why tease him? And that green and white polka-dot dress was a definite tease, being halter-necked, with a built-in bra that moulded and lifted her breasts into a cleavage that would have made Marilyn Monroe look under-endowed. Of course, it did have a small white bolero jacket which hid most of the curves and which she planned on wearing. But there would still be a hint of that eye-catching cleavage on show.

Gemma had made the decision not to wear the damned dress after all when suddenly Nathan's face appeared on the television screen before her. Startled, she stopped eating mid-chip, mouth agape when the camera panned to bring into focus the blonde whose arm was cosily linked with his and who was also smiling up into his handsome face with a sickeningly sweet smile.

'I'm so excited,' she was simpering. 'When Lenore decided out of the blue to leave the play come Christmas, I never dreamt I would get the lead role. But darling Nathan has faith in me, and I can only say I will do my level best to reward that faith in me.' This last little gem of gratitude was accompanied by a look that no one could mistake. It had 'I'm yours, darling, as often as—and in any way—you want me' written all over.

Before Gemma could stop herself she threw what was left of her plate of chips at the screen and leapt to her feet. 'You lying bastard!' she screamed. 'You're sleeping with that whore and now all the world knows it!'

At her explosive tirade, Jaws had jumped to his feet as well, whimpering with confusion before stopping to gobble up the chips that were gradually sliding down the television, dropping one by delicious one on to the floor.

'Traitor,' she snarled at him, then slumped down on the cane sofa and burst into tears.

Don't jump to conclusions, a tiny little voice tried to reassure her, but without much success.

'This isn't a jump,' she sobbed aloud. 'It's a tweenie weenie step!'

She wept noisily and angrily, but her hurt and her anger eventually turned into a full-on blaming of herself.

What did she expect him to do when she'd rejected him and virtually given him permission to be unfaithful? Nathan was not a man to go meekly to bed every night without the comfort he obviously found in a woman's body. She had been a fool to think he wouldn't. And a fool to think that when he did she wouldn't feel like killing him.

Because she did. She wanted to get in her car right at this moment, driving down to Sydney and scratch his eyes out. As for blondie—nothing was too good for that slut! Gemma fantasied about superglueing her lips together, so that she wouldn't be able to perform, either in that play or on other women's husbands!

She's only giving him what you never would, that awful little voice said again.

Gemma groaned admission of this. How many times had Nathan subtly suggested she take a more aggressive role in lovemaking, only to have her shrink away like a blushing virgin? God, what a fool she had been! What a fool she still was, pushing Nathan away in the one area where they were compatible. They could be even more compatible if she could get over her squeamishness when it came to certain activities.

No, it wasn't squeamishness, she realised as she pondered the problem. It was more a lack of confidence. When Nathan was making love to *her*, she would spin out into another world, but it was a world of mindless receiving, not giving. If *she* started making love to him, she would be taking responsibility for *his* pleasure. It was a daunting thought. What if she was no good at it? What if, when one came right down to it, she was a fumbler and a bumbler? What if she lacked the courage to go through with whatever she started?

By this time Gemma was pacing the room, Jaws trailing behind her. Around and around the lounge they went, till Gemma suddenly ground to a halt, looking down at the dog with some amusement at the picture they would have presented to an outsider.

'This is a damned silly way to take you for a walk!' she pronounced, then laughed. 'Come on, I'll get your lead and we'll go for a real walk, then I have some deciding to do.'

SUNDAY DAWNED with the promise of a hot summer's day. November had slid into December in the few days since Gemma had seen Nathan, and with it the weather had been consistently fine and warm. Beach weather. Only Gemma was not overly fond of the beach, or at least not the surf. Having been brought up in the outback, she found the sea intimidating. Nevertheless, she'd come to quite like walking along the sand, and even around the rocks when the tide was out and there were no crashing spraying waves to frighten her.

Nathan had said he would arrive no later than eleven-thirty, but it was nearly noon by the time his Mercedes pulled into the driveway. Gemma, who'd been fully made up and dressed by eleven, was hopelessly agitated by this time.

'You're late,' she snapped, glaring down at Nathan over the balcony railing as his golden head appeared out of the car.

He glanced up at her, grey eyes lazily amused. 'And hello to you too,' he drawled. 'I really like the "I'm so glad you've arrived safely—did you have a nice trip?" greeting.'

For all her determination to be cool and sophisticated about the Jody situation—she had resolved not even to mention it—Gemma suddenly found herself seething with jealousy and a desire to say something cuttingly pointed. She controlled that urge, but was still left with a sour disposition.

'I was worried,' she complained crossly.

'There was an accident on the expressway which held things up for a while,' he said as he strode around the car to mount the steep front steps. 'And I'm not that late, Gemma.'

'You should have started out earlier,' she told him waspishly. 'Or did you have a particularly late night?'

This last remark brought a sharp look. 'No later than usual on a Saturday night. There's always extra curtain calls on a Saturday night.'

He reached the top of the steps and Gemma allowed herself to look at him, *really* look at him.

For a man in his mid-thirties, he had no right to look so damned good, she decided. He still had all of that thick golden hair, he wasn't carrying an ounce of flab, and any lines on his face only seemed to enhance his looks, rather than detract in any way. Dressed as he was today in dark grey trousers and open-necked, short-sleeved shirt in the finest cream lawn, he looked no older than thirty and every inch a man other women would throw themselves at.

Gemma's eyes travelled back up his body again finally to meet puzzled eyes. 'Is my fly open or something?' he said.

She tossed her head somewhat irritably. 'No, I was just

thinking how well preserved you were for a man of thirty-five.'

'God, you make me sound like a bottle of pickles,' he said ruefully. 'And I'm not thirty-five any more, either. I had a birthday a couple of weeks back.'

Gemma looked stricken.

'Now don't start going all sentimental on me,' he went on impatiently. 'I've never set much store by birthdays. Only children get hurt when people forget their birthdays. Adults don't give a damn.'

But I'll bet you were hurt often as a child, Gemma thought. I'll bet that drug-addict mother of yours forgot your birthday more times than I've had hot dinners.

'I've made a booking for twelve-thirty,' he continued, 'so we might as well get going straight away. It's gone noon and, while it'll only take a few minutes or so to get there, it'll take an eternity to find a parking spot at this time of day on a sunny Sunday.'

'Where are we going?'

'The Holiday Inn at Terrigal.'

'Oh, good, I haven't been to Terrigal yet. I hear it's very nice.'

'I would say it's the prettiest place I've ever seen. I'd have bought a house there if the surf were better. Speaking of pretty...' He looked her up and down, his eyes finally settling on her cleavage. One eyebrow arched, before his eyes lifted back to hers. 'I was about to say that was a very pretty dress you're wearing but I doubt the word *pretty* is adequate. Where did you get it? I don't recall seeing it in your wardrobe before.'

'I bought it yesterday.'

'With our lunch date in mind?'

Gemma quivered inside, both with apprehension and excitement, but it was too late to go back now. She looked him straight in the eye. 'Yes,' she said simply, and with that word told him all he needed to know.

Yet his reaction was odd. His grey eyes darkened to slate, narrowing thoughtfully on her face. Oddly enough, she didn't think he was really looking at her face. His mind seemed to be somewhere else.

'What are you thinking about?' she said, her snappy tone jerking him back to the present.

The hint of a sardonic smile pulled at his mouth. 'I was thinking I should have brought Kirsty with me.'

It came to Gemma then that he didn't realise she meant to go through with it. He probably thought she was just teasing him. Or maybe *testing* him. So before fear—or a lack of confidence—could set in she walked forward, wound her arms up around his neck, went up on tiptoe and kissed him.

His lips felt startled and stiff under hers at first, neither did he make any attempt to put his arms around her, so she tightened her own grip, leant fully against him, then sent her tonguetip forward as he had often done to her, stroking his lips till they groaned apart.

Up till that moment, Gemma had been rather cool and calculating in what she was doing, but the split-second she actually slid her tongue forward and into his mouth an incredible explosion of raw desire mushroomed up through her, taking her by surprise. Her moan was the moan of naked passion, as was the way her tongue started moving, darting deep into his mouth again and again in a feverish echo of what she suddenly wanted his flesh to be doing inside hers.

Her senses leapt when she felt his hands on her, spanning her tiny waist and squeezing it. She welcomed his roughness, loving the feel of his fingertips digging into her skin. Till suddenly he was lifting her away from him, her mouth wrenched from his quite violently.

'No, Gemma,' he said in an astonishingly composed voice.

She started up at him, aware of her hot tingling mouth

and her hot tingling body, aware of herself as a woman in a way she never had been before. How could he be so calm when she wanted to tear the clothes from his body, wanted to *devour* him, wanted to do all those things she had never wanted to do before?

'Why not?' she groaned. 'I don't understand...' Her eyes dropped away in the confusion and misery of acute frustration.

'Because you don't really want this,' he said starkly.

Big brown eyes flew upwards. 'My God, how can you say that? Did you think that was *acting*?' The word 'acting' catapulted the reason for Nathan's control into her mind with the sting of a scorpion's tail. Reefing herself away from where his hands had been resting lightly on her waist, she scowled her disgust at him. 'I know why you don't want to make love to me,' she spat. 'You don't need to after screwing dear old Jody into the early hours of the morning.'

His pretend shock made her doubly angry. 'Oh, don't bother to deny it,' she flung at him. 'I saw you both on television the other night and I saw the way she was looking at you, not to mention what she *said*. One didn't have to be a genius to put two and two together. I stupidly blamed myself for forcing you into the arms of another woman but now I see that's where you'd prefer to be. God, she must be good! Or is it that dear old inexperienced Gemma is just so pathetically boring? Well, maybe I can find someone who doesn't find me so boring. Maybe I'll go find myself an ego-booster as well!'

For a few seconds, Nathan's face turned a ghastly shade of grey but then he rallied, his expression one of apology and concern. 'If you got the wrong idea with that interview, Gemma, then I am deeply sorry. What can I say except to repeat that there is nothing between Jody and myself on a personal basis? Nor any other woman for that matter. There has been no other woman for me but you, since the first day we met.'

'Pull the other leg, Nathan,' she scorned. 'It yodels.'

His eyes went hard and flinty as he battled for control. 'I'm trying to be patient with you—and with Jody, in a way—because I realise the initial fault was all mine by acting with her the way I did at the party, then taking her home afterwards. I had every intention of sleeping with her that night. I admit it. But I knew, the moment she walked into our apartment and sat down in *your* chair, that I couldn't do it. I gave her a drink, told her I was sorry and called her a cab.'

'Then why did she act like she was your mistress to the television interviewer?'

'She'd still like to be. She'd like to be the mistress of any man who could do for her career what I could. She's a very ambitious actress. She also happens to be a very good one. So when the opportunity presented itself, I gave her what she wanted in the hope that she wouldn't keep chasing me. Unfortunately, she hasn't got the message yet, but I'll be a little blunter in future. On top of that, come January, the play moves on to Melbourne and I'm not going with it.'

'You're not?'

'No. I've had a gutful of directing. I'm going back to writing.'

'Oh?' Gemma's heart leapt at this news. It was what she had wanted him to do, knowing how involved he got when he wrote. No way would he look at another woman once he had his nose buried in the computer screen. 'A new play, or that old one you have trouble with?'

'A new one, I think. I have a story in mind, full of conflict and erotic promise.'

'Sounds good. What's it about?'

Nathan's smile was mischievous. 'It's about a man who's married to a beautiful young girl many years younger than himself, and whom he's completely potty over. But things begin to go wrong and they become estranged for a while. She thinks he only wants her for sex, you see, and she won't have him back till he proves to her that his feelings run much deeper than that. He's dead determined to do just that, even though she makes it pretty hard on the bloke by wearing these seductive clothes and doing stupid things like French kissing him in the middle of the day.'

'Really? How inconsiderate of her!'

'That's what the husband thinks. He needs to prove to her, you see, that he can control himself in that regard, because he did something once…something that made him weep with remorse afterwards.'

At his confession the bleakest clouds gathered in his eyes and her heart turned over. 'Oh, Nathan,' she murmured, her own eyes filling with tears.

When her tears seemed to perturb him greatly, she quickly blinked them away and summoned up a smile from somewhere. 'Enough talk of plots and plays. If we don't leave soon, we'll be late for lunch. I'll just go put Jaws out the back, then get my jacket and purse.'

He brightened at this. 'That dress has a jacket?'

'Yes.'

'Thank heaven for small mercies!'

CHAPTER ELEVEN

NATHAN was right about Terrigal. Gemma agreed that it had to be one of the prettiest places in the world. The beach itself was delightful, curving round to end in a small protected cove which Nathan told her was called the Haven. She could see what he meant by the surf, however. Its waves were rather gentle and more suited to family enjoyment than daredevil board riders.

There was no shortage of families that day, a myriad umbrellas and bodies dotting the white sands, and many more sitting on rugs under the stately Norfolk pines which shaded a grassy area at the edge of the beach.

Opposite these pines stood the majestic and quite magnificent Holiday Inn, whose Mediterranean architecture made one think of the French Riviera. Not that Gemma had been to the Riviera, but she had seen plenty of pictures. And Terrigal, she fancied, would not be misplaced there, especially with the way the hills hugged the shore, houses built all over the steep hillsides to take advantage of the panoramic view.

Nathan drove slowly down the main street past the hotel, then turned a couple of corners that took them round to what looked like the back of the hotel but which, as it turned out, housed the main entrance.

'My God, a parking spot!' he exclaimed, zipping the Mercedes into a space between two cars. 'Wonders will never cease. You must have brought me good luck, Gemma. This never happens when Kirsty is with me. We always go round and round the block for ages, then end up parking miles away and having to walk.'

'We can only stay here for two hours,' she warned him, looking up at the sign as they both climbed out.

'I think we should manage to finish lunch in two hours, don't you?'

'I should hope so, provided the service isn't too slow.'

Nathan slid his arm through hers. 'Didn't I tell you? It's buffet-style. You serve yourself. And you can go back for more as often as you like.'

'Mmm. Sounds marvellous. But very fattening.'

'You could do with some fattening up. You've lost weight.'

'Not from everywhere,' she said drily.

His eyes slid down to the deep valley between her breasts. 'Yes, so I noticed.'

'You're making me blush,' she chided.

'You're making me do a few things too.'

'Nathan, stop it.'

'Can't, I'm afraid.'

'What…what are you going to do?'

'Steer you through these revolving glass doors, with you firmly in front while I try to think of other things and hope for the best.'

Gemma was so busy trying to keep a straight face as Nathan did this that she didn't initially appreciate the cool spaciousness inside the hotel, or its quite splendid décor which was oddly Victorian, rather than Mediterranean.

'Keep going,' Nathan said through gritted teeth and urged her past Reception and up a wide staircase which divided into two at the first landing, sweeping left and right in semi-circles up to the first level, where signs indicated various restaurants and convention rooms. Gemma also spotted Ladies' and Gents' rest-rooms.

'You could always go to the Gent's for a while,' she whispered to Nathan.

'I'd rather go the Ladies',' he growled. 'Look, let's just lean over this railing for a minute or two, then I should be all right.'

They did so, in silence, Gemma pretending to look around, all the while torn between laughter and a touch of lingering guilt. If she hadn't been wearing such a revealing dress, Nathan wouldn't be in the awkward situation he was in right now.

Yet it was really his own fault, wasn't it? They could have been, at this very moment, back at the beach house, in bed. This was what he had chosen to do. In a way, she was almost enjoying his discomfort, which was rather wicked of her. But justified, she imagined. My God, she had suffered a lot at this man's hands. Shouldn't he suffer a little?

'Right,' he said testily after a full five minutes. 'Let's go in now.'

'Which way?'

'Right behind you.'

It was called the Conservatory, being a largely glassed-in area with huge windows overlooking the beach, and a glass ceiling which had some kind of protective shade-cloth draped over it, probably to keep the heat down. Perhaps such a design would have been better suited to an English hotel rather than one in sunny Australia, Gemma thought, though it was spectacular to look at.

The smorgasbord menu was arranged on tables to the left and right as one walked in. Gemma was agog at the splendid array of dishes, both hot and cold. Everything looked mouthwateringly appetising.

'Down this way, Gemma,' Nathan directed, taking her arm and practically dragging her away from the food and down the steps that led into main body of the restaurant. Nathan gave his name and a waitress led them over to a table next to one of the windows—one of the few empty tables left.

Gemma was happy to see that the atmosphere was casual. There weren't even tablecloths, their small circular table having a black marble top of which the cutlery setting was directly arranged, the green chairs equally casual and countrified with wrought-iron arms, wooden slats up the back and cushions to sit on.

Once seated, Nathan ordered a glass of Riesling for Gemma and a light beer for himself.

'We'll have a drink first, shall we,' he suggested, 'before getting up to select our first course?'

She nodded her agreement and was content to wait for their drinks in silence, admiring the view of the pines below and the beach beyond. The water was a deep blue-green under the bright sunshine, the sky a softer blue than an outback sky.

'It's so beautiful here,' she murmured at last.

'I'll bring you here to stay some time,' he offered.

She smiled. 'Yes, I'd like that.'

Though the food proved as delicious as it looked and the ambience very relaxing, the next two hours provided absolutely no opportunity for Gemma to have anything approaching an in-depth conversation with Nathan. Their table was not far from three other tables, one on either side and one behind. Anything she said could easily be overheard, so, in the end, all they talked about was what they ate, or what Gemma's plans were for filling in her time up at Avoca alone.

'You don't have to make your own dresses, you know,' Nathan said over his dessert. 'I'm sure there are boutiques in Sydney which specialise in individually designed maternity wear. I could bring you down to Sydney one day and buy you all the outfits you might need.'

Gemma counted to ten. 'I *like* sewing, Nathan,' she said firmly.

'Then make baby clothes,' he ordered. 'I don't like the idea of my wife wearing home-made clothes.'

'I'm only making things to wear around the house,' she said with a sigh.

'Is it a crime to want my wife to have the best?' he asked. 'Besides, it gives me pleasure to see you wearing beautiful clothes.'

'I'm not a dress-up doll, Nathan,' she reproached.

'Oh, I see,' he snapped, angry now. 'This is another of the many things I did wrong as a husband. I bought you beautiful clothes. God, what a bastard I am to do such a terrible thing. Do forgive me for being generous and wanting to make you happy.'

Gemma groaned before putting down her spoon and staring blankly out at the horizon, a weariness seeping across her mind. Would Nathan never see that *things* didn't make a wife happy? When she said as much, he scowled. Gemma looked away in disgust.

'Does it hurt to let me give you things,' he went on irritably, 'if it makes *me* happy? And who knows, maybe there are some things I can give you which *will* make you happy?'

Her expression became exasperated as she turned back to face him. 'Such as what? There's only so much clothes and jewellery a girl can wear. She can only drive one car and live in one house at a time. Everything else is sheer extravagance and indulgence. I wasn't brought up to riches, Nathan, and while I do like to be comfortable—who doesn't?—I do not need to have luxuries lavished upon me to be happy.'

'I see…' He began playing with his dessert, clearly put out by her answer. Had he already been planning more presents in an attempt to win her back?

She reached over and covered his hand with hers, stilling it. 'You've already given me one of life's most precious gifts, Nathan,' she said softly. 'A baby…'

He winced, then glanced up at her, that old cynical gleam

in his eyes. 'I'm still to be convinced you're thrilled about that,' he said curtly.

Gemma's hand withdrew on a gasp of shock, her own face growing hard with hurt. 'Then that's your loss, Nathan. I'm not going to try to convince you of it.'

'No…no, I don't suppose you are,' he said agitatedly, then glanced around till he attracted the waitress's attention, asking for coffee and the bill in the same brusque voice. Ten minutes later saw them walking in frozen silence back to the car. Once they were both seated, Nathan threw her an exasperated look.

'For God's sake, don't go giving me the cold shoulder,' he growled. 'I don't want to go back to Sydney with you being angry with me when I've been doing my damnedest all day to do the right thing by you.'

Gemma wearily shook her head. 'I'm not angry, Nathan. More frustrated. You just don't see so many things.'

'But I *am* trying. And perhaps there are things *you* don't see. You're not perfect, Gemma. Stop demanding perfection in return.'

She stared at him. Was that what she was doing? Demanding perfection?

His suddenly tender smile scattered her already confused thoughts. 'You must realise, my love,' he said gently, 'that you don't have all the answers to life, because you haven't lived all that much of it yet. You are looking for a Utopian existence which no man worth his salt can give to you. Men and women are by nature very different individuals. They don't always complement each other. Sometimes they clash. You want me to pour out my soul to you, but I don't feel comfortable doing that. You'll have to learn to trust me without knowing the ins and outs of every moment of my life before I met you.'

'I don't want to know the ins and outs of every moment of your life before you met me,' she argued. 'Just a few crucial ones.'

'Such as?'

'Such as what happened between you and Irene? What *really* happened?'

'Aah...so Damian wins, does he? The bastard is dead, but you still believe him and not me.'

'No! I *did* believe you when you told me you didn't sleep with her. But I'm not a fool, Nathan. Something else happened. Maybe I'm just being a typical female but I can't seem to get it out of my mind. I need to know.'

'And if I tell you, my love, what else will you need to know, I wonder?'

Her mind flashed to his mother and she coloured guiltily. Luckily, Nathan wasn't looking at her at that precise moment. He had leant forward to start the car and was even now easing it away from the kerb, looking over his shoulder to the right.

'I will tell you if you insist, but don't blame me if you don't like what you hear. I don't pretend to be a saint, even today, but this happened many, many years ago, at a time in my life when I had little pity for women, and none at all for a certain type.'

Gemma gulped. *Did* she want to hear this?

Nathan glanced over at her but it seemed her curiosity was greater than her fear, for she said nothing.

'I knew from the first day I came to live at Belleview,' he began as he drove home, 'that Irene was the biggest two-faced bitch of all time. She was absolutely vile to Ava, vicious to Jade, but sweet as apple pie to Byron. I dare say she did love him in her own warped way but it was plain to anyone with a brain in their head that he didn't love her back. Oh, he tolerated her remarkably well, but there was no real warmth in his dealings with his wife, and certainly no passion.'

'How could there be?' Gemma remarked. 'He was in love with my mother, with Celeste.'

'So it seems. But he hadn't had anything to do with her

for some considerable time, so I have no doubt Byron slept with his wife when he was at home. I doubt, however, that she ever felt that she'd been ''made love'' to. Consequently, she hated anyone or anything she believed took Byron's love away from her. Celeste. Ava. Jade. All of them had been victims of her jealousy. When Byron adopted me, she pretended to be all for the idea, whereas in truth she was violently jealous of me as well. I think she decided to seduce me as a kind of revenge for Byron not loving her. On top of that, I think she may have been titillated by what Byron had told her of my lifestyle when he first met me.'

'What...what lifestyle was that?' Gemma asked tentatively.

Nathan's laughter was mocking. 'Come now, you mean Ava hasn't already told you of my living with some woman old enough to be my mother? I find that hard to believe.'

'She...may have mentioned it.'

'I'll bet she did. And it's true,' he added quite ruthlessly. 'Lorna was forty-two when I moved in with her, while I was a tender sixteen. Since my own mother had only been thirty-three when she died, that made Lorna more than old enough to fulfil a parental role if that was what she wanted. And there was a degree of mothering in the way she treated me...at first.'

Nathan chuckled darkly and Gemma swallowed.

'But the circumstances of my eventual deflowering are hardly relevant to the story of Irene and myself,' he went on savagely, stunning Gemma with this revelation. 'Deflowering' suggested he'd been a *virgin* before moving in with this Lorna person.

Before she could stop herself, her eyes snapped round, wide and shocked. 'But I thought—' she blurted out.

'Thought what? That Lorna couldn't possibly have been my first? That with the sort of upbringing I had, I must have had plenty of opportunities for sexual experimentation before that?'

'Yes,' she said in a small voice, though inwardly relieved that the horrors she had been imagining were not true.

'Oh, believe me, I had scores of opportunities. I was a well grown lad by the time I was fourteen. My mother's friends starting coming on to me around that time. And I don't mean just her women friends.'

'But you resisted them?'

'Yes, I did—surprise! surprise!—despite some of the women being quite young and very sexy. One or two were almost as beautiful as my mother who, believe me, was something to behold, despite her drug-taking habits. She was like a golden goddess, with long blonde hair and a body men would kill for. Yet it was her aura that drew them like magnets, that irritatingly innocent aura which made them think she couldn't possibly have been humped by as many men as she had.'

Gemma cringed at his crude words but said nothing to stop the outpouring.

'God, but she was a promiscuous bitch! I can't remember a time when I didn't lie in my bed at night and hear her with some creep in the next room. Do you know what it's like to hear your mother moaning and groaning like that, Gemma? Can you imagine how I felt, lying in my little bed, forbidden to come out of my room but worried sick that she was actually being hurt? And then, as I grew older and I knew damned well what was going on, I would lie there, hating her. And hating the excitement it gave me listening to my own mother...'

'Oh, Nathan...'

'Don't get me wrong,' he snarled. 'I loved her too. And she loved me. She used to put me in boarding-school when she was involved with anyone who wasn't nice to me. It was her way of protecting me, yet all I wanted to do was protect *her*, so I would run away and make trouble for whatever bastard was screwing her at the time and he would ultimately leave. Then, for a while, we would have a great time together, till another jockey came on the scene.'

He stopped to scoop in several steadying breaths, Gemma moved to tears for the boy who must have been in torment most of his childhood. But at least he hadn't been abused as she had feared he might have been. His mother had loved him in a fashion, and he had loved her, which meant he was capable of love, capable of giving his heart, even to an unworthy recipient.

'You know, I'll never believe she overdosed deliberately,' he went on. 'She wouldn't have done that. It was probably an accident. Someone must have given her some heroin that was stronger than she thought it was. Hell, when I found her dead that day I was devastated. I cried and cried, and then I went out and got roaring drunk.'

'And is that when you got tangled up with Lorna?' Gemma suggested softly. 'When you were at your most vulnerable?'

He nodded, slowly, wryly. They were not far from Avoca at this stage and suddenly, Nathan pulled over to the side of the road and cut the engine. Inside the car became deathly quiet except for Nathan's ragged breathing.

'She was a friend of my mother's,' he grated out. 'One of the only women who had never come on to me. I thought I was safe with her. And I was, for a while.' He gave a low, dark chuckle. 'I had this fantasy, you see, that I would stay a virgin till I fell in love and married. I guess that's what happens to boys with mothers like mine. They either become just as promiscuous, or they do the exact opposite. I had always vowed I would never be like my mother. What a naïve young idiot I was! One night, Lorna showed me what a fool's paradise I was living in. Boy, did she ever show me.'

His cold laughter left her stunned and speechless.

'Damian didn't try an original technique with you, my dear,' he continued caustically. 'Using drugs to turn a person on against their will is hardly new, especially when combined with alcohol. One night my devious den-mother got me drunk then gave me an added little something. I must have passed out because when I came round I was lying spread-eagled and starkers on her bed, where she proceeded to show me that sex with a woman you didn't love was far from repulsive.

'Admittedly, at first, I was not altogether comfortable with what was happening to me. My mind kept saying no, but all the while my body just kept on saying yes. I even bawled like a baby when I couldn't help coming under those rapacious lips and hands. Yet any remorse did not stop my youthful body from becoming aroused again within minutes, neither could I find the will to stop her from taking me as if I was nothing but a thing to be used, over and over and over.'

Gemma's whole mouth had gone dry with the tale, her eyes wide, yet her mind racing with new and understanding thoughts. My God, doesn't he know he wasn't to blame for any of that? What that evil old bitch had done had been tantamount to rape!

Yes, of course he realised that, she accepted with the dawning of wisdom, which was why he was so appalled at himself for raping *her*. And why he was so worried about her having anything to do with the likes of Damian, who had no conscience where women were concerned. She had been as sexually naïve as Nathan had been back then, both of them ideal victims for unscrupulous and debauched people like Lorna and Damian.

Nathan broke into her train of thought with a dry laugh. 'I can see the cogs of your fertile and forgiving brain working, Mrs Whitmore, but don't whitewash me totally yet. I went on living with Lorna well after the drink and the drugs wore off. She taught me everything I know about sex, the conniving corrupting bitch, and I enjoyed every damned moment. You also don't know what I did to Irene, which I knowingly and deliberately planned and executed.'

Gemma bit her bottom lip as everything inside started churning ominously.

'Well you might look worried,' Nathan said ruefully. 'Are you sure you have the stomach for the rest of this? You're looking a little green around the gills.'

Gemma lifted her nose and her chin. 'I want to know *everything* about you, warts and all!'

'Do you, now? Well, don't say you weren't warned!' he laughed. 'It's not a pretty story and I have no intention of watering it down. Irene came to my bedroom one night a few weeks after my adoption. It was very late, Byron was away on business, and she was wearing a very transparent négligé. Have you ever seen a photograph of Irene when she was younger, Gemma? No, you wouldn't have. That vain bitch got rid of all her early photographs when her looks began to go. She was extremely attractive and very sensual, with black hair and eyes, and a tall voluptuous figure. Let me assure you that nearly twenty years ago she looked very enticing in that sheer gear.

'If she was nervous, she didn't show it. She boldly stood with her back against the door and told me that if I didn't do what she wanted she would tell Byron I had made indecent advances to her while he was away. Given my background I naturally thought Byron would believe his wife, not me, and that I would be thrown out on the streets. She then went on to tell me what she wanted, and I felt sick with shame and fear.'

'Well, of course you did!'

Nathan's sidewards glance was withering. 'Not because of what you're thinking. Because I was so damned tempted! Lorna had done her job very well. I only had to look at Byron's near-naked wife and I was immediately stunningly aroused. Fortunately, I had a dressing-gown on over my pyjamas and Irene didn't notice. But this time, my respect for Byron was far greater than my desire for his wife. I hit upon a plan which I hoped would stop her in her tracks and guarantee that she would never tempt me again.'

'What...what did you do?'

'I told her I would be only too happy to do what she asked and that I thought she was the most beautiful, sexy, desirable woman in the world and that I hadn't been able to think of doing anything else except making love to her since I arrived at Belleview. Then I told her that Lorna had taught me an oriental technique which would intensify her pleasure. I explained to her that if we delayed our lovemaking for twenty-hours, during that time anticipation of what was to come would heighten her arousal to such a pitch she would never forget the experience.'

'Good lord!'

'Is that an exclamation of shock-horror or interest at the technique?' Nathan drawled.

'I...I—er—um...' She licked dry lips. Which *was* it?

'Never mind,' he snapped. 'I made it up, but it sounded plausible enough. I needed time to get my equipment together.'

'Equipment?' Gemma squawked.

'Not *that* equipment. I had to get my hands on a tape-recorder.'

'A tape-recorder...'

'That's right. I hired one from a local rental shop, put in a blank tape and hid it under the bed. When the time approached for my rendezvous with Irene, I turned it on. She showed up five minutes later. With great difficulty, I talked her into just sitting on the side of the bed while she told me in lurid detail everything she wanted me to do to her, and everything she was going to do to me. I convinced her this was part of the technique, and if she had enough grit to wait one more night without release the experience would blow her mind. The next day I had copies of the tapes made, one of which I gave to her, explaining what was on it and that if she ever came near me again I would give a copy to Byron. In a sudden inspiration I also told her if she laid a hand on Jade again the same thing would happen.'

'What…what was her reaction?'

'She cried. She ranted and raved. She begged me, then cursed me. In the end, she just seemed frightened of me. I have to admit I took great pleasure in her fear. I had never had anyone afraid of me before and I like the feeling of power, of being in control. I vowed to remain in control of my life—and my sexuality—from that moment on.

'By and large I have kept that vow. Only once…' he slid a black glance her way '…did I lapse, but I don't have to tell you about that, do I? In fact, I think I've told you far and away too much already. I dare say you'll try to psychoanalyse every damned thing I do from this moment on. You do have a tendency to want to analyse the whys and wherefores of my behaviour. In that respect you're very much like your father. Byron used to probe endlessly about my past when I first met him. Thank God, he soon gave up that idea and let me get on with my life. Now it's time for us to get on with our lives, Gemma, which means I'd better start up this car and get you home. The afternoon's sliding away and I still have several things to discuss with you.'

'Such as what?' she asked a little distractedly, her mind whirling with all Nathan had told her.

'Such as exactly what story we're going to be telling Byron and Celeste. I received a call last night saying they had a buyer for the boat but the man wants to take possession immediately. They're flying home tomorrow.'

CHAPTER TWELVE

THE moment Celeste arrived in Sydney and found out about Gemma's pregnancy she was up at the Avoca beach house as if she'd been shot out of a cannon. Byron was with her, but of course his attitude was one of smug satisfaction, whereas Celeste could not hide her concern underneath her congratulations, so much so that soon after their arrival Celeste contrived some errand for Byron to do down the road so that she could be alone with her daughter.

Gemma was left to face her mother with some trepidation, knowing Celeste was sure to ask her all sorts of awkward questions, including the one Gemma did not want to answer. In fact the moment Byron left Celeste launched forth.

'So what's going on here, Gemma?' she asked bluntly. 'I don't believe all that garbage Nathan fed Byron about you and he being totally reconciled, and that you were both thrilled about the baby. If that's so why aren't you living with Nathan down in Sydney? And I certainly don't believe his excuse that you were staying up here because you'd been feeling poorly and the sea air was good for you. You look as fit as a fiddle to me. Blooming, in fact.'

'Well, I...I—'

'For pity's sake don't feed me waffle,' Celeste interrupted impatiently. 'Just give it to me straight. I can't abide people beating around the bush. I love you, darling, and I'll stand by you, no matter what, but I must know the truth.'

Gemma knew that any hope of either hedging or colouring the situation differently had been well and truly dashed.

Celeste would spot her lies a mile off because she knew too much. Not for the first time, Gemma regretted having told her mother about that incident with Nathan. But she had, and nothing was going to change that.

'Nathan and I *are* having a sort of trial reconciliation because of the baby,' she answered matter-of-factly. 'But I didn't want to live with him because I'm not sleeping with him at the moment. I want to see if he can learn to care for me as a person, not just a bedmate. And yes, for your information only, the baby *was* conceived on that afternoon at Campbell Court. And no, that doesn't bother me one iota. I want this baby and I will love it as much as I love its father.'

Celeste's eyebrows shot up at this. 'I thought you hated him!'

Gemma's smile was wry. 'Now, Mother...coming from you, that's almost funny. How many years did you go round saying you hated my father?'

'Mothers don't want their daughters to be as dumb as they've been,' Celeste grumbled. 'Loving Byron gave me many years of heartache.'

'And many years of happiness...from now on.'

Celeste nodded slowly. 'I suppose so. But that's because Byron loves me back. Can you say the same for *your* husband?'

'No. Not yet. He wants to love me, I think. He's just not sure how. But he's trying, Celeste. He's trying very hard. And he's talking to me, telling me things he would never have told me before.'

'Really? I'm surprised. Nathan has never struck me as a confider.'

'No, he's not. Normally. But I've been able to get him at a vulnerable moment or two when he said more than he intended. Not that he tells me everything. Often I have to try to fill in the missing pieces and sometimes I'm way off beam, but I'm getting there. In time, I think I'll be able to put the complete puzzle which is Nathan together. He had a very rough childhood, you know. He needs a lot of understanding and compassion.''

Celeste frowned. 'You had a rough childhood too, Gemma. Everyone's had a rough something or other at some time in their lives, but in the end you have to go forward, not back. Don't probe too deeply, love. Maybe there are things you're better off not knowing. And maybe there are things you'd be better off doing.' So saying, she gave her a sharp look. 'You're *really* not sleeping with him?'

Gemma tried not to blush. 'No.'

'And he's going along with that?'

Gemma recalled his rejection of her offering herself on a silver platter and an embarrassed heat gathered in her cheeks. 'Yes, he is,' she said staunchly, which brought another disbelieving look from her mother.

'He's not still sleeping with that Jody woman, is he?'

'He never did sleep with her.'

'Is that what he told you?'

Gemma could not help smiling at her mother's cynical scepticism. 'Yes, that's what he told me and I believe him because he didn't have to give me any such reassurance. I'd already told him he could sleep with other women if he wanted to.'

Celeste blinked her astonishment. 'Good God, are you *crazy*?'

'Yep. Crazy about him. So crazy I'm prepared to do just about anything to win his love.'

Celeste was shaking her head. 'Dear girl, I think I will have to tell you the facts of life where men are concerned. You never *ever* give them permission to sleep with other women. They're likely to take you up on the offer.'

'Nathan won't.'

Celeste threw her hands up in the air. 'The girl's gone bonkers!'

'You don't know Nathan.'

'And I aim to keep it that way.'

'He told me he didn't think too badly of you any more. In fact, I think he rather admires you.'

Celeste stared at her daughter, her cat's eyes narrowing. 'Are you conning me?'

'Never!'

'Hmm. I suppose I might have to try to get along with him too, now that he's fathered my first grandchild.'

'Yes, Grandma,' Gemma teased.

Celeste grimaced. 'Gosh, that sounds awful, doesn't it? I'll be forty next week too. I'm getting old, Gemma,' she wailed.

'The only thing you're getting,' her daughter returned, 'is more beautiful every day. Marriage suits you.'

Celeste flushed with pleasure. 'Really? You think so? I...I've put on a bit of weight lately. All that lazing around on deck and drinking champagne.'

'Sounds blissful.'

'It was,' Celeste sighed.

'So why sell the boat?'

'Oh, it wasn't the silly boat that was blissful,' she said dismissively. 'It was...' She broke off, her eyes flying to her daughter's. For the first time, possibly in her entire life, Gemma imagined, the outrageous head of Campbell Jewels looked embarrassed.

'Mother,' Gemma said laughingly, 'what have you and Daddy been up to?'

Daddy chose that precise moment to return, a flagon of sherry in each hand. He stood outside on the front balcony, tapping one of the flagons against the sliding glass doors and mouthing for them to let him in. Gemma did so, giving him an all-encompassing glance as she did so. Golly, but he was looking fantastic. Tanned and relaxed and very youthful. No one would believe he was fifty. From Celeste's reaction, he hadn't been acting as if he was fifty, either.

'And what are you grinning at, daughter? Or maybe I

shouldn't ask. Been talking about me behind my back, have you?' he threw at both of them as he walked over to put the flagons on the counter separating the kitchen from the living-room.

'Couldn't find the brand you asked for, Celeste,' he went on, reaching up to slide back the doors of the glass cabinet above the counter and bring down three glasses. 'The man in the bottle shop said he thought they stopped making it back in 1922, so I bought these two instead. He recommended them as similar in taste. One's cream sherry and one's sweet.'

'Thank you, darling,' Celeste purred, knowing full well that the brand she'd asked for didn't even exist. It had simply been a ploy to keep Byron busy while she'd questioned Gemma.

'Let's have a tipple, then,' Byron went on expansively, opening the cream sherry and filling the three glasses. 'Later I'm going to take my two lovely ladies out to dinner.'

'You don't have to do that,' Gemma protested. 'I can cook, you know.'

'My dear,' Celeste said with a rolling-eyed glance of exasperation, 'if a man offers to take you out to dinner then don't object. Truly, I think I need to take you in hand in matters concerning the opposite sex.'

Byron gave Celeste a look that could only be classified as *classified*!

'I think we'll leave Gemma's education in the opposite sex up to Nathan, don't you?' Byron drawled. 'And speaking of Nathan, he told me to tell you he'd be up on Friday night.'

'F...Friday night?' Gemma stammered.

'Yes. And so will Jade and Kyle. Nathan's invited them for the weekend.'

'Oh...' Gemma didn't know whether to be relieved or worried. Wouldn't Jade and Kyle think it odd if she and Nathan slept in separate rooms? Or didn't Nathan intend sleeping in a separate room? Maybe he'd changed his mind about that...

'How nice for you to have company,' Celeste murmured, her knowing eyes telling Gemma exactly what she was thinking. 'You must get lonely all week up here without Nathan.'

'Actually, I quite like living alone,' she said swiftly. 'I'm used to it.'

'Is that a hint for us to leave?' her father asked.

'Not at all! I'd be horribly disappointed if you didn't stay a couple of days at least.'

'Good, because we're going to. We both planned to be away from our respective offices till the end of the week, didn't we, Celeste? So we'll stay up here with you till Friday, then pass you over to Nathan and Co. Now come over here, both of you, and get your sherry.'

'A hundred dollars you don't make it through the weekend without succumbing,' Celeste whispered to Gemma as they walked over to the counter.

Gemma was startled at first, then amused. Selecting the nearest sherry, she lifted it to her lips, meeting her mother's dancing eyes over the rim of the glass. 'Make it a real bet,' she whispered back as soon as she got the chance. 'Or aren't you that confident?'

'Will you ladies excuse me a moment?' Byron said. 'I'm going to take my sherry out by the pool and say hello again to that great dog of yours, Gemma. I can see now how he managed to get over the fences at Belleview. Never seen such a big dog in all my life, but I like him.'

'Go right ahead. I'm just glad he likes you back.'

'Oh? Has he been vicious with anyone else?'

'Only Nathan so far. And I wouldn't say vicious. But it's daggers drawn every time they meet. Jaws doesn't try to bite him any more, but he still growls a lot.'

'But he took to me right away,' Byron said, sounding puzzled.

'He liked the pool-cleaning man too. I think it's just Nathan.'

'Whatever did he do to the dog?'

'Nothing, really. I think maybe Jaws is a frustrated guard dog and he seems to think I need guarding from Nathan.'

'Smart dog,' Celeste muttered under her breath, but fortunately Byron didn't hear as he made his way out of the room.

'So what was Nathan doing to you,' Celeste asked with suspicion in her voice, 'that made the dog think you needed protecting?'

Gemma sighed. 'Don't jump to conclusions. He was only kissing me.'

'There's kissing and there's kissing, daughter, dear. I presume you were trying to fight the bastard off and he wasn't responding.'

Gemma laughed. 'I wasn't fighting at all and *I* was the one who was responding. Jaws has my undying gratitude for intervening.'

'Aah, so Nathan *isn't* happy with this "no bed" rule you've made.'

'I never said he was *happy* about it.'

'Just as I thought! You haven't got a chance of holding out against him for a whole weekend, Gemma, not when you're in love with the man. I hope you realise that.'

Gemma shrugged. 'As I said, I'm willing to bet on it.'

'All right. How much *do* you want to bet?'

'You decide, since you're so sure of my capitulating.'

'All right. If I lose, I'll give you the Heart of Fire…'

Gemma's mouth dropped open, her hand freezing around her sherry glass. Celeste had paid two million dollars for the Heart of Fire. Gemma had once coveted the magnificent black opal, had indeed thought she had inherited it for a short while. She'd been badly disappointed when she'd found out it was stolen property. She could still remember the first moment she'd turned it over in her hand, and been captivated by its rare splendour.

Would the chance of really owning that priceless gem be enough to stop her from making love with Nathan if he changed his mind and set his sights on seduction over the weekend? Gemma doubted it.

'And if I lose?' she asked.

Celeste's smile was quite smug. 'If you lose, I get to name the baby.'

Gemma blinked her surprise at such an ill balanced bet.

'I...I never got the chance to name you, you see,' her mother explained, a wealth of emotion in her voice and her face.

A lump immediately formed in Gemma's throat. 'All right, you're on,' she agreed, and wondered if she might deliberately try to seduce Nathan again herself, merely so that Celeste could win her bet.

Celeste put down her sherry, her eyes glistening. 'I...I think I might go and freshen up,' she said a little shakily. 'Would you mind going and asking your father what time he wants us ready for dinner, and remind him to make a booking to wherever he's taking us?'

Gemma found Byron relaxing on a lounger under a tree, Jaws stretched out by his side and thoroughly enjoying a gentle stroking of his ears.

'Don't get up,' she said as she approached and pulled up a deckchair to sit down beside him. 'Celeste said to remind you to book the restaurant. She also wants to know when you want us ready by.'

'No need to book on a Monday night,' he returned confidently before glancing at his watch. 'It's twenty after five now. How about we leave around seven?'

'Sounds good to me.'

'Can't understand why Nathan doesn't get along with this dog,' Byron puzzled aloud. 'He's as gentle as a lamb.'

'I think it might have something to do with his never

having a dog or a pet when he was a boy,' Gemma tried to explain. 'He never developed any rapport with animals and an animal can sense that. I'll bet you had a pet as a boy.'

Byron seemed to ponder this, nodding slowly up and down. 'Yes, you're right. I had a lot of pets over the years, including a dog once. He was a Labrador, a big fat lazy dog, and I loved him to death.'

'Nathan never had anything to love as a child except an unstable nymphomaniac who couldn't possibly have given him a good example of what real love was like. He's been struggling ever since to learn how to really love, especially when it comes to women. Nathan's idea of intimacy begins and ends with the physical.'

Byron sighed. 'I had hoped he might have thrown off that evil bitch's influence by now,' he muttered. 'It wasn't his body she corrupted, it was his view of himself as a male.'

Gemma frowned. 'Are you talking about Nathan's mother?'

'No, though, as you say, she's got plenty to answer for as well. I'm talking about Lorna Manson.'

'Oh, *her*.'

Byron's eyes snapped round in surprise. 'You *know* about Lorna?'

Gemma nodded. 'I'd heard rumours from Ava but it was Nathan who told me the grisly details. That woman as good as raped him!'

'Yes, she did, but it was the eventual rape of his mind that did the most harm. Did you know that bitch used to tell him he was a bad seed, just like his mother? That he'd inherited her weakness for sex and that no woman would ever want him for anything else but sex, just as no man have ever wanted his mother for anything other than sex.'

'Good God! No, I didn't know that.'

'I didn't think so. Nathan broke down and told me one night soon after I met him. He was quite drunk at the time.

He kept telling me over and over that he wanted to be good, but he was afraid he was programmed to be bad.'

Gemma was appalled that anyone would play with a child's mind like that, especially one as vulnerable as Nathan would have been. But really, it explained so much. No wonder he'd gone off the rails after he did what he did to her. He would temporarily have thought he'd reverted to type, to the depraved and uncontrollable animal this Lorna person had tried to convince him he was.

Did he still think that? Gemma wondered. Was that why he too was trying hard to keep their relationship platonic for a while? Maybe he was trying to prove something to himself, not her. Still, knowing this made Gemma feel so much more confident that she was doing the right thing in not sleeping with Nathan. Her feminine intuition had steered her in the right direction, and, bet or no bet with Celeste, she vowed again to keep sex out of their relationship for a while longer.

'I did my best to convince him that wasn't true, of course,' Byron growled, 'and I genuinely thought I had gotten through to him. But maybe I didn't. Maybe down deep he still thinks he's not fit to be truly loved, that all he can offer a woman is what's between his legs. Oh, God, I'm sorry, Gemma. That was a crude thing to say. I forgot who I was talking to. Sorry.'

'You don't have to apologise. I appreciate your being frank with me. And I don't want you to worry about Nathan. He'll be fine. *We'll* be fine.'

Byron shook his head. 'You're such an optimist. Either that or you're as stubborn as a mule.'

Gemma grinned. 'Do I get that from my father or my mother?'

'Oh, definitely your mother. That woman would try the patience of a saint. She—'

'What is this?' Celeste loomed up over them suddenly, hands on hips, face full of exasperation. 'I send Gemma down here to find out a couple of simple things and she's gone a week! Hello, dog,' she added, idly patting Jaws who had stood up and had started nudging his nose against her hand.

'I think he likes her too,' Byron told Gemma drily.

'I think he does. Nathan's going to spit.'

'I'm the one who's going to spit if I don't get a straight answer.'

'To what, darling?' Byron asked with mock innocence.

'To what you two are up to, huddled together down here all this time. What's so engrossing?'

'We were discussing dogs, actually,' Byron said, 'well, bitches to be more precise.'

Celeste looked perplexed. 'But Jaws here is a dog dog. Isn't he?' She peered under him to make sure. 'Yes, he is.'

'I was thinking of getting him a companion so that he won't be lonely,' Gemma said in support of Byron's distortion of the truth.

'Better to take him to the vet,' was Celeste's advice. 'Have him fixed up.'

'Ouch!' Byron exclaimed. 'Did you hear that, Jaws? Better start running, lad.' Giving the dog one last pat, he stood up. 'I suppose I'd better go and have another shave before we go out.'

Celeste watched him go with suspicion on her face. 'Why do I get the feeling I've just been lied to?'

Gemma looked at her mother and made a decision. 'Perhaps because you have. No, don't get mad. Byron was just protecting Nathan.'

'Protecting Nathan? I…I don't understand.'

'No, I can appreciate that, and it's unfair to you to keep you in the dark. Nathan is your son-in-law and he's going to be your son-in-law for a long time so I think you deserve to know what has made him into the man he is today. But you have to promise me to listen with all the kindness and understanding that I know is in your heart. You pretend to be tough, Mother, but you're not. You're as much a softie as Jaws here...'

Some time later, Celeste lifted teary eyes to her daughter. 'I...I didn't realise... Oh, the poor boy...'

'He's not a boy any more, Mother. He's a man. A very decent and very good man. But he needs those around him to really believe in him for him to believe in himself. People say you have to love yourself to love others. I think Nathan finds it hard to love himself because of what that woman did to him at a crucial stage in his growing-up years.'

'That was wicked...what she used to tell him. Really wicked.'

'Yes, it was.'

'I...I want to call that bet off, Gemma. It...it's not nice. You do whatever you think right, darling. You seem so wise where Nathan is concerned. I'm sure you'll make the right decision. And you can have the Heart of Fire anyway. I want you to have it.'

Gemma slowly shook her head.

'But why not? I can afford it.'

'It's just a thing, Mother. I don't want things. Why don't you sell it? Give the money to Byron's charity for street kids. Let it do some good, not rot away in a safe somewhere.'

'Are you sure?'

'Yes, I'm dead sure. Oh, and Mother...I would still be honoured for you to name my baby.'

Celeste's eyes flooded with tears, her hands flying to cover her mouth in a vain attempt to stifle a sob. 'You don't know...how happy...you've made me,' she choked out.

Gemma went to total mush inside, her own eyes swimming. 'You don't know how happy you've made *me*,' she managed to get out before both women threw their arms around each other and wept.

CHAPTER THIRTEEN

BYRON and Celeste spoiled Gemma outrageously that week, not allowing her to cook a single meal and fussing over her like mad. The weather became steadily hotter and they spent most afternoons beside the pool before going out each evening to dinner.

In a way, by Friday, Gemma was relieved to see her parents go, sure that she must have put on a few kilos. With Ma's advice about alcohol in mind, she'd refused to join in with all the sherry before dinner, wine with every meal, then port as a nightcap before bed every night, but her soft-drink substitutes had been just as fattening. Celeste burnt her calories off, churning up and down the pool in endless laps, but Gemma had never been much of a swimmer, and it was too hot for long walks.

An inspection of her figure in the bathroom after her shower on the Thursday night had shown a definite all-over rounding in her curves. It also revealed what looked like a couple of stretch marks on the undersides of her breasts. The sight had upset her. God, what would she be like when her stomach started ballooning? Visions of wall-to-wall stretch marks, sagging breasts and saddlebags loomed in her mind, so as soon as Celeste and Byron drove off she dashed down to the shops and bought a video of exercises for pregnant ladies as well as a moisturising lotion guaranteed to keep her skin supple and elastic.

'You look tired,' was the first thing Nathan said when he walked in that evening shortly after seven. Jaws growled at him from in front of the television set, and Nathan scowled back. 'Just keep your distance, dog, and I'll keep mine.' He turned back to Gemma and gave her a peck on the cheek. 'So what have you been doing? I thought Byron and Celeste were supposed to be looking after you but you look exhausted.'

Gemma didn't want to tell him that she might have overdone things that afternoon with the exercise video, having only just stopped, so she simply shrugged. 'I…I haven't been sleeping well lately.'

His expression was rueful. 'That makes two of us. But seriously, Gemma, I hope you're looking after yourself properly.'

'Pregnant women aren't invalids, Nathan,' she snapped, annoyed with herself for looking at him and thinking sex immediately. But dear heaven, he did have that effect on her. Still, in her defence, he'd obviously had that effect on a lot of women. Mother Nature had given him the face and body of a golden god, in much the same way his mother had been a golden goddess. Even when he'd been only sixteen, he'd inspired uncontrollable lust in a woman old enough to know better.

But Lorna hadn't, and in the pursuit of that lust had almost destroyed Nathan's faith in himself as a human being. With this firmly in mind, Gemma renewed her vow to show Nathan how much she cared for *him*, the human being, not just the superstud.

Which she was hardly doing by snapping at him.

Remorse brought a silent groan before she managed to dredge up an apologetic smile.

'I probably look a bit hot and bothered because I've been in the kitchen, cooking. I know you said not to make dinner, since Kyle and Jade won't be here till late, but I couldn't stand the thought of going out to eat again, so I popped a chicken in the oven with some baked veggies. I hope you don't mind.'

'No,' he smiled warmly, and her heart flipped over. 'Why would I? I love your roast chicken dinners.'

'Good, then why don't you go put your feet up and I'll get you a drink? I can imagine what that drive up from Sydney is like, especially on a Friday night. What would you like? Coffee? Beer? Some white wine perhaps?' Having been a good little teetotaller all week, Gemma decided the odd glass of wine or two this weekend wouldn't hurt.

'What I'd like is for *you* to sit down while I get *you* a drink,' Nathan returned. 'Is there a bottle of wine in the fridge?'

'Lots and lots,' she admitted, thrilled by his consideration. 'I think Byron and Celeste are bordering on alcoholics.'

Nathan's laughter was dry. 'Could be. Something must be making them so happy together. I'd rather blame it on their being pickled all the time rather than disgustingly in love.'

Gemma's insides contracted at this last sarcastic remark. 'I don't think they're in love at all,' she said, and Nathan's head whipped round to stare at her.

'Why do you say that?'

'Because being "in" love sounds like a very temporary state, like an illness which they will soon develop an immunity for. They love each other, Nathan. They had loved each other for over twenty years.'

He snorted his scorn. 'I think good old lust has a strong hand in their feelings for each other. Byron can't keep his eyes off Celeste.'

'Or his hands.'

'Gemma!'

'But that doesn't mean they don't love each other, Nathan,' she argued hotly. 'Lust is just another side to love. I would hate to love a man and not lust after him as well.'

It was a brave thing to say, considering the man she was saying it to. Nathan's eyes narrowed, sweeping over her flushed face then down her suddenly breathless body which was, at that moment, encased in bright pink shorts and a matching T-shirt. Her hair was swept back up off her face in a rather haphazard pony-tail and her feet were bare. She wore no make up except a quick dash of pink lipstick.

'What about the reverse? Could you lust after a man yet not love him at all?' he asked with a sardonic arch of one brow.

'Yes,' she admitted. 'But not indefinitely. I would eventually want something more.'

'I wouldn't be too sure of that, Gemma,' he drawled. 'Lust, by its very nature, is a corruptive force. It can make one want all sorts of things. And *do* all sorts of things.'

Gemma's heart lurched. Was he just being cynical or was he delivering some sort of dark message?

'Why don't you sit down and put your feet up,' he went on brusquely, 'and I'll get you that glass of wine? I might have one myself. It's been one hell of a week.'

Gemma decided while he was uncorking the bottle and pouring them each a glass that she would not try to find some secret message in what he just said. It was probably just an instinctive remark, born from his troubled past. But it underlined his ongoing mistrust of his own emotions, and perhaps hers. What would it take, she wondered and worried, for him to believe she loved him, and that he loved her?

For they did love each other. If they didn't, they wouldn't be here at this very moment. Together.

Yet Gemma's own certainty about their feelings did not give her peace of mind. If anything, it brought an added burden not to foul things up, not to do anything to spoil what they could have together for the rest of their lives, as long as she didn't do anything stupid at this juncture. It came to her with a stab of dismay that Nathan didn't need to see her lusting after him in any way, shape or form. She had been crazy even to bring up the subject of lust.

'Thank you,' she said crisply when he handed her the

glass and settled himself into the chair opposite. Jaws, who was lying on the rug not far from Nathan's feet, gave him a filthy look and crawled closer to Gemma.

'I see I'm still as popular as ever,' he bit out. 'I suppose he drooled all over Byron and Celeste.'

'Well, not exactly drooled...'

'But he didn't try to turn them into Long John Silvers.'

'Er—no...'

'I thought not. It's said animals have an instinct about people. Do you think he's trying to tell you something about me?'

'Only that you're as wary of him as he is of you. One day you'll look at each other and decide how foolish you've been not to be friends.'

Nathan chuckled. 'That'll be the day.'

The telephone rang. 'I'll answer it,' Gemma offered, putting down her wine and getting to her feet.

The telephone was at the end of the kitchen counter.

'Hello?' she answered.

'Gemma, it's Kyle. Problems this end, I'm afraid, so we won't be up. Jade had a bit of a dizzy turn at work today and the doc has ordered complete bed rest over the weekend.'

Gemma frowned her concern. 'She's really all right though, isn't she?' Jade was nearly eight months pregnant and in Gemma's opinion shouldn't be at work anyway. But there was no telling Jade what to do.

'Yes, she's fine. Naturally, I've been trying to get her to delegate at work till after the baby's born but what with Byron having been away she felt she had to go in every day. Still, Byron will be back on deck come Monday and I think between us we should be able to persuade her to take it easy from now on. So how are *you* keeping, love? Nathan tells us you haven't been tippy-top either.'

'Oh, I'm not too bad. I still get the odd spot of morning

sickness but my doctor says that should hopefully pass off soon.'

'I must say I've never seen a man as emotional about his wife expecting as Nathan was when he told us,' Kyle commented. 'You know, Gemma, people sometimes get the wrong impression of Nathan. He seems very cool and controlled but might I say from personal experience that it's often the men who seem the most cool and controlled who underneath are the least?'

'I know what you're saying, Kyle, and I think you're probably quite right.'

'Jade wanted me to pass a message on to you specifically. She said to tell you to be gentle with Nathan, whatever that means. I would have thought she should be saying that to him. You're the one who's pregnant. Still, you know Jade. She works on instinct and intuition so perhaps you should listen to what she says.'

'I will, Kyle. I will.'

'I'd better go, Gemma. I have to pop down the corner shop for some assorted chocolate bars. Madam Mother-to-be has a case of the fancies. Has that struck you yet?'

'Not yet.'

'It will,' he sighed. 'I'll have to give Nathan a list of items to have on hand so that he doesn't have to go roaming the streets in the middle of the night in search of an all-hours shop. Has he arrived there yet, by the way?'

'Yes, a few minutes ago.'

'Looks like it'll just be the two of you for the weekend, then.'

'Yes.'

'I doubt Nathan will mind that,' he chuckled. 'Well, bye now, sweetie. Look after yourself.'

'You too, Kyle. Bye.'

Gemma hung up and turned to find Nathan looking over at her with frustration on his face. 'Don't tell me,' he growled. 'They can't make it.'

'Jade had a dizzy spell at work and the doctor's confined her to bed for a couple of days.'

'Stupid damned girl! Why doesn't she ease up a little? I'll bet she'll be back at that miserable desk at Whitmore's within days of the baby being born. I can't understand women who have babies then don't want to stay home and look after them.'

'Don't be so narrow-minded, Nathan. Jade won't neglect her baby. Kyle would have something to say if she did. But she has a right to work if that's what she wants to do.'

'What are you saying, Gemma?' he returned sharply. 'That you will want to go back to work after our baby is born?'

'No, I'm not saying that at all! I've always planned on being a full-time mother. I also planned on having a lot more than one child.'

Nathan's eyes rounded a little. 'How many did you have in mind?'

Gemma shrugged. 'Oh, I don't know. Five or six.'

'Five or six!' Nathan shot forward on the chair, his wine almost spilling. 'Good God, woman, I'm thirty-six years old.'

'Yes, I know,' she returned quite calmly. 'But I'm only twenty. And it's me who has to have them, Nathan. Your part of the process won't take much out of you, will it? Besides, I thought you liked being a father.'

Nathan slumped back into the chair, looking stunned for a few seconds before his face slowly cleared of shock and he looked up at her, grey eyes steely. 'I think we'd better take this one baby at a time, don't you?' he said, and abruptly stood up. 'I'm going down to the study to work. Call me when dinner's ready.'

Gemma watched, taken aback, as Nathan strode down the hallway and disappeared into his private cave. The slamming of the door behind him obliterated the sense of optimism that had been growing in her heart since Nathan arrived. Now she saw that nothing had been solved yet. Not in Nathan's eyes. He was still as unsure of their relationship as he had always been. Maybe he still believed her feelings for him were bound up in lust. Maybe he thought she was still too young to be truly in love. Who knew what he damned well thought?

From that moment on, the weekend was ghastly. Nathan came out of the study only to eat and go to the bathroom. His behaviour propelled Gemma back to their honeymoon, when, out of the blue, he'd started writing, his complete absorption in his work bringing their honeymoon to an abrupt end. This time, there was no honeymoon to terminate, but Gemma still felt just as hurt, just as rejected. She'd thought they had gradually been reaching out to each other since she had come back from Lightning Ridge and now, suddenly, all their progress seemed to have come to nothing.

By Sunday afternoon, frustration and anger sent her storming out of the house and down the beach which was, unfortunately, far from deserted. Gemma felt like stomping along the sand, kicking it up and generally taking her feelings out on her physical surrounds. Instead, she had to carefully sidestep her way around sunbathing bodies till she was at the water's edge, where she tried to cool her temper and her toes at the same time. If she'd had her swimming costume on, she might have gone further, but she hadn't thought of changing her shorts and top for a bikini.

'Mrs Whitmore? Is that you?'

Gemma spun round at the highly unfamiliar male voice to stare into a vaguely familiar male face. She frowned as she struggled for recognition. He was thirtyish. Not an overly handsome man, but a well built one, with an interesting face, if a little hard.

'It's Luke Barton, Mrs Whitmore,' he told her, a charming smile softening his features in a very attractive manner. 'From Campbell Jewels.'

Of course! The man who had rescued her from Damian that awful night.

His intelligent grey eyes flicked down her bare legs and up again, not bothering to hide his admiration. But there was no leering in his gaze and Gemma smiled back. 'Yes, I know who you are,' she said warmly. 'And I know what you did for me. I never did thank you properly, Mr Barton.'

'Your husband did.'

'Aah, yes, my husband,' she said a little coldly.

Luke Barton seemed to pick up on her coolness, his expression turning speculative. 'Are you up here on holiday?' he asked.

'No. I'm not on holiday. I live here now. And no, Nathan and I haven't split up,' she added before he jumped to conclusions. 'He lives down in Sydney during the week and joins me here on the weekend. He's busy writing at the moment.'

'I see. I'm on holiday till the New Year, thank God. The boss has been away for a month and it's been bedlam without her, but she's back on deck tomorrow.'

'Yes, I know,' Gemma said, grinning at his surprise. 'Celeste's my mother-in-law, now that she's married to Byron.' There was no need to go into the more private tangles of their family relationships.

'Good lord, so she is!'

They laughed together, Gemma thinking he didn't know the half of it. They were standing there in the shallows, still laughing, when one of those rogue waves hit, totally soaking them both. It didn't matter with Luke, since he was only wearing swimming trunks, but Gemma's clothes were not the water-resistant type, their material going all soggy when wet, clinging to her in clumps.

'Oh, yuk!' she exclaimed, flicking the salty water off her fingers and flapping her T-shirt away from her chest. 'I'll have to go home and change.'

'Is it far? I'll walk with you. Maybe you could get your costume and we could go for a swim together.'

Gemma didn't have to think too hard to know what Nathan's reaction to that suggestion would be. 'Er—I think not, Luke. I can call you Luke, can't I?'

'If I call you Gemma,' he countered with that engaging smile of his.

'I don't see why not.' And suddenly, she didn't! Why should she be feeling guilty about talking to this man, or walking with him, or even swimming with him? He wasn't a stranger, and he had already proved himself a decent human being, a trustworthy human being. Despite what had happened with Damian, she had not become a total cynic. She still believed there were good people about—unlike Nathan, who didn't, especially in the male gender. But she couldn't spend the rest of her life avoiding male company just because Nathan might worry, or get angry, or jealous. That was no way to live. That was like being in a self-imposed prison.

'Of course you can call me Gemma,' she chided gently. 'I certainly don't want you calling me Mrs Whitmore all the time. Come on, this way. The house isn't far. It's just over on the side of that hill there. We'll go and surprise Nathan.'

Surprise was not exactly how Gemma would have described Nathan's reaction to her bringing home a semi-naked Luke Barton. Her husband's manners were perfectly polite, but she felt the underlying chill. Luke didn't seem to, however, and perched up on one of the kitchen stools, chatting away to Nathan about his play which he'd been to see the previous week.

'I took my sister, Mandy,' he said. 'She recently split with her boyfriend and was feeling down so I thought a night at the theatre would give her a lift.' He chuckled. 'A *lift*! It blew her mind away. Truly, she couldn't stop talking about it afterwards. Or should I say, she couldn't stop talking about the leading man? Personally, I thought the leading lady was much more eye-catching. But then I would, wouldn't I?' he grinned.

'Lenore's my ex-wife,' Nathan said drily.

'Really?' Luke's startled gaze slid from Nathan to Gemma, who was trying to relax, but couldn't.

'I must get back to my writing,' Nathan said on finishing the cup of coffee Gemma had originally cajoled him into having with them both. 'Nice to see you again, Luke.'

'I thought I might go back to the beach with Luke for a swim,' Gemma said quickly, and held her breath.

Nathan seemed to freeze for just a second before he turned to look over his shoulder at them both. 'In that case keep an eye on her, Luke,' he said. 'She's not the best of swimmers, are you, Gemma?'

'Er—no, I'm not.'

'I'll look after her,' Luke reassured.

'I sincerely hope so.'

Was Gemma imagining it, or had there been a dark warning in Nathan's parting words? Whatever, Luke seemed less comfortable with her after that, keeping his distance and not saying or doing anything that could even remotely be considered flirtatious. Gemma found that any enjoyment in his company had been spoiled, though maybe this was more tension on her part than on Luke's. In the end they parted company, Luke going off with some girl who'd been eyeing him up, and Gemma, relieved to go home alone.

Relief was also Luke's reaction, though he hid it well. He'd been a fool to go back to that house with Gemma Whitmore, especially knowing her husband was there. A man needed his brains tested! He'd seen for himself the sort of feelings Nathan Whitmore harboured for his wife the night he'd brought her home. He wasn't the sort of husband who would take to any male admiring his wife, even from a distance. He looked cool on the surface but there was an underlying emotional intensity about him that could be quite frightening.

Luke berated himself for being so stupid. It wasn't as though he'd been looking for any serious involvement with the woman. She was lovely to look at but really not his type at all. His type was smiling at him right now. Late twenties, a brunette, a go-getter who didn't want to be tied down any more than he did. Taking her hand in his, he drew her, laughing, into the waves, any thought of Gemma and Nathan Whitmore instantly behind him.

NATHAN SEEMED TO know the moment she walked in the door, for when she went into the kitchen to pour herself a glass of wine he materialised behind her.

'Have a nice swim?' he asked.

'All right, I guess,' she replied somewhat curtly.

'Luke up here on holidays, is he?'

'Yes, he is.'

'I don't want you going out with him.'

Gemma turned to look Nathan straight in the eye. 'I'm a married woman. I wouldn't go *out* with any man. But if I see Luke down the street or on the beach, I'll talk to him.'

'And swim with him? And bring him back here for coffee?'

'Maybe.'

'I don't want you to do that.'

'Do what?'

'Bring him back here for coffee. I don't want you being alone with him.'

'Why not, Nathan? Don't you trust me?'

'It's not a matter of trusting you. I don't trust the situation. Luke's a modern man and he fancies you.'

'But I don't fancy him.'

'You might…in the right circumstances.'

'My God, what kind of a woman do you think I am?'

'A very frustrated one, I would imagine.'

She glared at him, fury and, yes, frustration sending the blood pounding through her veins. 'Well, maybe I am but that doesn't mean I'd seek solace in the arms of another man. Sex isn't the most important thing in the world, Nathan. Neither is it necessary for one's sanity. I can do without if you can.'

'Maybe I can't any more,' he muttered, his face darkening. 'Maybe I can't stand another minute of being around you and not having you.'

'Then you know what to do, don't you?' she flung at him.

'Yes,' he snarled. 'I do!'

Gemma stood there, breathless with anticipation, her pulse-rate soaring at the way he started looking at her. An uncontrollable passion zoomed in his eyes, quickly followed by an oddly heart-rending torment. Then he did something that stunned her. He strode over to the refrigerator, snatched up his car keys from the top, and charged out of the house.

When she heard the car engine start up she raced out on to the front balcony but he was already reversing out of the driveway. She called out to him but if he heard her he ignored her shouts, burning rubber as he accelerated off up the street.

He'll come back, she told herself shakily. He's left his writing and his clothes behind. He's sure to come back once he's cooled down.

But he didn't come back. Dusk came and there was no sign of the Mercedes, or Nathan. Depressed, Gemma fed Jaws then brought him inside. The dog seemed to sense her mood, lying quietly at her feet when she settled down to watch the television blankly, unable to eat, unable to do anything except mentally castigate herself over everything she had done wrong.

She had been insensitive over the Luke issue. Of course Nathan would feel a little insecure at the moment. Why hadn't she reassured him instead of goading him? God, but she was an idiot!

Seven o'clock came and went. Eight o'clock. Nine.

He definitely wasn't going to come back. Gemma put

Jaws outside for the night, having stopped letting him sleep in her room this past week after she'd found a couple of fleas in her bed one night. She locked up the back door then tried Nathan's Sydney number, but there was no answer. Maybe he was there but refused to answer, knowing it would be her. Maybe he was punishing her. If he was, it was working.

In tears by now, she forced herself to have a shower, letting her misery wash down with the water. Afterwards, she dried herself then reached for the moisturiser she had bought, pouring a big dollop on to each breast, then working it in with a slow circular motion, her mind a million miles away.

When her eyes gradually refocused, Nathan's reflection was suddenly there before her in the vanity mirror. Shock sent her spinning round, the bottle of lotion slipping from her fingers on to the bathmat at her feet. 'You…you came back,' she gasped.

Nathan said nothing, simply stared at her naked body for some agonisingly long moments, especially at her oiled breasts with their darkly glistening nipples. Stepping forward, he bent to pick up the bottle, his face betraying nothing of his thoughts or his intentions as he straightened to stare at her some more. She couldn't seem to move, or breathe, a hot flush suffusing her body as his gaze swept over it once more.

'I think…' he said slowly, and tipped the bottle sideways, letting the creamy fluid pool in the palm of his hand '…that you should let me finish what you started.'

CHAPTER FOURTEEN

'CAN'T have my wife reduced to making love to herself,' Nathan went on in a low but seemingly calm voice, putting the bottle down on the vanity.

'But I wasn't!' Gemma protested huskily, her head whirling. 'I...I...'

'Sssh. Let *me*.' He dipped the fingertips of his right hand into the pool of cream and began smoothing it over her breasts, making her breath catch in her throat every time he grazed over one of her nipples. When the cream was all gone and he started using both his hands, massaging her, his thumbs rubbing over both tender peaks at the same time, she moaned softly and closed her eyes.

Dear God, but she had wanted this for so long. Please don't let him stop...

He stopped, but only momentarily, pouring more of the lotion into his hand and spreading it over her stomach. Gemma experienced a temporary pang of disappointment that he had abandoned her breasts. They were so deliciously swollen and sensitive by now and craved even more attention. But soon, the focus of her desires shifted, especially when Nathan started smoothing his oil-slicked hands down over her thighs.

'Move your legs apart,' he ordered.

Gemma blinked, lifting a flushed face to his oh, so cool one. The sight of his controlled countenance was like having a bucket of cold water thrown over her. Was this an example of the control he'd once vowed to have over his sexual desires in future? Or was it that he thought he had to be calm and careful, because she was pregnant?

Gemma didn't want him calm and careful. She wanted him as passionate as he had always been. She wanted him to want her and need her and love her so much that there was no room for erotic techniques or one-sided foreplay. She wanted him to strip off his clothes and reach for her with shaking hands, wanted him to kiss her till they were both mindless with the yearning to come together as men and women had been coming together since Adam and Eve.

It was on the tip of her tongue to say as much, her face perhaps betraying her feelings, when he did step forward and take her in his arms, capturing her mouth with a kiss that distracted her from her growing dissatisfaction. His lips were demanding, the hands sliding down her back equally so as they curved around her buttocks, lifting her body to mould against his.

The feel of his stark arousal pressing against her stomach came as a shock. So he wasn't so controlled after all!

His desire refuelled her own, sending a low groan from deep within her throat. Her mouth flowered open, accepting the immediate thrust of his tongue. When he eased her legs slightly apart and started caressing her intimately, she was soon beyond wanting anything but the completion of the journey he was mercilessly setting her upon. When he stopped kissing her to scoop her up into his arms, his desertion was only brief, his mouth returning to keep the heat in her veins at fever pitch as he carried her quickly back into the bedroom and over to the waiting bed.

There, he laid her gently down, the kissing continuing while he ran tantalising hands down over her tingling flesh. She whimpered her distress when he left her to discard his own clothing, despite his not taking very long.

'Tell me you love me,' she urged blindly when he finally covered her naked flesh with his.

His hesitation was marked, and it drove her crazy. 'Just say it!' she cried, and raked her nails down his back.

He gasped and rolled over, carrying her with him so that she was lying on top. Her hair fell around her face and she swept it back with a shaking hand. 'Why won't you tell me you love me?' she challenged. 'You do, you know, the same way I love you.'

'Is that so?' he said scoffingly. 'How do you know? Don't count on what you're feeling at this moment. That's not love. I could make any number of women feel exactly the same way.'

Outraged, Gemma went to lever herself up off him, but he grabbed her wrists and held them wide so she collapsed on his chest again. She glared down into his face which was only inches from hers. 'You're a bastard, do you know that?'

'Yes.'

'I...I hate you!'

His smile was wry. 'Now you're really lying. You don't hate me, Gemma, though perhaps you have every reason to. You still want me. That's one of the reasons why you came back to Sydney with me. The baby might have been the main reason, but this is the other. Calling it love won't change the harsh reality of the sexual chemistry between us. Forcing me to say I love you is just as hypocritical. Now why don't you shut up, my darling? I came back to make love to you, not to argue with you.'

'Why?'

'Why what?'

'Why did you come back to make love to me? Was it because you were afraid if you didn't I'd have an affair with Luke Barton?'

'Partly.'

'And what's the other part?'

'You need to ask? God,' he laughed. 'I've been climbing the walls this weekend with wanting to make love to you.

Lord knows how I survived it. Writing doesn't even work any more. *This* is all that's going to make me feel human again.'

So saying, he let her wrists go, reaching down to curve his hands behind her knees, pulling them apart and forward till she was straddling him, her hips raised provocatively so that the apex of her desire was hovering above his. His face twisted in a type of anguish as his flesh probed hers, steel into velvet, and then he was pulling her downwards, filling her with his hardness, impaling her and holding her captive in a grip of iron.

'For pity's sake don't move,' he commanded when she began to struggle.

'But you're hurting me,' she protested.

His face showed shock and bewilderment.

'Around my hips,' she told him breathlessly.

'Aah...' He relaxed his finger-biting hold, rubbing her flesh up and down. 'Sorry,' he rasped. 'I do get carried away when I'm with you.'

'I know,' she said.

'Don't sound so smug,' he muttered. 'And do shut up. I can't concentrate. You never used to talk when we made love,' he growled, moving his pelvis slowly up and down.

Gemma's mouth opened on a sucked-in gasp of pleasure. She had never been on top before and found the sensations incredible. Compelled, she echoed his movements with movements of her own. Nathan's moan of raw response sent a hot dizzying excitement flooding through her, making her want to hear that sound again, making her want to send him wild. Quite instinctively, her insides contracted, and with her flesh gripping his tightly the experience soared beyond description.

'Oh, God,' Nathan muttered, almost as though in pain.

When he reached for her shoulders and tried to pull her down to his mouth, she resisted, not wanting to stop what she was doing. His hands slid down to her breasts instead, playing with them as they rocked to and fro with her increasingly frantic movements. Gemma had never experienced anything so compellingly exciting. Everything inside her mind seemed to become focused on that part of her body housing his, in the build-up of pressure that was agony and ecstasy combined. She would not have stopped if the room had disintegrated around her.

'Yes,' she groaned when she felt her body tighten even further. 'Yes,' she gasped when everything started exploding in her head. 'Yes!' she cried aloud as her flesh followed, convulsing and contracting in a series of violent spasms, propelling the male flesh within her to an equally cataclysmic climax.

It wasn't till several minutes after she had collapsed upon Nathan's chest and her breathing had almost returned to normal that an odd sense of unease crept in. Was it Nathan's silence that worried her, or the mention of her own wanton wildness? For a while there she had been totally lost in her own pleasure, uncaring of anything but the achieving of her own satisfaction. Was that love, or simply lust? Was Nathan lying there, thinking that she had just proved what he'd been saying all along, that what she felt for him was mostly physical.

When his lungs expanded then fell in a weary-sounding sigh, Gemma feared the worst. She felt impelled to say something; anything to break the awful tension that she imagined was slowly invading the room.

And then.

'Are you going to stay, Nathan?' she asked somewhat gingerly.

'The night, you mean?'

'No. Not just the night. Though of course I do want you to stay the night,' she added hastily.

'I thought you might,' came his dry comment.

'If you're not going to be directing the play any more,' she went on, staunchly ignoring the pain and panic his caustic words had evoked, 'couldn't you move up here to Avoca? It's where you wanted to live when we were first married. You don't have to sell the apartment at Elizabeth Bay if you don't want to. We could keep it as a Sydney base.' Gemma said this, though she didn't want to ever go back there. She'd never really been happy in that place.

'No, I think I'll sell it.'

Gemma smothered her intense sigh of relief. 'Whatever you like.'

'I'd like a shower,' he said bluntly. 'And I expect you to join me.' Cupping her face, he lifted it so that she was forced to look into his eyes. What she saw there horrified her. An almost bitter cynicism gleamed in that steely grey gaze, accompanied by a decidedly wicked resolve. She'd crossed an invisible line with him just now when it came to their sex life together and he didn't intend to let her go back. There would be no more virginal blushing. No more shrinking away from his more imaginative demands. No more 'I'd rather not's'.

He clasped her close while he swung his legs carefully over the side of the bed. As he stood up, one arm moved down to cradle her buttocks, one wrapped tightly around her waist, supporting the full weight of her body. Which was just as well, she decided dazedly, since they were still fused together.

He carried her that way into the bathroom where he had her turn on the shower taps and adjust the temperature before he stepped inside the cubicle.

Gemma gasped as the hot jets of water cascaded over them both, Nathan moving their stance so that it mainly poured down between them, over his chest and her breasts. At this point he kissed her, uncaring that the water now splashed over their heads and poured down their backs. It was an incredibly erotic experience, especially when she began to feel his flesh stirring within hers again. She responded by tightening and releasing her internal muscles and would have stayed that way forever but he chose to withdraw and ease her down on to the floor.

Gemma took a moment to find her feet, a jelliness having invaded her thighs. Once she stopped swaying Nathan picked up a cake of soap and a sponge, lathered up the latter, then handed them both to her. 'Wash me, wench,' he commanded thickly.

Her hand shook when she started, moving the sponge tentatively over his chest at first. But gradually any shyness dissolved and, emboldened by her own escalating desire, her hand moved downwards till she was confronted with his quite stunning maleness. At this point she dropped the soap, groaning at her clumsiness.

'Leave it,' he rasped, then moaned when she lightly pressed the wet sponge against him, making another raw moan break from his lips.

God, but it drove her crazy to hear him moan like that. Now she enclosed the moist sponge around him more firmly and began sliding it up and down. He swore under his breath and braced himself against the tiled wall, his flesh quivering beneath her touch. Still, it wasn't enough for her. She wanted him to shudder with uncontrollable pleasure, wanted him to not be able to stop as she was never able to stop once he started making love to her. She wanted him to be hers, utterly and totally. Even if it was only this way.

'No!' he protested when she threw the sponge away and sank down on her knees before him, the water cascading over her head and down her body.

She ignored him, bending forward to kiss the top of each thigh before cupping the weight between them with her hands then planting softly teasing kisses up and down his straining body.

'Don't,' he groaned.

But she was without mercy or conscience, her own excitement and arousal so intense that what had once seemed like the ultimate in abandonment now seemed like the most natural thing in the world. She exulted in tantalising him with her tongue, to the way he trembled when she parted her lips and took him oh, so gently between them. Only an inch or two at first, then further and further till he was consumed totally within the hot cavern of her tender yet tormenting mouth.

When he seemed to freeze for a moment, she was suddenly overtaken by an urgency to propel him quickly over the edge, to make him surrender, if not his heart, then his body. She would not allow him to draw back, to retreat, to reject.

Her lips increased their pressure. Her hands found all sorts of intimate little places.

Suddenly, the water was snapped off and Gemma was being hauled upwards, lifted out of the shower cubicle, wrapped in a huge towel then carried back into the bedroom.

'If I thought you'd done any of that with any other man,' Nathan growled as he tipped her on to the bed and snapped the towel out from under her, 'I'd strangle you with my bare hands!'

Gemma took a few moments to find her voice, the blood still whirling in her head, her heartbeat racing with an arousal that refused to be either squashed or side-tracked. 'You know I haven't, Nathan,' she insisted huskily. 'You spoiled me for any other man. Quite deliberately, I imagine. You made me what I am. You made me totally and irrevocably yours. Don't tell me you're afraid of your own creation. This is what you always wanted me to be, isn't it? Your very own sex slave, ready to do whatever you want. Why did you stop me? Let me please you,' she pleaded, levering herself up on to her knees and wrapping her arms around his naked waist. 'Let me make love to you…'

She began by kissing the droplets of water that clung to his ribs, licking his skin dry as she gradually moved her mouth back down to his still throbbing desire.

'I want to do this, Nathan,' her lips whispered as they moved over him. 'And you want me to,' she rasped. 'Let me…'

He let her.

CHAPTER FIFTEEN

'DOESN'T Ava look beautiful?' Gemma sighed.

'All brides look beautiful,' Nathan returned, then slanted her a frowning look. 'Do you regret not having been a traditional bride with a traditional ceremony in a church?'

'In a way. It would be nice to look back on. But it's too late now, don't you think?' She smiled, patting her gently rounded stomach underneath her apricot silk sheath. She was just over four months pregnant, and beginning to show. She was also remarkably happy, had been ever since Nathan had moved back into her life as her husband two months previously.

At first she had been worried that their relationship hadn't changed, that it was still just a sexual thing, that he didn't really love her. But Ma had been right when she said what they needed together was time. With each passing day, Gemma became more convinced of the depth of their feelings for each other. Nathan might not have told her in so many words that he loved her, but he showed her every single day. Not only in his lovemaking, but in everything he did. Gemma could not have asked for a better or more considerate husband. Even Jaws had warmed to him, choosing to lie at Nathan's feet most nights in front of the television, instead of hers.

Of course it would be nice if he *did* say he loved her one of these days. But Gemma wasn't going to be greedy. Neither was she going to keep hoping for miracles. Clearly,

Nathan didn't feel comfortable with the word love. Maybe he never would.

Her attention shifted back to Ava, who was standing in front of the altar looking up into Vince's face with a look of such heart-felt adoration that a lump immediately formed in Gemma's throat. When Ava actually started making her vows, her voice shaking with emotion, hot tears pricked at Gemma's eyes.

'I'm going to cry,' she warned Nathan.

'Don't you dare.'

'I am, I tell you,' she sniffled. 'I can't help it. Give me your handkerchief.'

'Haven't you got a tissue?'

'No. I didn't bring one.'

Sighing, he gave her the silk kerchief out of his breast pocket. Gemma blew her nose, at which Jade turned round from the pew in front of her. 'You're not crying, are you, Gemma?' she said accusingly. 'You *are*. God, that does it! I'm going to cry too now. Here, Kyle, take the baby. I'm about to dissolve into mush.'

Kyle was only too happy to take his precious Dominic into his arms, looking down into his sleeping son's face with even more adoration that Ava was looking into Vince's. Only a month old, Dominic Henry Gainsford already had his parents twisted around his chubby little fingers, so much so that Jade had put off the idea of having another child for a while.

Gemma had no such plans to spread out her babies. She intended having one after the other till her family was complete. She wanted her children close and she wanted lots of them. Maybe they'd have to sell the house at Avoca eventually and get a bigger place, but she wasn't going to worry Nathan with that thought just yet. He'd seemed startled enough by her original announcement that she wanted half a dozen children. She'd let him get used to that idea first before she dropped any more bombshells.

Having composed herself with thinking of her future family, Gemma refocused on the wedding ceremony, just in time to hear Ava and Vince being pronounced man and wife. It had been a very traditional ceremony, and a very moving one, so much so that Gemma did feel a pang of disappointment that she had never been a white bride with all the trimmings.

Still…her arm slipped through Nathan's and she smiled up into his handsome face…she really must stop wanting to have it all. She was already one of the luckiest girls in the world. One year ago she had come to Sydney with nothing. Since then she had found two wonderful parents in Byron and Celeste, fallen in love with a wonderful man in Nathan, gained a wonderful sister in Jade, and was now having a wonderful baby.

'We can sit down,' Nathan said once Vince and Ava moved over to start signing the register and marriage certificate.

Everyone sat down and immediately the organ music started, haunting in its angelic tones. Gemma glanced around the mêlée of guests. She hadn't met Vince's relatives till today, but there were enough of them to fill the groom's side of the church. The bride's side was not nearly so packed, though there were a lot more people than might have come to a wedding of Ava's six months ago. Since meeting Vince she had really blossomed, both in her personal life and her career. Her art exhibition the previous month had been an enormous success with her being touted as one of Australia's most exciting up-and-coming artists. Byron was so proud of her, as was everyone else in the family.

Gemma wished Melanie had been able to be here today. She'd been more of a friend to the Whitmores than a housekeeper, but since Melanie had just given birth to a baby girl three days before that was hardly possible. She and Royce had sounded ecstatic on the telephone, saying they had named the baby Tanya. They had also faithfully promised to make the trip out from England after Gemma's baby was born so that everyone could have a big get-together with their respective children.

Gemma wondered what sex her own baby would be. She and Nathan had decided not to ask when she had had her sixteen-week ultrasound. They wanted a surprise. As for names…since Gemma had given Celeste the privilege of naming her grandchild, she tried not to think of names she liked herself. All she could hope was that her mother didn't come up with anything too weird. If she did, they would just have to find a suitable nickname to use. No child of hers was going to have to go to school with a weird name!

'Byron tells me Celeste gave the Heart of Fire to the Australian Museum,' Nathan commented quietly as they sat there. 'He said she offered it to you but you didn't want it.'

'Yes, that's right, I didn't.'

'I suppose you're going to tell me that two-million-dollar black opal was just another *thing*,' he said drily.

'Well, it is, isn't it?'

'Only *you* would think that.'

She frowned up at him. 'Are you angry with me for not taking it?'

'I'm angry with you for being so damned right. I only hope I haven't done the wrong thing.'

'About what?'

'About something I've bought you.'

Gemma cringed inside. He hadn't bought her a single thing since they'd got back together again, except at Christmas, and she'd been very happy he hadn't. Finally, she'd begun to feel like a real wife, instead of an expensive mistress.

'What have you bought me?' she asked, trying not to look worried as she smiled and waved over at Lenore and Kirsty.

'Maybe I should have mentioned it earlier,' he hedged. 'Maybe I should have consulted you.'

'Nathan,' she said through gritted teeth, 'if you don't tell me this very moment, you can spend the night in the study. *Writing*!'

He gave her a look of such horror that she almost started to giggle. In truth, his writing output over the past two months had been so negligible that it was just as well he had inherited a fortune from his grandparents. It was also just as well that Cliff Overton had bought the Hollywood rights, not just to *The Woman in Black*, but a few other plays as well.

'Belleview,' he said, almost bleakly. 'I bought you Belleview.'

Gemma's mouth dropped open as she stared at him, her heart stopping, her eyes blurring.

'I thought you might like to live there,' he went on, his own eyes worried. 'You seemed so sad when you heard Byron was selling it. I thought...oh, hell, I've made another *faux pas*, haven't I?'

She shook her head and dabbed the tears away with his kerchief. 'You couldn't have done anything to make me happier,' she choked out.

'You mean it? You're not just saying that?'

Gemma's answer was really to burst into tears. Fortunately, her weeping was looked upon with indulgence by all and sundry. Why not? Most of Vince's Italian relatives were crying by this time anyway.

Nathan put an arm around her shoulders, drawing her against him. 'At last,' he sighed, 'I did something right.'

GEMMA LAY IN BED later that night, tired but happy. The drive back from Sydney to Avoca after the reception had seemed very long and she was glad to get her clothes off, shower and tumble between cool sheets. February had been as hot as January, and, while there was a sea breeze wafting into the room, the house was still warm from being closed up all day.

'You were quick into bed,' Nathan teased as he came into the room, pulling at his bow-tie. 'Dare I hope that's a hint?'

'Come near me tonight and I'll have your guts for garters,' she warned, yawning.

'How's that for gratitude? I buy you a three-million-dollar mansion and I don't even get a reward.'

'I'll reward you in the morning.'

'I might be dead by morning.'

She pulled a face at him. 'Don't you ever take no for an answer?'

'No.' He ripped off his shirt to reveal his magnificent chest, tanned to a golden bronze from all the swimming he'd been doing. Gemma had always thought his body was beautiful with its wide shoulders that tapered down to slender hips and long lean legs. She especially liked his lack of body hair, his skin like satin beneath her hands.

When his hands dropped to undo the waistband of his trousers. Gemma began seriously to reassess her weariness. By the time he'd stripped off his trousers, throwing them on to a nearby chair, she'd rolled over to watch him avidly, slyly pulling the sheet down a little so that one dark ripe nipple peeped out at him. Gemma had long given up wearing any clothes in bed, having found it a waste of time. They were never on by morning.

Nathan's steely gaze travelled down to the stiffened peak, one eyebrow lifting. But he said nothing, merely stared for a moment then turned and walked into the *en-suite* bathroom. The shower jets came on in full force and Gemma rolled over on to her other side with a resigned sigh. Damn the man. It would be just like him not to touch her now that he'd stirred her interest. He could be contrary that way sometimes. Or was it that he always found her much more accommodating after he'd teased her for a while, after he'd made her wait?

She listened for the water to go off. When it did, she tensed a little. Any moment he would—hopefully—join her in the bed. He would curve his cool nude body around her back and start playing with her breasts. In no time, he would have her panting for him so that when he eased her legs apart and slipped into her she would be totally lost in a sea of desire. He'd been doing it that way lately, telling her it was less likely to disturb the baby. She'd found the position incredibly exciting, loving the feel of his hands on her while they were fused together.

God, just thinking about it was making her so hot and wet! She moaned softly in her need, aching for him.

And then he was there, scooping her back against him and taking her without preamble, exulting in her instant need for him, groaning his own pleasure when she started undulating frantically against him. They both rocketed to climax within seconds, leaving their mouths gasping wide, their chests heaving. Nathan stayed inside her, however, stroking her softly till their breathing calmed and that glorious feeling of peace washed through her. Her sigh was deep and full of satisfaction.

'You have a funny way of saying no,' he whispered, kissing her on the shoulder.

'Mmm.'

'How's Junior?' he asked, and started caressing her belly.

'Growing.'

'My God! Did you feel that? The little blighter moved. That's the second time this week.'

Gemma yawned. 'Probably protesting at all the action.'

'He'd better get used to it,' Nathan said drily. 'I'm not giving up his mother till the doctor orders it.'

'How do you know it's a he?'

'I don't, but *he* sounds better than *it*. Next week I'll use she. I'm an equal-opportunities father.'

Her laughter was soft and warm.

'Are you really happy about my buying Belleview, Gemma?' he asked. 'Naturally, we'll live here till the baby's born, since your doctor's up here, but then I thought we'd move back to Sydney during the week, and keep this place for weekends.'

She twisted her face around to look up into his eyes. 'That sounds wonderful. I love that house. And I love you.'

He kissed her. But he didn't say he loved her back. For the first time in ages, it really hurt. Perhaps he sensed her pain, for the kiss suddenly turned more hungry, his hands finding her most sensitive places till renewed desire obliterated everything and she ceased to think.

But only till it was over. Long afterwards, she lay wide awake in his arms, listening to his heavy rhythmic breathing and wondering if he would *ever* say he loved her again. Her thoughts went to Ava, who would also be lying in her husband's arms tonight. Vince would have told her he loved her. Gemma did not doubt that. He would have told her so many times that Ava would be dizzy with the words.

When Gemma finally fell asleep, her lashes and cheeks were wet. So was her pillow.

THE FIRST PAINS started when she was at home, alone. It was a Sunday, and only mid-June, with the baby not due for another two weeks. Nathan had driven to Sydney for the day to help Byron and Celeste move out of Belleview, since they had at last bought a unit they both liked.

At first Gemma thought it was just another backache. She'd had a few of those. But when the dull nagging ache suddenly turned into a gut-wrenching contraction, she knew the baby was on the way.

Trying not to panic, she dialled Belleview, only realising when there was no answer that she didn't know Byron's new number. Or even his address! Nathan had it written in his little black book but that went with him everywhere. When she tried Nathan's car phone, and received no answer on that either, she began to panic. For a few moments, she didn't know what to do or who to call.

'Jade!' she cried aloud, and rang her sister's number. Luckily, Jade was in.

'It's Gemma, Jade,' she said quickly, doing her best not to sound frightened. 'I've gone into labour and Nathan's not here. He's helping Byron and Celeste move today and I haven't got their number and…and…' Another contraction started and Gemma couldn't help gasping with the pain. It felt like something was sticking a knife into her and twisting it. 'Oh, God, Jade, the pain's bad. I mean, *really* bad.'

'I know, honey, I know. I couldn't believe it myself. Why do you think I'm not signing up for seconds in a hurry? Now you listen to me. Call a taxi straight away and get yourself to hospital quick smart. Which hospital are you booked into?'

'Gosford District.'

'Right. I'll find Nathan and the rest of them and send them straight to the hospital. When you get there, demand they give you every painkiller that God and man invented. And then some more. Forget all that natural-childbirth crap. I think men invented that idea out of revenge for us making them fathers. Now have you got all that?'

'Yes, Jade,' she whimpered, almost in tears with the pain.

'Now hang up and ring for that taxi, pronto.'

'I will.'

'Good girl.'

The taxi driver took one look at her, paled visibly, then bundled her into the back seat and drove as if the hounds of hell were after him. Fortunately, it being a Sunday in winter, there wasn't much traffic around and fifteen minutes later he was zooming up the ramp into Casualty, fortunately without killing both her and the baby. By this time, she was in a bad way indeed, one contraction hardly seeming to end before the next began, each successive one more intense. She kept biting her bottom lip in a vain attempt not to moan, but occasionally a small sound would sneak through.

Hunched over, she managed to make it inside, where the

admitting nurse immediately called for a wheel-chair. Ten minutes later Gemma was lying in a hospital bed, showered and robed. She kept thinking the birth must be imminent, so when her doctor finally arrived and examined her, then told her that the birth could be some hours away, she stared at him in stark horror.

'I'm...I'm not sure I can stand this for that long,' she cried.

He patted her hand while he instructed the nurse to prepare an injection of pethidine. 'We'll do what we can to make you more comfortable, Gemma. First babies can be slow in making an appearance. It would help matters considerably if you would try to relax.'

Relax! How could she relax when her insides were being torn apart?

'You've been going to breathing classes, haven't you?' he said.

'Y...yes.' Her face twisted with pain, everything inside her tensing.

'Then pant during your contractions, deep even breathing in between. This should help as well...'

She hardly felt the needle in her thigh, yet she hated injections. The torment she was enduring put insignificant discomforts like injections into perspective. They could stick needles in her all over if only this agony would go away.

She wanted to cry, but pride kept the tears at bay. Women did this kind of thing every day. What was the matter with her? Was she extra-weak? A coward, perhaps? Or was there something wrong? Maybe the baby's head was too large. She wanted to ask the doctor all sorts of questions but he was called away to perform what he calmly called a 'Caesar'.

Images of their having to cut her open to get her baby out filled Gemma's mind. Oh, God, where was Nathan? Where was Celeste? She wanted her husband. She wanted her mother. She...

A type of haze suddenly began to infiltrate her mind. The pain was receding a little. Maybe she would live after all. She sighed, letting all the tension flow from her body. Fifteen minutes later, she began to feel like pushing.

WHEN NATHAN RECEIVED the call from Jade, he nearly died. Gemma, in labour. His darling, all alone and possibly afraid. God, he could have killed himself for leaving her. He should have known something like this could possibly happen. Where were his brains?

Luckily, he'd been driving back to Belleview at the time, Jade catching him on his car phone as he approached the Mona Vale Road turnoff. Leaving instructions for her to call Byron and Celeste at their new unit in Mosman, he raced through the intersection and up the Pacific Highway, going north. Within minutes he was on the expressway. Nathan glanced briefly at the speed-limit and decided a fine was worth it. His foot came down and the Mercedes leapt forward.

Half an hour later he was screeching to a halt outside the hospital and racing inside.

'Maternity section!' he demanded breathlessly of the first nurse he saw. Taken aback but with a typical female reaction to Nathan, she dropped everything and showed him the way, even finding out what ward and room Mrs Gemma Whitmore had been placed in.

Nathan didn't know what to expect when he burst into the room. Certainly not an empty bed.

'She must be in Delivery,' the ward sister informed him when he cornered her at her desk. 'You'll have to be scrubbed, masked and gowned before you're allowed in there.'

'Then scrub, mask and gown me, woman. That's my life you're talking about!'

'Don't you mean wife?'

'No, dammit, I don't. And if anything bad happens to my Gemma I'm going to tear this hospital apart!'

'PUSH HARDER RIGHT in the middle of the next contraction,' the doctor instructed. 'Go with the flow.'

Gemma glanced over her shoulder at the delivery-room door, which was shut. 'Is my husband here yet?' she breathlessly asked the nurse for the umpteenth time, then screwed up her face as another fierce contraction took hold. 'Please,' she gasped. 'Please go and see…'

The nurse glanced down at the doctor, who nodded. She bustled out and Gemma tried to concentrate on pushing. But she had an awful feeling she was somehow holding on to this baby till Nathan arrived.

'Push, Gemma,' the doctor commanded, sounding annoyed with her.

The contraction eased off, and right at that moment Nathan was ushered in, the nurse still doing up the ties on his mask. 'Here he is, Mrs Whitmore.'

Nathan hurried over and took her nearest hand in both of his, anxiety and apology in his eyes. She smiled weakly up at him and would have said something if a contraction hadn't seized her at that moment.

Nathan was appalled at the agony on her face. When a smothered cry burst from her lips, the sound turned his insides.

'Push hard, Gemma,' the doctor said firmly. 'Push.'

Her fingers dug into Nathan's palms, the nails biting deep. But he said nothing, glad to share the pain she was obviously enduring, anything to lighten her load.

'That's good,' the doctor praised. 'A few more good pushes like that and it'll all be over.'

Nathan stared down at her pale tired face, at the dark rings under her eyes, at this beautiful brave young woman whom he loved more than life itself. Lord, how could he not have known how much he loved her? How could he have stupidly kept fearing it was only lust that moved him every time he looked at her?

There was no lust in him for her today. Only admiration and tenderness and caring. Only love.

He bent down and pressed his lips through the mask against her forehead. 'You can do it, darling,' he urged. 'You can do it...'

He saw her gather all her reserves of strength, saw her make another supreme effort, then another.

The sound of a baby crying took him by surprise. He'd almost forgotten about the child, his worry all for Gemma.

'You have a son, Mr Whitmore,' the doctor announced proudly. 'Here, Nurse, let Gemma hold her boy. She deserves it. She's had a pretty rough time.'

Nathan watched as all the exhaustion left Gemma's face, her eyes sparkling with maternal joy as her arms reached for her son. 'Oh, Nathan,' she cried, drawing the infant to her breast. 'Isn't he beautiful? Isn't he the most beautiful thing you've ever seen?'

Nathan swallowed. Yes, he thought. He had never seen anything as beautiful as his wife and son together. His heart squeezed tight for a moment when he thought of how his son had been conceived, but he quickly realised that none of what had happened in the past mattered any more. Nothing mattered but what he said and did from this day forward.

A resolution formed in his mind that he would marry his Gemma again. She would come to him down the aisle of a church, on her father's arm and dressed in white. Everyone would be there to watch them take solemn vows—even that ghastly old Ma—and afterwards they would have a fantastic reception before going away on a proper honeymoon then coming back to live happily ever after at Belleview. But the most important resolution of all was that he would not let a day go by without telling Gemma how much he loved her.

'What do you think Celeste will call him?' she asked, interrupting his train of thought.

'Alexander,' he said straight away. 'Your mother called me on the car phone while I was driving up here so that I could tell you. Alexander, if it was a boy, and Augusta if it was a girl.'

Gemma blinked up at him, then laughed. 'Thank God it was a boy.'

Nathan had to smile. 'Amen to that.'

'In that case pass me little Alexander,' the nurse said, smiling herself. 'I think he needs a bath and some clothes.' She carried him away, cooing and clucking.

Gemma sighed. 'I can see Alex is going to be a ladykiller. Just like his father.'

'I think he takes after his mother.'

'Oh? In what way?'

'By being instantly, infinitely lovable.'

Gemma's breath caught in her throat. It was so close to his saying he loved her. So close.

Nathan reefed the mask over his head, then bent down to kiss her on the lips, so softly that it was like feathers brushing over her mouth. 'Have I told you lately that I love you?' he murmured.

Her heart stopped. 'Not…not lately,' she managed to say in a strangled voice.

'I love you,' he said simply.

Gemma closed her eyes, then let out a shuddering sigh. How many moments could be as wonderful as this? How often did one have it all? How many miracles actually happened?

'I love you,' he repeated, his voice trembling.